**W9-DEY-246**

Going EAST

Nan A. Talese DOUBLEDAY

NEW YORK LONDON TORONTO SYDNEY AUCKLAND

→ Going E A S T

MATTHEW D'ANCONA

PUBLISHED BY NAN A. TALESE
AN IMPRINT OF DOUBLEDAY
a division of Random House, Inc.

DOUBLEDAY is a trademark of Doubleday, a division of Random House, Inc.

This book is a work of fiction. Names, characters, businesses, organizations, places, events, and incidents either are the product of the author's imagination or are used fictitiously. Any resemblance to actual persons, living or dead, events, or locales is entirely coincidental.

Book design by Terry Karydes

Going East was first published in 2003 by Sceptre, a division of Hodder and Stoughton, London.

Library of Congress Cataloging-in-Publication Data
D'Ancona, Matthew, 1968–
Going east / Matthew D'Ancona.—1st ed.
            p.   cm.
1. Young women—Fiction. 2. Loss (Psychology)—Fiction.
3. Alternative medicine—Fiction. 4. East End (London, England)—Fiction. I. Title.
PR6104.A83G65 2004
823'.92—dc22   2003055559

ISBN 0-385-51049-7

Copyright © 2003 The Serpentine Publishing Co., Pty. Ltd.

All Rights Reserved

PRINTED IN THE UNITED STATES OF AMERICA

August 2004

First Edition in the United States of America

1   2   3   4   5   6   7   8   9   10

FOR SARAH

Not every man has gentians in his house
in Soft September, at slow, Sad Michaelmas.

—D. H. LAWRENCE,
"BAVARIAN GENTIANS"

I guess part of me or a part of who I am, a part of what I do,
is being a warrior—a reluctant warrior, a reluctant struggler.

—ASSATA SHAKUR

→ Part ONE

THE PARK

Chapter ONE

DARK THOUGHTS coursed through the mind of Jeremy Taylor: It was a time to kill. He stretched and flexed his body, calculating the precise force and trajectory required for the strike to be fatal, the blow to administer justice. He began his lethal swing. But just as he was about to send his son Ben's green croquet ball singing into oblivion, his murderous reverie was punctured by his wife's voice. A hundred feet from the wicket and cluster of balls over which he loomed stood Jenny Taylor, clasping a gingham cloth in one hand and a box of something in the other. No second summons was necessary. And even at a distance, he could tell from her very posture—the position of her left leg in respect to her right, as it happened—that no such summons would be forthcoming.

Thirty-five years had taught him what each such configuration meant. He was an expert in the private semaphore of her body language and gestures. In her mauve cardigan and white shirt, she communicated the simmering impatience which was rarely given the chance to boil into fury. All was ready with the feast, he knew, but the croquet game was not over. The timing of the Taylor family, as ever, was just a little askew, and he wished, with a moment's flash of irritation, that, for once, this were not so.

"Come on, Dad," said Ben. "If you're going to kill me, kill me."

Closing in on their father, and swinging their mallets high above their heads, the twins approached to see what he would do. The green ball touched the blue and was ripe for vicious despatch. Though the turf of the park was shockingly uneven and offended Jeremy Taylor's deep love of a game he had mastered on the lawns of his father's Oxford college, there was no doubting his opportunity. Even his son could see this and, with the suicidal impulse that sometimes overtakes a player in a match he knows he has lost, longed to see his own murder carried out with beauty. His father began to swing and then, looking over to the copse of ferns, planted his mallet in the grass.

"No," he said. "I want to make you suffer. Afterwards."

"Afterwards?" said Ben. "It's five o'clock already. It'll be too dark when we're done eating. Come on, Dad. Don't be wet."

"Kill him, Dad," said Caitlin. "You know you want to."

"For God's sake, Dad," her sister Lara said. "This is it. Kill him before he turns thirty. It's too old anyway. Put him it out of his misery before he's an old man."

"No. Tempting as it is, I think we should eat. We can postpone the slaughter of Benjamin Taylor, aged twenty-nine, till after the feast. And I don't want to be slaughtered by your mother. She would make an unconvincing single mum."

He stretched his arms high, still an impressive figure of a man at sixty-two. He remained a trim six feet and, though his fair hair was now thinning fast, his features had hardened into a look of timeless Roman distinction. Jeremy Taylor was, by common consent, an imposing individual, whose gangly frame had settled over many years into a physique tinged with patrician menace. Distracted for a moment by the late-afternoon sky and its first streaks of apple pink, he noticed for the first time that there was a small hole in the elbow of his cashmere jumper.

He looked out at the road beyond the park railings and watched a woman in a translucent windbreaker walking a little dog, which led her along at a furious pace. The woman's face, he could see, was etched with unfathomable fury as she made her way along the pavement towards the pub, where young people sat outside, smoking and chattering into their mobiles. The pub, formerly known as the George, was now called @Organic: Ben had explained that this was a mark of the area's creeping gentrification rather than, as his father suggested, the decline and fall of Western civilisation. What Jeremy meant by this was something of which he had begun to feel intimations in the past few years: that this was no longer his world. I am a guest now, he thought, and a landlord no longer. A new age has come, and one which acknowledges no debt to me.

Leaving the wickets and stakes in place, the four Taylors made their way over to the little oasis of shade and opulence which Jenny had been constructing for the past hour from the contents of three wicker baskets. The sun, though low in the sky, was still beating powerfully upon the parkland and wearing down the jaundiced sports pitch beyond their picnic site. A handful of die-hard sunbathers lay scattered on this bleak football field, the puce markings of sunburn crisscrossing their skin like strange tattoos. A mother and three young children argued by the far goalposts, apparently over a push chair which the smallest was crashing repeatedly to the ground with impressive force. Undisturbed, only a few yards from them, a man wearing only khaki shorts, socks, sandals, and a porkpie hat slept. His eyes were concealed by a newspaper whose pages fluttered hectically.

On the Taylors' right shimmered a pond of blackish green, barely worthy of the name lake but described as such on boards emblazoned in gold lettering on flaking blue paint. By its edge, the detritus of park life mingled with the reeds and the fronds of parched vegetation: cans, wrappers, leaflets advertising closing-down sales. A few hungry ducks quivered optimistically as they passed by, hoping for food, their paddling just visible below the ripples caused by the easterly breeze. The twins, clad in matching denim jackets, skipped as they now did only on such family occasions. In their Hammersmith basement flat, with their set of school and university friends, such unself-conscious behaviour would have been inconceivable. But here, a return to the habits of childhood was permissible. Lara's hair was short now, styled in a bob, while Caitlin had stuck with the long blond tresses which had been their shared hallmark for so long. It made their father laugh, as he watched the two young women cackling hand in hand, that their occasional efforts to cut the umbilical which had linked them for twenty years only emphasised its resilience.

"At last, Jeremy," said Jenny as they reached the blankets she had set on the ground. "At bloody last. I do wonder about you sometimes." She reached over to pick up a little pot of gentleman's relish, which she offered to him absentmindedly, before reaching for a canteen of cutlery.

"Only sometimes, darling? That's progress. I shall have to call our marriage counsellor at once with this exciting news."

She chuckled. "Don't bother. I bloody well sacked him while you were playing."

"Oh, really? And doubtless paid the severance money from the joint account."

Ben Taylor smiled at this exchange as he foraged in one of the baskets for the first bottle of champagne. As far back as he could recall, such badinage had been the warp and weft of his parents' relationship. It comforted them both, for sure: It was their way of making safe—in the sturdy encasement of English irony—the accumulated tensions of three and a half decades of life together. But it was primarily, Ben also knew, for their children's benefit, a well-honed means of signalling to the four young Taylors that all was well, even when it was not.

He remembered that tone of voice from the past. It returned to him like a pebble dancing across the surface of a limpid pool, the inflexions in his father's voice whenever he reassured his son. It reminded Ben of long afternoons in Jeremy's study and the private magic of that room at the end of the corridor on the second floor. On his father's knee, he had learned the rudiments of chess and listened to the Narnia stories. He had discovered how to do crosswords and what a Welsh rarebit was. Sometimes, on Sundays, Jeremy would let him sit and read a comic as he worked or completed correspondence. At the end of the day, as dusk fell, he might even be allowed to play a game of darts with his father, lobbing the red-and-blue arrows high up at the board which Jeremy had screwed to the back of the door against Jenny's protestations. Naughtiest of all—astonishingly so, Ben now thought, with the clarity of hind-sight—his father would very occasionally show him and his sister the lit-tle collection of guns, some of them antique, which he had inherited from his uncle. There was a musket, a wartime revolver, and a few more modern pieces, some of them quite valuable. He explained to them how these firearms worked, how to dismantle them, clean them, and respect them. He said that they would never have to use guns, as his own fa-ther's generation had been forced to, but should know about them. Ben and his sister were speechless with reverence during these rare sessions, which they regarded, correctly, as a ritual of trust rather than as a reck-less form of playtime. In other circumstances, their father's demonstra-tions might have seemed psychotic. But they were evidence of his confidence in them—their mother could not possibly be allowed to know—and his belief that they should be aware of everything about their family's past and its role in their present. It taught both of them, too, that their father was capable of keeping secrets. This was the basis of the covenant between Jeremy Taylor and his two older children.

In those days, Ben remembered, the walls of the den were lined with "Spy" cartoons and pictures of his father posing with eminent men, the financiers he worked with and the politicians whom he had befriended when they were undergraduates together. A medical skeleton, a Christmas present from his surgeon brother, Gus, grinned manically in the corner, wearing a homburg given to him by his children but never

really worn. Behind was an old notice board, with the warning PROP-
ERTY OF ORIEL COLLEGE: KEEP OUT, a memento of a drunken evening
more than four decades ago now. The shelves told the story of Jeremy's
life as a literary pilgrimage, from the volumes of Walter Scott, Tolkien,
and C. S. Lewis of his childhood, via the Cyril Connolly and Orwell
of his teens, to the first editions which he prized above all else and
could now afford to collect. Above the desk hung an old print of
Constantinian Jerusalem, bearing the motto *Hierosolyma Urbs Sancta.*
On the desk was an old-fashioned green reading light and a beautiful
piece of Russian amber given to him by Jenny when she was a diplomat
and they were courting.

The champagne was good, Ben noticed. A vintage Krug, one his father drew from the cellar only when he was feeling exceptionally well
disposed towards life in general or someone in particular. In this case,
the imminent passing of his eldest child into his fourth decade had evidently prompted a flush of generosity. He opened the first bottle with a
tea towel, losing only a little liquid as the gas seeped out. He poured into
five plastic flutes, leaving his own till last.

"Did your sister call?" asked Jenny.

"Yes," snorted Ben. "This morning. You know she said she was going to take the day off work? You know, definitely, absolutely, for sure?
So she could be here on time? Well . . ."

"Mia wouldn't take a day off work just for someone's thirtieth," said
Caitlin. "Even if they were her brother. Far too grand these days."

"Just because she's short," said her twin. "And never has sex with
anyone."

"Oh God, La," her father said. "Do shut up. Just because your sister
doesn't lead the life of feckless hedonism which you and Cai have chosen for yourselves doesn't mean she isn't normal."

"It's true, though. She lives in the office. She's such a bloody spinster.
I got her a ticket to this club the other day and—"

"Yeah," said Lara. "Cai got her a ticket, twenty quid, all-night gig in

Clerkenwell, and we all went. There were even a couple of single guys we lined up, just in case she got faced and decided to behave like a normal human being for once. And she called two hours before we left and said she couldn't make it after all. Work. Work? It was bloody seven o'clock on a Saturday night." Lara shook her head in sincere bafflement. This was truly incredible behaviour, a mutilation of the most basic opportunities life offered.

Jeremy Taylor sipped his Krug and laughed inwardly. The twins ought to have been his burden, the late, unplanned-for children who had raised hell and rebelled throughout the middle age which he had set aside for quiet enjoyment. They had kept him up at night in his forties, got drunk in his late fifties, and forced him into a disagreeable round of chauffeuring around London, often very late at night. Caitlin and Lara had rampaged through adolescence, in constant need of collection from some middle-class home or other, deserted by unfortunate parents who would return after the weekend to find it desecrated by hormones and vodka. And yet Jeremy had derived only joy from the twins, not least because their worldview was so spectacularly at odds with his own, one which he shared with his two elder children. Ben and Mia sought out dragons to slay and crusades to fight. They had their father's gnawing ambition secreted in their marrow, and they competed passionately with each other to match his example. The twins' symbiosis, on the other hand, was of a completely different order: Their intimacy only reenforced their shared sense of complacency and their scepticism of unnecessary effort. From time to time, a smitten man would threaten rivalry between the two girls: One impossibly handsome suitor had pined for both twins for a full year before retreating in total defeat. But Lara spoke for her sister as well as herself when she sneered at the very notion that "some poxy bloke," even a twenty-five-year-old foreign exchange banker on a million a year, should come between them.

In Hammersmith, down the stairs behind the black railings, they had created a ménage of apparent disorder, although it was actually one founded on strict rules and regulations. "No dogs, no Italians, no cheap white wine" was one of the more explicit bylaws of the flat, as Caitlin had once explained to him. There were things which she and Lara would permit, and things they would not. Jenny and the two other children worried that the flat, with its clothes strewn everywhere, unemptied ashtrays, and resemblance on a Monday morning to a pub at closing time, would be the undoing of the pair. They would sink into untidy immobility, their lives an increasingly barren round of partying, idleness, and lost opportunity. But Jeremy knew better. He could see that the twins had wit and resolve on their side and that, while the paths of their lives would be utterly unpredictable and must, of sad necessity, include more heartache in the years ahead than either bargained upon now, they would both be all right. He felt sure of that as he watched Lara doing a merciless and brilliant impersonation of her elder sister dancing, badly and sadly, at a ball two years before.

"Even Anthony Foster wouldn't dance with her!" Caitlin said as her sister gyrated. "I mean, please. Anthony Foster. London's saddest man. I walk up to him and say, 'Ant, for Christ's sake, dance with my sister. She's gorgeous and she's single. You're the one for her.' And Anthony turns to me, Mr. Halitosis himself, the man who threw up on Clare Singleton at her own wedding, and says, 'I would, but she's mad!' I mean, what can you do?"

Lara shook her head again in exasperated agreement and drained her glass. She was hungry, and by now one of the blankets was covered with the feast to celebrate Ben's thirtieth. There were cold cuts, smoked salmon, a tin of beluga (a present from Uncle Gus at Christmas, saved for this occasion), blinis, salads, and her mother's special quiche. There were pickles, relishes, cheeses, and bottles of Badoit. Jeremy was already nibbling at a cracker smeared with the gentleman's relish. A second bottle of Krug was making the rounds. He noticed that the screaming family had departed, leaving the unconscious man in the sandals to his dream. The newspaper had now completely disintegrated and was spreading across the pitch in sections.

"Well," said Ben. "The point is that she's coming, but of course she's going to be late. Apparently, her man—"

" 'Her man'?" said Caitlin. "Shome mishtake shurely, Benjamin."

"Not that kind of man. Her politician. The golden boy. He's on telly in the morning and he needs a briefing. So, of course, fingers snapped, and off goes little Mi with her pencil and her revision notes to help him prep up. She's been working on the questions and answers so she can hand them to him before he goes on. He'd be eviscerated if she wasn't there for him."

"Is he any good?" asked Jenny. "This—what's it?—Anderson."

"Anderton," said Ben. "Miles Anderton. Yup, he's pretty good. Not much older than me, and already a parliamentary aide. He's made a name for himself bashing Islamic militants and banging on about child poverty. All very scripted. He's a complete chancer, of course, and a world-famous shagger apparently, which'll catch up with him one day. But he'll be in the Cabinet, or so Mi says."

"She would," said Lara. "She talks about these people as if they were pop stars, when they're just middle-aged men in crap suits."

"Not so crap in Milesy's case, La," said Ben. "She's got him shopping for the best threads now. That was step one, apparently. Robinson wouldn't take the account unless he promised to spend ten grand on a new wardrobe."

"I don't see how it works," said his mother. "How could an MP possibly pay for Z Robinson? I mean, most big companies can't afford the ridiculous rates they charge."

"True, Mum. But the point is that he doesn't pay, or at least he doesn't pay properly. They charge him a mate's rate—almost pro bono—and their calculation is he's going to be a star. Milesy keeps banging on about dangerous mullahs and poor wee children up a chimney in Barnstaple. The whips notice, he gets into a big job, and—hey presto—Robinson are laughing. Mia's the link man, so she's happy. That's what Claude told me, anyway."

Claude. With a couple of glasses inside him and the licence of the birthday boy, Ben felt entitled to mention the name of the man who had hired Mia from Oxford, nurtured her at the firm, wooed her, and then dumped her. Jenny, in particular, having met Claude Silberman early in this cycle of grief—at a drinks party at Merton, where she had gone to meet her daughter one summer day—found every stage wearyingly predictable. She considered Silberman an all-too-familiar character: suave to the point of parody, handsome in a merely feminine way, and utterly untrustworthy. Her unimpressed mumbles when asked about him by Mia had, she later realised, only heightened his attractions to her daughter, and that caused her a frisson of guilt. But she and Jeremy thought Ben's decision to continue socialising with the man who had broken his sister's heart very poor form, and told him so. There were few fissures between the Taylors, but Ben had drilled one into the family's rock face by staying friends with this indubitably wicked person.

"Him?" hissed his mother. "What does he know?"

"He wears hats," said Caitlin. "What a wanker."

"Wanker," chimed Lara. "He's like something out of a crap sixties film."

It was true that Claude wore hats, one of many affectations which verged on the intolerable. Slender and immaculately dressed, he had the perfect manners and air of utter insincerity which marked the true dandy. He had the infuriating habit of saying "Of course, of course." But Ben liked him. They had got to know each other through his sister, but their friendship had quickly grown, completely independent of the faltering romance. They had gone out for a tentative drink in St. James's one night and got into a completely unnecessary fistfight with a couple of Americans. The brawl's origins were mythic and had become the subject of almost-theological debate between the two young men at subsequent gatherings. But it was agreed that the two Americans, sitting at the next table in T-shirts and expensive bomber jackets, had taken exception to Claude's volubility and asked him "to keep the fucking noise down." Claude, had he not drunk as much as he had by then, might have acceded to their request—"Of course, of course"—or simply brushed off the provocation with what Ben later learned he called the "Silberman stare." But they had racked up a bar bill of well over a hundred pounds by then—the kosher vodka was going down a treat—and were therefore deaf to the warning signals which would normally have been screaming in their ears.

Claude turned on them with a look of comic iciness. "Are you talking to me? Are you looking at me? Because I don't see anyone else here."

Ben could not believe that Claude, the silken strategy adviser in his foppish overcoat and thousand-pound suit, had unexpectedly been transformed into Travis Bickle. He was suddenly out on the town with Taxi Driver, an unlikely impersonator of De Niro, missing only the Mohawk and the marine veteran's jacket. How had this metamorphosis occurred? Ben could not say, although most of what he needed to know was gathered in a glass forest on the marble table in front of them. Though the bar was dimly lit, he could see that American One—who had issued the original challenge—was as astonished as he was, but nowhere near as amused.

"Funny guy, eh?" said American Two, who was not remotely fazed. "Funny loud guy?"

It always intrigued Ben that real fights were so messy and initially undramatic, with none of the choreography you expected from a lifetime's movies and television. For a moment after this riposte—which was not a riposte at all, of course, but a statement of violent intent—both tables had fallen quiet and all four men had looked at their hands, the American team fidgeting nervously with their chunky frat house rings. Then, most improbably of all, Claude had stood up and slapped American One hard on the top of the head. This could not have been particularly painful, Ben thought, but had served its purpose admirably, humiliating American One in the most stinging way possible. A girl standing nearby had laughed out loud at the bizarre sight of the lanky young gent slapping down his burly adversary so contemptuously. This was very funny, and also very bad news.

For what seemed like several minutes (but which Claude and Ben later calculated must have been no more than sixty seconds), the four men pummelled one another with little skill and much foul language. Glass was smashed and a chair broken. Kosher vodka spilt on the floor. Ben took a fist full in the face and felt no pain, just something warm trickling from his nose. Claude, he noticed with odd detachment, was on the floor, taking a kicking from American One, and would probably have been badly hurt had two big security men in puffer jackets bearing the legend SANDINO'S BAR not rushed over from the other side of the room and broken up the fight. To their relief, Ben and Claude quickly found themselves bleeding and barred for life, but safely on the pavement, freezing and laughing their heads off. Claude patted Ben on the back as he was copiously sick in the gutter, then helped him into a taxi. When he woke up outside his flat in Primrose Hill, he found that the driver had already been paid and handsomely tipped: so handsomely, in fact, that he waited until Ben had walked through the front entrance of the mansion block before driving off.

The next morning Ben had awoken in a terrible state, badly shaken by the fight, hungover to the point of suicide, and convinced that he had committed at least four criminal offences at Sandino's. He looked in the mirror, to see a man he did not recognise, grey from the after-effects of drink, sporting the black eye and cracked lip of a failed amateur boxer. He wondered if his nose, still clogged with blood, was broken, or merely agonising. He also seemed to be suffering some sort of palsy, which made it very difficult to make coffee, brush his teeth, or pick up the paper. When the phone rang at two o'clock, he assumed with exhausted fatalism that it must be DCI Bastard of the local nick, giving him advance warning that he and his colleagues were on their way round to collar him and end his liberty forever, and that Ben might like to use the minutes of freedom remaining to him to call his parents to say good-bye. But it was Claude, chirpier than seemed possible for an ordinary human being who only twelve hours before had been taking ferocious blows to the head and stomach.

"Well, young man, you seem to have made your bones rather quicker than I anticipated. You've got your sister's temper, I see, but your right hook is better. You deserve a reward. Let's do the same again tonight." And so, against Ben's better judgement, they had.

Claude had introduced his protégé to a milieu he found intoxicating in every sense: not the skiing and skunk set of the Fulham Road, with whom Ben had run in his teens, those boys in their cricket jumpers drinking Japanese beer and dreaming of Porsches full of blondes. Claude's world was the best that Soho and Mayfair had to offer. He would pick Ben up from work on a Friday night, drive him to the West End, where they would meet his coterie for dinner. Then they would move from club to club, from Shaftesbury Avenue to Jermyn Street to Berkeley Square, downing Stoli martinis until sunrise or later. Sometimes they would end up in the dives of the East End, where Claude's circle of acquaintances included some unlikely hard men who evidently found his incongruous presence in their clubs amusing. Then, sometimes in the company of one or two of these gorillas, they would head for the market pubs, which had early licences, for a few last pints and a fry-up first thing.

This friendship had long survived Claude's affair with Mia, which had, in truth, not lasted as long as she had pretended to her parents. What Ben chose not to reveal to them was that although Claude was indeed a disastrous boyfriend and had technically at least been the one to end the liaison, Mia had more or less forced him to do so. She had made clear to him more than once that she felt next to nothing for him and that their affair, while it satisfied some of her needs, was very much a phase as far as she was concerned, and that he should not get his hopes up. "Of course, of course," Claude had said. But he had known as soon as he heard the first of these speeches that he would have to end it quickly. Which, at a sushi bar in Park Lane one clear November night, he had done, with no tears on either side. They had resumed their strictly professional relationship at Z Robinson with functional frostiness. Ben, of all people, knew this to be for the best. He also knew that his sister was now smitten by another, and that the memory of Claude was a very distant one. Only the other Taylors believed that Mia had been traduced.

"Let other men make money faster in the air of dark-roomed towns," sang his father in a passable baritone, opening the last of the champagne.

"Oh God, he's off," said Caitlin.

"I don't dread a peevish master; though no man do heed my frowns," sang Jenny. Then, together with her husband: "I be free to go abroad, or take again my homeward road—"

They were both interrupted by a singing voice which still had the enchantment of a child's: "To where, for me, the apple tree do lean down low in Linden Lea."

"Mi! Darling!" Jenny enveloped her daughter with an embrace of sheer, unrestrained delight. She had not seen her, she suddenly realised, for months, and the sight of her little blond girl, shoeless, in a trouser suit, and carrying a briefcase, filled her with melancholy and relief. She had, Jenny thought, lost weight, which was no surprise, given the ridiculous intensity with which she lived her life. Mia reminded her of herself, and that was a cause of worry to her. She knew that she had needed an anchor in life and had found one in Jeremy. Mia, for all her accomplishments, drifted on the choppy waters of life with little to link her to the seabed.

"How do you know those words, Mia Taylor?" asked her father, bending over to kiss his daughter. "You're not supposed to sing songs like that till you're more than forty."

"Well, on that basis, Mia's probably been singing them for ten years," said Caitlin.

"Listening to you in the bath, Dad. Piss off, Valley Girl," she said, hugging her younger sister and then Lara, who immediately began to examine the new set of earrings Mia was wearing.

"These are nice. Very nice. Suspiciously nice."

"Oh, those . . . Do you like them?" Mia played with her right earlobe nervously.

The twins looked at her, then at each other, and then at her again: "Boyfriend! Boyfriend!"

"Anthony Foster!" said Caitlin in triumph. "He changed his mind!"

In spite of herself, Mia smiled and threw her arms up in despair. "God, I'm not that desperate. So, Benj, I am here. I said I would be. Gasping for a drink."

"Good God, aren't you Mia Taylor? Didn't we exchange E-mails once about two years ago?" He smiled and put an arm around her. "Only three hours late. I'm glad you're here. This all right?"

There was a glass left in the last bottle of Krug. She nodded. Preparing the briefing notes for Miles's television appearance had worn her out. Miles, Miles. Would he see the point? He was a great actor and a nimble political operator. He had already caught the eye of the press with his passionate outbursts on child deprivation—the trip to Liverpool had gone particularly well—and his ferocious attacks on Muslim militants in London. He had dared to name individual Muslim leaders like Omar Aziz and Dr. Saffi Muhammad, and taken them on in person, live, on Channel 4 News. He was fearless in his march towards the racial front line of the country's inner cities; he did not flinch from the hatred and anger that simmered on its ugliest streets.

It was difficult to catch Miles out. But she wanted more of him, much more. She wanted him to shine in the dull political firmament and for the shine to be seen as her work. It was an open secret that he was being groomed at Robinson, and just as well known—because she had told several journalists she trusted, and a few she didn't—that she was the groom. There would surely be a reshuffle by the end of the year, and Miles had to make the leap from lippy bag carrier to a middle-ranking job in government if he was to remain on track for greatness. He was not the finished article yet and could not see that his answers in interviews, unlike the speeches she wrote for him, were still too defensive, lacking visible passion and purpose. There would be no sparkle in his performance tomorrow, she feared. But there ought to be enough confidence to catch the eyes of the hacks and the whips, which was all that was necessary. She needed a few more stories in the nationals saying he was "tipped for promotion," "a rising star," or "the next leader but one" and she'd be home and dry. Unless Milesy blew it in his interview, that ought to be sewn up in Monday's press.

She drank the champagne in three gulps and searched in the baskets for something else to drink. She needed to put a firewall of warm feeling between the stress of the day so far and the celebrations of the hours ahead. Her father had laid out a fine Chassagne Montrachet for the lunch proper, but Mia would have drunk from a wine box at that moment. As the Krug took effect in her limbs, she looked out at the makeshift croquet pitch, saw for the first time the cluster of balls, and realised that the game must have been interrupted at a crucial point. Gazing through the railings beyond, she could see the growing crowd outside the pub, young money in T-shirts escaping from their loft conversions to enjoy the preamble to a serious Saturday night. A couple, Mediterranean in their beauty, held hands over glasses of white wine. It was six o'clock. Families were beginning to make their way slowly from the park, out beyond its old and dilapidated bandstand to the Georgian terraced houses which looked over its lawns and ponds to the amber glow of east London's evening. The two tribes of the area went their separate ways: the young out to find pleasure and trouble in the night, the middle-aged back to their homes to avoid such things. Mia brushed some grass from her suit jacket, then took it off, folding it neatly from habit.

So often, she thought, she had watched day turn into evening with her family in this way, eating on a hillside, in a park, on a Cornish beach, by a French lake. Jenny told her that the ritual picnicking came from her father's side and that the tradition had annoyed her enormously when she met him. The Druids—her name for Jeremy's father and his greybeard uncles—would gather in Kensington Gardens or St. James's and feast on special occasions. She remembered them as particularly joyless events, enlivened only by very occasional moments of spontaneity. When she was pregnant with Ben, one of Jeremy's great-uncles had suffered a spectacular seizure under a tree in Holland Park, a situation which had initially been treated by his relatives as a nuisance, disrupting as it did their *déjeuner sur l'herbe*. Jenny had ended up administering first aid to the poor man—ponderous and breathing heavily herself—while one of Jeremy's uncles trudged off lugubriously to find a public telephone to call an ambulance. The old man had not died that day, lasting another five years before expiring over a book of Mandarin proverbs. At the time, Jenny had been horrified by the indifference of the family she had married into, and by its embarrassment that one of its members should bring chaos to such an occasion. Now, years on, she found the incident hilarious. And she recognised how much the tradition mattered to Jeremy and the happiness with which he invested it once it had been wrested from the Druids' chilly grasp. As they had brought up their children, alfresco eating had become an almost-sacred part of their partnership: Birthdays, anniversaries, and even sad events which needed to be forgotten were marked by picnics. The age of the Druids passed and yielded to the age of Jeremy and Jenny. A rite of grim patriarchy was made a rite of spring.

The sight of the baskets and the bottles reminded Mia of these little rituals which had been the punctuation marks of her upbringing. She remembered her thirteenth birthday on a touring holiday in Heidelberg: After a morning in which her father had explained to Mia and Ben the perils of student duelling, with dramatic moments of swashbuckling reenactment, the family had pitched camp in one of the little town's squares and eaten wurst, bread, and cheese, with beer for the adults and apple juice for the children. One of the twins had been stung by a wasp, plunging the festivities into disarray and delaying the moment when the cake could be presented to Mia. But it was the extreme heat of that day which she remembered most, the blurring of the pale stone of the town under a baking sun. For her twenty-first, Jeremy had thrown a series of parties, but the one that mattered most was for the family itself, including her elderly grandmother, in Christ Church meadows. They had watched the undergraduates make their way down to the river for Eights Week and drunk Pimm's laced with mint and borage—made, as Jenny insisted, with ginger ale, not lemonade. Her grandmother had given her a silver brooch of unremarkable design but the deepest family significance: a gift from her own mother, long before she had met Jeremy's father and been claimed by the Druids, as Jenny had been a generation later. That occasion, in the sight of the windows from which Antoine Blanche had read "The Waste Land" through a megaphone, captured for Mia the end of her Oxford years much more than the call from her tutor later that summer to tell her she had got her First.

So now the family was gathered again. Henty had once called it the "golden thread," the glittering fibre which encircled them all and bound them together, these Taylors. Jeremy had scoffed at this whimsy when he first overheard the nanny explaining it to the older children at bedtime, but he was secretly pleased. All his work, the mountain he had climbed to provide for them all and raise them as healthy and mostly happy, was vindicated in that phrase coined by a childless middle-aged woman from the Black Country who had a gift for sentimental observation.

His father might have been the leading philologist of his generation and an Oxford luminary, but Professor Taylor had died penniless, supported in later life by a modest college pension and the subsidy of his children. Jeremy had built from scratch, determined that Jenny should not have to work or want for anything. Her final posting before they married had been Paris, and he had visited her almost every weekend for six months. She had wanted to remain in the diplomatic service, she said, and a woman of her intelligence, two decades later, would have meant it. But Jenny did not mean it. Her decision to marry Jeremy was a decision to withdraw from the fray of telegrams, speech writing, and Foreign Office politics.

When they had met at a Fitzrovia cocktail party, she was twenty-three and wanted only to climb the gilded ladder until she was appointed to a big ambassadorship. She spoke of Rome, Bonn, Moscow, Washington, as if these were merely preordained pit stops which lay between her and the chequered flag of glory. Her unfettered ambition had been one of many things which Jeremy found attractive. She was not like the cool blondes in head scarves with whom he had previously consorted, whose only goal in life was to be heavily subsidised and mistaken for Jean Seberg. Jenny, an immaculate brunette with heels of just the right height, knew she did not have to strain for effect to draw men into her orbit, and she realised from the moment she caught Jeremy's eye, across a room thick with Gauloise smoke and London chatter, that he was hers for the taking. But, once taken, she also knew he would draw to a close everything she said she wanted that night. The ambassadorship would not be hers, but a life of true contentment, which suddenly seemed to be on offer, might just prove an acceptable alternative.

Jeremy's career in banking had been in its very infancy when they met. But he already exuded the invincibility of a man for whom success was a given. This was not, as it happened, what he felt at all. Raised by a man of supreme intelligence, if not of worldly accomplishment, he doubted his own abilities profoundly. Like his father, he had built his life from books, but Jeremy felt only self-disgust at the inadequacy of the results. He looked up at the marbled intellectual tower of the professor and felt like a humble outhouse in his shadow. It was only with Jenny's gentle chiding and encouragement that he grasped how far he could go in the City, and how quickly; that his intellect had practical application; and that his sheer presence as a man gave his cleverness real power. By the age of forty, he was a senior partner at a famous investment bank, with a large house in the Boltons and two children at public school. He could indulge himself and his brood, take them on holiday, buy his wife a run-around sports car on a whim. His cloistered upbringing in a semidetached house on the outskirts of Oxford seemed a dream of many centuries ago, a strange fantasy of golden stone and men padding quietly to libraries across perfectly kept grass.

UNLIKE HER FATHER, Mia was open in her affection for Henty's idea of the "golden thread." She took to it instantly and grew to love it more and more over the years, nurturing it as if its appointed custodian. It seemed to her to conjure all that was simple and true. But, to the precocious teenager she quickly became, it also had satisfying overtones of myth and magic, of Ariadne waiting for Theseus in the labyrinth built by Daedalus, and of the *Aeneid*'s golden bough. Such thoughts, she knew, struck her father as hopelessly pretentious and just the sort of nonsense that gave an expensive education a bad name; or that, at least, was what he said to her from behind his newspaper. "Oh, no, not that again," he said on one occasion when Mia, back from school, had drawn these allusions at supper. "You'll give Henty the idea that she's a classicist." But Mia could see that his official intolerance of her literary whimsy did not outweigh his pleasure at the myth growing round the nanny's idea that something rich and strange bound the Taylors together and warded off evil.

Mia was also smart enough to see that affluence played a part in that. Her father was a man of considerable wealth by the time she was old enough to grasp what that really meant—to understand that not everyone lived in the same comfort or made the same assumptions as she did. School had given her a dim sense that the life of the Taylors was not the life of all: The scholarship girls dressed a little differently, spoke a little differently, boasted less about where they had been on holiday when term began. But it was only at Oxford that she had understood fully what privilege was, and that she was its beneficiary. She understood this not from what people said, but from what they did not say; from the minor irritation she could generate in some of her fellow undergraduates simply by saying where she lived or where she had been to school. "Christ, listen to yourself, darling—all you talk about is the things you own," one fellow fresher, a girl with purple streaks in her hair and many badges on her jacket, had said to Mia during her first term as she babbled nervously about her life at some society open evening or other. Never before had she realised that her very countenance, and the good fortune it communicated, could be a provocation. On the other side, an earnest man in John Lennon spectacles had declared to her, without invitation or explanation, that Max Weber was "primarily a dialectician." He had tried to ply her with warm Blue Nun as she recovered speechlessly from the girl's attack. Mia had felt, for the first time, a true impostor, lonely in a way she had never before encountered.

And yet she knew that there was more to the Taylors' strength than money. Her parents had built something in their years together, an anvil on which they had forged their family, and they had done so with more than material wealth. This was not the work of sentimentality, she had realised over time, but of ferocity. Jeremy and Jenny Taylor had protected and nurtured their four children with teeth bared at the world, determined that no deliberate harm or random misfortune should come their way. Now they were all adults, or at least trying to be. But that had not diminished her parents' instinct to scar savagely any creature who came near their young. Claude Silberman never stood a chance.

By now, the six Taylors were feasting happily, their conversation subdued for a while as they ate the birthday lunch that—as a direct consequence of Miles Anderton's political ambition—had become a birthday tea. Caitlin and Lara squabbled in their monosyllabic private language over who had had more caviar, and whether quiche was more calorific than pizza. Ben got mustard on his white cotton shirt and swore with a lack of restraint so total that even his mother laughed. The Burgundy, cool and smooth, wove the early evening together and bred affability. The croquet game was forgotten as the light deteriorated. Beyond the copse, the ochre games pitch was now deserted, the last sleeping sunbather having awoken and marched off in his socks and sandals as if to a business appointment. Although the park stayed open till nine o'clock, there were few people left within its boundaries now, and, as day drew to a lazy close, it began to seem less like a public space, a place to observe and coexist with other people, and more like a private realm, an enchanted family fiefdom. The breeze brushed at the surface of the water and caused the greenery of the rhododendrons nearby to shiver. But it was still warm.

"So are we really going back to yours, then?" Caitlin asked Ben.

"Yes, Cai, and don't sound as if you're visiting the poor relations and doing them a great favour. It was a bloody expensive house and I've spent a mint tarting it up."

"Well, it's still miles from anywhere."

"No, it's miles from Hammersmith and Fulham and that funny little comfort zone where you and your airhead friends insist on living. It's got five bedrooms, and a drawing room bigger than the whole of your flat."

"So what's the plan, exactly, Benj?" asked Mia. "What have you planned for the midnight hour, when you officially become an old bastard?"

"Finish up here, then back to the love shack. We can have a late supper and then toast my bus pass at midnight. I've laid in a few bottles of decent fizz, which even Dad might deign to drink."

Ben Taylor's house was a cause of deep fascination and some suspicion in his family. Mia, who lived in a split-level flat in Islington, understood why he had moved so far east: as a smart investment, of course, but primarily to signal his distinctiveness. His financial services business—whatever that meant, exactly—was diversifying fast and he was doing well, perhaps even better than he had yet let on. He had prospered during his years in the City, constantly running into men who knew his father and smiled upon him, but somewhere down the line, he had managed to find the backers and the nerve to go it alone. A little venture capital—did she detect the hand of Claude and a late-night deal with a half-cut contact?—had started him up in his new trade and he was already succeeding. The house was a declaration of friendly independence from his past, and his plans for the night he turned thirty were an integral part of that: He wanted his family to see what he had done on his own and for them to celebrate that, as much as his passage into full adulthood and the commonwealth of the self-sufficient. But the other four Taylors felt he was either being purely perverse or mysteriously ingenious in moving out of their geographical orbit. Jeremy had got lost twice on the long journey from the Boltons and was worried now that he should have driven the six-year-old Volvo, rather than the newer Bentley. Parked beyond the railings, it stood out among the secondhand BMWs and battered Golfs, a conspicuous totem of real wealth amidst the spoils of mere aspiration.

"I don't know," said Jeremy. "In the East End after dark. It all sounds very dangerous." Ben rose only partially to the bait. "Don't worry, Dad. You can go home with a police escort after you've drunk my health at midnight. You'll be back in a civilised post code before you know it. And I promise not to drag you back until I'm forty."

"That's a relief," said Jenny. "It means I don't have to worry about your father ripping out pages from the *A–Z* and swearing like a navvy for another decade." She was amused by Ben's little plan, curious, too, to see how he had refurbished the house and whether there would be any telltale signs of a woman in his life. His flat in Primrose Hill had been almost comically that of a bachelor, combining the outward signs of disposable income—gadgets, expensive sofas, a new kitchen—with an ingrained squalor that defied the power of money to shift grime. Relieved at last of his eighteen-hour days in the City, and suddenly flush with cash, Ben had begun to understand the notion of home and had even talked to her about his burgeoning interest in the art market and the local galleries he had started to frequent. In his stained shirt, chinos, and deck shoes, Ben still looked like the teenager who had confessed all his anxieties to her and cried in her arms more often than she would ever have told the others. But he was no longer that teenager, she knew. Of the others, Jenny understood that only Mia grasped how Ben had moved on in the past year in the most profound ways, and that his benign purpose that evening was to take his loved ones on a tour of his new world and seek their approval. It pleased her that, like Jeremy, he had chosen his own path, albeit one about which she knew much less and could never be fully certain.

Mia bit her nails and wondered how to broach the matter with Ben. He would be angry, she knew, but if she waited much longer, he would be furious. She had thought of coming clean when she had called earlier, but she'd been able to tell that he was disappointed enough that she would be late. Her plans for the latter half of the evening would compound that disappointment. But she knew that if she got it out of her system now, he could be brought round and would not throw what the twins called a "Big Ben." These tantrums, of which she had almost three decades' experience, were to be avoided if at all possible, if only because it usually took her brother several days to revert to normality. Such an outcome was unthinkable on a night like this. She could not be responsible for ruining the afterglow of the picnic, the present giving, and the toasts.

"Benj," she said. "Benj." Her father and mother were arguing about where the car was parked, and the twins were trying to make a conspiratorial call on Lara's mobile. It was as good a moment as she was going to get.

"What?"

"There's something I didn't mention when I phoned earlier. Please don't be cross. Please. I have to go quickly—"

"Go? Bloody hell, Mi, you've only just arrived."

"I know."

"What about the house? And the toast?"

"I'll be there. I have to run an errand first."

"An errand. What is it about you and Saturday nights? Don't people at Robinson ever go off duty? Or is it choosing Milesy's underwear for him?" He pushed his plate aside. Even in the fading light, she could see that his eyes were already gleaming with bitter exasperation.

"It's not work."

"Not work?" Somehow, illogically, this made a difference, perhaps because it was so surprising.

"Well, not really. Oh come on, Benj. You know what's going on."

"It is Miles."

"Of course it's bloody Miles. I have to pick him up from the airport and give him his notes. He's in Frankfurt today and—"

"Nice earrings, by the way."

"Fuck off." She grinned. "Am I making a complete fool of myself?"

"No. Yes. I don't know. Does he like you as much as you like him?"

"God knows. I do like him. I wish I didn't sometimes. It's very unprofessional. But I do. And I have to pick him up from the bloody airport tonight."

Ben laughed and then put his hand to his mouth, realising that she was not ready to make this disclosure to the full tribal council of the Taylors.

"Look, you are a complete nightmare. I don't see why you can't work for somebody without jumping into bed with them, but—"

"Low blow, birthday boy."

"Joke. Sorry. Anyway, I forgive you. Thousands wouldn't. And listen, Mi, just bring him along. There's no point in going to pick up Milesy and then dumping him. Bring him with you for the toast." He caught her eye and guessed that she already had invited him and was in agony as a result.

Mia had indeed already asked Miles to the late-night drinks one afternoon in bed when they were supposed to be in his office in the Commons working on a speech. Jean, his secretary, had called him three times to ask where he was and when he was planning to return. He had held the phone to his lover's ear so she could hear the ill-concealed impatience of his PA. Ah, Jean: the best secretary in the Commons, or so they said. Miles's protector and the matriarch of his vibrant little world. If Mia was the sculptress, it was the more dogged, knowing Jean who secured the plinth of his political ambition.

That day, as she and Miles lay together, Mia's exuberance had got the better of her, and he had lazily agreed to go with her to Ben's party, quite oblivious of the honour she was paying him and the risk she was taking. She had even forced him to write the address and time in his private diary, and found his amusement at her excitement vaguely demeaning. She could have kissed Ben for detecting what she was really saying, and for letting her off the hook so elegantly. Even so, she went through the motions. "What will Mum and Dad say? They think I'm still in love with Claude. I'm not sure they're ready for an intolerably pushy MP at a Taylor family gathering."

"Leave it to me. I was singing his praises earlier. When you're gone, I'll say I insisted. And if they make a fuss, I'll say it's my house and my birthday. Which happens to be true." He rolled over in the grass with an air of self-satisfaction, having turned his sister's annoying revelation into an opportunity to assert himself.

Their giggling conspiracy invited attention. "Too much champagne, children?" asked Jenny.

"Pathetic," said Jeremy. "When I was your age, I could drink three bottles of champagne and still sit an exam."

"Bollocks of the highest order," said Ben. "When you were my age, you slept in your office and fell over when you had more than a glass of Tio Pepe. You were never a hard man of rock'n'roll, Dad."

"True, sadly," said Jenny, running her fingers through her husband's hair. "You were very well behaved."

"Well, I don't know. I struck myself as pretty wild, actually."

"Mi was just saying she's got to run an errand," said Ben. "Work, of course. Typical Mi. But she'll be back for the toasts and—dare I presume?—the presents."

"Oh, Mi," said Caitlin. "Not a-bloody-gain."

"Can't it wait, darling?" asked their mother. "Just this once? We never see you. Can't you put it off just this once?" Jeremy made no attempt to conceal his frustration. He said nothing, but Mia knew he thought she was behaving badly by the way he examined his striped cuffs and his watch.

Her mouth was dry. "Look, I have to go; there's no way round it. But I'll be back for the festivities. I promise."

"Well," said Jenny, who was starting to pack up. "See you are, my dear. It's not every day that your brother turns thirty and not every day that we all get together like this." There was a sharpness in her words which Mia immediately recognised. It was the frost of acquiescence in something deeply undesirable, grafted onto a warning that her daughter had better make good her promise. To miss the midnight toast would now be considered a serious offence.

The matter settled, or at least frozen in a truce, the Taylors set about dismantling the little haven of their afternoon. Dirty cutlery was returned to its canteen, plates were cleared and stacked, blankets folded, leftovers put in plastic bags. Ben and the twins carried the many empty bottles over to the nearest bin while Mia and Jeremy uprooted the croquet wickets and stakes and collected the balls. By now, the light had almost gone and the park had fallen completely quiet. Across from the copse, the terraced houses were lit up and the pub was a throng of activity. The late-afternoon crowd, making their first pit stop of the evening, had been replaced by those who would stay till closing time, drinking real ale and spritzers. Cars sped by. Mia looked at her watch and knew that she must catch a cab soon or end up displeasing everybody. She had no idea whether she would be returning alone, but she was determined that she would return, in time to give her brother the cuff links on which she had spent a week's wages.

"I'm off," she said. "See you all in a little bit."

"All right, darling," said Jenny. "Be back soon."

Leaving the rest of her family to their tasks, Mia Taylor turned round and began to walk towards the park gates. It was brisk suddenly and she put her jacket on as she made her way to the two tall Victorian lamps which marked the entrance. Only now did she notice how wrecked and squalid the bandstand was, apparently a home for tramps, its boards broken and what remained of the platform a maze of smashed bottles. No music had been played in its pavilion for many years. On one of its steps, an old man in a grey gabardine coat talked to himself and swigged from a brown paper bag. His beard was flecked with spittle and booze. He sensed her tension as she walked past, and he shouted, "Good evening to you, darlin'!" She quickened her pace and headed towards the light.

Out on the road, she waited on the corner of a roundabout for a cab. She was near enough to the pub now to make out the faces of the drinkers at its outside tables and to catch snatches of their conversation: the arguments over trivia which marked such evenings and the high-pitched laughter of women being plied with drink by optimistic males.

Suddenly, she wished she did not have to go and meet Miles, wished she could turn round and spend the evening unbroken with her family, wished that she did not have a gift for making things more complicated than they need be. Miles, Miles, Miles: Who was she trying to fool, thinking that she and Miles could make a go of it? She felt a stab of guilt, too, that she was even contemplating such an interlude in so carefully choreographed and long-planned a celebration merely to indulge the ego of a man who had no inkling of its tribal significance. She remembered, too, the tone of her mother's voice and the thinness of the ice onto which she was now careering. If his flight was late, she was done for. If he was too tired to go back with her, she was done for. And if he decided to join the party after all, she was probably done for, too. Who did she think she was, bringing an outsider into such a gathering?

On the horizon, an amber light was growing slowly in size. With the reflex of a native Londoner, she lifted her arm before she realised what was happening. A few seconds passed, and then the driver flashed his headlights. This was a relief. She would make it in time to pick up Miles, and then the rest would have to sort itself out. The cab drew up and she gave instructions to the driver before tugging on the door, which was stuck. She tried again and it clicked open. Mia clambered in, set down her briefcase, and ran her fingers through her hair. She breathed a sigh of minor affliction. This was proving a stressful day and she wanted to negotiate its final complexity as quickly as she could. The cab drove off, and she looked out of the window at the Bentley as she passed. Her family had not yet packed the car and must still be under the copse, probably talking about her abrupt departure and her hopeless performance. Well, nothing she could do now. She had made her peace with Ben, which was what mattered most.

She thought she heard a car backfire behind her, or a flock of birds rise as one in a sudden burst from the surface of the water. But when she looked round, there was nothing.

Chapter TWO

THE ROTATING BEACONS of the police vans and
fire engines sprayed crazy beams of light onto the smoking embers of the
building. She could see all this from the end of the street, and her cab-
driver muttered an expletive in a quite different spirit to those with
which he had bored her on the journey back from the airport. A cordon
had been set up, and beyond it the street was full of police officers, firemen, and numb residents, evacuees from their own homes, wandering
aimlessly in the preposterous clothing of those who are forced to dress
quickly at night. She ought to have felt at least a twinge of horror, the
nausea of foreboding, but she did not. This was a moment of such total
dislocation, such unfathomable shifts in the foundations of her life, that
all she could feel as she walked towards the light was curiosity.

At the cordon tape, she asked a policeman in a bright yellow jacket
what was going on, and he told her that the situation was under control
and asked her to move on. So persuasive was he that she almost did as
she was told and walked off into the night. But, of course, she persisted
and explained that she was the sister of a resident in the street. Which
number? Twenty-five. She saw him stiffen and mutter into his hissing

radio as he let her through, escorting her to the cluster of vehicles above which plumes of smoke curled towards a frozen black sky. She walked with all the poise she could muster, conscious somehow that all eyes were suddenly upon her, even though she could not see anybody looking directly at her. Her fist clenched and unclenched around the handle of her briefcase. The refugees of the street, clad in sweatpants, bathrobes, and—in one ludicrous case—a three-piece suit but no shirt or shoes, looked at her with the solemn, instinctive knowledge that her story intersected somehow with whatever horror had occurred in the house down the street. Two policewomen with clipboards were trying to herd this temporarily displaced tribe out of the road and towards waiting vans. But the fascination of Mia's arrival—the captivating sight of a person making a rendezvous with death—made their work impossible. A small child ran across the road and was intercepted by the gloved hand of one of the WPCs.

By then, the scale, though not the nature, of what had happened was becoming apparent. She could see Ben's house and the house adjoining much more clearly now that she had passed a cluster of trees whose foliage had obscured her view. Both buildings, she realised, had suffered vicious fire damage, centred on the ground floor. Most of Ben's living room was gutted and the frames of the windows had disappeared entirely, as had much of the brickwork. All she could see within was singed debris and shattered glass, none of it bearing any relation to the interior of the house as she remembered it. What looked like a lamp stand, charred and splintered, jutted from what remained of the windows, a crazy remnant of chic domesticity. In the drive, there was rubble everywhere and livid fragments of timber, which still glowed. Firemen wearing masks walked from one house to the other, dousing what remained of the flames, sending a charge of steam into the night air each time they did so. Another cordon had been set up across the two adjoining properties, along which mingled more police officers. Looking down at the other end of the street, she could see a much brighter light shining towards the scene, which she realised was a television camera. A man whom she imagined to be a plainclothes officer saw the intrusion as she did, and he instructed one of his men to deal with it immediately. The policeman marched off towards the offending light, his body a silhouetted spectre against its powerful beam.

"Excuse me, miss. Are you Miss Taylor?" The voice came from nowhere, and, for the first time in what she realised was less than three minutes, she felt a stab of shock. The noir fantasia she was looking at—a twilit nightmare, rather than a rational experience—had no space for dialogue with another human being. Its sheer detachment from anything she had ever seen or contemplated had deadened her to any reasoned consideration of what it could mean. She turned round with a start, to see another man in street clothes. He was tall, balding, and wore a long gabardine coat. Even in the poor light, she could see how crumpled his suit was and how yellow his teeth. He smiled at her without conviction, shuffling his feet as he did so. "Miss Taylor? I am DCI Warwick. Have you just arrived?"

She opened her mouth and wondered what to say. She could think of nothing and so just nodded.

"I see. Perhaps I could have a word, Miss Taylor. I . . . As you have obviously guessed, I am afraid there has been a dreadful accident."

She absorbed what he said and realised that she had not guessed anything. A dreadful accident? If you say so, Officer. I seem to be in the wrong place, actually. Can I go now? This is what she wanted to say. Still, she could not muster words.

"Perhaps if we go over to my car. I'm afraid there isn't a proper situation room established yet." He smiled again, clearly prompted by some inner script of what was proper on such occasions. "We can speak a little more privately. This must all be a terrible shock to you."

DCI Warwick led her to his car and opened the passenger door for her, then closed it after she had got in. He walked round the bonnet, barking an instruction as he went, and got in on the other side. How often has he braced himself for something like this? Mia wondered. Does it get any easier to tell people the worst thing in the world? "That's better. Miss Taylor, as I said, my name is DCI Warwick. I am afraid I have very bad news. There has been a fire at your brother Benjamin's home which has caused considerable damage to the adjoining house, as well. We believe that the adjoining house was empty. However, it is my sad duty to inform you that there were at least four fatalities in your brother's home."

At least four. Did that mean only four? Or that there were really more than four dead and he did not feel she was ready for the news? At least four—that could mean that one was still alive. Still alive. Still alive. Speech returned.

"You said four."

"Yes, Miss Taylor. I am afraid we have been unable to identify any of the—"

"Who's alive?"

"I think . . . Miss Taylor, I am afraid that details are very sketchy at present. I can tell you that a young woman was taken to the Royal London Hospital a little over an hour ago and—"

"Caitlin or Lara?"

"I'm sorry, Miss Taylor." DCI Warwick was perspiring heavily. He ran his finger around the grubby collar of his shirt and coughed.

"I have two sisters. Twin sisters. Caitlin and Lara. They both would have been here. In the house. My brother was having drinks to celebrate his thirtieth birthday."

DCI Warwick pulled a notebook from his pocket and began to ask her questions. It was at that point, in her memory, that the strange glitch in space-time, the phantasmagoria into which she had strayed, suddenly began to acquire some of the features of reality. She had not strayed at all. This was not a dream. Day would follow night again. Life would continue, somehow, insultingly. What had happened—whatever it was—was not, after all, a despicable feat of the imagination, but a real virus that had somehow drilled into her bloodstream and would never go away. This much she realised, tugging at her ring and staring down at the *A–Z* at her feet.

The policeman's little red notebook and the biro with which he wrote changed everything. A surreal interlude began to be transformed into something all too real by dates, names, times, missing persons, telephone numbers, addresses, and the thousand other details that could not begin to explain what had happened but which pinned it down in a net woven from little facts. In this man's ugly, looping handwriting, the biggest thing in the world was reduced to small details and question marks in the margins of each page. It was a lie that death brought drama. Its face was banal and ignominious. She heard herself reel off answers to his questions with the voice of an automaton. Yes, Benjamin Taylor. Age? Thirty. . . . No, twenty nine. Height: five eleven, or maybe five eleven and a half. Occupation: financial adviser. Jeremy Taylor. . . . So it went on. This was only the first of many interrogations that would follow, but it was the most important. Her elegy over the ashes of her family was not an oration, but a series of monosyllabic answers, helping a policeman shrink them down to a list in which their true selves were completely silenced.

It was Lara who had survived. The main blast of the fire—for blast it had been—had somehow not reached her. She had been found by the first policeman—semiconscious in the hallway, suggesting that she had been coming or going. Perhaps, DCI Warwick speculated helpfully, on her way to or from an errand. In any case, she had survived the incendiary wave which had swept viciously through Ben's house and into the neighbouring building. Even so, Lara had suffered burns on 85 percent of her body and, Mia learned when she arrived at the hospital, was critically ill. She spent the night by her bedside, unable to hold the hands that were bandaged, watching the blips on the machines, the slow draining of the drips and the whirring of the automatic drug dispensers. From time to time, Lara's features twitched. A priest came and went, politely asked to leave the small dim room by Mia. The consultant warned her that Lara's survival was in itself a miracle, a judgement with which Mia took private issue. There was, she could plainly see, next to nothing of her sister left. And though her chest rose and fell with the pulse of the ventilator, the girl who less than twelve hours before had been imitating Mia was already gone. What remained of her could not, her elder sister grasped at once, be reeled back to dry land on the hook of medicine and prayer. She was trapped in a miserable antechamber, waiting to join the other four, delayed only by some botched bureaucracy of the afterlife. At seven o'clock that morning, Lara died and Mia wept for the first time, briefly, privately, and exclusively from a sense of relief. She would not cry again for months.

So ended the first night and began the first day. As she waited to sign forms at the hospital, two men in casual clothing—leather jackets, open shirts, and jeans—arrived at the hospital to talk to her. They gave names (Brown and Jones) which were so obviously not real that she almost laughed. They offered no indication of what official agency they represented, and evidently felt no obligation to do so, briefly flashing identity cards of some kind on their arrival and nothing more. In the days and weeks that followed, she came to realise that the smartness of the people who came to see her was inversely proportional to the importance which the authorities were attaching to the incident. The astonishingly shabby Brown and Jones came when parts of Ben's house were still steaming with heat, and anything seemed possible. Six weeks later, all her dealings would be with uniformed officers who plied her with tea and platitudes.

But Brown and Jones, whoever they were, came from a higher authority, one that took for granted her compliance and sought no permission. Brown was little more than five five and had a generous beer belly; his hair was too long and hung in a lank fringe over his brow. He spoke softly with a mild Birmingham accent, and asked her often not to be alarmed, scraping his plimsolls along the floor of the hospital canteen as he did so. Jones was taller and craggy: He must have been a good-looking man once, she thought, and he knew it. While Brown consoled her, Jones spoke in the agnostic tones of the London middle class and offered her nothing but routine condolences. She asked about DCI Warwick and whether she would have to go through everything she had said with him again. Oh no, said Brown. No, no. That was not it at all. The thing was this: They had reason to believe that the fire was not an accident. Not, Brown said, the result of a faulty electric system or a gas leak. Indeed, he continued, she was probably aware that her brother's house did not *have* gas. And the thing was this, although he should not, he said, be telling her: Their forensic people had already *found* evidence of an incendiary device at the back of the house. One of considerable *power,* Brown confided, wiping his nose with a serviette. Enough to kill four people and destroy the ground floor of two houses, to put it bluntly, and sorry for doing so. Now, Brown said, this was very odd and very disturbing. And it was their job—no, he apologised, their sad duty—to find out why something so odd and disturbing had happened to such an apparently innocuous, well-to-do family holding a party to celebrate their eldest child's thirtieth. It was, he hoped she agreed, a very odd thing. She nodded assent, her head whirling once more at the way in which utterly unexpected things generated more utterly unexpected things. You might think that horrors such as this one—had there even been such a horror?—would compel people to act normally, to make a special effort to mend the tear in the universe, to go out of their way to smooth out the wrinkles. But no: Oddity bred oddity. Weirdness loved company.

What Brown and his sidekick wanted to know was—how could he put this?—what they were dealing with. I mean, said Brown, was there anything *unusual* about the events of that night that she could recall? Did her brother have any *enemies* that she knew of? Had she *seen* any-body at the park? Flailing around, desperate to offer them something, anything—anything to head off the italicised questions—she told them about the sunbathers and the children and the couples at the pub. *"Sunbathers?"* said Brown, raising his eyebrow, and made a note. Jones nodded grimly, as if this constituted a lead, if not a breakthrough. They asked her why she had left the party in the park, then returned later, and she explained that she had been to the airport to meet a friend—well, a boyfriend, actually—but that she had been late and missed him. So she had gone back alone. They seemed satisfied by this and did not press the matter. She saw no reason to involve Miles, having already forgotten the molten fury she had felt that he had not waited for her at Arrivals. She wondered for a second if he had heard what had happened, and whether the television camera she had seen had been the first of many and whether the world now knew, as she did, that everything had changed forever.

They thanked her and left without saying what would happen next. She never saw Brown and Jones again, although there were times in the weeks that followed that she came to miss their sparkling wit and forthcoming manner. She lost count of the men (and very occasionally women) who came to see her and the questions they asked. Special Branch, CID, uniformed officers, bereavement counsellors, probate lawyers, insurance investigators—on and on it went, merging into one long question-and-answer session. Some wanted to find out who had committed the crime; some wanted to reassure her that it was not a crime; some wanted to comfort her; some wanted to withhold money from her, even while pretending that their only wish was to see her compensation expedited. Brown and Jones were the first and shabbiest of a phalanx of intruders, people with whom she became practised in dealing.

She became expert, too, in judging whether her case mattered much to them. Brown and Jones had been worried that this event had some meaning which eluded them and which might signify something more broadly terrible. Their successors, increasingly, looked like men clearing up a mess, performing a duty with as much diligence as they could muster but no visible sense of alarm. Within days, the urgency drained from their enquiries, although those enquiries continued to be protracted and tedious for many weeks to come. The facts were so bald and so resistant to interpretation that she wondered at first why they kept asking her such basic questions. And then she grasped that it was all a ritual, that the proper procedures had to be observed and would be. Nothing more. Holding court in the small sitting room of her flat, she made tea for these functionaries and answered their questions and realised that it meant nothing. This was the mourning party of the state, sent to offer its condolences and present the official face of sympathy to the taxpayer. She had not yet absorbed the greater loneliness to which the fire had condemned her. But the glazed eyes of the men in grey overcoats introduced her to a defiant form of solitude, which was the solitude of the person who is beyond help and for whom only routine comfort is on offer.

The press got there first anyway. Two days after the fire, a national newspaper discovered that Ben's neighbour, a Mr. Ronny Campbell, was a businessman from Ulster with strong connections to hard-line Protestant Loyalists: Indeed, he was hoping to stand for Parliament. Mr. Campbell, it turned out, had been away from London on the night of the explosion, although he had returned the morning after the blast to find his pied-à-terre a burnt-out shell. It was pointed out by the newspaper, which seemed to have good police sources, that the device had been placed in a part of Ben's house which abutted directly with Mr. Campbell's. Naturally, its report continued, as an Ulster politician of outspoken views, he had taken basic security precautions, and it would have been hard to break into his home without detection. Not so the unlucky Mr. Taylor, whose home had been easy prey for the arsonists. At first, the police poured cold water on this speculation, calling it "irresponsible" in their official statement. But the following day, a little-known Republican organisation in Northern Ireland that had not declared a cease-fire claimed responsibility for the blast and, via its

Derry brigade, sent sympathy to the Taylor family, or what remained of it, for "falling victim to the armed struggle and the terrible consequences of continued British occupation of the Six Counties." Within hours, Sinn Fein had condemned this "totally unacceptable abuse of the Republican cause committed by a maverick group which in no way represents the wishes or grievances of the Irish people." All parties engaged in the peace process agreed that this unspeakable act would only stiffen their determination to find a political solution. Mr. Campbell, meanwhile, announced that he would not bow to terrorism and gave an angry interview to the BBC's *Today* programme, in which he promised that he "would not rest" until the "cowards and murderers" who had made an attempt on his life and taken five others in the process were brought to justice. He also wrote a ten-page letter to Mia, which she opened and then threw away without reading. A while later, she saw in the paper that he had bought a large house in Hampstead and had also been selected as a prospective parliamentary candidate for a fringe Unionist party. That was when she stopped reading the press.

After the Republican group claimed ownership of the crime, it was clear that the police would do no more than go through the motions, evidently satisfied that the case was closed. At that point, Mia knew that she must get out of the country for a while. History had not only tapped her on the shoulder but was now mocking her. Ulster? How could this be? "The dreary steeples of Fermanagh and Tyrone": She had learned this phrase at school, along with Yeats's portentous lines about too long a sacrifice making a stone of the heart, and peace dropping slow, and all that. But this had precisely nothing to do with her or her life or with the family she had lost because her brother had chosen—not even chosen— the wrong next-door neighbour. Could the ending of it all, of all the love, of all the conviction, of all the accomplishment, have been more absurd? A bunch of Paddies burning down a house when their target was out of town? I mean, please. How could one take such a denouement seriously?

With the funerals out of the way—a small family occasion, at her request, attended by only half a dozen people—she went to New York for a month, where she knew there would be no police, no reporters, no bereavement counsellors, or at least none with any interest in her. Tanja, a friend from Oxford, had landed a plum job on a glossy called *Live* and had rented a tiny apartment down an alleyway in TriBeCa. She had a spare room, which she had offered to Mia as soon as she heard what had happened. Normally, Mia would have found the suggestion impertinent, but it happened to suit her needs completely. On the morning of Tanja's message, she had telephoned the chief executive of Z Robinson, Alan Kingsley, and asked for a month's compassionate leave. He had given it to her with an alacrity which reflected, she felt, something other than compassion. The Taylor tragedy had drawn attention to the agency, however obliquely, and that was never welcome. She knew that they would not want to lose her but that they would not let her work for them as long as the story was running. Better to absent herself; and better to postpone the reckoning with her pain that she knew must come but could not face just yet.

In New York, she refused to wear the weeds of an orphan or even to accept the minor celebrity of the victim, though she knew that such celebrity was hers for the taking. On the first day, when Tanja picked her up at JFK in her Mercedes convertible, Mia asked that what had happened remain, if not a secret, then at least a private matter. She did not spell it out to her friend, for to do so would have seemed unspeakably heartless—but she had come to New York to have fun. She could see on the horizon of her life the pale froth of a tidal wave approaching, an irresistible force which would sooner or later wash her away to a dark place of its choosing. Until then, as long as she was possessed of the strange composure which is often death's first handmaiden, she wanted to explore the full range of human experience for what she assumed would be the last time.

For a month, Mia had followed Tanja around the cocktail parties and book launches and fashion shows that made up her professional life. She had drunk more than she had ever done before, taken drugs she had scorned at Oxford, and slept with men who found her accent interesting, and some who didn't. For four weeks, the apartment in TriBeCa was a shrine to expensive hedonism, a scene from someone else's life. She made a fool of herself and of others. She mocked the afflicted, flirted with hysteria, and spoke with a sharpness that made her feel sick afterwards. Tanja indulged her, lacking the emotional depth to see that Mia was playing a game which was not only a funerary rite but a preparation for something else: a last fling before darkness fell and she walked off into the labyrinth of a new and different life. She did not know about the monkey of history sitting on Mia's shoulder, and it was better that she was too shallow or self-absorbed to see what was happening to her houseguest. Mia left as abruptly as she had arrived, full of self-disgust but wise enough to know that she had done what was necessary at the time.

And so she had returned to London and what she knew in her heart would be a failed campaign to start afresh. At first, her strength astonished all around her, colleagues and friends alike. It seemed that when Jeremy and Jenny Taylor had died, their surviving daughter had become a vessel for all that was best and most steadfast about them. That, at least, was what people said: that she was their truest legacy, the angry fist they waved in triumph at the world of hazards and violence. Mia was their last will and testament and their greatest achievement. So they said.

She went back to work, first on smallish accounts, working three days a week, and then the tougher jobs which had been her forte. Miles finally contacted her, tearful on the phone about his failure to wait at the airport that night. He hoped she would understand that he had simply assumed she had forgotten to come and get him, and, because he was exhausted, he had gone straight home. His was a voice from the past, and she could not muster the strength or interest to argue with him. He had rung off, but not before passing on love from his secretary, Jean, and promising to call again, saying this in such a way that she knew that he would not. She was glad that he would not. He had failed her that night, and there could be no forgiveness.

It was six months before she was ready to accept what had been done to her. The truth is that, by then, she was too exhausted to defer the moment any longer. She had expended too much effort keeping it at bay and could not, she realised, wait any longer to open the shutters and let in the light of horror. What she had not counted on was the manner in which this would happen. One grey September day, on the fifteenth floor of a building on the South Bank, she had been preparing to make a pitch to a big publishing firm which was launching a TV guide. Her presentation, which she had rehearsed meticulously, to the point that she knew it by heart, was fantastically provocative. She planned to tell the suits from the firm that their ideas were junk and that they had to start from scratch if they wanted a saleable product in a market which was already ruthlessly competitive. Her first slide, linked into her laptop, said WHY YOU ARE WRONG ABOUT EVERYTHING. She hoped to antagonise, deflate, encourage, and then seduce. It was a familiar act, carried in this case to its extreme. She felt good about the pitch and had no doubt that she and the others from Z Robinson would walk out with the contract.

Much of that period had blurred in her memory into a series of disconnected tableaux, the synopsis of a much more detailed story. But as she sat on the steps of Christ Church, she could still visualise the boardroom in precise detail, one side a wall of glass through which one could see the landmarks of London and look down on the choppy brown river with its tugs and pleasure boats. Vast abstract paintings lined the other walls of the room, the kind of art that such companies bought by the square metre from agencies for crazy prices. The suits—four of them— sat at the near end of the long teak table, drinking lattes and sipping mineral water. Flanking them were her two assigned junior consultants on the project, Kim and Steven, both rising stars at Z Robinson, who had worked hundreds of hours between them on the presentation she was about to give. Neither of them would have dreamt of speaking of her recent past, but she knew that both—"little Oxford shits," as Claude called them—were worried that they were hitching themselves to uncertainty as well as proven talent. She could see it in their eyes as they watched her make her final preparations, Steven turning his fountain pen nervously in the fingers of his right hand and catching Kim's eye occasionally. I know what you're thinking, Mia reflected. I know only too well. You little *bastard*: I'll show you how it's done, just so you'll know that you'll never be able to do it. Watch and learn.

So what happened to her in the next minute surprised her utterly. She had felt poised and braced for action as she prepared to click the mouse of her laptop and display the first, mocking slide. These were the days she enjoyed most, when the peril and brutality of work crowded in and pushed away all that was quiet and deadening. She felt safe with her adrenaline surge and the vista of faces to whom she would now address her stinging thoughts.

Except that she would not. Not then, not ever. As she stood at the metal lectern, mouse in hand, an absolute form of knowledge descended upon her. She could not deliver her presentation under any circumstances. Her breathing was level; her pulse did not race. The room did not swim around her; there was no dizziness or panic in her limbs and breast. No, this was a matter, it seemed, of philosophy, not physiology. It was revealed truth, not a rebellion of the body or nervous system. What it said to her was nothing more or less than: I cannot do this, and I shall not.

"I cannot do this," she said to her audience. A second or two passed, and the chief suit, a burly man in Armani, chuckled.

"Don't blame you," he said. "Hate all that technology myself. Can I help?" He stood up and approached her.

"I cannot do this," she repeated. The other suits joined in the genial response of their boss, amused at what they imagined to be female incompetence and immensely relieved that her assault upon them would begin from a position of weakness. Kim and Steven, however, exchanged glances of preemptive horror. They knew more and they had more to lose. The antennae of ambition were sharp and had picked up the danger that was now twisting and curling into the air.

"I cannot do this," said Mia, for the third and final time. Calmly, she switched off her laptop, packed it away, and put her papers in her briefcase. This took little more than a minute, she guessed. The room was now silent. Steven stood up and motioned to Kim. "Mia, shall I take over? Sorry, chaps, we'll have this sorted in a second." Mia walked past them all, left the boardroom, and took the lift to the lobby. She hailed a cab and was home in less than a quarter of an hour. She stopped counting the number of times her mobile rang after the first twenty. When she got to her flat, there were five messages flashing on her answering machine. But she did not listen to them. Instead, she undressed and went to bed for a week.

During those seven days, she rose very occasionally, only to take the most basic sustenance, splash water on her body from time to time, and watch soap operas, whose plotlines she was able to pick up with pleasing speed. She did not want to speak to her colleagues or listen to their fake sympathy, even when Claude dropped a handwritten note into her letterbox and peered through the side window for any sign of life. On the first day, she wrote a one-paragraph letter to Kingsley, thanking him for his support over the years and tendering her resignation; she faxed the letter over without hesitation. Kingsley's office called her repeatedly and then Kingsley himself left several messages: Nobody, he said, blamed her for what happened. On the contrary, all her friends and admirers at the firm were worried about her and wanted to help. She was an integral part of the team. She had been through hell; he could see that. Would she call? She could phone him at home if she preferred. And he left several numbers.

On the seventh day, a letter from Kingsley arrived on the fax, accepting her resignation with great regret and wishing her well for the future. For only the second time, she wept, once again from relief.

Thus released from the pretence of normality, Mia was free to get on with the business she knew lay ahead. She asked Uncle Gus to sell the house in the Boltons, trace all her father's assets, and put the whole lot into trust for her. She would not, she said, be up to organising anything for a while, so she asked him to look after the many millions Jeremy Taylor had accrued over the years, and to arrange for a modest wage to be paid to her from the interest to cover essentials. She also asked him to help Henty, who had continued to live in the attic of the family home, find a new place to live and to pay for it up front from the principal. All this was accomplished very fast.

While Uncle Gus got on with the paperwork, she asked to be admitted to a discreet clinic in west London—chosen more or less at random, because she had read about it in *Vogue*—to get on with what she knew she had to do. Mia was too much of a rationalist and too much of a pessimist to believe that the people there, with their open-neck shirts and loafers, could do much for her. Their therapies were, at best, a balm. But she knew, with the clarity only her mother had shared with her in the Taylor family, that she was now good for nothing else. Her soul had some chores to do and she needed time to get them done. Let the shrinks and the counsellors analyse her, drug her, get her to write diaries about her pain, compose letters to those she had lost—as long as she was in somebody else's care, where nobody would bother her. That would be fine for a month or two, maybe longer. She remembered little about this time, except the sometimes-insufferable cheeriness of it all, the limitless supply of herbal tea, and a rather bloody suicide on her floor, which the clinic managers had tried feebly to conceal from the other patients.

When she finally discharged herself, after three months of expensive care, she returned to the flat in Islington and realised, to her surprise, that she wanted to work again. She remembered Kingsley's promise that he would take her back anytime, and realised that he had not meant it, and that it would not matter if he had. What she wanted was fresh occupation, something that was not solitude but was also not her old life. A week or two after her return, the instructor at her yoga class—a class recommended by the clinic—had told her over coffee about her friend Sylvia, who was looking for a deputy manager. She had slipped Mia the number of the Echinacea Centre across the table and smiled. Mia had promised to visit Sylvia and see if it was something she might like.

→ Part TWO

THE EAST END

Chapter THREE

NANTES STREET was almost deserted beneath a sky of resilient melancholy. A young man, wearing headphones and singing to himself, pushed a buggy with a sleeping infant through the puddles, down towards the small green at the end of the cul-de-sac. A couple of Asian schoolkids were skiving by the bench where the street met the road, arguing in Bengali over an impossibly early fish supper from the chippy around the corner. One, heavily overweight, was wearing a school blazer that was embarrassingly small for him, but he did so with obvious pride as he sat shovelling chips into his mouth. His friend—lean, his hair gelled back, the hint of a moustache already showing—engaged in an acrimonious discussion with him. He kicked his trainers against the bench in syncopation with the beats of his diatribe. Chels could not help feeling that the chip shoveller was having the better of the bout. Gel Boy was trying hard to contain his frustration and failing miserably. He reverted to English to clarify his position. "You are so fucking wrong," he said, his voice shrill now. "She never said that." The chip shoveller smiled and continued to stuff his face. This was clearly the response he had been working to elicit from his companion.

Chels walked past them to the end of the street and over the road to Top Price, the open-all-hours shop, which lived up to its name inadvertently in the sheer scale of its markups. Emerging from the door was Tommy Bonkers, carrying a bagful of his day's drinking supplies. He was wearing his usual uniform of old suit trousers, held up by a necktie, a sweater of indeterminate colour, and a threadbare raincoat draped over his diminutive frame. With his bald head and wispy beard, he looked, she thought, a little like a figure from Dostoyevsky, a man in a trance, but one from whom holy wisdom might unexpectedly emerge. Except the truth was that Tommy Bonkers was not going to dispense wisdom, or anything else, to anyone. He was off, she knew, to his spot on the green to knock back a bottle or two of pear wine and then pass out, probably till midafternoon, when he would shuffle into the Echinacea Centre in his sandals and be given a cup of tea by the centre's founder, Sylvia.

As he passed her, he smiled beatifically and raised one hand, covered in a fingerless glove, in greeting. This was as close as Tommy ever came to communication and he did so only when he was in an exceptionally good mood. Yes, he was definitely off to get stuck into the bottles that clinked cheerfully in his Top Price bag. His clothes and bearing were those of a man in the pit of existence, but his grin was that of a king surveying dominions of limitless wealth—in this case, two bottles of Thunderbird and maybe, if he was treating himself, a couple of miniatures to get the party started. He shuffled off towards his own lethal little arcadia.

She bought milk and turned back to make her way down Nantes Street, past Prospero's, the pub, to Ringo's shop. The kids had gone somewhere else to continue their row, leaving only the greasy paper remains of their vile morning feast. The metal shutters were still down at the pub, although she could hear the sound of a vacuum cleaner coming from within. Monsoon Records, in contrast, was open—more open, she suddenly realised, than it was meant to be. The plate glass of its door

had been smashed in overnight. The CLOSED sign was still showing, but
the door was ajar and Ringo was on his hands and knees, sweeping up
the fragments, cursing sulphurously to himself. Seeing him so preoccupied, she wanted to abort the mission and creep back across the road to
the centre. But her shadow had already fallen into the shop, and he
craned his neck round to see who was there. His face was a study in im-
potent fury, and she felt a stab of guilt as she realised that she absolutely
did not want to hear what had happened or to have to deal with another
minor crisis before lunch.

"Chels," he said, getting up. "Chels, man. This is so fucked."

"Are you all right?"

"What's it look like?"

"Sorry, I meant—"

"No. No." He stood up, brushed off a few shards and flakes of paint
from his jeans. "I'm sorry. Shouldn't snap, man. It's just . . . Can you believe this? I mean, again?"

"I know. Was it Aasim?"

"What do you think?"

She looked inside and could see the word NUFFINK spray-painted in
large blue letters on the wall of Ringo's shop. This was the call sign of
Aasim, the toughest of the local Bengali gang leaders, who headed a
posse of six or so kids, none older than sixteen. A vicious imp of a boy,
he epitomised the new East End and the fresh fault lines baked into its
cobbles by the irrepressible sun of change. Once, these streets had paid
homage only to cutthroat white men in suits, the villains of local folk-
lore. Now, those men had gone—or were seen no longer, at any rate.
Their old manor shuddered with new forces. Bengalis, Somalis, refugees, artists, writers: All had come to settle around the ancient source of
the city, clustering by its earliest foundations and its first spring. Old
tensions had faded and new ones had arisen in their place. Cockney and
Muslim rubbed shoulders, sometimes growling as they did so. A third,
quite different tribe—soft-handed and middle-class—had insinuated it-

self between them, colonising the lofts and cottages, its members staring at the pavement whenever trouble arose. Millionaires looked down from penthouse apartments on the welfare nation beneath. There was fresh affluence, and fresh menace. Racists seethed and poor whites muttered as Asian boys strutted across this ancient terrain and claimed it as their own.

Aasim's gang roamed between the top of Hackney Road and Mile End Road and around Brick Lane all day and much of the night, hot-wiring cars, committing petty theft, and breaking and entering wherever they felt like it. They hated Ringo, a Gujarati, whose real name was Jay Patel. He was twenty years older than Aasim and his cronies and completely unimpressed by the swaggering path they cut through their little patch of the East End. The middle-class whites in their cottage ghettos were weak, Ringo said. They put up with Aasim and his brother Ali setting off firecrackers on their estates and breaking into their cars. Ringo had thrown them out of his shop more than once, and they hated him for it. A brick through the front door and a sprayed message were par for the course. He had stopped telling the police, who had sent a forensics team to his shop a few times but left him in no doubt that they would never catch the vandals unless they had a witness.

"I don't know, Ringo." Chels stepped into the shop and walked down its main aisle of records, all vinyl, all twelve-inch. Above the counter hung a huge poster advertising the last album by Asian Dub Foundation—Ringo's favourite group—and a political banner from some march or other, bearing the legend ISLAMABAD, KABUL, LONDON. Even in his fury, Ringo had put the music on—bhangra with a hard bass beat—and this was something she admired in him very much. He mocked her for the music that she listened to on her CD player while walking to work—Groove Armada or, much worse, chill-out compilations—but he liked the fact that she listened to music at all, and that she asked him what was new and what he recommended. His shop always thundered with some rare imported record or other, and he had a dedicated clientele of enthusiasts who admired his taste. He made his money—what there was of it—from mail-order sales and from running Old Skool discos in clubs and at weddings, where he would spin and sample records he privately despised to make ends meet. But he didn't really care, as long as he could play what he liked in his shop. It would take more than a brick through the door to stop him.

"Tell you what," he said. "I'm thinking maybe I'll get me some protection."

"Protection?" she said, taken aback that Ringo should utter such a word. "Is there such a thing anymore? I thought that went out with the Krays."

"You can get it. The old pub was supposed to be one of Jack Dove's."

"Fat lot of good it did it. Christ, Ringo. It was always being trashed. Drugs all over the shop. Or so Sylv says. Anyway, does Jack Dove exist? I thought people like him and Freddy Ellis and Stratford Terry were just legends. All that stuff ended thirty years ago. You've been spending too many evenings in the Blind Beggar. Or watching too many movies."

"Yeah, well, maybe. When I had my shop in Dalston, there was a crew who said they worked for Dove. Came round once and threatened to do the place over if I didn't give them a piece of the action. 'What action?' I said. I was earning nothing. No punters at all. They said they'd burn me down if I didn't pay up."

"Did they?"

"No." Ringo bowed his head in partial defeat and went behind the counter. "But you know what I mean, Chels. Don't be all . . ."

"I won't be all . . . if you cheer up. I'm sorry about the window. That boy needs a good slap. And his stupid brother. They only do it because you stand up to them, which is more than can be said for all the soft white boys who go to our yoga classes. Aasim and Ali key their Saabs while those boys are in there with Erica, and they don't say a word. Scared shitless of him. He must be thrilled."

Of all the characters that she had met in her three years at Nantes

Street, Ringo was her favourite. He had been called Ringo for most of his adult life, supposedly because the other two employees in the first record shop where he had worked were called John and Paul and had said that he did not look like a George. Sylvia disputed this and said that Ringo was a family nickname, the origins of which his mother, Mrs. Patel, refused to divulge. It didn't really matter. It was somehow true to the spirit of the street, a place of sanctuary, escape, and alter egos, that he should go by such a splendidly inappropriate name. He was not a drummer, not a Liverpudlian, and he hated the Beatles. He didn't have a moptop and he spoke with a Cockney accent. It was perfect in every respect.

He ran his hand through his cropped black hair and smiled at her. "You hiding, or on an errand?"

"Both. Sylvia got rid of an instructor this morning, so I'm making myself scarce for a bit. My excuse is that I'm buying milk and visiting you in search of a roll for the till. We've run out again. Have you got one?"

"Yeah, sure." He ducked under the counter, rummaged in a box, and resurfaced with what she was after. He was, she thought, an attractive man, tall and lean, with dark eyes and an appealing roughness of complexion. Perhaps it would have been fun if he had not always behaved as the perfect gentleman. But then, she had to admit, she would never have trusted him, or got to know him. He appealed to her because his charisma concealed no threat or demand whatsoever. Ringo handed over the roll.

"You want to see a movie next week? I'm taking Sanjay. There's something good on at the Lux he wants to see. French, I think. You can pretend to be his auntie, with Uncle Ringo by your side."

She laughed. "Sure. Let me know which night."

"I will. See you."

She left the shop, stepping over what remained of the mess from the break-in. As much as she liked Ringo, she wondered how much of

Aasim's war of attrition he could really stand. He was on his own, lived on his own, only had the shop, and the local hooligans had decided that they were going to drive him out—no less, no more. He would never get Jack Dove's protection, she knew, wouldn't know how to get it even if he wanted to, even if Jack Dove really existed and wasn't just a name people in the area invoked when they became tearfully nostalgic about the days when you could leave your front door open and the local villains were good to their mothers and only preyed on their own kind. But Ringo needed some help, or he was going down. That was the truth. Aasim's NUFFINK said it all.

On the street, the puddles and windscreens were glaring from the first hint of sun. A sharp-looking scooter with more rear mirrors than was strictly necessary was now parked outside Prospero's and the door was open. She looked onto the green and could see the huddled form of Tommy Bonkers, an empty already by his side, busying himself with the second bottle, which would take him to the insensate place that he most wanted to be. His sandals wiggled from side to side with the rhythm of true happiness. The path to self-destruction was, it seemed, paved with many pleasures, wicked treacheries of the senses, which kept people like Tommy on course to the annihilation which was their fate. She could not recall seeing a more contented figure, his private joy entirely at odds with the autumnal misery of the day.

As the seasons changed, so the anniversary drew closer. No getting away from it, no hiding from the day and its pitiless memorial. No respite. Once a year, a reminder, forever and ever, amen. The day, like a wound that opened according to the lunar cycle, would come and go for as long as she lived and beyond, when she, too, would be gone. The calendar was a vicious merry-go-round of the soul, permitting no escape and no exit. You could hide from people, she knew, but not from time itself. Time always crept up to tap its bony finger on your back and remind you of all that you had thought past, dead, and buried. But nothing was ever truly dead and buried. Nothing was more alive than death.

She crossed the road and went back into the centre. Sylvia was nowhere to be seen, and to Chels's relief, nor was Lorenzo, the centre's self-realization teacher who had quit with a flourish of Latin fury minutes before she had stepped out to buy milk and stop by Ringo's. It seemed that Lorenzo's students had also disappeared after Chels had reimbursed them for the remainder of the course. Even Irene—a short woman, a widow who always seemed reluctant to leave after each class, often catching Chels's ear to complain with proud vagueness of "nerves"—was gone.

But Erica, the yoga instructor, was on the phone and looked pleased to see her. "Yes, hold on a minute," she said. "I've just seen our deputy manager. Chels!"

She took the phone. It was another applicant for the assistant's job, a man called Rob, who said he needed the work and asked if he could come round the next day. He gave a few details. Trying to hide her irrational relief that at last a man was on the list, she told him to be at the centre the next morning.

"Yes, just ask for me. I'm in first thing," she said. "No, Chels is just a nickname. My name is Mia. Mia Taylor."

Chapter FOUR

THE FLAMES were licking at her feet, but she could feel nothing. There were six of them, six jets of fire, aimed at her naked body, arranged in an orderly fashion, three on either side. They looked like the flames from a laboratory or a crematorium, purpose-built, designed for some highly specific task. But there was no sensation to accompany this spectacle: no sense that her body was melting into liquid submission or hardening as the flames scorched and tightened her skin. No, there was nothing. No faces, either. Nothing. Was there a whispering? Or was she hearing only the hiss of the flames doing their invisible work? Her body was limp on a canvas bed of some kind, like a military stretcher; she could not move. Worse, she could establish no link between mind and flesh, no bond of loyalty between the body and soul. All was at odds with itself. Nothing mattered or made sense. Except now, perhaps, there was a hint of feeling, of heat, of something irritating at first and then unpleasant. She could feel her thigh, and then a sharp stinging beneath her arm. Prickling turned into discomfort, and then pain. The hissing had suddenly become loud, soon deafening. Now there was a connection between body and mind all right. Pain, pain, all flowing from these pitiless mechanical flames, pain dragging her towards what she supposed would soon be agony. Intolerable. Intolerable. And no faces anywhere. Nobody to witness the suffering and say something. Agony and loneliness shrouded in a silent scream. Lead me to Purgatory and then let me go forever. Now she was begging, begging for God knows what. No sign of mercy in this private abyss. Please, God.

Mia awoke. With the clinical detachment that often fills the moments immediately after horror, she realised that this had not been a bad one, not bad at all, really. She was not crying. The bed and her nightclothes were wet, but only from sweat. Her heart was racing, but not with the arrhythmic pattern—the stops and starts—that had made her feel that she was dying so often in the early days. All things considered, this was an unremarkable episode, just another dot on the chart of recovery and setback. By any normal measure, she had dipped a toe in the waters of hell. But these were waters whose vicious clasp one grew used to: Misery has its connoisseurs, no less than pleasure. There had been worse nights, and would be again.

She got out of bed and looked around the room for her pills. It still made her laugh that she had ever believed she could manage without medication. Boldness had been her greatest friend in the immediate aftermath, and then her greatest enemy. Courage had proved treacherous, assuring her of a resilience that was entirely illusory. For three and a half years, she had taken the little purple pills in varying doses, and she found it hard to imagine a life without them now. They were not, as she originally expected, analgesic in their effect, aspirin for the soul. Their function was more properly categorised as hallucinatory, in the very mildest sense that they changed her perception of things, took the edges off the world through which she moved. They permitted her the consoling delusion that she had not changed at all, but that everything else had, that her habitat had been made safe by some benign force. They answered fear with the limpid sensation that fear was redundant when the world was seen through the stained glass of a perfectly distilled pharmaceutical. She stumbled over to her dresser, where the little phial, with its label warning her against driving heavy machinery, had been all along. As she opened it and shook out two tablets, she noticed that her hands were trembling. Calm, she whispered to herself. Remember the exercises. Calm, calm. One step, two step . . .

Downing the medication with last night's water, she sat on the edge of the bed in her T-shirt and heaved two dry sobs. It would be all right in about a quarter of an hour, and the placebo effect of taking the pills would probably kick in even sooner. But for now, she was caught in that unpleasant interlude between the numb shock of awakening from the nightmare and the feathered chemical plateau onto which she would soon alight. She looked over at the clock and saw with relief that it was past six. The worst nights had been those when she would wake with insane regularity at three and find herself incapable of sleep, of reading, of watching television, of listening to music, of drinking, of anything. She would sit on the sofa and stare at the oil painting of the cob at Lyme Regis, retrieved from the Boltons, which she had put above the mantelpiece and the gas fire. She had once heard that more people died around 3:00 A.M. than at any other time, and, in those terrible months, she had come to understand why. Midnight might be the hour of incantation and witchcraft, but three o'clock belonged to death. It was a time of night—or of morning—stripped of the mercies of love, belief, and belonging; there was only the cruel joke of absolute emptiness. She had resented this punishment more than almost any other. Almost.

After a few moments, feeling the neurological gear change begin within, she stood up again and looked around the bedroom. On mornings like these, she wondered why she had never got round to hiring a cleaner for her flat. She worked every weekday and she was always too tired to keep the place tidy. She had also, she knew, become more prone to messiness and less mindful of cleanliness. At the centre, she tried to maintain a semblance of order, endlessly battling Sylvia's contrary instincts. But at home, for the first time in her life, she made little effort.

The basement flat had been her home for almost three years, and it served her needs perfectly adequately. But she had done nothing to make it welcoming or impressive, and expended almost no energy upon keeping it clean. She washed herself and her clothes, though she took little care in what she wore. She had not yet allowed true squalor to creep through her door. But the fastidiousness of her past life had gone, the edgy perfection of the flat off Canonbury Square. There were clothes, newspapers, and unopened mail all over the floor. She felt absolutely no need to clear them up. It was not as if she was expecting visitors.

She turned the light on and went into the bathroom next door, stripping her T-shirt off as she did so. The shower was faulty, but, unusually, the pilot light clicked into life immediately as she turned the dial and waited for the water to heat up. The blue bath mat from Conran's was now frayed to the point of disintegration, but she had brought it with her from her old flat and kept it for some obscurely sentimental reason. There were flecks of toothpaste on the mirror, which was steaming up, sparing her a sight which she knew would not be gratifying. She stepped under the water and lifted her face up to the flow. It was a good shower, surprisingly powerful for an ill-maintained rented flat, and its tiny pummelling massaged her brow and cheeks soothingly. Amazing how terror and its aftereffects are so physical, she always found. Little balms, tiny forms of release, were everywhere, just waiting to be discovered, and she had had time in the past four years to identify many of them. Ylang-ylang oil, a long shower, a crisp glass of good wine (rather than a bottle drunk in misery), an espresso on a summer's day—all had consolations, though none could be relied upon. There were no guarantees in the realm of the distraught.

She washed herself with a sponge and shaved her legs quickly. She looked around for shampoo, then remembered that she had run out. A rinse would do for now, though the sweat in her hair would not wash out properly. She would not look her best, but then it was so long since she had. Did Sylvia, who knew her so well, notice the little differences from day to day? Or Ringo, who said less than her boss but was perhaps more acute? Sylvia's old consort, and odd-job man Vic—recently deported, creating a vacancy—had sometimes called her "pretty girl," but only in the time-honoured tradition of the polite beatnik. Her fellows in exile were kind. But they must have detected something of her inner state from her appearance and its fluctuations. Her body was a canvas upon which her soul scrawled mischievous messages, hinting always at a lost elegance, hard won in past times, and now surrendered. One could not hide these things. One could only hope for generosity from those who looked, understood, but had learned to say nothing.

She turned off the water and towelled down, wondering what clothes were handy for her to put on. A pair of sweatpants and a hooded top were hanging over the chair at her dresser and there was a clean T-shirt on the rail in the bathroom (part of the welcoming pack from a big pharmaceutical conference she had attended more than five years ago, the relic of a former life). She found clean knickers and socks in her bottom drawer and pulled on her high-tops. With irritation, she noticed that the sole in the right shoe was about to wear through. There were few items of clothing Mia cared about now, but trainers were amongst them. It was simply not possible to live and work in the East End without decent trainers. Ringo had heard that, on average, Aasim spent at least fifty quid a week on shoes, and threw out each pair at the merest hint of shabbiness. Ringo wore sandals and hip-hugging bell-bottoms, and hated the style of clothes favoured by the local Asian youth, but even he understood, with grudging respect, where Aasim was coming from. So did Mia. She would have to go and draw out a hundred from the bank and pick up a new pair from the big shop near Aldgate East Tube station. This task would not wait: action this day.

The small living room and kitchenette still smelt of the pasta she had cooked for herself the night before, and there were videos scattered on the floor, evidence of an unsatisfactory effort to settle down in front of a film. She and Ben had shared many things, but what they'd enjoyed most together was to spend the evening in affable silence watching a movie they had seen a dozen times before. It was not the same sitting through *Withnail and I, Get Carter, Wild Strawberries,* or *Some Like It Hot* without him, although she tried often enough. She kept coming up against the lines he loved to quote to her, having that bizarre power for total recall of the trivial which is a distinctively male attribute. They would watch *Apocalypse Now* and he would remember every word. " 'This was the end of the river all right,' " he would hiss as Martin Sheen bowed down before Marlon Brando in the mad colonel's compound.

Sometimes she would rent a movie from Raj Videos, the local shop which specialised in Bollywood blockbusters but normally had a copy of the latest Western release. There was occasionally pleasant diversion to be derived from such a film, and she had discovered for the first time in her life that she found mindless action pictures restful: By nothing more than accident, she had been initiated into the joys of Schwarzenegger and Van Damme, of *Mortal Kombat* and its sequels, of laser guns and androids that would not die, of buildings that exploded to the orgasmic sighs of blond American actresses. Her brain had unexpectedly welcomed and taken to the soothing horrorshow of these films. Last night had not been successful, however: an unexpectedly earnest Russell Crowe movie about a kidnapping had failed to grip her in any way. She had gone to bed early, which was often a mistake, allowing her subconscious, however strapped in it was by drugs and cognitive restraints, the time it needed to break free and torture her.

Well, she thought. Well, I cannot stay here. I have to keep moving, blow away the wreckage of the night and try to embrace the day. She opened a back window to air the place, threw on a long woollen coat and a scarf Sylvia had given her as a birthday present, and locked up. As she walked up the wooden stairs to the railings and the pavement, she noticed that a dumpster had materialised overnight. No, not possible. It must have been there the night before when she had got home, after stopping by Prospero's. She, Sylvia, and Erica had sipped their half-pints of cider and shared a "Caliban Ploughman's Lunch." They had stayed in Prospero's for an hour and a half, until a party of young women, noisy and apparently lost, had sat down at the table next to them and started ordering rum and Cokes, clearly as the prelude to an extremely loud evening out. She and Sylvia had left without discussion, insufficiently drunk to tolerate what they knew was about to happen.

Still, Mia hadn't noticed the dumpster when she got home. Above it was a new billboard advertising conversions ready for habitation in the New Year, and giving a Web site address for the lucky few who would be able to afford such accommodation. Not, she reflected, anyone local. But then, who was she to talk? She was known as Chels because Sylvia had referred to her by no other name than "Chelsea Girl" for the first trial month of her employment. The experience had been similar to what she imagined square-bashing to be like: a brutal induction to the community of the Echinacea, with Sylvia as the ferocious NCO, seeing how far she could push the rookie and whether she would make the grade. Fortunately, a fondness had developed between the two women rather more quickly than either had expected. Sylvia had been in no doubt of Mia's intellect and managerial power, but she feared that she would not understand or respect the eccentricity of the centre. Mia had liked Sylvia's shabby panache but worried that her badly applied makeup and catastrophic Laura Ashley dresses were signs of hopeless disorganisation. And yet an affinity was quickly born in their badinage, from Sylvia's wise intuition that Mia was broken in some way, and Mia's recognition that she would be safe with Sylvia for the time being. She had arrived at the centre with a sports bag over her shoulder and a few boxes in her car, and, somehow, three years had already passed.

The dawn stuttered through a pale mist above the tall buildings of Brick Lane and the little roads which were its arteries. She wanted a cup of tea and so turned left under the bridge and past the open warehouses. THERE ARE NO INNOCENT BYSTANDERS declared a recently painted message on a billboard, surrounded by stickers advertising local raves and club nights. The DJs' names always amused her. Tank Wally and the Sunkiss Crew. DJ "Abby" Absolute. Maximum Steff. These were the sort of people Ringo knew well and sometimes performed with. They lived in an entirely sealed world of obscure vinyl, sampling, and fantastically technical discussion about the merits of the equipment they used. And the loyalty some of them inspired, she knew from Ringo, was religious in its intensity. The mosques in the area competed with the club residencies in their claim on people's souls. Everybody has their faith, as Ringo often said. You just have to find it. Too right: There are no innocent bystanders.

Mia walked up to the twenty-four-hour bagel shop and saw a few of the tarts leaving with their takeout at the end of a long night's shift. She thought she could count four at a distance, swaying off to God knows where after enduring their allotted hours of God knows what. She had heard that the intersection of Brick Lane and Bethnal Green Road round the dark tunnel of Wheler Street had been a red-light district since the time of Nell Gwyn, perhaps longer: an area smaller than an acre, sweating with London's seediest desires and populated by its most desperate women, year after year, decade after decade, century after century. These were not call girls, these shambolic ladies; they were not even in the same class as the fishnet caricatures who waited for curb crawlers in King's Cross. Most, you could see, were pathetic crackheads who did what they were told in return for food and shelter, and a rock to smoke at the end of the night. They wore denim and mascara and stuck together. After three years, she recognised one or two of them, though the turnover was rapid. Mostly teenagers trying to look a few years older than they were, their skin already rough from the terrible variety of abuses to which their bodies were daily subject. Occasionally, one would smile at her if they passed early in the morning. But only sometimes. More often, their eyes were glazed over from drugs or, just as likely, the distance they had to put between themselves and the world in order to bear their lives. Mia heard two of them giggling loudly as they crossed the road and headed off, leaving behind them the strange hybrid aroma of salt beef and strong cheap scent.

She bought her tea and turned back down the street. Brick Lane was beginning to fill with vans and lorries as the restaurants and wholesalers unloaded their supplies. An old man poked his head out of the door of a little mosque and stared at the passersby. At the newsagents, a pile of newspapers in English and Bengali had already been dumped, taller than she was. There was still little traffic, but the tradesmen shouted jokes and abuse to one another; over the noise they made, you could just hear the slow hum of the city waking up, its irrepressible, foul-breathed yawn. "Don't you have any fruit?" a shopkeeper asked a man with a van. "Course I don't have any fucking fruit," he said. "Do I look like I sell fruit? What does it say on the side of my van? Muppet." He was half joking, but the disgust was real. He wasn't a fruit salesman, and anyone who thought he was could expect an earful. They could expect, in fact, to be called a muppet.

Mia made her way past the Vibe Bar, which in the evenings was a noisy joint full of dotcom kids. She sometimes took Sylvia here after a really bad day. Then she walked across the little arcade of scooter and clothes shops. A Japanese boy with National Health spectacles and improbably blond spikey hair slouched past her, lost in the music pounding through his earphones. His mobile telephone was going off, squawking the tune of one of the big hits from the year before, a song she could not quite place. But there was no chance of him hearing it. Nice trainers, though, and obviously new. She repeated her vow to herself to get the trainers problem sorted before the day was out. Perhaps, if she was feeling bold, even before work.

First, though, she would perform the little pilgrimage which she always made after a bad night. Turning down Fournier Street, she walked towards the church, the Hawksmoor which she had learned to love. To approach Christ Church from the east was to appreciate its marvellous

Gothic monumentality, especially at this strange hour, when streetlamps and natural light competed eerily to reveal its brooding magnificence. She passed the rector's house, and the intersection with Wilkes Street, and stood for a few moments by the railings and looked up at its portholes, the eyes of the stone beast glowering over its dominion. Some said that Hawksmoor had ripped off the design of Christ Church from Alberti's San Francesco at Rimini. But she had seen the pictures and did not buy that for a moment. The magic of this church was unique, and lay in its sheer defiance, the scorn with which, she had read, the architect had treated the critics of its "Solemn and Awfull Appearance." Its very design anticipated and dismissed the doubters.

She turned the corner and looked up at the great steeple rising like a Georgian minaret, calling the poor and the mighty of the city to prayer and to judgement. The portico, with its arched centre, was no less wonderful to her eyes, Palladian or Venetian, or whatever the guidebooks called it. You could read as many architectural treatises as you liked, but none gave the slightest sense of the living quality of this building. It was both monument and organism, an act of creation begun almost three centuries ago and still heaving with life. The air around the church's columns, its arcades, its clerestory windows crackled with the architect's will—his fury, really. He had created a mighty stone beast as well as a place of worship, a beast he had chained to the earth of the immortal city and left behind him to growl and scrape its tethered claws against the ground long after he was gone. She had always found solace in this place.

The church was closed, but she walked up its steps to the doors and sat down, looking down towards the Fruit Exchange and the tall crystalline towers of the City. Three years before she had sat in the same spot and decided to stay at the centre and work for Sylvia. It had been a Sunday, and she had watched swarms of shoppers drift in and out of the covered market opposite, carrying flowers, organic food, and beeswax candles. The city revolved around her that day—or rather, around the steeple—like some axle lodged in time and space to give meaning to the chaos around it. She had sipped on bottled water and listened to the sound of couples arguing and children laughing, and she had thought, I can hide here for a while. I can be safe. I can stop asking myself what I must do, and do something else instead. Nobody will find me, unless I want them to. This may not be a place of sanity. But, on the steps, in the shadow of the slumbering Gothic beast, she had realised that this was perhaps a place of respite.

Was it a mistaken decision? Three years on, she still did not really know. It had seemed right at the time. It was impossible for her to live as she had been doing, the curator of a family's memory, and the object of universal sympathy: broken and pitied. That way of life presented her with a map heading only towards slow self-destruction and confusion, a misery beyond grief. She had started to hate living in her old world, submitting to the habits of a patient and a victim, surrounded by the people she knew, or thought she knew, who pretended that there was no stigma attached to her new status even as they branded her with it and whispered behind her back. She had learned to hate the friends who were most apparently solicitous, most sensitive to her needs, most understanding of her moods. They were the ones who enjoyed it most.

How do you explain to people what it is like when history crashes into you? Unless you have heard the thunder of its approach and seen the splintering glass and smelt the burning flesh of its attack, all discussion is pointless. The night of Ben's party, she had left the park a neurotic young professional, surrounded by the love of her family, and returned to her brother's house only a few hours later as something quite different, a quite separate person. The change was not manifest to her for some time, but she realised, when she became aware of the transformation she had undergone, that she had played no part in it at all. History had followed her out of the park that evening like a stalker and claimed her as its own, or at least as one of its footnotes, even as she worried about the trivia of her behaviour and the etiquette of bringing a new boyfriend to a family party. It had planned inexplicable horrors for her while she tried to make sense of small inconveniences.

Now she drained the dregs of her tea and wrapped her coat around her. It would soon be a full four years since that night, the night that she had driven back to Ben's house and found that most of it was no longer there.

Chapter FIVE

"**WHERE HAVE YOU BEEN?** He'll be here any minute." Sylvia stood at the door of the centre, arms folded, brow furrowed. She was wearing one of her vintage cardigans over a paisley dress, tapping the toes of her Birkenstock sandals together edgily. Mia noticed that one of her two strings of beads—African, probably—was twisted. A nervous wreck already, and not even 9:30.

"I've been buying some footwear. Unpostponable. Bloody good they are, too. Do you want to see? I'm well pleased. Only eighty notes."

"What are you talking about?"

"Trainers. God, I needed them. Now I can look the East End in the face again."

Sylvia let out a sigh of exasperation and slumped against the door frame. "I don't know what you're talking about. I have no idea why you are telling me about your shoes. Do I greet you in the morning with a speech about my sandals? No, I don't."

"That's because you're ashamed of your shoes. I could help you. I know a man who can help you."

"Chels. You know I once said to you that I bet I'd probably only ever have to pull rank on you once or twice."

"Oh, yes. The first time was two years ago, when I tried to get us sponsorship from an organic wholesaler."

"Correction: an *unethical* organic wholesaler," Sylvia said. "A wholesaler who could afford to sponsor us only because he was paying his staff less than minimum wage."

"Oops. Yes, I remember now. Mr. Calloway, the green fascist. Bit of a faux pas, that. Got rather carried away. Guess you can take the girl out of the capitalist system, but you can't take—"

"Yes, yes. Well, that was the first time. And if you don't shut up about your trainers and come inside, you're about to experience the second."

Mia laughed and edged past her flustered boss. This was excellent, if mysterious, entertainment. Sylvia, fidgeting between street and porch, appeared to be on the verge of having an out-of-body experience. Two young men in matching jeans and Diesel T-shirts, yoga mats in bags over their shoulders, brushed past her and out onto the pavement, but she barely registered them or their mild irritation at her obstruction. She pulled a piece of toilet paper out of her cardigan pocket, looked up at the uncertain sky, and blew her nose with an expression of pure affliction. A bus on its way to Stratford droned past the end of the street. She looked at her watch and shook her head dramatically.

"You're late; he's late," said Sylvia. "I may as well give up." Mia put down her plastic bag. Oh dear, she thought, are tears imminent?

"Well, I'm here now. And who's he?"

"Him. *Him.* The bloke."

"Which bloke?" Mia saw Sylvia's look of agonised frustration. "Oh, Christ. Of course, the *bloke.* What was his name? Rob something."

"Rob Eastwood. He's local and he's keen. Or at least that's what he told you, if you remember. Said he'd be here at nine-thirty."

"Yes, it's all coming back to me. How could I forget? Well, I'm sure he's caught in traffic or something."

"Chels, love. He only lives a hundred yards down the road. With his mum, on the estate. If he's late, it probably means he's not coming and he was lying and we are stuffed and—"

She linked her arm through Sylvia's. "We are absolutely not stuffed. We are so unstuffed, it's not true. This is an unstuffed health centre. Now, either our boy is coming and he's a candidate for this fabulous job or he isn't and we don't want his sort anyway. The chance to work with a couple of duchesses like us? Come on. What red-blooded male wouldn't leap at the chance?" This made Sylvia laugh, in spite of herself. They went inside to the back office and Mia put the kettle on. What she really wanted to do was spend a good half hour lacing up her new Nikes and enjoying their perfect fit. Smooth, white, clean: just so. But she could see that the owner-manager of east London's premier alternative therapy centre was herself in need of a bit of alternative therapy.

Sylvia slumped on the sofa and put her feet up on a plastic chair. "Do anything after we left the pub?" she asked Mia.

After three years, her deputy had learned to answer such questions economically. She did not want to lie to Sylvia, who knew enough of her history not to ask too much. But she did not want to conduct a post-mortem after every bad night. When each day of your life is post-mortem, she had once told Ringo, you get weary of explaining yourself: every wrinkle and rub of emotion, every assault of memory. She could have said that she had taken a powerful sleeping pill, passed out, and woken up convinced that she had just visited hell in its most vividly fiery, medieval form. That would at least have had the merit of accuracy. But she did not want to explain herself, and she loved Sylvia for having learned so quickly not to press her on such matters. The deep bond between the two women lay in what they did not say to each other. She poured the tea.

"Afterwards? No, I tried to watch a movie but got bored. I had nightmares about Erica, though. I dreamt that she came to my flat in her green leotard, stole my cash, and cut off my gas and electricity."

"You may laugh, my girl, but if I have any more days like yesterday, you'll be looking for bar work before you can say P45. I tell you, she ought to be in the City, that Erica, not teaching pregnant women how to stand on their heads. Merciless she was. I have no money. Which means we have no money."

"What about the new guy?" She corrected herself instantly. "I mean, assuming we hire him."

"There's a tiny bit left from what I was paying Vic. We'll manage. I got an arsey letter from the bank the other day, but nothing too bad. I just said we had some cash-flow problems, and nice Mr. Webber of the small-business unit said it would be okay for a month or two." She paused and finished her tea. "Actually, I'm more worried about this, to tell you the truth."

Sylvia leapt from the sofa and rummaged in one of the piles of paper on the shelves, cursing quietly to herself until she found what she was after. "There," she said, handing the letter to her deputy. "I'm worried by that. Should I be worried? Tell me whether I should be worried."

It was a letter from the local authority, dated the previous Tuesday, from a Maureen Stove (Mrs.), in Environmental Services, warning the manager of the Echinacea Centre that it had come to the attention of the council that the business was "apparently deficient in a number of aspects vis-à-vis planning regulations and proximity of residential buildings under the new legislation." Mrs. Stove added that the centre faced a number of penalties if the "deficiencies"—which had been brought to the attention of the department by an elected councillor—could not be dealt with "in the approved manner." It was, Mrs. Stove added, her "sad duty to inform you that the legislation requires closure of facilities judged by the local authority to be deficient, except in highly exceptional circumstances." She signed off, "Yours faithfully" above a complicated reference number.

"Bloody hell," said Mia. "What deficiencies?"

"I have no idea. We had some trouble a few years back about the foundations of the place. Supposedly, the structure was unsafe or something. Ages ago now, before I got upstairs going properly with all the classes. Anyway, it turned out that somebody on the council didn't like some of the meetings we were having here; it was all political. The whole thing got forgotten pretty quickly. It had completely slipped my mind, to be honest. I daresay the building isn't the sturdiest in the world. It was a bloody disaster area when I bought it, that's for sure, and I couldn't afford to start from scratch. Painted a bit here, mended a bit there. It's not a health hazard. What's brought this on, I have no clue."

"Somebody's out to get us, or make a point. Bastards." Mia read the letter again. "Mrs. Stove is no wordsmith, that's for sure. Listen to this: 'Pending further investigations, you should await further notification under the terms of the legislation, with a view to resolution concomitant with the act.' Fine, thanks. Concomitant with your arse, love."

She tried to imagine Mrs. Stove sitting at her word processor in the town hall, mouthing the words to herself as she composed. Thin-lipped, a little too much makeup. A two-piece suit from BHS and a drab blouse. Flat shoes, and a thermos of tea. Yes, and the kind of glasses worn only by the truly vicious, those with a gift for cruelty, which has been nurtured over the years. Mrs. Stove, in an airless office, living her airless life, her hair pulled back in a bun, despatching letters around the borough, with the sole purpose of inflicting the maximum amount of grief conceivable "under the legislation," and then returning to the flat shared with her mother since the day Mr. Stove went out for cigarettes and never came back. Mrs. Stove, her eyebrows pencilled in, making the world pay, "pending" the justice that would never be meted out to her.

"What does it mean, Chels?"

"Nothing, for now. I don't think this is a death warrant. More of an exercise in psychological warfare, I'd guess. Mrs. Stove is putting the frighteners on us, and somebody's egging her on. Let's wait and see whether it gets forgotten. The last thing we want is council officials poking at the plaster and taking humidity readings round here." She looked up at the ceiling and its filigree web of cracks. It was true: An inspector would have a field day at the centre. The key was never letting an inspector near the place. But Mia could see her boss did not share her confidence that this could be ensured, was not able to muster her deputy's scorn for bureaucracy. Sylvia was of a generation that saw bureaucrats as the enemy, rather than as a nuisance to be swatted aside. Mia could tell that Sylvia believed in her heart that this letter marked the beginning of some ghastly nemesis. All the joints she had smoked, all the demos and marches she'd been on, all the leaflets she had handed out—and now Big Brother was finally striking back and would obliterate everything she had worked for with a flick of Mrs. Stove's vengeful pen.

"Excuse me—are you Mia, or Chels, or whatever?" The two women turned round. "I wasn't sure whether to knock or not. I'm Rob."

"Oh, hello. Yes, come in, please. Sorry, we were just doing some admin. My name is Sylvia. I'm the manager, and I think you spoke to—"

"Mia, or Chels, or whatever. That's me. We spoke yesterday. Pleased to meet you." She smiled briskly at the young man and extended her hand, which he took with a grip that was a little too slack for her liking. He was tall and fair, unshaven, his hair shorter than it should be, and the gold stud in his left ear an instant indication to her of his youth. Twenty-one? Twenty-two? No more. The baseball boots and faded jeans were a giveaway, too. He was broad-shouldered, but his bearing was not that of a confident adult. Even as he walked into the little office, she noticed that his eyes darted nervously between the two of them. He shifted ever so slightly from foot to foot as he stood, brushing the leaves of a wilting rubber plant. Was he up to it? No, no, stop. She had to check herself—or rather, the habits of her old high-octane profession. God, she thought, I must stop judging people like this; those days are over. We're looking for somebody to man the desk and change the lightbulbs, not a speechwriter for a chief executive or an account leader to work eighty hours a week.

"Thanks for coming in," said Sylvia. "Do sit down. I'm afraid the place is a bit of a mess. I could pretend to you that it isn't normally, but I'd be lying." Mia cleared a pile of Xeroxed leaflets off a chair for him. "Thanks, Chels. So . . . Rob. Would you like some tea?"

"No, I'm fine," he said. "Sorry I'm late. I . . . Well, since you're not lying, I won't. I slept in." He laughed a little too loudly, and took off his leather jacket a little too quickly, revealing a skinny body and tattooed forearms. His T-shirt bore the slogan WARWICK BEERSOC SUMMER PUB CRAWL: I SURVIVED! Mia could feel her nose turning up involuntarily and tried to control herself. She sat on her hands, for fear that they would give her away. At least, she thought, I won't ask him which college he went to. I won't ask him a question like that. I'll be good.

"Yes," said Sylvia. "Yes, well, never mind. You're here now. So, Rob, tell me—tell us—how you found out about the job?"

"A mate saw it in a mag and sent it to me. Your ad. I finished uni not long ago, and he knew—my mate—that I was looking for something local, so, you know . . ."

In the dreary light of the office, looking through the particles of dust frozen in time by a lonely sunbeam, Mia wondered why it was that there were some things in life that were so instantly and intrinsically annoying. There was the time it took cabdrivers to find change, sighing heavily and grimacing, as if they had never before had to do something so inconvenient as offer coins in return for a note. There was the way in which couples at the cinema talked about what refreshments they wanted, loudly and at length. There was the way in which florists commented upon the private messages you sent with flowers, as if their opinion was of interest to you. And now there was Rob.

"What did you read at university?"

Sylvia shot Mia a look of quizzical horror. Why was her deputy asking this? Mia was not sure herself.

"I don't think that matters actually, Rob. But do tell us about yourself," Sylvia said.

He drilled Mia silently with an expression of well-honed hostility, his blue eyes suddenly aglow with reflex ferocity. The look made clear that, in case she was wondering, he already had her number, thank you very much; had probably had her number when he heard how she spoke on the phone the day before. The Oxford girl, lost in Mile End for some reason: Mia, or Chels, or whatever you call yourself. It was a look of amused contempt and surprise that she should offer such a weak opening gambit. She thought she heard his East End accent thicken ever so slightly. "I read politics, actually. Since you ask."

She blushed at his insolence, feeling all power in the little room drain from her and towards him. "No, Sylvia's quite right. I was just curious. Do go on. You were saying that you're living round here."

"That's right." He returned his attention to Sylvia, put his hands behind his head. "After I graduated, I moved back home. My mum is getting on, so she's glad of the company. And I don't mind. My dad bailed years ago, so we get on well, Mum and me. Have to, I suppose. And living there suits me for now. It's a bit cramped. I could do with getting out during the day, to be honest." He drummed his fingers on the table's edge, then flicked some dust off absentmindedly.

"Do you know much about alternative health?" Sylvia asked.

Mia could see him tense a little. "Well, I did a bit of yoga once. Or at least I had a girlfriend who did. Used to go to classes near our digs in the morning. A lot of people at college were into crystals and aromatherapy. What can I say? I'm no expert. I mean, you know, I read the papers, so I know a bit about it. Not much. Does it matter?"

"Look, Rob," said Sylvia. "The fact is, we're a man—I mean a person—short here. We used to have a wonderful, wonderful chap called—

well, never mind about that now. But the point is that we need somebody to sort things out, help with the desk, keep the place in order. We
have a lot of customers. It's a busy place and it needs a bit of upkeep."

"So, what . . . I'd be a caretaker?"

Yes, thought Mia, that's right, my son: You'd be a caretaker, second
class. And after ten years, you might get the full title, if we're feeling
really generous. If we haven't sacked you for having tattoos and an ear
stud. And surviving the Beersoc pub crawl. "Good heavens, no," said
Sylvia. "No, you'd be . . . assistant manager. Chels is deputy manager, so
you'd be assistant manager. Does that sound fair?"

"Oh, yeah," Rob said, stretching his feet out, not noticing as he
knocked aside a pile of old *Time Outs*. "Sounds very fair."

"I'm sure you can pick up a bit about the ethos of the place—you
know, our values—along the way. We definitely have a set of values here.
It's not just a business. There's also a pretty mixed clientele. Some very
much, you know, young professionals, others more into the spiritual
side, some locals, all kinds of people. What are your interests, Rob?"

He pulled his cigarettes out and put one on his lower lip, a painful
imitation of James Dean. Oh no, thought Mia, could it be worse?

"Actually, I'm trying to get a band together." Yes, it could. "That
keeps me busy in the evenings. We've done some gigs. I mean, they've
been okay. But I need a few days' work a week while I get things sorted.
I can't survive on the dole. Can I smoke?"

"Yes, but not in here," said Sylvia. They laughed at this feeble witticism as he put his Marlboro Lights back in his jacket pocket. "Sorry, but
the punters take it for granted these days that the centre's a no-smoking
zone." She leant over and, to Mia's horror and Rob's visible amusement,
patted him on the knee. "Between ourselves, I have been known to light
up in here when we're closed. But you know how it is."

"Oh, yeah," he said, nodding cheerfully. "I know how it is. Used to
be big rows about it at college. Can't smoke here, can't smoke there.

Nearly made me give up. But not quite." Sylvia laughed in a way which Mia realised with some shock was almost kittenish.

A sense of unspecific desolation crept through her bones. She could tell that Sylvia liked him already, which meant that the job was his. Where she had instantly detected chippiness and fecklessness, her boss had seen only boyish charm and the prospect of a mild flirtation which would brighten her days. She looked on with resignation as Sylvia, babbling and squirming, described what the job entailed and what his terms would be. She did not bother to ask him if he had any bookkeeping or computing skills, and it would not have mattered either way if he had turned out to be a fully qualified chartered accountant, or unable to write his own name, or, indeed, not entirely sure what his full name was. The die was well and truly cast.

Mia could also see that Rob had already worked out that he was onto a good thing here. He probably thought that she and Sylvia were mad spinsters, one young and uptight, the other superannuated and off her rocker. But that would not stop him making the centre his base for a while, a cushy little stopover until he could bear his mum no longer, or got his band together and moved out. Watching Sylvia cavort on Vic's grave, she felt a little sick. But then she had only herself to blame. Her petty question about his degree course—the bigmouthed Oxford graduate within jumping out to ruin things—had bonded him to Sylvia instantly. Vic? Vic who? The era of Rob had begun that very moment, when she had forgotten to shut up. His triumph was total.

"So Rob," she heard her boss saying. "Do you have a number where we can reach you? To let you know?" They were already standing, leaving Mia sitting there pathetically, like a patient absorbing the news of a dreadful diagnosis. "Tell you what. Why don't you give it to Chels. She'll probably be handling things from now on."

"Oh, fine," he said, putting on his jacket. He picked up a scrap of paper and wrote on it. "Here you are—is it Chels?"

"Yes," she said with more feeling than she wished to disclose. "I mean, nobody calls me anything else round here."

"Right," he said. "When will I hear?"

"Oh, very—" Sylvia caught Mia's eye and shifted gear. "Well, quite soon. Once we've seen the other candidates. You know."

Rob knew she was lying, but he went along with the fiction. "Sure. I understand. It's an attractive job. Anyway, fingers crossed."

"I'll show you out," said Sylvia.

" 'Bye, then," said Rob. "Hope to see you soon." He smiled at Mia as he left. Was it her imagination or did he wink? No, that would be too ghastly.

Left alone in the room, she grabbed the plastic bag with her trainers in it like a safety blanket. She took the box out and inspected them, finding the smell and texture of the new shoes moderately soothing. This would have been a good day to pull a sicky, she decided. She could have stayed at home and watched daytime television, soaking up the recipes, the advice on life and love, and the soaps. As it was, she had been treated to the sight of her boss, the matriarch of Nantes Street, fawning at the feet of a man less than half her age, who was wearing a beer T-shirt and baseball boots and threatening to "get a band together."

"And what, exactly, has got into you?" Sylvia, who so recently had been slumped on the porch, now stood at the door of the office, arms akimbo, righteous and—as she would have it—"empowered."

"Nothing," Mia replied, standing up in order to escape a showdown. "Nothing's got into me."

"Bollocks, nothing," Sylvia said, blocking her way. "You couldn't stand him. And I can't for the life of me see why. He seems nice enough."

" 'Nice enough'? Well, that's an understatement. You were all over him like a cheap suit. There I was, thinking we were interviewing for a staff member, when all along we were going on a blind date. Only next time, take someone else as chaperone."

"Bloody cheek, young lady. You know full well we won't do any better. And you nearly scared him off with your smart-arse questions about his degree. Who cares what bloody degree he did? He's going to stand at the desk and deal with people like Irene, and hose down Erica when she gets moody, and tidy up the workshops. For next to no pay. It doesn't matter if he's got a degree in computer science, or pottery, or jumping up and down on the spot. *I don't care.* I just need somebody to work here."

"Fine. Well, there's no need for a discussion then, is there? You've obviously made your mind up. So I'll just get back to work then, if that's all right."

"Now, look, Chels—"

She rounded on Sylvia. "No. No, you look. I'm going to get on with my job now. If you have any queries, please take them up with your new *assistant manager.*"

There was nobody in the shop area, so she decided to storm out properly and get some air while she was at it. The row would probably blow over as quickly as it had flared up. But she wanted to make Sylvia feel just a little nervous about her victory, to pay for what had happened. She knew, as sure as free-range eggs were free-range eggs, that she herself would have to phone Rob later that day and offer him the job. That was her punishment. But she didn't want to make it too easy for her boss. What Sylvia had signalled was nothing less than the transformation of a duumvirate into a triumvirate. Rob, who evidently had none of Vic's docility or his genius for receding into the background, would be the new and unstable element in the management of the centre. Two had become three, with all that that entailed. Sylvia did not know about such things, but Mia, with seven years of office politics behind her, most certainly did. Oh well. She had done her best, which, as it happened, had turned out to be her worst.

On the street, a bright day was unfolding. The sun's reflection in the plate glass opposite stung her eyes and almost made her turn back for her shades. But she chose instead to go and see Ringo, who was invariably good company after a row at the centre. He was a good listener, Ringo. That was what he did for a living and, in his free time, what made him a good friend. A talent for listening.

Wrapped up in her reverie, she noticed that he had company only when she was much closer to his shop. Outside Monsoon Records, Aasim and three of his gang were posing, smoking and admiring what was obviously their leader's new scooter. One, she noticed, was Ali, Aasim's younger, goofier brother. The machine was a dazzling silver, a Vespa of sleek beauty, and, like everything Aasim owned, flawlessly clean. Even his clothes, she felt, were of a different order from those his henchmen wore. His trousers were shinier and more perfectly pressed, his Adidas hooded tops newer, his Kangol berets less sullied and frayed.

Aasim lived in Mile End, but he wore the uniform of Compton or the Bronx. His uniform was an homage to those places he had never visited and never would, but whose voices he heard in music and with whose fury he identified instinctively. This was what he imported to London: It was his challenge to it. He loved the street from which he had sprung and the control he exercised over it. But he rose above its grime and its contaminations. He laid claim to his dominions by exempting himself from their ugliness. On another teenager, his pierced eyebrow and his severe buzz cut would have looked ridiculous. And yet on Aasim, they were badges of menace, clean and spare and perfectly judged. He was small, no more than five six. But the gang members who pranced around him were not the only people in the neighbourhood who feared him. He knew how to make others feel nervous and he respected only force. That was why he tortured Ringo: because he could not, would not, tolerate anyone, least of all an Asian man, who refused to bow to him. Until Ringo submitted, his windows would be broken and his walls would be defaced. That was how it worked.

To the glee of his three accomplices, Aasim was revving up his scooter to deafening levels, smiling to reveal his gold incisor. Ali shouted something to his older brother. She noticed that Aasim was wearing a matching chain, which she thought was new, and that his hands were freighted with more jewellery than she remembered. You ponce, she thought. You look like an Essex girl on a Saturday night. But did she dare to tell him? Perhaps not. Not yet anyway. The three henchmen screeched with laughter as Aasim whispered something to Ali which appeared to be miraculously audible in spite of the roar from his moped. Poor Ringo. She wondered whether he was inside the shop, struggling to pretend not to notice the provocation outside.

Aasim saw her and turned his engine off at once. He had spotted her going into Ringo's shop a few times, or out to a pub with him, and made clear that he hated her merely because of her association with the Gujarati. They had barely exchanged a word, and she had no desire to do so now. But she felt the full force of his panther eyes as she walked towards them, and she wished that she did not feel as unsettled as she did.

"Looking for your boyfriend?" he asked as she passed them.

"No," she replied without thinking, or catching his eye. "Are you?"

One of the cronies laughed at this lèse-majesté and then was silenced savagely in Bengali. She did not turn round, but she could hear Aasim spitting furiously on the ground and a hissed "Bitch" just loud enough for her to catch. She pushed the door open, noticing the wood that had replaced the smashed pane, and was glad to be inside the shop.

Ringo, who was reading a magazine behind the counter, looked up. "Christ, you seen a ghost?"

She laughed. He was playing hip-hop—Dr. Dre, if her amateur's ear did not deceive her—which was a sure sign that he was rattled himself. But his defiance impressed her. Outside his shop stood four sinewy teenagers who had shown every intention of smashing up his property and possibly kicking his head in, too. And there he was, leafing through a copy of *Q* magazine and listening to his favourite music. A pile of unsorted twelve-inch records, the day's consignment, not yet subjected to

Ringo's meticulous system of categorisation, stood reproachfully at his side.

"Not a ghost, just a gangster. Jesus. I'm glad I got through that gauntlet alive. How can anyone as small as Aasim be so scary?"

"He's not scary; he's just a vicious little bastard."

"An interesting distinction, my friend. How long have they been there?"

"About an hour and a half, I reckon. Oh man. Will you look at him on his scooter?"

"No, I think I've done enough looking at Aasim for one day, thanks."

"Well, he's still looking at you." Ringo smiled. "Actually, he's really looking. . . . I think maybe he likes you."

She picked up the magazine and started hitting him as he collapsed in laughter. "You know what you can do, Ringo?"

"Mercy, man, mercy! Okay, I give in, I give in. He doesn't fancy you. Really." He recovered himself.

"Thank you very bloody much."

"Well, not as far as I know. Not much anyway." She made to strike him again. "No, man, only joking. Only joking. So. What you doing here?"

"Came to see you. Bored. Pissed off. All three."

"Trouble again?"

She told him about Rob and what had happened. As she described the scenes of the morning and saw his grin, she realised that she was getting worked up about nothing, and that she would have to make up with Sylvia sooner than she had planned. Why was it that sulking became harder the older you got? Ten years ago, she would have extracted a week's standoff from such a slight, or perceived slight. At Oxford, she had avoided the High Street for an entire term in order to snub a boy at Brasenose who had wooed her and then committed some obscure infraction of her code. They had run into each other in their mid-twenties at a Notting Hill housewarming and she had apologised, only to discover that he had met a model in London a few days after their row and had had a brief but utterly wonderful affair with her. Mia had sulked about that, too. But now, less than an hour after locking horns with Sylvia, she regretted her obstinacy and was already worrying that she had damaged a treasured friendship. Ringo reassured her, which only made her feel worse: Here was a man under siege by the nastiest little hoodlums in the area, who was considering paying imaginary gangsters money to protect him, but was still able to comfort her over her ridiculously trivial troubles. Maybe Rob wasn't so bad, he suggested. Why not give it a try?

Why not indeed? She looked out of the window and saw that Aasim and his posse were still watching them. The four gang members were completely still as they scrutinised their prey.

"Doesn't it do your head in?" she said.

"What?" He moved out from behind the counter, and she noticed he was barefoot.

"That. Them. Looking in. I couldn't do it."

"Actually, I'm going to shut up shop in a minute anyway." He looked at her and put his hand on her shoulder. He had a warm touch. "Listen, you know why you came here. So let's get it out of the way."

She knew what he meant, but she asked anyway. "What?"

"Oh, come on, man. Just make it up with her. Bet you she's in a state now. Just say sorry. You will eventually, so why not now?"

She looked at his kindly face and smiled. "You're right," she said. "You're right. You're right. You're right." She looked back at Aasim's posse. "You'll be okay?"

"Hey, count on it," said Ringo. "Catch you later."

She marched out of the record shop, head down, and passed the boys. Their silence made her feel sick, and, as she got closer to the centre, the sound of Aasim himself screeching with laughter and revving his scooter triumphantly came as a relief. Better that they should be crow-ing than speechless with vicious intent. By the time she got through the porch of the Echinacea, she was almost running, and beyond caring who saw it.

In the shop area, she could smell the dense fog of lavender and knew at once what was happening, and what was required. Only in her darkest hours did Sylvia use her Neal's Yard burner during the day, and the pungent aroma in the outer room revealed that she had really gone to town, squeezing many drops of her favourite essential oil into the water and lighting a tea candle beneath it, doubtless with shaky hands. There was nobody on the desk, which did not matter, as there were no customers. She could hear the muffled sound of a class chanting upstairs. Mia lifted the barrier and went inside.

Sylvia was sitting on the sofa, an expression of complete bereavement on her face. A trail of toilet paper stretched from the cushion to her cardigan pocket and, though her head was turned, Mia could see that her eyes were red. She was clutching her hands together, oblivious of the fact that her deputy had walked in. A wisp of smoke curled from the burner by her side, bubbling away in busy consolation. It smelt like an explosion in a lavender factory. "Hey," said Mia. Sylvia turned around and then turned her face away, embarrassed by her emotion and the ludicrous figure she presumed herself to cut.

At such moments—and they had been plentiful over the three years—Mia always feared she would burst out laughing at her boss's lack of resilience, and in the event, she always found herself full of pity. Sylvia was not a robust woman and she felt things deeply. To take her on in verbal contest was invariably to hurt her. She had none of the defence mechanisms and regenerative powers that Mia had taken for granted in people before getting to know Sylvia; she lacked an emotional immune system. Rationally, Mia was annoyed that a grown woman should be so pathetic over so little, so easily thrown off beam by trivia. But she was prepared to forgive Sylvia much, knowing that she owed her something that she might never be able to repay explicitly. She walked over, ignoring her boss's instinctive cringe, and placed a hand on Sylvia's shoulder, which trembled at her touch.

"Can I just say that I am an ungrateful, spoilt, unworthy girl and that I apologise unreservedly?" She paused. "Well, how's that for starters?"

Sylvia's tears flowed anew, but this time with a dash of laughter. She picked up a sheet of toilet paper and blew her nose explosively.

"Better out than in. Have you been on your own in here?"

Sylvia nodded, and turned to face her. She looked dreadful, like a war widow or a lonely woman in a police station waiting room. Her life is held together with bits of string and packing tape, thought Mia. It could fall apart with the smallest shove, lie in pieces on the ground, unnoticed until somebody came to sweep it up and away. Each of these incidents, she realised, was a little tragedy for Sylvia, a tiny dramatisation of her greater failures and the loneliness that lurked within, like the child she would never have. I must take care with her, Mia thought; I must take care of her, as she has of me.

"I was an idiot earlier," Mia conceded. "You're quite right. He'll do just fine, and we need him. Let's face it: We need a bloke." There: She had said it.

Sylvia nodded again.

"So if I call him, will you cheer up?"

Another nod.

"All right, deal. But I want to take the afternoon off. I fancy a walk. Fair?"

Nod, nod.

Mia pulled out the scrap of paper with the number of Rob's mobile on it. She unfolded it and was horrified to see that he had written underneath, "Mia/Chels/Whatever: Smile! It may never happen." Did he realise that it already had? Did he, in fact, grasp that he was it? Probably not. But that was her problem, not his. Her job was to make things right with Sylvia and restore order to the troubled little cosmos of the

Echinacea. Apart from anything else, she was worried that one of them might pass out, finally overwhelmed by the lavender fumes.

Deep breath. She dialled the number, and he answered almost immediately.

"Hello, Rob speaking." He sounded so much like a telesales rep, so breezy and helpful in tone, that she wanted to say that, yes, she was interested in the seventies compilation advertised on the shopping channel and, yes, she had her credit card ready. But she bit her lip and proceeded.

"Yes, hi, it's Chels at the Echinacea here."

"Oh, hello. Didn't expect to hear from you so quickly."

Yes, you bloody well did. "Well, you made a good impression on— on us. We'd be thrilled if you would take the job." She remembered her drama classes at prep school: *This time with feeling, Mia.* "Really, we would."

"Great. That's brilliant. I'm all made up. Thanks. So when do I start?"

"The sooner the better." She saw Sylvia nodding vigorously. "Sylvia's nodding vigorously! How about Monday?"

"No problem. Fantastic. Well, I'll see you then." He paused. "Bye, Chels."

She restrained herself, glad of her deeply ingrained ability to do so. "Yup. Look forward to it. Bye for now." *Click.*

It was done. The Rubicon of Rob was crossed and Sylvia could not complain. Mia had done her boss's bidding and cooed as much as she could bear over the new recruit. What would it be like working with this teenaged Neanderthal? Would there be more annoying T-shirts, more tales of the new group, more flirtation with the helpless Sylvia? Probably. Certainly. But that was a dilemma for another day. She had steered the ship through choppy seas and could now slump at the wheel.

Sylvia got up and came over to embrace her. "Thanks. I mean it." She sniffed. "It'll be fine, I promise. And I promise not to come over all maternal. I'm sorry if I made a fool of myself. I just couldn't believe we'd actually got the problem sorted. You know what I'm like. I get carried away."

"I know what you're like." Mia smiled at the bedraggled woman before her. "That's why I work here. And now we've got a big strong man to work with, too, I won't have to do half as much. On which note, I intend to leave you to dream of your hunky new employee and depart. I'll swing by later on. Adios."

Not for the first time, she had made the peace. It was a skill she had learned at the Echinacea, a practise which had seeped into her over the months and years. She recognised it as a worthy thing—to turn the other cheek, to shirk conflict, to seek resolution. But she also understood that she needed this skill more than she had in her past life. It was part of the new scaffolding she had erected around herself to keep herself sturdy, to prevent herself from lashing out, and to ensure that she behaved well. For she had learned, with sadness and some shame, that her reflex now was to see harm being done to her, to scent conspiracy, to detect enmity. There was no logic to this: She was surrounded by love, albeit of a disorderly sort. But she could not help the poison within: the fear and doubt that had been pumped into her through the syringe of inexplicable bereavement. She saw things in the shadows; she expected them to be there; she was sure they bore her ill. She did not want this, but she could not prevent it, either. The shadows ambled behind her, try as she might to throw them off her trail. They were always there, in the recesses of rooms, around the next corner, and in the perceived sarcasm of the last remark. The threat was nowhere. It was everywhere. She carried paranoia in her belly like a phantom child.

Mia walked through Bethnal Green and down Columbia Road. She stopped at another one of the stations of her occasional pilgrimages: St. Leonard's in Shoreditch. She watched the mothers out in the unseasonal sun with their kids in the church's garden. The tulip beds were grey and barren, and it was hard to imagine the riot of colour that this small retreat would become by the spring. On one of the benches, beyond the railings from the pub with the mock-Tudor facade, Tommy Bonkers was sitting, apparently asleep or in communion with some deeper force. He had a scarf wrapped round his neck and mouth and appeared to be breathing heavily beneath it. He's off his usual patch, she thought, then realised that she really had no idea what Tommy's daily itinerary might be. It was a good half-hour's walk from the church to the centre, perhaps twice that when you shuffled at Tommy's pace, stopping every hundred yards or so to pick up something or deposit an empty. But what was that when you had twenty-four hours to kill, seven days a week? It was a journey of no consequence, from one half-safe place to another. When your world lacked a centre, all places were the same, and the flow of time ceased to mean anything; perhaps it stopped altogether, all moments crowding into one colourless second, to the sound of a distant sigh. She wanted to wave at Tommy, then realised that he was too far away, and too far gone. She carried on walking.

It was late when she returned to the Echinacea. The centre was still open, and she remembered that the advanced Mysore Astanga class was due to start in half an hour. There were no lonely-heart Irenes in that group. In the evening, it was strictly young professionals, career women, men in love with themselves or each other, bankers desperate for a burn, and bored with the gym. Erica was at home with such people, businesslike and focussed, concealing their narcissism in the camouflage of Eastern teaching. That was the unstated contract between teacher and class: Make us beautiful and we will buy your snake oil, all of it. Things were smoother in the evenings, Erica always said.

She was standing at the desk when Mia walked in. "Oh, hi, Chels," she said. "Were you looking for Sylv? You just missed her."

"No, no. I've just popped back to pick up my stuff."

"Actually, I'm glad you're here. There's somebody waiting for you. He's been here for twenty minutes or so. Said he'd wait."

"Oh. Is it Rob? We hired this guy today."

"I don't know. Tall bloke. He's upstairs in one of the little rooms. Thought he'd be more comfortable up there reading his paper." She turned back to her own paperwork.

"Okay, thanks, Erica."

It could only be Rob, of course, but she wondered why her nemesis had come back so quickly and what was so urgent. Perhaps he simply wanted to gloat. Perhaps he wanted to sue for peace. Perhaps he had developed a sudden urge to learn about alternative health and the wisdom of the Orient. Whatever it was, she hoped it would be over soon. She was ready to go home, try on her trainers, and have a bath. She went up the stairs, taking them two at a time, and saw that the door of the back room was ajar, light flooding from the crack onto the landing. Mia noticed that the floor was filthy, as usual, and steeled herself to point this out to Rob as one of the first tasks he must attend to on Monday. It would be a good way of imposing her authority without being churlish. She pushed the door open.

"Ah, at last," her visitor boomed. "The prodigal returns." All she could do was smile. "Hello, Claude," she said.

Chapter SIX

CLAUDE WAS NOT impressed by his Big Macbeth. "This is not what I call a burger," he said, holding up a limp piece of iceberg lettuce in disgust. "Why did you make me eat here?" He gestured at the mock-Tudor interior of Prospero's with his free hand.

"Because you said you were starving," Mia replied.

"I said starving, not desperate. Why couldn't we go and get an Indian in Brick Lane? This place is like some sort of nightmare you have when you're doing English exams at school. All these oh-so-hilarious Shakespearean gags. The long winter evenings must just gallop by."

"Welcome to Nantes Street, Claude." She peered into her pint of cider, already three-quarters empty. He had barely touched his glass of dry white wine, which she had known as she ordered it would not satisfy his dainty palate.

"Some welcome. This is my reward for months of detective work, tracking you down. A burger named after the Scottish play. Ha bloody ha."

He had not changed, not really. The hairline had receded a little, and the clothes were even better cut than before: His chalkstripe suit was a thing of beauty, she had to admit, the kind of elegance that comes only from the best tailoring and the most discerning taste. His tie, a dark blue with a key pattern, was more restrained than she remembered, but his shoes, reassuringly, were the same Lobb brogues that he had always worn. The coat folded at his side on the pub bench looked new, but it was the same capelike affair that she associated with him as he swept in and out of rooms. And, of course, the trademark hat which had so provoked her sisters. Yes, she thought, still a wanker after all these years.

"So, Claude. What brings you to these benighted parts?"

"I come here all the time, my dear. I knew the East End when you still thought that east London was anywhere beyond Kensington Church Street. Some of the best pubs in the city are round here, and the lock-ins are proper lock-ins. Easy to get a pint and a packet of crisps at four in the morning. You just have to know the right people."

"Which, of course, you do."

"Of course, of course. That's my speciality. But I have to say that nobody has ever mentioned this . . . exclusive establishment to me. I'll chalk it up to experience."

"Just don't go bringing any of your friends here, Claude. This is our boozer. We don't want a bunch of ponces spoiling it."

He drew himself up to his full height and dabbed his mouth with his paper napkin. "Well, well. We have become quite the eastern queen, haven't we? Lock, stock, and two smoking trust funds. Excuse me for trespassing on your manor, Mrs. Kray."

"That's quite all right. Just show a little respect, and you might get out of here with your teeth in the right order."

"Hmm. Well, I'm glad this time away from planet Earth has had such a civilising effect on you, Taylor. Makes all the effort it took finding you worthwhile, really."

She was intrigued; that much, she had to concede. The sight of Claude after more than three years had spooked her, naturally, and she deeply resented his capacity not to be thrown by such things, to greet

her after such a long time with such insouciance. It had taken her a pint
and a half of cider before she had felt able to converse with him on
something approaching equal terms. In the meantime, grumbling about
his food and disdainfully silent about the quality of the wine, he had
talked at length about what was going on at Z Robinson, how his accounts had improved in size and prestige, and how much Kingsley
missed her and would have her back tomorrow. It was a lie, she knew—
Kingsley would rather die than see her back at his firm—but she appre-
ciated the lie anyway. Claude had always grasped one of the essential and
simple facts of life, which was that people liked to be lied to when the
lie was flattering. He had deduced that if—as is so often the case—the
truth hurts, it follows that falsehoods are very often pleasant to hear and
rewarding to promulgate. This was one of the reasons why he was so
successful professionally, and why his clients adored him: Even as he
filed reports, telling them what they were doing wrong, he made them
feel that they were right, right, right. When he killed, he killed with
cream.

Still, she could not work out why he had come. His company was
not objectionable, and the feline speed of his ripostes reminded her
agreeably of the life she had once led. It was like listening to a tape of
oneself five years before, or discovering a photograph of a long-forgotten
night out. Trading minor insults with her former boss—former lover,
God help her—she replayed the highlights of her old existence, all the
stress and tension artificially filtered out by the passing of time and
Claude's charm. She could envisage spending the entire evening with
him, allowing herself to become drunk as he narrated the continuing
saga of ordinary west London folk, a scene from which she had exited
three years before. But, no, that would not do. Claude had not come to
provide her with a synopsis of the events she had missed, still less to hear
what she had been up to herself. He was too selfish for that.

He returned from the bar with a gin and tonic for himself—the
wine, now warm, abandoned—and another half-pint for her.

"I can't believe it," he said, opening a packet of pork scratchings. "There's actually a framed picture of Judi Dench as Elizabeth the First behind the bar. This is a seriously terrible place."

"Well, you must feel at home." A silence fell between them as he prodded the remains of his food. "Look, Claude, it's getting late. Why are you here? I mean, really, why are you here? No bullshit, okay?"

He snorted. Claude remembered this tone in her voice, and also remembered that it was something she had inherited from her mother. Fraught and insistent, and yet not remotely hysterical. A sign of sheer will, he had come to realise, rather than petulance, as he had first suspected. In the beginning, he had found this side to Mia's character sexy, and then, once their brief liaison was under way, deeply irritating. Her desire for clarity—for life to be written with clear punctuation marks—had grated against his own desire for the unexpected, his addiction to the spontaneous and the contingent. When Mia said something like "No bullshit, okay?" he wanted to scream that the bullshit was the whole point; it was what made life worth living. It was clarity that dragged you down in a mire of tedium. Mia wanted full stops; Claude wanted question marks.

"I have to tell you," he said between mouthfuls of scratchings. "No, let me start again. I have to salute you. You are not an easy woman to find."

"That was the general idea. I didn't want to leave London. But I didn't want to lead the same life anymore. Simple as that. So I moved. I moved on. I'm not the first person to get a new job, Claude."

"Ah, yes. Your job. This health centre. Yoga and carrot cake. Well, if it makes you happy."

This was a deliberate and gratuitous provocation, but she could not be bothered to rise to the bait. "It does. Go on."

"Well, I thought it was time I looked you up. So I asked all the old crowd—Natasha, Lulu, even David and Mands didn't know where you were. Not a clue. Lulu thought you had joined a New Age sect and were living in the West Country. By the way, David and Mands have a little boy now. Hugo. Must be coming up to two."

"I haven't seen any of that lot in years," she said quietly. The names of these people, all of whom she had seen every week for almost a decade, were like the inscriptions on tombstones, a roll call from another age. Inseparable? They had said it so often of one another, and in the end it had meant nothing.

"One big blank," said Claude. "So. I thought, First principles, and went back to the house in the Boltons."

"You went to my home?" This was intolerable. She was not sure why.

"Yes. And it isn't your home anymore. Things have changed round there."

"What do you mean?"

"I knocked and the door was answered by the queeniest man I ever met in my entire life. I mean, short of wearing a diamanté G-string and singing 'YMCA.' You should have seen him. Smoking jacket, scarlet trousers, Quentin Crisp hair, cigarette holder. Middle-aged. Astonishing sight, really. He was called Kent and he was holding a yappy dog called Dover, which would have seemed funny if it hadn't been pissing down outside. Eventually, he let me in, out of pity, I think. At least I hope it was out of pity."

The sale of the house had been handled by Uncle Gus, and all she knew when she signed the sheaf of papers was that a QC had bought it for cash. Mia hadn't even registered his name. "Did he look like a lawyer?" she asked.

"Kent? Christ no. I doubt he'd done a day's work in his life. No, he said he was Mr. Vincent's assistant and asked me to wait downstairs. Which I did. And boy, they've given the place a whole new look. *Makeover* is not the word."

"Like how?" She smiled, wanting to cry.

"Well, if I say *Cage aux Folles* meets the Dome, you'll get the idea. Loads of gadgets and lava lamps and chrome stuff. Dodgy African statuary of young men everywhere. Suspicious mosaics here and there. Tiled floors, all those wonderful old floorboards ripped up and gone. Modern art on the walls. He's redone the whole thing. Unrecognisable. It must have cost him a fortune."

"God, how awful. I feel sick."

"Not as sick as I did when Kent brought his friend down."

"Vincent?"

"That's what I was expecting. But no. The friend was called George and said he was Mr. Vincent's handyman. Which I have no doubt he was. Very handy. He looked like a gym instructor. Preposterously muscly and wearing nothing but a T-shirt and skimpy shorts."

"And the three of them live there?"

"So it transpired. They offered me a drink, which I have to say I took very gratefully. Although I was worried they might slip something in it and that I'd wake up in the boot of a car somewhere in Devon a week later. If I was lucky."

"I hate it. I grew up there. That's my house."

"It *was* your house, Mia. It's Mr. Vincent's house now. Very definitely Mr. Vincent's house. And when he finally came down from his study after a good thirty minutes, I was half-cut on the White Russians they'd been mixing. Kent perched on this sort of metal chaise longue and George sat at the other end, with his feet on Kent's lap. And Mr. Vincent came in, looking like this perfectly ordinary bloke, some well-heeled lawyer enjoying his weekend. You know, Lauren shirt, nice loafers. No rouge or feathery boa or anything. And there are these two Mardi Gras characters. And me."

"Poor old Claude."

"Thank you. So I explained, in my deepest voice, that I had once had a walk-out with the daughter of the man who used to own the house. I hope you don't mind my presumption in dragging you into it, but I was desperate. There were three of them, and only one of me. And Dover, the dog, occasionally growling in my direction."

"No, I quite understand."

"So Mr. Vincent—it was pretty clear by then that Mr. Vincent doesn't have a first name—he said he didn't know anything about the vendors because he had dealt entirely with a trust."

"Uncle Gus."

"Uncle Gus. But he said he felt sorry for my wasted journey and asked would I stay for dinner. And he stands up and starts to walk towards me."

"God. What did you do?"

"It was one of those moments when I was glad that I am so mad and paranoid and have 999 stored on my cellular. Because I could see things might be about to get a bit hairy. I mumbled something about my secretary wondering where I was, and Kent pointed out that it was a Saturday. And I said my office was open seven days a week and our business never closed, which none of them believed."

"Did Mr. Vincent keep walking towards you?"

"Yes, but only to put on a CD, it turns out. Edith Piaf, of course, which is only one notch up from Marlene Dietrich."

"These dead?" Tony, the barman, loomed over their table, his expression deeply disapproving, as if he had been eavesdropping or, more probably, because he didn't like the look of Claude.

"Yes, thanks, Tony," Mia said, handing him three glasses. They waited until he had moved on to the next table. Claude leant over conspiratorially, chin perched on his hands. He was enjoying his story.

"As you can guess, I was dying to get out. I mean, dying. Because I could see by now that Mr. Vincent was by far the most sinister of the three. I mean, there was Kent, looking like a pantomime dame, and George all toned and bronzed, very much the gay boy pinup. But Vincent had this weird stare: you know, that weirdness that really ordinary-looking people can have. Funny little bifocal glasses. Satanist twitch in his cheek. He looked like he might pull a knife at any moment and tell me that, on balance, he had decided that I was too pretty to live."

"Which would have made him the desperate one."

"Yes, well. So I fumbled badly, trying to think of something to say. And then I finally remembered that Henty had stayed on in the attic for a while before the sale, and so I asked them if they had a forwarding address for her. And that was it, bingo: the three of them squealing and running around, looking for the piece of paper. Yes, said Kent, the nice lady, they had met her, *such* a nice lady, *such* nice manners, don't see nice manners like that very often these days. Oh yes, said George, *very* nice. The dog stopped growling at me. Mr. Vincent disappeared into what used to be the dining room but I assume is now a fully equipped dungeon and returned with Henty's details. It was like pressing a button. I think she saved my life, actually, the dear old thing. I really wouldn't have liked to die in there. I have a feeling they may have a whole room upstairs full of stuffed young strategy consultants."

Mia laughed. As upset as she was by the news that her old home had been so desecrated—upset, in truth, that other people lived there at all—the story was funny. She wondered how much of it had actually happened, how outrageous Vincent's companions, and Vincent himself, had really been. In all likelihood, the door had been answered by the impeccably soignée Mrs. Vincent, who had got the housekeeper to make Claude a cup of tea and introduced him to her middle daughter, back home from Benenden, before writing Henty's address on a yellow Post-it. But it didn't matter. There was something oddly touching in Claude's tale, the deft way in which he let her know that he really had gone out of his way to find her.

Her head was beginning to spin, but she did not care. The evening had already acquired a surreal tinge, which would have been inconsistent with sobriety. The cider was cushioning the whole experience nicely. Claude's unexpected visit might have been—could yet be—the spur for trauma. But the booze, in conspiracy with her medication, kept that well at bay. For now, she was able to enjoy the fascination of his story and the mystery of his appearance in Nantes Street.

Henty, it turned out, had been an even harder nut to crack than the Vincent ménage. Claude had visited her a few days later in her top-floor flat in Earls Court. The purchase of the property had barely dented the Taylor trust fund, but Henty considered herself honoured beyond words by the gift. She called her three rooms and kitchenette "a palace," although it was, Claude said, more like a shrine to the Taylor family, with photographs of the four children at all stages of development beautifully framed on every available surface. A portrait of Jenny by a friend had pride of place above the mantelpiece. In the bathroom was a finger painting which Mia, aged four, had presented to her beloved nanny at Easter. It had yellowed over the years but was now protected behind glass, a splash of colour preserved forever in the formaldehyde of an old woman's heartbreak.

Claude had always done his best to get along with Henty, knowing how integral she was to the Taylor family machine. Though scarcely a chatelaine, she nevertheless had powers to suggest and advise that far exceeded those of a normal family servant. Her veto was deadly; a word in Jenny's ear about one of the children's suitors had usually proved decisive. Conversely, those she took a shine to generally prospered in the little world of the Boltons house. It was always a wise investment to call on Henty when visiting, and Claude had done so many times—not least because he knew how unpersuaded Jeremy and Jenny were of his virtues.

So he had gone to Earls Court after work, armed with a bottle of fine Madeira, remembering that this was her favourite drink. He took a risk and did not call in advance, knowing that it would be better to catch the old nanny off guard than to give her the time to fret about the purpose of his visit, or, even worse, to refuse to see him at all. The gamble paid off, at least as a means of gaining access. Claude pressed the entry phone's buzzer and had to announce himself several times before Henty had remembered who he was. "It's Claude, Henty" had got him nowhere, but "Mr. Silberman, Ben's friend" had triggered some deeply buried memory or other, and the door had clicked open. Four floors up, he regretted not taking the lift, but his puffing and wheezing had caused her amusement when she opened the door for him. Henty told him that he should take better care of himself, and that a young man should be able to climb a few flights of stairs without needing a lie-down. It wasn't so long ago, she reminded him as he took his coat off, that men of his age had had to carry backpacks into battle in Normandy and couldn't afford to pant and wheeze. Claude was sorely tempted to remind her that, in actual fact, it was a very long time ago, and that she had only been two years old on VE day and could therefore scarcely claim to have vivid memories of the war. He had, however, held his tongue. It was part of Henty's rich legend that she pretended to be much older than she was, or at least to have lived through most of the great events of the twentieth century. Such claims had always been indulged by the Taylors, who had treated her as a majestically timeless figure.

Claude had opened the Madeira and settled in one of the armchairs in Henty's sitting room. The furniture, he realised, was all from the Boltons. An old three-piece suite from the large spare room, a mahogany sideboard from Jenny's dressing room, and a chest of drawers that Claude could not quite place. Over these relics from the Taylors' home, Henty had draped her own chintz and fussy paraphernalia: Photographs, framed needlework, and ceramics cluttered the little room. It was stuffy from the gas fire at its centre, in front of which an aged cat slept, oblivious of Claude's unscheduled intrusion.

Henty had sat, as ever, with her back straight and hands folded over her knees to listen to what Claude had to say. He had asked after her health and she had waved the question away as a silly irrelevance. In truth, she had looked bone-weary, a much less ebullient figure than he remembered from their coquettish exchanges in the past. The creases in her face that used to multiply when she smiled, which was often, were now just creases. Her clothes were the same, though: beige and dowdy, a large pin in her tartan skirt and her flat shoes kicked off. A romantic novel in a plastic cover from the library lay open on a table by her armchair, beneath the colourless frames of her reading spectacles. He wondered how she spent her days and what she thought about during the long, empty hours. It was obvious from her stiffness that she was not visited often, although the flat was immaculate. She cleans all day, he thought to himself. She cleans all day for those who never come.

Claude propped up the conversation, telling her unbidden about his work and letting slip that Mia's colleagues still talked about her in awed tones. He sensed at once that she found his presence troubling, but he also gathered that she did not want to squander the chance to talk to someone with whom she had once felt comfortable. After a couple of glasses of Madeira, Henty had relaxed a little and asked him where he was living and how he had been keeping outside his career. He entertained her with the story of a recently dropped girlfriend, whom he had taken to Paris at great expense and then discovered was already engaged to a doctor, temporarily absent in Saudi. Claude avoided such complications in his private life with neurotic care. Henty told him with a chuckle that he "should have asked the young lady before taking her on such a treat, with all the carry-on." Good, thought Claude: He had manoeuvred her into a position where she was once again the wise woman, and he the feckless pupil in the ways of the world. He topped up her glass and amused her further with the story of the Vincent ménage and the strange things that must have happened at the Boltons in the past three years.

And so, having mentioned Mia once, he mentioned her again. The fact was, he explained to Henty, he rather wanted to get in touch with her, hadn't seen her in a while, and none of the old crew had the foggiest where she was. Usual story with Mia, he said: one step ahead of the rest of us. He'd tried to make light of it, but he knew he was inviting Henty to break one of the most basic protocols set by the benefactors who had given her her little home. Mia was not to be disturbed. Mia was to be left alone. And yet he knew that she would not dismiss his request out of hand, that she saw him as at least a peripheral member of the tribe of whose memory she was curator. Henty knew that Claude, for all his drama and his self-aggrandisement, would not harm the precious girl whose hand she had held on long childhood walks and then, in darker times, when they were the only two left.

The nanny stalled by saying that she never met Mia where she worked or lived. This was true. They saw each other three or four times a year on neutral territory, usually somewhere that Mia knew Henty would like. The last time had been tea at the Savoy, the two of them sitting side by side on a velvet couch with what Henty described to Claude as "a lovely little stand of delicacies, all done as nicely as you could ask." Mia had looked beautiful, she said, a little thin but obviously very healthy and enjoying her job. Claude asked as casually as he could what Mia's job was, and the nanny's eyes had narrowed. "Management," she replied.

And so, after a couple more attempts to edge Henty towards disclosure, Claude had given up. He realised that discretion on this point had become one of the guiding principles of the old nanny's life. Perhaps, he thought, she does not even know her true whereabouts, just waits for the call every few months to arrange the next meeting at some prim hotel or other. In any case, he accepted defeat. He had hoped that Henty would regard what he sought as an indiscretion which might be teased from her with a certain amount of effort. But their conversation and the turn it had taken told him otherwise. She would not betray Mia's confidence. She would never betray the last of the Taylors. He felt foolish for having thought that she would.

Defeated, he stayed with her to finish the Madeira, swapping stories of the years when they had seen each other often. They spoke with careful banality, joking about little things and small incidents, as if the people of whom they spoke might be expected to telephone or knock on the door at any moment. Henty picked up her needlework as they talked and Claude slumped on the sofa. The cat did not stir. Another hour and a half passed before he realised what the time was and how late he was for drinks with friends in the West End. He did not want to leave abruptly, but he also did not want to stay any longer, his visit such a conspicuous failure. Woozy from the Madeira and depressed by his mis-judgement, he wanted to start drinking expensive cocktails immediately, as far away from the enveloping gloom of Henty's flat as was humanly possible. He wanted to be in a neon-lit bar with people like himself, talking nonsense, running up a crazy tab on his American Express card. He wanted to eat late, then resume drinking, probably all night. With a trace of bitterness, he realised that he would feel terrible the next day as a direct consequence of Henty's moral fibre.

She led him to the door, walking down a corridor of, he thought, un-speakable bleakness, a fading rug from the second-floor landing of the old house stretching all the way to the little hallway. He put on his hat and leant down to kiss her on the cheek. She opened the door and said good-bye and then, as if it was the most natural thing in the world, spoke again: "She has done very well for herself, you know. Running a gym or health centre, or whatever you young people call it. In the mid-dle of nowhere, Mile End or Stepney or somewhere. Gracious, she was always a bold one. I think she's far too busy to need disturbing, though. You understand, don't you?" Then she shut the door, leaving him in the stairwell, which was quickly plunged into darkness as the timer ran out on the light.

He did understand. He understood that Henty loved Mia enough to want her at least to have the chance to see people like Claude again. That was what she had been thinking about as she embroidered ugly let-ters in front of the fire. Considering the risk of steering him in the right direction, weighing up the different ways of protecting a person: from interference or from isolation. He also understood that she could not bring herself to say exactly where Mia was, that Claude would have to clear the final hurdle himself. But in truth, she had not set it very high. What remained was a nuisance, rather than a secret. There could be only so many places that matched Henty's description. Six, as it turned out. And the third he had called had been the Echinacea.

"So here you are," said Mia, running a finger around the rim of her glass.

"Yes, here I am," he replied. "Quite a story, even by own standards, I think. I must say I was rather pleased with myself."

"You are a pest, Claude. She must have wondered what you were up to."

"I think she rather enjoyed my visit, actually. Self-evidently, if you think about it."

"What are you up to?"

"More drink. First, we must have more drink."

He disappeared to the loo and then returned with another half-pint for her and what looked like a very large gin and tonic. She remembered from their brief courtship that Claude ordered trebles only when he was nervous.

"Christ. If my colleagues saw me, they'd be appalled. Drinking in their local with a Sloane in a hat."

"Never mind your colleagues," he said. "I assume they're busy cooking up a bong somewhere. Actually, I'm pretty appalled myself to find you knocking back the cider. Whatever happened to Cosmopolitans and Bellinis?"

"Not much call for them round here, I guess. Although Tony, the barman, mixes a mean Dark Lady."

"A cocktail inspired by the sonnets. Classy."

"And I think there's one called Ophelia's End. That's got rum in it."

"Stop, please stop. I give in."

"Good." She giggled. "So. Out with it."

"Actually, I just wanted to ask you on a date."

She sat back. Should she slap him? No, that would secretly please him. True punishment for Claude was to be starved of drama. For the past two hours, he had built up to a finale which, it turned out, was a pathetic squeak. No revelation at all, but an insult disguised as an invitation. He had traced her, run her to earth, disturbed a person she loved, simply to ask her out for the evening. Did he grasp the scale of his blunder? Almost certainly not. Cold with fury, she remembered all that she had disliked most about Claude, the compulsive game playing and the fantasies which he found endlessly funny but which always seemed to involve recklessness with the emotions of others.

She coughed, then sipped her cider. "I see. A date. Well, there it is."

"What were you expecting?"

"I'm not sure, Claude. I wasn't expecting you to turn up. I'm not sure I like the way you found me. I'm not sure I'm glad you're here now."

He was silent for a few moments, but she could see that he was genuinely perplexed.

"Look, Mia. I know it must seem odd, me rolling up like this. I absolutely accept that. Of course, of course. And if you want the truth, I wouldn't have dared look for you until now. I—everyone—understood you needed space. Don't you think people would have tried if they thought you wanted to be found?"

"I think most of them were glad to see the back of me." She looked him square in the eye. "That's what I think. What do you think, Claude?"

"I think you're drunk. I also think you're reacting the wrong way. I came here because it's been three years and I thought you might be ready to see some of your old friends. I thought you might be ready to see me."

Ready to see old friends. She wasn't sure about that, either, not sure at all. And did Claude fondly imagine that she could just reenter his world, which used to be hers, without burning up? Did he know how far he had truly travelled in his search for her and how far was the journey back? No, of course he didn't. Claude thought he was just a ten-pound cab fare from Soho, on an errand up east, where the curries are cheap and the lock-ins brilliant. A place to bring his friends when they wanted a change of scene and Cockney accents to laugh at. He had no idea how deep in the jungle he truly was, and how pointless his mission. Henty had understood, though. Henty understood everything. She had realised that at some stage Mia needed to hear this, to confront it, and to be angry. Mia had expected Claude to make her feel uneasy, but now she felt only contempt for his presumption.

"Well, now I've seen you, haven't I?"

Claude squirmed. "Not like this. I mean properly, an evening out."

"Round here, this is an evening out." She gesticulated, spilling cider on the table.

"Careful, you might get me beaten up. Look, Mia, I can see I've upset you, although I'm not quite sure why. I wanted you to come to the Bracknell with me. A friend of mine has got a table, and I don't have a date. It's in six weeks' time. I just thought you might enjoy it. That's all."

He stood up, struggling with his coat, getting his arm stuck in one of the sleeves. He was visibly annoyed at his own loss of equanimity, and there was sweat on his brow. Their meeting, strangely amicable for so long, had descended into something nasty. She had made him feel terrible. She was glad. But she was not absolutely sure that she wanted him to leave. She had to be sure it was not her demons speaking, that her judgement was right.

"So you're just going to go?"

"I think so, yes. It was a mistake to come here, I'm sorry. I've wasted your time." He looked at her and then at the pool of cider on the table. "And mine."

He started to leave and then turned back. "Look, I still have the tickets. If you decide you want to come, you know where to find me. Good night."

The Bracknell. She hadn't expected to hear those words again—or rather, she hadn't thought of them for so long that their very mention seemed odd, to the point of lunacy. What possible use could she have for the Bracknell Ball, the winter party in Battersea Park organised by the all-powerful Bracknell Committee? There had been a time, of course, when missing it would have been equally unthinkable. It was years since the Bracknell family had run the event—they hadn't run anything since selling off their enormous global distillery business in the eighties—but they had allowed the sponsors and the charities to retain the name, and therefore keep the brand going. How many Bracknells had she been to? Eight, nine? One year, three members of the committee had been friends of hers; that had been a matter of pride, no denying it. Another year, she had sat next to a famous American novelist, who had whispered an unspeakably obscene proposition to her over the main course of poached halibut on a bed of spinach vermicelli in mussel broth. She had not answered back, but was unsettled a few weeks later to see a picture of the two of them apparently revelling in each other's company in *Tatler's* two-page spread on the ball. The next photograph showed the novelist's glamorous wife—a minor English aristocrat—laughing hysterically at some witticism uttered to her by a corpulent Cabinet minister.

The very idea that she might go to such a gathering ever again made her feel nauseous. Was Claude deranged? It was too ridiculous for words. The thought that, after three years helping Sylvia plan yoga classes and sell therapy tapes, she would want to spend an evening in the company of people who would laugh at her if they knew what she did for a living . . . The poor boy really had lost it. He had come all this way to tell her something nothing short of stupid. He had found her, merely to remind her why she had wanted to be lost in the first place. She knew, too, that he had not told her the whole truth about his visit.

Looking up, she noticed that the pub was almost empty. There was an old man on a bar stool, and a couple in the corner, barely acknowledging each other. Tony cleaned glasses and watched football on a small television set by the till. Was it her imagination or had he dimmed the lights? It seemed dark suddenly. When she got up, a five-pound note fell out of her pocket, and she could only just bring herself to pick it up. She walked home, melancholy and drunk.

ON MONDAY, Mia arrived early at the centre. The trainers were a perfect fit and she felt good in them, almost as if each step she took contained a little extra spring because of her clever purchase. There was a new begonia on the counter, apparently put there by Sylvia over the weekend, but no sign of her boss. Mia had wanted to be there when Rob arrived, if only to impress upon him that he was entering her territory and should tread with care. The first lesson of the day, however, was that Rob was not an early starter. She was on her fourth cup of tea when he arrived, looking, she was pleased to see, a little flustered.

"Morning, sorry, sorry," he said. His hair was not long enough to reveal whether he had just got out of bed or not, but his T-shirt—which bore the much less offensive slogan TOKYO 75—looked as if it had been pulled on in a tearing hurry.

"Don't panic," she said, barely looking up from the magazine she had been reading. "Sylvia's not even here yet. You're safe."

"Thanks. Thanks. God, I must learn how to get up early. It's been such a long time. You know?"

She wanted to say that it had been more than three years since she had slept after 6:30, except on the rare occasions when she had taken enough sleeping pills to flatten a horse. Instead, she smiled and returned to her reading.

Rob ducked under the counter and into the back room, where he dumped his satchel. He looked at the computer screen, scratched his belly, and walked back out. He was nervous. This was good.

"So," he said. She smiled again, leafing over an article about Nicole Kidman for the fourth time. "So, so. Well, what do you want me to do?"

"Well, maybe we should wait for Sylvia. I'm sure she'll want to give you a proper induction."

"Sure. Okay. But since I'm here and she's not, why don't I get cracking on . . . on whatever it is you want me to do."

The filthy floor—of course. She remembered the filthy floor upstairs, a subject which she had planned to raise with him on Friday night, when the person waiting upstairs had turned out to be Claude. She could now resume her plan for Rob, with the bonus that he had invited it upon himself.

"All right, then. The thing that really needs doing is the carpet on the top floor. It's a mess, and I think both of those rooms are going to be used today. Needs a really good scrub, I'm sorry to say. You'll find all the cleaning gear in the utility room in the basement."

Rob was about to speak—to register protest or to acquiesce, she could not tell—when Sylvia arrived. She had, Mia counted, four plastic bags in her hands and a basket over her shoulder. A few strands of hair poked out from the navy blue beret she sometimes wore and which did her no favours.

"Well!" she said, dropping her payload of food and files. "Well, well! That's a sight for sore eyes. The new assistant manager and the deputy manager of this great centre, busy already."

"I was just saying that the floor upstairs needs a good scrub."

"Oh, never mind that," said Sylvia. "I need the two of you to go over to the wholesaler's and pick up the new yoga mats. They don't deliver, and the mats have been sitting there waiting for collection for three weeks."

"Okay, I'll go and get them," said Rob, brightening as his duties moved up the scale from menial to manual.

"No, no, it's a two-person job. You'll both have to go. That's why we couldn't do it before. Is that all right, Chels?"

"I'll get the keys. Come on, Rob. Let's go."

She led him to the lockup alley which the centre shared with a local hardware store as a parking space for Sylvia's old Transit. It was a useless vehicle, in Mia's view, and one which the centre could ill afford. But Sylvia had fond memories of trips to festivals in it and could not bear to part with it, even though she drove it no more than five times a year. Journeys such as this one—the collection of twenty-five brand-new yoga mats—were cited as reason enough to keep it. But Mia knew this was nonsense. Once again, sentimentality prevailed over sense.

"What a wreck," said Rob, inspecting the bashed bumpers and liberally dented bodywork. For once, she completely agreed with him. "What colour is it? Or is that a rude question?"

"It's not rude. I just don't know the answer."

"Looks like it'll fall apart the minute you turn the key in the ignition."

She backed the van out of the alleyway, noticing that there was a new pile of scrap metal and an abandoned fridge. Rob held the gate and then jumped in. He lit a cigarette, drew on it heavily, and offered her one. She shook her head. The truth was that she would have loved a smoke but would have hated the intimacy involved in accepting one from him.

"Amazing, really amazing."

She turned into Roman Road and headed towards the Underground station. "What is?"

"This motor. I mean, this beats the old bangers we were driving at college."

"Well, it's all we've got, so get used to it." She slowed for three veiled Bengali women, two with push chairs, at the zebra crossing.

"I suppose I expected a big van with the corporate logo on the side."

"I wouldn't say that around Sylvia. She's not big on logos. You'll get a half-hour speech on globalisation if you're not careful."

"Right, right. Where are we going?"

"Up Kingsland Road to Dalston. There's a place we get all our kit from. We've needed these mats for ages. The truth is, I'm not sure we can afford them. But the old ones are going mouldy. Your predecessor—

Vic—used to hose them down once every few weeks in the back garden."

"Something to look forward to. Does the radio work?"

"God knows. Try it."

Rob turned the knob on the ancient stereo and tinny music filled the van instantly. He fiddled with the bass to dampen the hiss and then with the tuner to get a station. She found this irritating after a while, particularly when he settled for one playing loud New Wave music and began to dance jerkily, drumming the dashboard in time to the staccato guitar and whiney mid-Atlantic vocals. "Excellent," he said. "Excellent. The Hives. Do you like them?"

Here we go, she thought. Teenage bands none of us has heard of: noise, noise, noise. She could not wait to set Ringo on Rob, Ringo with his effortless knowledge of all that was worth listening and dancing to, and his contempt for precisely the sort of racket that her new colleague obviously liked. It would be a pleasure to watch Rob shrinking in size as Ringo audited his musical taste. A rare treat.

"I don't think I've ever heard of this lot," she said. "Actually, can you turn it down a bit? My head is pounding. And it *is* Monday morning."

He obliged but was disappointed. "You have to listen to a band like that loud. You'll see. You just have to give them a chance."

I did, she thought. I gave bands like that a chance at school discos when I was sixteen. And now I don't have to listen to that sort of stuff.

Why did he rile her? She could not quite place it. All he had done, after all, was to share his love of a band with her and invite her to listen harder: scarcely a mortal insult. She had experienced this before, mostly in her old workplace. A colleague would become irritating, to the point where anything he or she said, however innocuous, seemed an act of outrageous hostility. She would hear herself complaining about this associate or that trainee. And you know what he did then? He *bought me a coffee*! Plain as day! The cheek of it! In only a few days, Rob had apparently joined this category of the irredeemable, for reasons that were far from clear. Apart from an inexcusable T-shirt and a certain freshness of manner, what had he actually done?

She looked over at her new colleague who was still hammering away at the dashboard in time to the frenzied rhythm of the track. Absorbed in his little dance, elbows jutting out and head nodding furiously up and down, he looked anything but threatening. The eyes were softer than she remembered, and his features less mocking than they had been during the standoff at the interview. Stubble crept up his chin and threatened to coalesce into a goatee. He was enjoying himself. He was, more enviably, completely unfazed by her scrutiny.

She turned into Kingsland Road and put her foot on the accelerator. Even then, the van could manage only a querulous forty miles an hour, its joints groaning and the engine heaving with unnatural effort. The road widened as they passed the rank of Vietnamese restaurants and headed north. Shabby chic gave way to something else: The concrete looked greyer, the pedestrians slower in their step. The lava flow of London money had not reached this far. But it would soon enough, bringing new bars and design studios and estate agents who could not believe their luck.

"Is this the sort of music your band plays?" Was she really interested? Not much, but it was impossible to say nothing.

Rob's little jig slowed somewhat. He was surprised to be asked an apparently neutral question by someone he assumed was allergic to him, and he didn't want to say the wrong thing. "This? Well, I like this kind of stuff. But the idea of the band is really to get back to playing instruments, you know, to get a raw edge back."

"I see. So I take it you don't like much of the stuff there's been the last few years?"

He reflected on this and drew on his cigarette. Was she setting a trap? "No, not much. I think the whole DJ thing is bullshit. Turning them into cult figures. They're just sampling stuff. It's not music. It's as if they think that nobody will ever make music again, that that's all over, and now it's just variations on a theme. It's such—"

"Such what?" His outburst made the prospect of his first encounter with Ringo all the more appetising.

"It's such *arrogance.* You know, to think that music ended in the 1990s and now all that's left is for a few blokes in luminous T-shirts to rearrange the order it was played in for the rest of time. I mean, there's loads of good music still to be made. Loads. Mind you, I'm not saying we're the best band in the world." He paused and looked out of the window at the breeze-block landscape speeding past. "Actually, if the truth be known, we're crap."

They both laughed, and then stopped almost immediately, disconcerted to find themselves in agreement for the first time. Mia disliked it more than Rob, and she pretended to be concentrating on the traffic at the crossroads and a lorry that was performing an arthritic U-turn. They drove on. Not wishing to seem hostile, she broke the silence again.

"So what are you called? I mean your band?"

"You'll laugh." He smiled and looked down.

Yes, she thought, but not in front of you. "Course I won't. Go on, tell me."

"We're called Thieves in the Night."

Shit: This was not in the script. Rob's band had a good name. They should have been called something studenty and embarrassing. Not so. Not so at all. This was annoying. Rob was fast clambering out of the box she had prepared for him, what with his speech on DJs and his band's cool name. She felt the beginnings of a headache.

"You see?" he said, shaking his head and rolling down the window to throw out his fag. "I knew you'd hate it. I should never have told you."

"Actually," she said, turning off the main road, "I have to admit that it's rather good."

She looked over and saw that he was speechless with surprise.

"You like it?"

"Sure. I mean, it's not every day you hear of a band which takes its name from Saint Paul." She pulled up outside the wholesaler's. "Rob. You can close your mouth now. We're here. There's lugging to be done."

"Oh, God. Sure, sure. It's just . . . I didn't . . . Right."

"I'm full of surprises, as you'll discover. Come on."

The wholesaler's premises was a dingy building which, it seemed, used to be an interior-decor shop. They specialised in gym kit and martial arts equipment, which kept them in business. The owner, Jim, had explained to her on a previous visit that three-quarters of their business came from kickboxing classes, which were proliferating across the city. Mia enjoyed the irony of a firm which could afford to cross-subsidise mats for Yuppies looking for peace and harmony by shifting martial arts gear which encouraged urban warfare.

Jim was behind the desk. He was a beefy, overweight man, his paunch spilling out from a short-sleeved maroon shirt which revealed fading tattoos. It was cool in the shop, but beads of sweat clung to his forehead, alongside strands of unwashed grey hair. He looked like a Buddha just back from a very short and exhausting jog. Jim's view was that exercise and fitness were greatly overrated—although he was glad that they were, since he had bought a nice little maisonette in Leytonstone on the proceeds. He liked beer and football himself, preferably enjoyed simultaneously, and happily declared to anybody who cared to listen that he expected to pay for it sooner or later with a spectacular cardiac arrest. He was one of the few people Mia had actually heard use expressions like "Can't take it with you" and "You only live once." She liked him.

"Chels! Where have you been for so long, my darling? Haven't seen you in donkey's. Was it something I said?" He closed his *Sporting Life* and rubbed his hands together.

"Never, Jim. How could you possibly upset me?"

"You've got to be careful, young lady. Very easy to offend these days. Very easy not to be PC, say something that old men like me think is gallant but turns out is out of order, and then you're in trouble. All sorts of bother. Know what I mean?"

"I do, I do," she said. "But you could never offend me, Jim."

Rob, she noticed, had pointlessly put on his sunglasses and was casing the joint nervously. There was very little to case. Jim was not trying to attract off-the-street business and his shopfront was little more than functional: a counter and a till, with a few old punching bags slumped forlornly in the corner.

"Who's this, your bodyguard?" he asked, pointing at Rob. Rob turned round and took off his shades, smiling feebly. He looked ridiculous.

"No, this is Rob. He just started at the centre this morning. This is Jim, Rob. Jim supplies us with everything. Couldn't do it without him." The two men shook hands, Jim surveying Rob with ill-concealed scepticism.

"Nice to meet you, young man. Well, you're very lucky to be working with this charming lady, I must say. Not so sure about that Sylvia, though. She's a caution."

"Now, Jim." Mia laughed. "Sylvia gives you loads of business. Don't be like that."

"Gives me loads of grief, more like. God, I thought those mats were going to be in my storeroom forever. Called her last week, I did. And she gives me ten minutes of bunny about how she's got no staff. So I says to her, 'There's only me here, doll. Tell me about it.' And I need the space. Got a shipload of teenage ninja crap arriving tomorrow. I assume you *are* here to pick up the mats, Chels."

"That's it. All paid for, aren't they?"

"Months ago, my love, months. You just need to sign for them and then you can stretch and flex, or whatever it is you lot do, to your heart's content."

Rob and Jim obliged by loading up the van. Mia could have joined in, but she realised that there was no need and no rush. Twenty-five mats, probably eight or nine separate journeys from the storeroom. She hoped Jim would not expire from the effort, but she also wanted to pull rank on Rob. The pettiness of their first encounter had not drained from her yet, and she still wanted him to feel that there was a gulf of years and status which separated them. He might have a cool-sounding group— he did, didn't he?—but she was still deputy manager. That was what counted. Wasn't it? She leant against the counter as Rob bounded down the stairs with a mat and Jim shuffled behind him, trembling and looking as though his prophecy of a heart attack was about to come true at any moment.

The radio was on and she half listened to the news. She had lost her political antennae completely—or rather, had surrendered them. Stories that would once have had her sending E-mails to clients within seconds and writing memos to her superiors about market opportunities now seemed distant and irrelevant. At Robinson, she had read every national newspaper and listened to the *Today* programme with a religious regularity that had infuriated her boyfriends. She had surfed the Net for tips and business gossip. But news no longer enthralled her; she was free of its promiscuous grasp. Radio and television headlines that would once have held her rapt in silence now washed over her like an indifferent tide. There was civil unrest in the Ukraine; the dollar had taken a tumble and the Fed was concerned; Downing Street had offered "unreserved backing" to a minister accused of offering lucrative government contracts to a company in which his cousin had a controlling interest; civil liberties and Muslim community groups had condemned Miles Anderton, the Home Office minister, over his new crackdown on organisations connected with militant groups overseas; a famous sportsman was getting divorced; there was cold weather on the way. So it went, rolling over her.

Miles . . . It was odd to hear his name. Still at it, obviously. She wondered whether he knew what he was doing this time. Probably not. But he would love the publicity, as he always had, running towards the lights wherever he saw them.

"That's the last one, Chels." Jim stood before her, craving her approval. He was a wreck, his shirt soaked through. One of its buttons had burst off and a patch of lily white flesh was now clearly visible. Curiously, what hair he had was now standing up. "Oh, Jim. My hero. Thank you so much. Where do I sign? Here?" He panted miserably, struggling to compose himself. She wondered who his next customer would be and how long he would have to wait. Probably a few days would pass, and then a couple of tough nuts from one of the upstairs fight clubs in Hackney would come to pick up gloves and masks and nunchakus so they could go back and kick the crap out of each other. A strange trade Jim plied—no doubt about it.

She said good-bye and left the shop with Rob. He did not put the music on in the van, and, though they made a little small talk, he did not try to resume their earlier conversation or tell her more about his band. The Transit grumbled in disbelief at the new load in the back and made heavy weather of the journey home. But Sylvia was delighted when they returned. Mia could tell from her expression that she had seen the little trip to collect the mats in the crudest terms—as a bonding experience. Her boss beamed with the serenity of an Earth Mother whose brood is at peace. Rob unloaded the mats and then spent the rest of the day on chores, including the carpet cleaning.

She left as early as she could and walked home, stopping in Brick Lane for a coffee and an egg sandwich. It was cold, but she sat outside the café, alone on the bench. The waiter brought her her food and gestured to the heavens as if to say that she was mad. She thanked him but stayed put. She liked the place and enjoyed watching the other customers. Inside, a man in a black leather coat, who reminded her a little of her brother, shared a beer with a striking blonde. She laughed at almost everything he said. Their fingers touched across the table occasionally and then they would lose physical contact as his next bon mot sent the girl into happy convulsions. There was no tension between them at all. They were totally at ease with each other's bodies, and she was obviously content to be the audience for his show. The man slapped his forehead and she laughed again.

Mia finished her sandwich and walked the last few hundred yards home. It was dark already and, she realised, cold in a way that no longer contained the ambiguity of autumn. Only a few days ago, the season had quivered and the sun still played its treacherous game. But now the sharpness of winter pricked at her fingers and the sky spoke only of doleful change. This was when she wanted to lie down and sleep, to lose herself completely. But she kept walking. There is no escape in a city, she thought. There is no hibernation.

At her flat, there was a pile of junk mail and a letter from an estate agent asking her whether she wanted to sell her property. She was, she noticed immediately, behind with her laundry and needed badly to shop for essentials, too. The flat was in a state, but she could not be bothered to do anything about it before morning. The answering machine was flashing, but she decided not to listen to her messages just yet. There was, as she had thought once before that day, no rush.

She made herself another cup of tea and put on a CD of the *Diabelli Variations.* The Beethoven captured her and transported her from her forgettable day. She enjoyed the complexity of the music, its challenge to her brain. She liked the fact that the pianist gave the composer no quarter and accomplished his frightening task with such ferocious, subtle accuracy. It fortified her to hear the struggle of two geniuses across the centuries, one man's hands flying across a keyboard in response to marks laid down on paper by another, the latter half-mad with the forces within him, unable to hear what he was creating. No room for failure, not a trace of it. A performer who would never countenance such a thing. This was something that she could not explain but which she understood.

The CD finished and she sat for a long while on the sofa. Then she got up and called Claude to say that she would go with him to the Bracknell.

Chapter SEVEN

CITIES SURVIVE by heading west in pursuit of the setting sun. They conquer fresh dominions, settle their children, and then, when they can conquer no more, they perish in the cooling desert or in the slow stranglehold of the suburbs. But not London. For more than a century, its energies did indeed flow west, draining the old Roman stronghold of its lifeblood, leaving only the rusting graveyard of the docks and the airtight financial quarter of the Square Mile, from which the city's plutocrats and barrow boys scurried away in the evening. The old working class of the East End, or at least those who could afford to, evacuated its dying homeland, founding new pebble-dashed colonies in Essex and beyond. For a while, all that could be heard was the howling of the wind that raged down the Commercial Road from the old docks to the City, an artery once swollen, now suddenly bloodless.

No longer, though. The white labourers and taxi drivers had been replaced by Asian families who worked twice as hard and made twice as much money. Their wholesale shops now lined streets which had been deserted for years. Meanwhile, the artists had moved from Hampstead and Chelsea to Hoxton and Shoreditch. The artless middle classes had followed quickly, looking for loft space and bohemian scenery. The brush strokes of indigent painters and the concept art of their sculptor colleagues were a mighty engine of regeneration. As the millennium approached, a new tribe had staked its claim to the East End, and the swirling currents of the city changed direction once more. London still had its Checkpoint Charlie at Fleet Street, where East met West in nervous détente, but East no longer cringed as it looked over the wall of the law courts and deserted newspaper buildings.

These were not the forces that had brought Mia Taylor east, but she understood them. She sensed the plates beneath the city groaning and shifting as they did once a century or so, as wealth and talent regrouped and redirected itself within the ancient, infinite city. Her own story was one of accident, the treachery of fate. But it had cast her unwittingly in a bigger story, a modern legend of migration and change that would carry on for a few decades, run its course, and then metamorphose into something else entirely as the children of her generation scorned their parents' decisions and chose a quite different path.

She took the steps down to Bethnal Green Tube two a time, embarking on one of her rare journeys west of London Bridge. On the midway landing, a young man with a dog begged for small change, his hands curling and uncurling under a blanket. Leaning against his ankles was a battered piece of box cardboard with "Homeless and hungry" written in a desperate jumble of upper and lowercase letters. The dog, better fed than the young man—who would doubtless starve himself rather than see it go hungry—slept soundly amidst the cascade of human traffic. His master's hair was streaked with blond, and matted from weeks without water other than rain. She absentmindedly tossed a pound coin into the cap, but not before checking that she had enough change for her ticket.

She needed to go west, because she needed a new outfit for the Bracknell. There was no way round it. A pair of trainers to match Aasim's could be found in Whitechapel, but not a dress to knock them dead in Battersea Park. Her wardrobe had nothing to offer, and even if it had, she would have wanted something new anyway. It was one of the subsidiary rituals of this greater rite, observed every year for many years, that she should buy a new outfit. New shoes, perhaps some earrings, everything. She had two and a half grand in her pocket, drawn out of the bank that very morning. Uncle Gus need never know. Would he approve? Probably, but for the wrong reasons. He would think that Mia's extravagance, and her decision to go to the Bracknell at all, was the first sign that she was coming home. He would hear the fidgeting of keys in the lock of her self-imposed captivity. They all would. They would think that her madness was at an end. They would not know whether to feel embarrassed or smug at what they imagined was her return to normality.

On the platform, the board flashed EALING BROADWAY: 1 MIN. She looked across the rail to a poster inviting her to make sense of life at a series of meditation classes in St. Pancras, then at another declaring the virtues of Portuguese wine. A rat scurried across the trench as the train approached—so small a creature, one would have thought that the noise alone would pulverise it. She got on board and sat as far away as she could from a bedraggled woman who was singing an aria from *The Marriage of Figaro* for loose change, well enough for the music to be identifiable, but not well enough for it to be worth listening to. The woman, who was wearing a pitifully threadbare dress and cardigan, walked through the carriage, breaking off between phrases to thank the passengers who were giving her nothing, hiding behind their newspapers or staring ahead as if she were not there. She isn't really there, thought Mia. Not really. The music comes from nowhere and she is its transparent vessel.

The train moved off and she wondered again what she was doing. Claude's visit had disturbed her deeply. For a start, it showed that she could be reached quite easily. For all the confection of his story, he had not had to work very hard to track her down at the Echinacea. Her safe haven was nothing of the sort—or rather, it was safe only as long as people chose to leave her alone. Claude had wanted to see her, and she could still not work out why. His date for the Bracknell Ball? Well, it was nice of him to pretend. But he had been to such parties on his own many times, and left accompanied many times. The notion that Claude needed a woman on his arm when he arrived at these events was the opposite of the truth. But he had known that the offer would be hard for her to decline. It was not that she longed to see her face in *Tatler* again, or to renew contact with any of the people whom she would now, inevitably, have to confront. It was that the challenge was too great for her to refuse. He knew her well enough for that. To tempt her back, the bait had to be big enough, frightening enough for her to be unable to refuse. Clever Claude.

Liverpool Street. The train disgorged a few passengers and admitted many more. A teenager wearing an Adidas top and carrying a football sat next to her, fidgeting so that his elbow dug once or twice into her ribs. She turned and glared at him, which calmed him down temporarily. She caught her reflection in the window opposite and saw the face of her mother: She had used the expression Jenny had deployed so often with the four of her children to still the boy. Not cruel, but unbending, her features instantly communicating a sense of unbudgeable will. Is that what I have become? she thought. Are the other five within me, trapped inside me, each scrambling to the surface of my being occasionally to be glimpsed in mirrors? No, that was too glib. Human personality did not work like that. Each of them had always contained parts of the others, their characters commingled in the busy stew of a family. Now there was only her, with no one else to make sense of the likeness or to laugh at the affinity.

Such brooding annoyed Mia, but Claude's visit had provoked much of it. She was dwelling once more upon matters she had forced into the sidings of her life, confronting questions to which there could be no answers. It vexed her that this should be so, for she knew after so long that to stray into this maze was always to court pain and frustration. Those who spoke of "closure" did not understand the nature of loss, not true loss. They did not grasp the final truth: that there were no answers, no symmetries, no final acts. There were only daily tactics, the mastery of evasion and the struggle simply to keep moving. The only question worth asking was, When will I stop asking questions? Still, she thought, as the train rattled to a halt at Bank, I cannot blame Claude entirely. It would be so convenient to hold him responsible, as the first intruder to trample into the little shelter she had built for herself. The unwanted pioneer. But he was not the first. No, that particular honour fell elsewhere.

A year and a half had passed since the coming of Beatrice Brown. Had it been April or May? She could not remember. Spring, anyway, and warm enough to go to work in T-shirt and shorts. The lone cherry tree in the garden of the centre was in full blossom, and there was a pitcher of lemonade full of ice cubes on the front desk. All the windows were open and electric fans whirred in the studio and workshops. Even so, the oppressive heat of deep summer, when the city became an infernal prison and men naked to the waist leaned out of the windows of twenty-storey tower blocks in boozy desperation, still seemed an age away. Spring suited the East End, and the children who raced around the little green at the end of Nantes Street.

It was Vic who first noticed Beatrice, who was sitting on a bench on the other side of the street. He was peering out of the front window, as he did when he had nothing to do, which was often. A sly roll-up concealed in his left hand, he puffed smoke out to the pavement. In his black denim shirt and old paint-spattered cords, his hair pulled back in a ponytail, he looked like a jazz musician down on his luck, or a roadie for a folk group. Either of which, Mia thought, he might well have been had he not ended up as the oracle and odd-job man of the Echinacea. Another drag, this time deeper, more contemplative. Something had caught his eye.

"Chels. Chels, man. Come here. No, don't make a thing of it. Easy."

She ducked below the counter and shuffled over to the window. When Mia had first seen Vic walk, she had suddenly understood, after years of misapprehension, what the word *amble* really meant: It was very specific, and, she had discovered, very difficult to do. All in the shoulders, waist, and hips. She wanted to amble over to him now. But the best she could do, more ostentatious probably than cartwheeling across the room with a traffic cone stuck to her head, was to scrape her feet along the floor, trying not to look too furtive.

"What? What is it?"

"Be cool, girl. Don't look so obviously. See? Over there." Vic gestured with his cupped hand, from which smoke curled mysteriously, as if from the magic palm of some Inuit shaman.

On the bench was a large woman wearing a large coat. She stared directly ahead, determined, it would seem, not to make contact with anyone or anything. Her hair was a shock of henna, almost a separate creature really, cast into an immobile and monumental shape. On her lap was an expensive-looking handbag, whose ivory handles she gripped ferociously with both hands. Even from this distance, Mia could see she was heavily made up, her true features concealed by a boldly applied stratum of foundation, blush, and mascara. But it was her coat that was most striking: a long fur creation, containing the many browns of the numerous creatures which had doubtless perished in its construction. Its fronds moved slightly in the spring breeze. Like the woman's hairdo, the coat seemed an independent entity. They made a strange trio.

"She must be bloody boiling. That's a coat for winter in Siberia."

"Well, she was wearing it yesterday," said Vic. He threw his fag out of the window.

"Seen her before?"

"Only the last four days." He turned to Mia, as if about to impart some story of the paranormal, so incredible that it would require an extraordinary suspension of disbelief. "I tell you, Chels. Most peculiar. *Most* peculiar. Four days in a row, I seen that old girl. First up, she's down by the green. Didn't think anything of it. I mean, she could be somebody's mum or gran, right? Weather's nice, so I see the coat first time and think, Well, maybe she knows something we don't; it's probably going to turn nasty. Whatever." He looked around conspiratorially, then took out his tobacco pouch to roll another fag. "But then the next day, I notice she's back."

"On the green?"

"No, man." He looked at Mia again. "Far from it. This time, she was looking in the window."

Mia could barely suppress her giggles. "The window, Vic? You mean, she was actually looking in the window? I mean, how weird is that?"

Vic did not miss a beat. He was too engrossed in the subtle manipulation of cigarette paper and tobacco. He also had the confident air of a man who knew things which would silence the sceptics once he decided to reveal them. Weird things. "She's looking in the window, but when she sees me looking at her, she bolts like a pony in a blizzard. You wouldn't think she could move so fast. But she came back the next day. And now there she is again."

"Is she stalking you?"

Vic considered this. "Me, doll? I doubt it." He looked out at the woman, staring at her hair and her coat again. "But she's after something. For sure. For sure."

The train pulled in to St. Paul's and the teenager got off. Vic had been right, although he would never have guessed the answer to the riddle of the Woman in the Coat. She was after something. The next day, she did not show up, and he and Mia had joked that they had driven her away and would never know what she was up to. But after the weekend, on a colder Monday morning, Mia had seen her again on the bench. This time, she wore a cashmere scarf and cream gloves. It was hard to say whether she looked defiantly splendid or merely absurd, done up as if on her way to a concert in Bath rather than, as she was, sitting on a bench sprayed with the word NUFFINK. An hour later, Mia checked again and she had gone. She told Vic, who shook his head and said he couldn't wait to tell his friend Steve the saxophonist: In his heyday, apparently, Steve had been followed around the jazz circuit by a madwoman who had declared undying love for him. Steve had politely declined her advances and she had thrown herself under a train. Or was it off a bridge? The precise details eluded Vic.

It was not until the next day that the saga of the Woman in the Coat ceased to be an amusing diversion and became something else entirely. Mia left the centre at six and set off home. It was a dazzling evening and she savoured the aroma of the season, of early flowering and hectic pollen, mingling with the changeless smells of the capital. In the little parks along her way, men and women lay holding hands, sipping from bottles of mineral water, while eighteen-wheel lorries growled to a halt only yards away. Pockets of tranquillity defied the fury of the city. She strode through the dappled shadows cast by the trees, wondering what to cook for herself for supper and whether she should buy a good bottle of Chablis on the way home.

Mia did not know what made her turn round, but when she did, she instantly felt the familiar squeeze of panic. Perhaps fifty yards behind her was the Woman in the Coat, bustling with evident effort to keep up with her. This act of undisguised pursuit was as ludicrous as it was unsettling. The woman could scarcely have stuck out more. Her lack of cunning was laughable. But it was also appalling. She wanted something badly enough to heave her way for half a mile through Bethnal Green wearing a fur coat and—Mia now noticed—heels. A circus act she might be, but she was obviously a determined circus act. Worse, it seemed now that Mia herself was the object of her manic fixation, whatever it was. What had started as a joke with Vic had suddenly become a personal violation. Mia dealt with many damaged people at the centre, people who treated it as a place of sanctuary; she was well acquainted with most of the local hostels and halfway houses, which were often grateful for help in finding some lost soul or other. But the Woman in the Coat was not in that category. She had the look of a wilful maniac rather than that of a victim. And this was not something Mia was prepared to tolerate in her life.

She started to march back towards the woman, who, realising she had been detected, was already frozen to the spot. At the pace she had struck up, Mia reckoned she would be upon her in under thirty seconds. It would be a short conversation, curt and to the point. Mia did not expect, or want, explanations. What she would say was simply this: that the woman was welcome at the centre if she wished to attend the classes, but was not entitled to harass or pursue the staff. The centre was a place of generous spirit, and nobody minded her hanging around if she wanted. But following people was not permitted. Would she please stop at once?

The Woman in the Coat wasn't going to let her off so easily. Preparing her little speech, Mia had not noticed the furry arm in the air, or the black cab gliding towards the curb. She was only twenty paces away from her confrontation now, but the woman was already clambering awkwardly into the taxi and giving frenetic instructions, waving her hands to make the driver go, go, go. As the cab sped past her, Mia called out helplessly, furious at this insolent escape. The car stopped at the end of the junction to turn left into Cambridge Heath Road. Mia looked at the traffic and considered running after it, knocking on the window, demanding an audience. But then the driver sneaked in between two buses and was gone. Mia stood for a while, quite unsure what had just happened and what to do next. After a few minutes, she walked to the supermarket and bought the Chablis.

When she related all this—minus the Chablis—to Vic the next day, he shrugged his shoulders in a way she found insufferably irritating. "Told you," he said, bending over a group of jars in which he was cleaning paintbrushes. "She's obviously a loon. It stood out a mile."

"Well, yes, Vic. I mean, I think I worked that one out last night. What I want to know is what I do next. I mean, that was no fun at all.

I am not up to being stalked by a fat woman wearing the pelts of a hundred squirrels."

He stopped his work and gave this some thought. "You've got to wonder what makes people do that kind of thing, haven't you? You know, the pain within? It's tragic, really. Did you know John Lennon once said that if there was half as much happiness as there was pain in the world, then there would be no wars?"

This was too much for Mia. "No, he didn't. *Obviously,* he didn't. And even if he did, I don't care. I don't care if the silly cow was abused as a child or dropped on her head or wrongly sacked. I just don't want her following me."

Vic stood up. "Chels, I can see you're upset. And I can see why. So that's why I'm going to leave you now to recover your space. And if you want to talk about it later, well, we can. Or if you don't, that's cool, too."

You useless beatnik fuck, she wanted to say. But of course she said nothing. Vic plodded off with a couple of the jars, leaving Mia in the garden, the vivid scent of cherry blossom her only comfort.

Chancery Lane. A group of clamorous schoolchildren carrying clipboards got on the train, herded by three exhausted teachers. "I don't care, Jennifer," said one. "You should have gone before we left." Jennifer looked up at the adult, considered her options, swept a blond lock from her forehead, and then, quite deliberately, began to sob inconsolably. Her hot breath left mist on the windows of the Tube carriage.

Mia had not expected the Woman in the Coat to return immediately after their encounter. The rules of the game had changed completely. But she knew she would be back. Whatever was driving her to this demented pattern of behaviour would not be sated by so inconclusive an episode and might indeed be provoked further. A week passed with no sign of her. It was tempting to think that she had been scared off, but Mia had seen enough to know that the woman, this hefty huntress, was wilful. Sooner or later, determination would overcome fear.

And so it did, a fortnight after her getaway in the cab. Mia was waiting for a bus on the main road when she saw the woman leaving a café only a two-minute walk from the centre. It stretched the imagination to believe that she was in the area for innocent reasons. More likely, indeed, that she was marking the end of another day of surveillance, carried out by more devious means now that her cover had been blown. At the first sight of the coat—a moment, if she was honest, she had been longing for—Mia bolted from her seat and ran across the road, provoking a furious profanity from a young man in a Maserati who was forced to screech to a halt. She did not care, waving her hand dismissively in his direction. She would not be denied her prey a second time.

"Hey!" Mia shouted. "Hey! I want to talk to you!"

The woman turned around and saw, with a mask of horror made comic by the extent of her makeup, that she had been detected again. She made a feeble effort to escape, scurrying away with, Mia noticed, a mild limp in her left leg. But there were no cabs this time, no hiding place for the heavyset fugitive. Mia ran towards her and then ahead of her, finally blocking her path. The two women halted at the edge of the curb, opposite a chemist's shop.

"Excuse me," Mia said, a little out of breath herself. "Excuse me. I want to talk to you. Do you mind stopping for a moment?"

The woman stared at her. Her eyelashes were magnificently fake, curling like paper in flames. She pulled her coat around her. It was just possible that she might not relent, might ask Mia what on earth she thought she was doing, and insist on stepping past her. But Mia was not to be cheated, and the woman could sense this. The standoff could not last much longer.

"You have no right to do what you're doing," Mia said. She realised that her voice was raised, and that her tone was unlikely to make this obviously hysterical woman declare her hand. She took a deep breath. "Please. I just want you to explain what's going on. And I want you to stop."

The woman opened her handbag and pulled out what looked like a vintage powder compact. It was silver and had a snakeskin design. She peered in the mirror and applied a few dabs to her face. Then she snapped it shut. "All right, dear," she said. "Let's go back and have a cup of tea."

The children, including the still-sobbing Jennifer, disembarked at Holborn. Mia was glad that they had gone. Their screeching had disrupted her reverie and distracted her from remembered detail: the gloss of the woman's coat, the dignity with which she walked back to the café, the vividness of her lips. Though Mia was technically the victor, she felt as if she were being escorted into custody by the woman, rather than vice versa. The chase finally over, she was struck at once by the force of her captive's character and the calm with which she carried herself.

They walked silently into the café, where they were the only people apart from a trucker in overalls, reading his paper over a fry-up.

"Forgotten something, love?" asked the man behind the counter.

"No," said the woman firmly. "What shall we have, dear? You look like you could use a cup of tea. Not to say a stiff scotch. Two mugs of tea, please."

"Coming up," said the man as Mia and the woman retreated to one of the tables with fixed orange seats and a chipped Formica surface.

Mia wanted to speak, but the woman once again assumed control. "I'm sure you've got a lot to say, dear. But let's just calm down, shall we?" She waited for Mia's assent. "No need for us to get into a lather, is there?" Mia paused, then grudgingly shook her head.

The tea arrived. The woman put three sugar cubes into her mug and stirred vigorously. She smiled weakly at Mia, who did not touch her own.

"You look pale, dear. Well, I'm sorry. There's no point in denying it's my fault and there's no point in denying that I'd feel the same as you, tables turned. Probably even angrier, if the truth be known. I've led you a merry dance, haven't I?"

Mia brought her hand crashing down on the table. "Look, who the hell are you? Do you know what you've been doing? What gives you the right . . . You have no right." Tears welled in her eyes. The trucker looked over, but he lost interest almost immediately: just some stupid posh bird having a go at her mum.

This time, the woman was visibly shaken. Her hands trembled as she reached for her mug, and she thought better of it. Instead, she put her handbag on the table, evidently as some sort of reflex defence. She stuttered and then tried again.

"I—I shouldn't have come. I know that. This isn't how it was meant to be. But I had to. I owed it to him. At least . . . It's hard for me, too. I know you won't believe that, but it's hard for me, too."

Mia regarded her with unconcealed contempt. "How can it possibly be hard for you? You hang around where I work, you follow me, you run away from me, and now you're obviously at it again. You chose to act like a lunatic, not me. I don't want to be followed. And if you knew the *slightest* fucking thing about me, you'd know how awful what you're doing is." She could feel her face flushing, the pricking in her cheekbones.

The woman drank her tea and then looked up. She had exceptional brown eyes, perfect ovals in a face that once must have been quite something, too. Mia suddenly grasped that the woman had probably been a rare beauty at one time: The coat, the hair, the makeup were all props, part of a nostalgic costume that kept alive the memory of some sort of glamour and the power it had once brought.

"You see . . . The truth is that I know a lot about you. I've known a lot about you since you were very small. All of it wonderful. So much love. So much love, you wouldn't . . . you couldn't believe it."

Mia listened to this gibberish and was suddenly frightened again. She looked up to check that the café owner and the trucker were still there. "Listen, whichever religious group you represent, I'm sorry, but I'm not interested. Thank you for talking to me, but I really would be grateful if you just left me alone. I have nothing to offer you." The woman laughed, throwing her head back a little with practised femininity. "Oh, goodness. Is that what you think? I don't work for a church, dear. God gave up on me a long time ago, I'm afraid. No, no. I don't want anything from you, either. Far from it. No, the reason I know about you is that I knew your father. I was a friend of his for many years."

The air around Mia thinned and her vision blurred a little. Of all the outrages which this appalling woman might utter, she had not expected this. "My father?" she hissed. "How dare you mention my father? What could someone like you possibly know about my father?"

"Try me."

"You must be joking."

"No, you're quite right. Why should you believe me? After all, I'm a perfect stranger. But try me anyway." She leant over the table with a candour that was compelling. "The point is this, really, Mia. You'll never know unless you do. If I get it wrong, then I'm a fraud and . . . well, you can call the police or have me committed, or whatever else you want to do to me. And if not, then perhaps we can have a chat together. But you won't know unless you try."

The woman's use of her name, as well as the way she spoke, caught Mia off guard. As disturbed as this woman clearly was, her logic was beyond reproach. It was, oddly enough, precisely the sort of logic that Jeremy would have used. This was coincidence, of course, but in a context of heightened emotion and gathering panic, it resonated. She looked up at the menu on a white board behind the counter, as if that might provide inspiration.

"All right, then. If you knew my father, you'll know what his father's first book was called." This would bring the ghastly encounter to a swift end. Then she could be off and forget it as quickly as her sanity permitted.

"Gracious. I thought you might ask me something easy first up, like his star sign or favourite colour."

"This is easy. If you knew my father, that is."

"Well, actually, it isn't easy. Which is why you asked me. He didn't buy me that particular book until I'd known him nearly thirty years. Would you believe? Said I wouldn't understand it, which is true, of course. But I wanted it anyway, because I wanted to share in every part of his life that I could, apart from the obvious. So I got my way in the end and we went to Waterstone's in Piccadilly one evening and he bought it for me." She closed her eyes in contented memory. "A lovely gift: *First Principles in Philology,* by B. T. Taylor. I still keep it in my lounge."

Mia listened to this and felt the plastic chair beneath her melt away. The foundations below began to crumble, giving way to soil, clay, rock, and lava. The world that once was new, was being sucked into a hole in the earth, at its centre a vortex of falsehoods suddenly expelled into oblivion with the utterance of a book's title. There could be no doubt about it: This woman had known her father. Her grandfather Bernard's first book was indeed *First Principles in Philology,* but, to his shame, it had not been the first book to find a publisher (that was a little Greek primer for sixth formers, still in print). He had had to wait five more years for the manuscript to end up between hard covers, a delay which grated with him until his dying day: Bernard Taylor's first book, turned down! Only somebody with intimate acquaintance of her family would know that fact, which was almost a guilty secret. How could this woman, with her face paint and her gaudy looks, be one of that number?

"I don't understand." She stared blankly at this woman, this destroyer of worlds.

"Who are you?"

"My name is Beatrice. Beatrice Brown. And I'm pleased to hear you don't understand, because I hoped this day would never come, really. You know, me meeting one of you, one of Jeremy's children. I'm still not sure I'm doing the right thing. But a promise is a promise."

"Who did you promise?"

"I promised your father—oh, more than five years ago now. I said that if anything happened to him and your mother, I would keep an eye on his children. Well, actually, he didn't make me say that, not exactly. It was odd. He was more specific. It was Benjamin he was worried about. Made me promise I'd look out for him, his boy, although goodness knows what he thought I could do to help."

"Ben? What are you talking about?"

"Jeremy—your father—always worried about Benjamin, you know. He always said he would get into trouble one day and need a firm hand. 'Beatrice,' he used to say, 'you've got a firm hand. Sort the boy out.' " She laughed again, with the same artful movement of the head. "Well, I can't imagine he thought it would ever come to that. But he believed that Benjamin was always up to no good, somehow, that he would take risks and get into terrible trouble. It kept him awake."

The last detail was not lost on Mia. But she could not bear to linger over it. "I can't imagine my father thinking that."

"Well, there it is, dear. He said it, not me. Then—well, then when he died, I didn't know what to do. I was devastated, you see. I can't explain to you how devastated I was. And for a long time, I didn't do anything about it. Kept away, shut up. Didn't tell *anyone* what I was going through. But then I thought, What did I really promise him? I promised to look after Benjamin. And Benjamin's gone, too, now. So am I free of my promise?" She paused and looked out at the dusk. "No, of course not. I realised that, late one night. I wasn't sleeping, you see. Terrible nightmares, taking pills, no good at all. And I realised that what the promise really meant was to check up on his children, all of them, any of them. Which meant you, my dear. Only you. Poor Jeremy."

"How did you find me? Nobody knows where I am."

"Your uncle does."

"I see. So now you know my uncle, too."

"As a matter of fact, I've never met him. But your father left a private letter for his executors' attention, vouching for me and asking, in general terms, that I be given any help I needed. The letter was very explicit that your mother should not be involved, were she still alive, and that if this proved unworkable, her interests were to come first. All very sensible. Of course, the trust assumed I was after money when I approached them and they found out that the letter was real. And I'm sure that Jeremy wanted to see me looked after. But I wasn't after cash. I was after peace of mind. Your uncle and I corresponded, rather angrily at first. But then we came to an agreement. He let me know where you were and I agreed to leave you alone once I'd seen that you were all right. But the truth is, I always intended to introduce myself. There was no way I could keep my promise just by staring through that shopwindow day after day. I needed to hear from you that there was nothing I could do. And if there was . . . well, I needed to do it."

"You did plenty, don't worry. You did my head in. As if it needs doing in."

Beatrice suddenly put her head in her hands. She was, at last, at her own limit. "Can you understand? Or at least try? All I had left of him was that promise. Nothing more. It kept him alive in my heart if I believed there was some chance I could honour it. I didn't know whether I could possibly help you, and I doubt now that I can. But if I hadn't tried . . . Do you see?"

Mia looked at the expanse of dyed hair in front of her and listened as the quiet sobs began. What strange ritual of expurgation was she witnessing? What guilt did this woman feel that made her commit such a folly? And yet, if what she said was true, what option did she have? If she had made such a promise, if Mia's faithless father had extracted such a pledge, then what else could she do? There was no choice. As much as Mia hated this woman for what she had already told her, she did understand what she was saying. That much she was prepared to give.

"I do," she said quietly. "I do see."

Beatrice looked up. Her face—or rather, her mask of makeup—was now a devastated battlefield of emotion, ravaged by tears, carefully de-

lineated areas of colour leaking into one another with disastrous consequences. "Thank you," she whispered. "Thank you very much."

Tottenham Court Road. She was nearly there, nearly at Bond Street,
where she would blow the equivalent of the Echinacea's monthly wage
bill on a frock and some trinkets. She patted the money in her pocket,
smiling, in spite of her better instincts, at the memory of the evening
she had gone on to spend with Beatrice Brown—who was herself no
stranger to spending Taylor money on clothes.

"This wine is very nice," Beatrice said. "Just like your father. Always
pick the best." They had moved to an Italian restaurant in Mile End that
Mia liked. She was exhausted, hungry, and badly wanted a drink. She
felt no debt to Beatrice, but she had too many questions simply to dismiss her, as she knew she had every right to do. She also knew that what
Beatrice would have to tell her would be painful. But the worst shock of
all was already over. An unspeakable secret had been revealed and had
rent a hole in the heavens. There was a whole side to her father's life—
to her father's self—that she did not know about. But it was precisely
because she was like Jeremy herself that she wanted to know the truth
in detail. Until a couple of hours ago, Beatrice had been an eccentric,
possibly even deranged, stalker. Now, it seemed, she was somebody
whose life story was intertwined with her own.

"Well, I like wine, and he did teach me a bit about it," Mia replied.
"And I won't deny I need a drink."

"Me, too." Beatrice emptied her glass. The coat had at last been
hung up. She was wearing a big blue sweater dress, chosen to conceal her
girth, and pearls which matched her earrings. There was a brooch, too,
probably a present. Everything was a little old, a little out of kilter.
Something musty fought through the wall of powerful perfume. She
looked, in fact, like the mistress of a man who had died suddenly a few
years ago. For Beatrice, time had stopped: She would always be wearing
the outfit she would have worn for her next discreet dinner with Jeremy.
These were her widow's weeds.

Beatrice nibbled on the bread sticks while Mia downed another glass of Frascati.

"Am I what you expected?" Mia asked.

This caught Beatrice off guard. "Expected? Goodness, dear, I don't know. I'm not sure I ever expected you to talk to me at all. After our little . . . incident with the cab, I couldn't see how I could ever speak to you. My original plan, God help me, was to breeze into your shop and say I was an old colleague of Jeremy's, in the area to see friends, and that I had noticed a family resemblance. Which there is, by the way. But I didn't think you'd buy that if you were a tenth as smart as he was. So I was a bit stuck."

"I don't think I'd have believed you were an old colleague of my father's, I'm afraid," Mia snorted into her wineglass. "No offence, but you don't look much like a banker."

Beatrice's eyes widened and she swallowed quickly to make her point. "Oh, but that's how we met, dear. I wasn't a banker, of course, I can't add up the fingers on my hands. No, I ran the stationery office on Jeremy's floor. One day—so many years ago—he came in to my office looking for pens and paper and he seemed very fraught about some deal or other."

"Fraught? My father?"

"Oh yes. Tense. And so I asked him about it, and made him a cup of coffee—just instant, no milk, no sugar. With a biscuit. And he sat down and told me how nervous he was, and please not to tell anyone. And I said I wouldn't. And afterwards, he said thank you, then padded off down the corridor towards all the posh offices."

"Did you like him?"

Beatrice smiled. "I thought he was wonderful. Everyone did, even then. He was married, of course. And he had two little children—you and Benjamin. But what I remember most was that he wasn't like everyone said. You know, aloof and awesome. He seemed like a lovely chap, worried about everything, someone who needed a cuddle."

The waiter hovered. Mia ordered for both of them, guessing from her expression that Beatrice would prefer this, was used to it perhaps. She asked for another bottle of Frascati and some water.

"A cuddle, eh?"

Beatrice, her makeup now fully restored after a full twenty minutes in the ladies' at the restaurant, arched a perfectly pencilled eyebrow. "Yes, dear, cuddle. This was almost thirty years ago. People didn't just . . . you know."

"Well, not at first anyway. Is that right? Cuddles first? And then . . . you know."

"I understand what you think of me. What you probably believe. You might be surprised by the truth. You know, your father was a good man. The best of men, actually. And all I can say to you—and you just *have* to believe me—is that he never betrayed any of you, not even your mother."

"Oh, come on. He betrayed us all, every one of us, even my unborn sisters, when he walked into the stationery office and caught a sight of your legs, Beatrice. I'm a woman. I can guess what you must have looked like then. And Jeremy was like an Adonis in those days. I still have the pictures. It must have been a bloody hormone explosion."

"Oh, I fancied him like mad. Always did." She put the palms of her hand on the checked tablecloth. "Till the day he died, and beyond. And I think it's fair to say that he thought I was easy on the eye, too. At least in those days, before I went to seed. But that's not the point. Why do you think I'm sitting here with you rather than lying in a grave with him? Why did I spend thirty years hoping he'd call, praying he wouldn't cancel because one of you was ill, or it was a sports day, waiting for him in places it's no fun to be a woman waiting on your own? You were in the Boltons. I was in a maisonette in Streatham. That's the way it was, and that's the way it was always going to be."

"Who made the first move?"

"Oh, I don't know. After the first time, he kept finding excuses to wander in. Always making jokes, lighthearted, you know, office banter. And then one time, when there was nobody else around, he lingered a little and invited me to lunch, just a sandwich. And we sat in the square by the office, in the shade of a statue, and passed the time of day. And it was—for me, it was heaven, bliss to be paid attention by such a man. And I could tell it was . . . well, I suppose, relaxing for him. Because I was so unlike anyone he had ever spent any time with in his life. I saw that at once. All the books and frightening relatives and pressures he lived with. I don't think he had ever realised how . . . how *easy* life can be."

"And then?"

Beatrice shrugged. "Well, then, after a while, I suppose it became something else. We saw each other more. We started to take care, because he knew how the office gossips would be. He always said he was protecting himself, but he was really protecting me. If the partners had ever found out, it would have been me who got the sack, because he was too important to them, too damned talented. But they never did. *They never did.* You have to understand that I am as amazed to listen to myself as you are. You are the first person I have ever spoken to of this. It is quite something not to speak, ever, of such a thing in one's life."

Mia shifted impatiently in her wicker chair. "I can't see how you could possibly keep something like this secret. My mother was a very observant woman. She was brilliant." She paused, then carried on. "Frankly, anyone who knew Jenny would find it completely mysterious that my father should want to spend any time with you. She was a dazzling woman. In every way."

"She didn't find out because . . . because there was no need to. Yes, I know how exceptional she was. Your father never stopped talking about her, the Foreign Office, her mind. Her beauty, too. But you see, dear, not all secrets are bad. That's the mistake people make. If I had been any danger to your family, your home, your mother would have found out somehow and been at me with a meat cleaver. But I wasn't, and she didn't. There was no need."

"Are you suggesting that my mother tolerated all this? Turned a blind eye? I mean, really. For Christ's sake."

"Oh no, I don't mean that at all. I mean that some things stay hidden because they should, because there's no use to anyone in them being known. And when that's true, it's easy to keep a secret. A secret is like everything else. It needs care; it mustn't be abused. We never abused ours. Your mother never asked whether your father was really having dinner with a client, or why he had been out of the office when she called, because she loved him and she trusted him. And she was right to."

"Weren't you ashamed? Carrying on with a married man? I mean, didn't you want your own family, instead of risking the breakup of someone else's?"

Beatrice sighed. She looked old suddenly. "I was worried sometimes, yes. I never wanted to ruin what he had. It was part of him, the most important part. But somehow I always knew that I wouldn't ruin it, not least because I simply couldn't. There was never a moment of betrayal, as I say. It wasn't like that. He was always kind, always giving me presents, money to buy clothes. But I was never competition. I was never a threat. He told me once about how you were all linked by something, by a magical thread—"

"The golden thread. That was one of Henty's."

"That's it. What you have to believe is that he told me about that as a warning. The point was that I wasn't part of it, couldn't be. He would never, ever, ever have done anything to harm any of you. He would have died for any of you, especially your mother."

The food arrived. The clams glistened in the candlelight, steam rising from the pasta as the waiter turned the pepper mill and then ground Parmesan onto their plates. Beatrice rolled some spaghetti onto her fork.

"I wasn't his bit on the side, you know. I was somebody who knew him, loved him dearly, for almost as long as you've been alive. As much as you must despise me, I'm afraid you can't wish away the fact that I was part of his life. I gave him something, however mean and contemptible it might seem to you. Even in the last years, when we were both getting older, we would meet when he could. Mostly in Streatham, at mine. We would drink a bottle of wine together and he would tell me about his worries."

Mia tried to imagine this: Jeremy telling this blowsy woman, her looks fading, about his worries. In the kitchen, chairs with vinyl seats, an old fridge, everything spotlessly clean; a calendar with dates ringed in red marker, exclamation marks, perhaps little heart symbols to mark birthdays and other significant dates. The afternoon drawing in outside, twilight approaching. All that Jeremy hated? No, no. That was not what she imagined, much as she wanted to. She could see him laughing, carefree, amused by this simple woman and her tenderness. She could imagine her father revelling in Beatrice's vulgarity, the effort she went to, the straightforwardness of everything, and the limits of her demands. Their own shared memories of many years, uncomplicated by money, plans, doubts, children. For a few hours, nobody knowing where he was, his suit jacket hanging on one of those MFI chairs, her lipstick mark on the wineglass, the ticking of a plastic clock on the wall. Jeremy and Beatrice laughing until their time together was up once more.

"I should hate you. I loved my mother very much."

"Yes. I can't stop you feeling that, either." Beatrice dabbed some sauce off the corner of her mouth. "Wouldn't expect to. But, you see, I never dreamt it would come to this. My health is not very good, and I thought your father would long outlast me. In fact, that was what I wanted. He was my life, you see. He was the reason I never married or had children. And so to survive him—well, that is obviously my punishment." Mia filled her glass. "Oh, thank you."

"And he worried about Benjamin."

"Benjamin was the only one of his children who really worried him. Not you, or the twins. Jeremy always said that Benjamin was a chancer. You know, he said that there were always little secrets in your family. Like the gun collection and letting you two see it in his study." She laughed.

"He told you that?"

"Oh, yes. He thought it was very funny. But it was because he loved you both so much. The secret was his way of letting you know that he did."

"It was great fun; there's no doubt about that."

"But he always said that he feared that Ben would end up having a big secret, something deadly. I mean, the fact is that I was Jeremy's big secret. He said as much. But he thought Ben's secret would end up hurting him and maybe others, too. It frightened Jeremy. He thought bad things could happen. He used those very words to me." She finished off her food. " 'Bad things, Beatrice.' That was when he made me make my promise."

"And now you're here, have you kept it?"

"I think so. I can't stop you from hating me. I would love to see you again, of course, but I think that's me being selfish. You do remind me of him, you see. In the strangest way, it's like being with him again." She looked intently across the candlelit table at Mia.

"How do I remind you of him?"

"Everything. Your cleverness, your looks, your sadness. It's the same, really. I remember it all from the day he walked in to the last day I saw him."

"When was that?"

Beatrice paused, her fingers playing with the neck of her glass. "About a week before . . . before he died. We went for a walk at lunchtime in St. James's. He'd had a meeting, which ended early, so he called me and I raced to meet him in a cab. It was such a lovely day. We ate sandwiches on a bench, with half a bottle of champagne from

Fortnum's. We watched the world go by. He always said that if you meet somewhere really public, nobody will notice you, and he was right. Never failed. Actually, it's funny: He talked about you a lot that day, and how proud he was of you. He said you were bringing on some MP or other who was on the news all the time, and that was thanks to you."

"Miles?"

"Yes, that's right. Jeremy said how lucky this chap was to have you. Your dad loved you so much."

Mia could hear the voice of her father, and she wanted to weep at the memory of the gentle baritone. She was angry with him, too, for leaving her, for leaving her to eat pasta with this wreck of a woman in a Mile End restaurant. He had kept his secret for three decades, but to no avail. His death had forced out that secret, and caused more pain. Not least to Beatrice herself. The big wilful woman of the chase had gone: Before Mia now was something much smaller, a diminished, half-drunk widow who could not even call herself that. Jeremy had not had the guts to be a bigamist, or to leave Jenny, or to end it once and for all with Beatrice. For three decades, he had persuaded her that what he was doing was poetic and special, and allowed her to ruin herself as he drained the life from her when it suited him. And now she and his surviving daughter sat around the flickering candle as the waiter cleared the plates away, trying to make sense of the unspeakable mess he had left behind him, his true estate and legacy. Oh Daddy, you bastard. You left me once, and now you have left me again. In death, you have visited treachery upon your child; you have sent a ghost to see me. Beatrice is the ghost, the last fleeting remnant of your towering vanity.

The train pulled in to Oxford Circus and suddenly filled with a herd of shoppers, laden with plastic bags, pushing strollers, arguing, sweating, jostling one another with the special misanthropy of the crowd. Two men, engaged in a row which had apparently begun on the platform, held on to adjacent straps, unable to meet each other's eyes in their profane fury. A child laughed hysterically just beyond them. She was nearly there, so near to her journey's end.

So, Claude, you are not so clever, she thought. You were not, as you took for granted, the first visitor, the first to find me. Yours was not the first bony hand to reach out from the past and grab my shoulder. It was Beatrice who found me, Beatrice with her coat and her makeup and her life lived in the shadows. Beatrice who had been watching me since I was a child through the lying eyes of my father.

After the waiter finished clearing up, Mia had paid as quickly as she could. There was nothing left to say, and she realised suddenly that she needed quite desperately to sleep. She also wanted to end the meeting without fanfare, to prevent it slipping into the intimacy which formal diplomacy can so often become, with neither negotiator noticing. She did not want a peace treaty with Beatrice, still less a friendship. There was a danger now of easy sentimentality, of kind words she did not mean. What she had learned sickened her to the pit of her stomach; and the pity she felt for this spectral woman could not eradicate the disgust. Beatrice Brown had shambled heftily into Mia's life, and now, on the pavement outside the Italian restaurant, it was time for her to shamble out.

"Here's your cab." Mia had asked the waiter to organise a taxi to Streatham while Beatrice was in the loo. A battered old station wagon driven by a middle-aged Asian man with bloodshot eyes pulled up, its horn tooting superfluously. "There you go, Beatrice. Safe journey home."

She turned to Mia with a face of infinite sadness. She was back in her coat, but now it looked like part of a comedy outfit, rather than the armour plating of a strong woman. The tears in her eyes shone in the harsh light of the streetlamp. "Mia, I—"

Mia raised her hand. "Don't. It's no use. I'm sorry, truly I am. I can see that most of your life has been a terrible injustice, the price you have paid. But I can't say any of the things you want me to. I'm going to call my uncle tomorrow and tell him not to speak with you again. Not ever. I think you were a fool to let my father use you as he did. I really do. But that is your business. Did Jeremy ever dream you would do something like this, that you would one day meet me? Not in a million years. He would have hacked you down as you tried. Would I have done the same if I were you? Maybe. I don't know. Have you kept your promise to him? How do I know? I don't. I don't care, either. It was all part of some sick, disgusting game he played on us all for thirty years. His family. His real family. Can I forgive you? Never. Do I want to see you again? Never. Don't come back here. Don't ever follow me again. Don't come near me. If you do, I'll find a way of hurting you. I'll find a way. Remember: I am his daughter. Now, here's twenty pounds for the cab. Take it; I can tell you need it. Get in and go."

All this was said in a voice as calm as Jeremy's when he was stating a fact, or a series of facts, as unavoidable as they were disagreeable. The tone was unmistakably his, and it silenced Beatrice utterly. It was as if the dead man she had loved so passionately, for so long, so pointlessly, was now speaking through his daughter, issuing his final warning, spelling out more brutally than ever he had in life that she was no part of his family. For the first time, Mia saw real fear in Beatrice's eyes. She took the twenty-pound note and got into the car without a word. Mia knew she would never see her again, and she was glad. The cab performed a preposterously showy U-turn in the empty road and lurched off at great speed. Mia thought she saw Beatrice's frozen hairdo shudder a little. She allowed herself to laugh.

"Bond Street. This is Bond Street. All passengers wishing to change for the Jubilee Line . . ." It was time to get out and time to breathe. Time to race up the escalator and the stairs to the waiting light and the retail playground above. She passed the shops in the station, the McDonald's, the sandwich shop, and the mobile-phone store, then went out to the street, where she could see Claridge's in the distance and, much closer, a pub so down-at-heel, it looked as if its very brickwork might burst into tears. At its tables, a few of which were still outside, men sat alone in the chill, nursing frothy pints of lager; she could smell the booze wafting through the grilles from the cellar below. She walked past the silent drinkers, who were oblivious of the morning sun, and then made her way down one of the side roads off Bond Street, where she had once spent hours and hours of her time, sometimes alone, sometimes with her sisters.

How long was it since she had walked along these cobbles? Three years, more. Some of the shops had changed, but not many. There were more coffee bars and a couple of new accessory stores, selling hats and scarves and glittering gimmicks to teenaged Sloanes in boots. Her eye was quickly caught by a gorgeous black evening gown, classic and pure, in the window of a shop she had often gone to in the past. She had always liked it there: the attentiveness of the staff, the luxury of the changing rooms, the indulgent rustle of the tissue paper as the clothes were wrapped and boxed. She looked again at the gown and, for no reason, thought of Rob. Strange. The tap of her subconscious was still dripping away randomly; she needed to turn it off and focus on the matter at hand. She looked round and noticed a middle-aged couple holding hands outside another of the stores. They were staring through the window at a magnificent, opulent squirrel red fur coat.

Chapter EIGHT

THE WAITING ROOM outside Councillor Phil Roberts's office was as depressing as the campaign literature scattered over the pine coffee table. One flyer asked, "Where did it all go wrong? Councillor Phil tells you." The cover of a flimsy booklet bore the headline EAST END FOR EAST ENDERS: DON'T LET PROPERTY PRICES DRAG YOU AND YOUR FAMILY DOWN. An older leaflet showed Councillor Phil with his wife and two small daughters. It simply said "Councillor Phil: Family Man!" There was a three-day-old *Daily Mirror*, too, although that was more concerned with the latest development in a pop star's love life than with Councillor Phil's little local difficulties. A dusty rubber plant stood in the corner of the room, unloved and slightly askew. There were no decorations on the wall except a picture of Councillor Roberts in black tie and bright cummerbund at a charity event, shaking hands with the prime minister, whose frozen rictus spoke volumes. It was not often that Mia felt sorry for the prime minister, but on this occasion she sympathised entirely with his predicament.

She wished that Rob would sit still. He was beside her, leafing through his *Guardian* and muttering to himself. Every now and again, he would cast the newspaper to the floor and leap to his feet, cursing everything and nothing.

"Rob," she said quietly. "Rob. Sit down. You can't see him like this. We have to be cool about it."

"I know, I know." He sat down and sighed, fingered the laces of his baseball boots. "I know. You're right. Of course you're right. But it just gets me that we're here at all, you know? I mean, look at this." He picked up one of the leaflets. "Listen to this: 'Councillor Phil cares about his local community. As a dedicated family man—husband of Shirley and dad of Laura and Charlene!—he welcomes prosperity and new jobs for all our children's future, but he strongly opposes the gentrification and estate agent terror which is pricing locals out of the market. Councillor Phil cares about you and your family.' Thanks, Councillor Phil. So why are you trying to close down a harmless health centre?"

She patted him on the shoulder of his leather jacket. "Rob. Listen to me. I don't know much, but I do know about politicians. I used to work with them a lot in one of my old jobs. Councillor Phil is trying to make a point. Councillor Phil doesn't give a fuck about his community, but he badly wants to be an MP, and to do that he needs to get selected. And to do that he needs to win some local battles by picking fights with people who can't win and aren't liked. He has chosen us because he thinks the local press will see us as hippies and Yuppies and interlopers, middle-class slackers who are driving up house prices and lowering moral standards. He may be right, too. It's a good little story for the local hacks."

Rob shook his head. "You seem to know so much about it all. How can you accept it? Doesn't it disgust you? I mean, that they can just come and close down the centre. It's Sylvia's life. And you've put enough into it. And then some fat fuck—"

"Keep your voice down. He's probably in there already."

"—and then some fat fuck comes along and shuts it down. Just like that. On the off chance that if he gets good press, he might get selected to be an MP. So he can do exactly the same thing on a national scale. Is that how it works?"

"That's exactly how it works." She blew the fringe of hair off her forehead. It was too long, but she was saving it for a proper haircut before the Bracknell. "Now what we have to do is see if there's something else that Phil the Family Man wants that we have to offer which is even better."

"Like what?"

She looked at him, and smiled. "Well, how the fuck do I know? You're the politics graduate."

In a matter of weeks, a cloud the size of a man's hand on the distant horizon of the Echinacea had blown into a raging typhoon. A dark and terrible time had come upon this ramshackle little community. Now she and Rob had been deputed by the others—by Sylvia, who was ill with worry—to protect the centre's foundations from the storm and save what they could from disaster. They were, in the eyes of their colleagues, the brave scouts sent out across the mountains to bring back a rescue party, the two Antarctic explorers despatched from the tent in search of help. It was Mia's opinion that they were more like Captain Oates, and might be gone for some time. When she had explained this allusion to Ringo, he had nodded sagely and asked her whether she had ever eaten husky.

The letter from Maureen Stove (Mrs.) in Environmental Services warning of "deficiencies" and their consequences "under the terms of the legislation" had been no idle threat. Two weeks later, Mrs. Stove had called Sylvia and asked why no reply had been received. Sylvia had panicked and, lying, said that her reply must have got lost in the post. Well, said Mrs. Stove with silken malevolence, that was a shame. A real shame. Because the legislation was very restrictive in the time allowed for resolution of "deficiencies." Could she send another copy of her reply? Sylvia had tap-danced furiously and demanded to see her in person. Mrs.

Stove, though generally contemptuous of her new adversary, had been mildly impressed by this riposte, not guessing that it was the product of desperation, rather than bravado. She had agreed to meet Sylvia and Mia the following Thursday.

The meeting had been a disaster. On the third floor of the town hall, Sylvia and Mia had sat opposite Maureen Stove and listened to an awesome litany of complaints about the Echinacea Centre, almost all of which seemed unanswerable. The council had indeed got hold of the ten-year-old correspondence between Sylvia and the department over the building's foundations, and correctly observed that the matter had been somewhat mysteriously dropped ("Only because I got drunk with one of the inspectors and kissed him," Sylvia later confessed in the pub: a crucial detail, in Mia's view, which she would have liked to have known before the meeting). Onto this ancient history had been grafted a variety of new and trumped-up charges. A number of locals had been encouraged—that much was clear—to allege that the centre was an environmental hazard, the cause of noise, pollution, parking problems, pedestrian congestion. A lone parent alleged that her children were kept awake by "rowdy" people emerging from the evening classes. A pensioner said that the centre had "ruined" an old-fashioned East End street. An epileptic man had even complained that a flashing light from one of its windows had caused him distress. "He had a fit?" Mia asked Mrs. Stove. "No, Miss Taylor," Mrs. Stove replied gravely, as if a fit was the last of the complainant's worries. "It caused him distress."

They sat in a small partitioned cubicle, lined with wall charts and timetables, meticulously marked and starred. Mrs. Stove was not quite as Mia had imagined her. She was badly dressed all right, wearing sandals and a pleated skirt. Her glasses were indeed those of the professional oppressor, thick and rimless, magnifying the danger in her cold, pale eyes. Disappointingly, however, there was plentiful photographic evidence on her desk of a Mr. Stove and a brood of Stovelets at home. Mia's original image of a life ruined by a husband's sudden departure years ago, and a subsequent campaign of arbitrary vengeance against mankind, was wide of the mark. No, it was much worse: Maureen Stove was not a woman scorned. She was an enthusiast, a woman who derived simple pleasure from the damage she caused and found daily delight in the limitless possibilities offered "under the terms of the legislation" to pursue the path she had chosen in life. She went home in the evenings and told her rapt and adoring family of the terror she had sown and the horrors she had wrought. Within minutes of their shaking hands, Mia realised, to her alarm, that she and Sylvia were dealing with something much more dangerous than she had feared.

Mrs. Stove's assistant, Eileen, arrived with cups of coffee. She was a vacant-looking young woman, wearing a black cardigan and the shortest skirt Mia had ever seen. Her complexion was poor, but her hair was long and blond, and it was not hard to imagine the effect she must have upon the sweaty male office workers who gawped over their computer screens as she sashayed back from the kitchenette. She wore a strong and distinctive scent, too—Angel by Thierry Mugler, Mia thought, and lots of it. Bought off the back of a lorry in Bethnal Green Road, she bet, or given to her by some lustful sugar daddy desperate for her favours. "Any milk?" Eileen asked. Mia nodded and Sylvia shook her head as much as her paralysis would allow. Eileen did not notice this twitch of the neck. "Any milk?" she repeated sunnily. Mia stepped in: "No, just for me. Thank you." Eileen smiled, then wafted off in her cloud of Angel to sit at a desk nearby. There, she began to shuffle some papers around with as much method as she could muster. When Mia looked over a few minutes later, she was painting her nails.

With the ritual of the coffee over, Mrs. Stove embarked like a gallows judge on her summing up: Mia could see the shadow of the hangman's noose looming behind her. Mrs. Stove noted the gravity, as well as the number, of the alleged "deficiencies" and reminded Sylvia and Mia that "under the terms of the legislation" such "deficiencies," if found to be as bad as alleged and not dealt with swiftly, would automatically lead to "closure of said facilities." These phrases tripped from Maureen's lips with immodest ease: They were her poetry, the words that made sense of the world to her. They were words that snared people who got above themselves, who tried one on, who thought they were special. That was what Maureen loved about them. She sat in judgement every day on the Sylvias and Mias of her parish, a great leveller, a bringer of justice. She was fulfilled by these daily acts of destructive democracy.

Mia recognised this and thought that she should address Maureen in those same phrases. She cleared her throat. That was all true, she said, and the alleged "deficiencies" were indeed shocking to hear. She and the manager of the Echinacea had a lot to think about, and they would obviously have to acquaint themselves immediately and intimately with their responsibilities "under the terms of the legislation." But, said Mia, was it not also the case that "in highly exceptional circumstances," the local authority was entitled to award a dispensation? Perhaps there was some way the Echinacea Centre could reprieve itself? Could, in fact, repair the damage it seemed to have done, however unwittingly?

Mrs. Stove's eyes narrowed. She looked over at Eileen, who was not following but who had obviously listened in specially to Mia's little speech. Their faces were as one: We know your game, you smart little madam, and you're fooling no one. Not here. Not in the Environmental Services department. Eileen crossed her long stockinged legs defiantly. Mrs. Stove turned her withering attention back to Sylvia and Mia. She was not to be deflected. That much was clear.

The legislation, she explained, did indeed make provision for exceptional discretion. But that was a matter for elected councillors, rather than officials. Off the record, she was in a position to tell them that the planning subcommittee had already reached a "strong provisional conclusion" on this matter—"pending full investigation," of course—and that it was highly unlikely that it would change that position. Councillor Roberts, the chair of the subcommittee, had taken a particular interest in the case. Naturally, it was open to the Echinacea Centre to answer the complaints listed to the satisfaction of the inspectorate, legal department, council architects, and relevant committees within the next ten days. There was also a possibility of appeal, should they wish to follow that course. But Mrs. Stove's view—again off the record—was that the unresolved matter of the foundations gave the subcommittee and inspectorate little option but to recommend closure forthwith, notwithstanding whatever remedial action the centre proposed to take to improve its "obviously troubled relations" with the lone parent, disabled, and other disadvantaged communities in the area. She advised them both, on what she called with relish "a human level," to consider the possible implications of the investigations for their own staff. I am Nemesis, she was saying to them both, a halo of fire around her head. Your moment is at hand.

Two hours later, Sylvia was still sobbing as she drank her fourth vodka and tonic. Mia had stuck to orange juice but was considering joining her boss in the hard stuff. It was a busy lunchtime in the Dove and Pigeon, the pub nearest to the town hall, to which the two women had rushed as soon as they had left Eileen in the reception area, the assistant smiling smugly and holding their plastic visitor's passes like scalps. Sylvia had been unable to speak for the first five minutes, and Mia had worried that she might hyperventilate, perhaps go into shock. In desperation, she'd bought a packet of full tar John Player Specials, which Sylvia had torn open and chain-smoked with undisguised gratitude.

"How could this happen?" Sylvia asked after a while.

Mia explained her analysis and the need to see Councillor Roberts very soon.

"I don't get it. I let that man have a kiss and a fumble. I thought it would do the trick. It did do the trick."

"I know you did, Sylv. At least I know now. But that was ten years ago. And I think things have changed since then. This isn't going to go away with a bit of judicious kissing. We're going to have to fight dirty. I can't see how yet. But we'll think of something."

"More booze, Chels. I mean it. I'm on the edge here."

Mia went up to the bar and ordered another double. "Your friend all right?" asked the barman.

"What do you mean?"

"That's her fifth. She doesn't mess about, does she?"

"Are you going to serve me, or shall we go somewhere else?"

"Please yourself." He turned round, and she thought she heard him mutter something like "snotty cow." But there were more pressing matters at hand. Rather than pick a fight, she ordered a vodka for herself, too, then sat down with her crumpled boss. They made a plan.

She and Rob would go to see Councillor Roberts. Had she really suggested taking Rob? Yes, she had. She was not sure why, but then she rationalised her strange proposal thus: Councillor Roberts would meet the two of them, and he'd think Rob was the hard man and she was the soft touch, the little blond chick with tears in her eyes. Whereas the opposite was, of course, the case. Diffident Rob would divert the councillor into a false sense of security while Mia thought of a brilliant plan—what brilliant plan?—with which to thwart this terrible act of destruction. They would see what Councillor Roberts was really up to. Maureen Stove was a pitiless machine, a Terminator of the town hall. And like the Terminator, Mia explained to Sylvia, Mrs. Stove couldn't be bargained with. She couldn't be reasoned with. She absolutely would not stop. But Councillor Roberts was a bald, bearded politician, full of clammy greed, vanities, and insecurities. There would be a deal, something, anything. This was what they needed to find, and fast. Maybe she could make some calls. Maybe there was a way of undermining him. She was not sure. Should she call Miles? No, tricky. Something else.

That something else still eluded her as she sat with Rob in the joyless anteroom to Councillor Phil's office. He had asked them to see him in what he called "a window" before his housing-advice sessions began. It was early evening. She was not sure whether he was in the office yet. The receptionist had explained that there was a back entrance to his room, which led to the car park, so they never really knew whether he was in or out. "He's a one, that Councillor Phil," she ventured. "He's going to bring a big smile to this part of town one day, you wait and see." She and Rob had not dared challenge this, lest the receptionist reveal that the demolition next Saturday of an obnoxious middle-class health centre was the first phase of this excellent campaign to make the East End smile again.

"Ah, Miss Taylor! Mr. Eastwood! Sorry to have kept you!" There at his white door with its frosted glass was Councillor Phil. He was more oleaginous than he appeared in his photos, balder, more grizzled. He was shorter, too. Did he wear platforms on public occasions? Probably. Today there was no tie, his shirtsleeves were rolled up, and he wore a pair of old grey suit trousers. His shirt, she noticed, had the curious translucence that some men who perspire too much impart to cotton, or, in this case, polyester, washed so often it had lost any recognisable colour. It looked as if he had been sweating recently, doubtless because of the electric fire she could see behind him. Even so, Mia had to agree with the receptionist: Councillor Phil was indeed "a one." He had evidently been in his room for some time, no less evidently enjoying the knowledge that they were outside fretting. He beamed at them with the portable sunshine of the politician. You're not very good, thought Mia. But you're still a big hairy fish in this little pond.

He shook hands with them both and ushered them in. She caught him looking her up and down and then dismissing her just as quickly. No, she was definitely not his type: too tiny, not enough meat on her. I only date members of the government, honey, she felt like saying, then realised that it would not help if she did. His office was tiny, little more than a big filing cabinet with chairs and a sagging oatmeal sofa. But what space there was had been given over to more memorabilia: pictures everywhere of Councillor Phil with moderately famous people, including a past snooker world champion. Photos of Shirley, Laura, and Charlene at various ages. Councillor Phil in the dads' race at the local primary school. Councillor Phil on a "fact-finding" trip to Cuba. Oh dear, she thought. All this, and you haven't even stood for Parliament yet. How old are you? Forty-five? More? We don't stand a chance. You'll do anything to get noticed: *anything*. You'd sell your granny into slavery if you thought it would get you onto a shortlist to stand for Parliament. Because if you don't, five years from now you'll be propping up the bar in your local at lunchtime, sinking pints with whisky chasers and shouting at the television when the news comes on.

"Thanks for coming in," he said, settling into a canvas director's chair. "So, how can I help you both?"

She could see Rob was about to start speaking, and she broke in before he could. "Thank you for seeing us, Councillor. We know how busy you are, and so we'll take up as little of your time as we can."

"No rush. Well, within reason! Fire away."

She rehearsed the basic details of the case, which of course he knew. She explained that the centre was a modest business with no plans for expansion, a small turnover, and a happy atmosphere, which of course he knew. The present investigation would spell disaster for the Echinacea, and bring to an end a fine enterprise run by a woman who had become a pillar of her community and had regenerated an entire street, with all that implied for the local economy. Which of course he knew.

The trouble was, as she had realised long before their meeting, he didn't give a damn. Not at all. He had probably never been near the Echinacea, but he had obviously stumbled on the old file about its structural defects and spotted an opportunity to score some cheap political points. The meeting was a bore for Councillor Phil, a formality for procedure's sake. He had made his mind up about this one months ago.

"Yup. Yup. Tricky. I see where you're coming from, Miss Taylor. I really do. And you have my complete sympathy. You like the centre; you work there. It's your livelihood and—let's face it—something more than that to you. And to you, too, Mr. Eastwood, I have absolutely no doubt. So here's my problem." He smiled, revealing a mossy dungeon of dying yellow teeth. "I represent all the people of this borough, not just some of them. Every day, I meet people like you, whom I like. You know— people I'd happily have a beer with, welcome in my home with Shirley and the kids. But the tough thing is that I still have to oppose something they're doing or disagree with them about something. And the reason is that the people I represent need me to do that for them. They need me to say no to people I like. It's the hardest thing, I tell you. The hardest." He reached over and drained what looked like a long-stewed cup of tea, with the bag still in it.

Rob was staring at the floor. He ran his fingers through the soft fringe of his hair, awkward and embarrassed. Ah me, she thought, he's going to be useless. I may as well have come on my own. She smiled at Councillor Roberts. "Don't think we don't appreciate that, Councillor. We do. But the fact is that the people you represent do benefit from this centre. Lots and lots of them. Look." She opened her shoulder bag and pulled out a petition with 150 signatures on it. It was a letter, written by her for Sylvia, for customers of the centre and local residents to sign. Ringo had delivered forty names, mostly friends of his cousin, who owned a restaurant in Brick Lane. It was an impressive achievement, not least because it had been drawn up at such speed. The councillor inspected it, leafing over the pages with undisguised displeasure. He put it down in front of him and linked his fingers beneath his chin.

"Yup. Yup. Some of these are your customers, I assume?"

She sagged a little, furious at herself for doing so in his presence. "Some, yes. Not all."

"Sure. Sure. Well, I've no doubt they feel as strongly as you both do. They use the place, after all. But the complaints about your centre are very serious, and it isn't open to me to ignore the feelings of residents—

the elderly, disabled people, lone parents." He frowned, as if the mere mention of such groups required a change in tone. "You also have"—he pulled out a brown file marked *Echinacea Structure: Background*—"an unresolved investigation into the structure of the building, which was unsound ten years ago. I can only wonder what state the foundations are in now." Another frown. "Actually, when I was reading the file, I couldn't for the life of me work out why the enquiry had been suspended then for no good reason."

Because, thought Mia, in those days, the price of a quiet life was a quick snog in the back of a cab, courtesy of the woman whose world you now propose to ruin. What's the price these days, Councillor Roberts? How has inflation affected grubby little men like you?

What happened next was so unexpected that it took her a while to register that it was not a trick of her imagination. She would never forget it, or the way in which it indirectly affected the course of her life. Much later, it would make her smile with an unadultered pleasure she had not felt for a long time. But, as Rob rose to his feet, she could not possibly have guessed his intention. Indeed, as she saw him standing up, out of the corner of her eye, she assumed that she was mistaken, that her senses were deceiving her. She was tired, after all. She was beginning to hallucinate.

But no. Rob was indeed on his feet. He was trembling violently, his whole body shaking with a fury she would never have thought him capable of. And suddenly, from nowhere, he was talking at a rate to match his rage; shouting, really, to be honest. Except that it wasn't just shouting. It was more than ranting. He was taking on Councillor Phil, the town hall, Maureen Stove, the legislation, Parliament, the courts, the press, the whole damned lot of them. He was questioning this revolting little man's right to jeopardise a fine local institution like the Echinacea and to swat aside Sylvia's life's work in the name of some stupid political ambition. She could see the openmouthed councillor brace himself to object. He was doubtless used to heckling, and was evidently about to unleash his standard patter. Though shocked, he had the air of a man who had tried to be nice and had now accepted that he must, reluctantly, remove the gloves.

But Rob was just warming up. Did he, Councillor Phil, think that anybody was remotely fooled by what he was doing? Didn't he know the contempt people felt for politicians when they did things like this? How dare he don the mantle of decency as he wallowed around in the gutter of thwarted ambition? And that was not all. Rob might not know much, and he certainly knew less than Mia, he admitted. But—and here he laughed with lethal scorn—he knew a man who would never be an MP when he saw one. He could smell failure and resentment and betrayal everywhere in the room. Yes, the councillor might close them down, ruin the Echinacea, score his point. But all the people who worked there would be back, doing good things, creating something, and injecting life into the place where they lived, rather than draining it. Did Councillor Phil realise what a loser he was? Did he realise how his petty victories were nothing of the sort? That each one of them was a terrible stain on his conscience and a corrosion of what passed for his soul? Did he really sleep at night? And—above all, above all—how *dare* he talk to them while wearing a shirt like that? Did he realise what an offence his shirt was, with its big sweat stains? Didn't it bother him seeing members of the public in such a state?

Rob sat down. She noticed that the veins on his bony hands were bulging and blue. Adrenaline was coursing through his body. She could even see the pulse on his neck throbbing crazily. He was in a state of profound agitation. But it was a state full of passion and suicidal dignity. Perhaps even some sort of beauty. Once again, he had surprised her, as he had on their trip to Dalston in the van. He had also, of course, almost certainly killed off the Echinacea Centre, and removed any chance she might have had of exploring the possibility of a deal with their chubby opponent. But for now, she was unable to feel any fury. There was an undoubted splendour in Rob's outburst, which had come from deep within and still hung in the air. And she could not deny that at precisely the moment that her heart should have been sinking, she had felt nothing but exhilaration. Now the room was thick with a silence that, she feared, could last for several years if somebody did not break it soon.

It was Councillor Roberts who did so. He was as pale as Rob and visibly unsure of what to say. There must have been part of him that was relieved that he had not been thumped as part of the performance. Slowly, however, his politician's instincts reasserted themselves and he resumed his platitudes. "Mr. Eastwood. Mr. Eastwood. Now, then. I'm glad you've sat down. Now, look. I'm going to do you a bloody big favour. Both of you." He glared at Mia to let her know that he considered her complicit in the psychotic behaviour of her colleague. "I'm going to pretend I didn't hear any of that nonsense. I have to tell you: I'm a politician, it's true, and I don't mind criticism. I welcome it, actually. Keeps you on your toes. But there's nothing I hate more than abuse. It's just not on, and I won't tolerate it. Least of all in my own office. But I'm a reasonable guy and I can see that emotions are running pretty high here." He picked up a pen and made a note, a vulgar attempt to signal his resumption of power in the situation. "So what I'll say is what I would have said anyway. You and your centre will be treated like everybody else. No favours, no grudges. Fair treatment. My middle names. I'll add your petition to the file. And I'll let Mrs. Stove know. You'll be hearing from her department quite soon, I imagine." He stood up. It was a dismissal. "Thanks again for coming in. You'll let yourself out, if that's okay."

Mia and Rob stood up. He shook his head in disgust. She took a deep breath and suddenly noticed something that she had not noticed before. It had escaped her attention entirely during her own exchange with the councillor, and Rob's astonishing performance. Was she right? Yes, absolutely. Yes. It was unmistakable now that she thought about it. Obvious, maybe, looking back. The sort of thing she should have spotted sooner. But she had spotted it now; that was what counted. And what it meant was splendid. But she did not want to mention it just yet. Let Councillor Roberts think himself invulnerable a little longer. Let him scratch his belly when they had gone, and call them fools under his breath, and make a few calls to his cronies on the council to say that, come hell or high water, that bloody health centre was coming down if he had to swing the demolition ball himself.

"Well, thanks for nothing," said Rob. "May I wish you only misery and heartache."

"Good-bye, Mr. Eastwood," said the councillor without looking up from his notes. "Miss Taylor."

"Come on, Rob," she said, linking her arm with her colleague's. "Let's go. Let's leave Councillor Roberts to his work."

They walked out in silence into the night. It was raining halfheartedly, the drops flying sideways on gusts of wind. A bus thundered past, a tableau of frozen faces peering from its windows. Rob was instantly apologetic, and she felt that she owed it to Sylvia to take him to task and ask what the hell he thought he was doing. But she didn't. She had found herself disconcertingly transfixed by his vigour and innocence. She had agreed with every word he had said. Worse, she had envied him for saying it. She had long ago forgotten how to say what she meant in such encounters. That honesty had been burned out of her by a thousand handshakes and a hundred deals. Her craft had been the manipulation of language and the identification of the darker motives which underpinned what people said. She had traded in perception. She had been an excellent practitioner of her trade. But Rob's instincts had been right. Councillor Roberts was indeed nothing more than a fat fuck. He would not listen to them, no matter what she said. There was no deal to be done.

She did not say this to Rob as they walked back towards the centre together. She could not quite bring herself to congratulate him, not yet. But she wanted to console him at least.

"I screwed up royally," he said, kicking a paper cup into the road. "I ruined it for you. I should have kept my mouth shut. It was just so hard—"

"Forget about it. He wasn't going to change his mind. You could have got on your knees and begged for mercy. I could have taken my clothes off and offered myself to him. It wouldn't have made any difference."

"So we're stuffed?"

"Officially, as of now, we are more stuffed than a row of Christmas turkeys. Not a prayer. But while you were tearing Councillor Roberts's head off, I noticed something which cheered me up a bit."

"What? What could possibly have cheered you up in that hellhole?"

"Did you notice the smell?"

Rob gave this some thought. He pulled his satchel over his shoulder. "Not really, no. Should I have? I don't have a great sense of smell. I imagine it smelt of him, which must be pretty unpleasant."

"You're a bloke. You're less sensitive to these things. Unless I'm deceiving myself, there was the unmistakable aroma of Angel by Thierry Mugler in that room."

"Angel what?"

"It's a perfume. Very strong. How can I put this? A certain kind of girl wears it. It's not the sort of scent you give your nan for Christmas."

"So what?"

"So when Sylvia and I went to see Mrs. Stove the other day, her assistant, Eileen, was wearing it. Buckets of the stuff. Drenched in it. A complete bimbo. Legs up to her armpits, clothes falling off. Blond. And this amazingly strong perfume. The kind that walks into a room five minutes before you do. You could hardly breathe when she came near."

"What are you saying?"

"What I'm saying, Rob, is that, unless I'm very mistaken, Eileen had come near Councillor Phil not long before he saw us. She had been in that room. A room with a back exit, don't forget. I think there'd been a bit of a tryst going on. Which, revolting as it is to contemplate, puts the state of his shirt into a new light."

Rob stopped walking. She looked up at him and saw that he was smiling.

"Councillor Phil, the Family Man?"

"Exactly." They carried on towards the Mile End Road.

"Husband to Shirley? Dad to Laura and Charlene? The man who cares about your *family*?"

"Got it in one."

"What are you going to do with this? Mia?"

She did not look up this time. "Very, very bad things."

THE PLAN would take longer to execute than it did to hatch. They returned to the Echinacea, where an already-weepy Sylvia was awaiting them, surrounded by scented candles. She wanted to get back to feed Ravi, and had to buy cat food, she said. Mia calmed her down. There was, she said, a way of persuading the councillor, but it was best left to her and Rob. Sylvia should go home, get some rest, and forget about it. Leave the whole thing to her loyal deputy manager and assistant manager. They would protect her, if she would trust them. Sylvia sniffed, said she did trust them, and burst into tears again.

The next day, Mia and Rob began the stakeout. They parked the van across the road from the car park behind Councillor Roberts's office. Mia reasoned that there was no chance of Phil and Eileen having a date before noon. But anytime thereafter was possible, and so they needed to be in place. She had warned Rob that it could take many hours and told him that he did not have to come. But he'd said that he wanted to see the thing through. He had arranged to meet her there. And he arrived only five minutes late, a thermos and plastic box in his hands. She opened the door.

"Get in, don't make a fuss." He had shaved, she noticed. His skin was downy and fresh. "What's that, a packed lunch?"

He looked down shamefacedly at his provisions. "Er . . . Well, actually, yes."

"You're kidding." She laughed. "A stakeout with a packed lunch. Did you bring an apple for teacher, too?"

"My mum asked me what I was doing. So . . . so, I sort of told her."

She giggled. "Bloody hell, Rob. You wouldn't be much use as a spy. What if your mum asked you when you were going to meet a Soviet defector or make a drop in Hyde Park? She'd be there checking you were wearing a vest."

He settled into his seat. "Unfortunately, that is completely true. She turned up at one of our gigs the other day to see if I was all right. You know, she'd heard from one of her bingo friends that the pub was a bit rough. I had to wrestle her into a cab. So embarrassing. I mean, how can I be a rock'n'roll suicide when my mum comes and stands at the back of my concerts? She'll scare the groupies off, for a start."

Mia looked in the rearview mirror and saw a car parked behind them pull away. "So you told her you were off to do a bit of surveillance with your colleague?"

"Not in so many words. But I said that we had a long job outside, and before I knew it, she'd done tea and bacon sandwiches for two."

"Very nice. I don't think my mum ever made me a bacon sandwich in her life."

Rob put his feet on the dashboard. "Really? Why don't you ask her?"

"Oh. No. She passed away a few years ago."

The feet came down. "I'm sorry. God. I haven't been doing very well lately, have I? Open mouth, insert trainer. You must miss her."

She looked across at him. For some reason, this was exactly the right thing to say. "I do. I do miss her. Thanks for saying so."

The afternoon was bleak and drizzly. There were about ten cars in the car park, mostly old hatchbacks. Mountain bikes lined the wall, jostling for space. A supermarket trolley had been dumped near to the door that she had worked out must be Councillor Phil's. It shifted forlornly on its rubber wheels as the wind grew stronger. She was glad to be inside the car.

Rob shifted uncomfortably. "Listen, I'm really sorry about the other day. I know I've already apologised. But I wanted to say it to your face again. I feel terrible. You know, as if I barged into this thing that you and Sylvia have created and just ruined it. My big mouth."

He looked infinitely sad. There was, she noticed, an eyelash on his cheek. She resisted the temptation to brush it off. "Rob, look. What you have to understand is . . . I'm not the person to apologise to. It's Sylvia's place, you know. I mean, I love it with all my heart. But I just sort of ended up there, a while ago. I've tried to help out and make things run a bit more smoothly. But that's it. It's all her. She's looked after me for quite a while."

He shook his head. "Come on. I've seen it. You prop her up. You hold the place together." He looked ahead. "It's remarkable really. Sylv says it herself: She'd be nothing without you."

Sylv: So the young Ganymede and his boss did have little chats, as Mia had suspected from the first. But perhaps they were innocent chats after all. Perhaps Sylvia's loneliness was such that she simply valued another youthful face to talk to. Someone else to take her seriously. Yes, that made sense. Mia still saw everything through the pitiless prism of competition: Those habits were too deeply seared into her consciousness to have faded. But perhaps the truth was simpler than she thought. Perhaps when Sylvia sat with Rob and talked, she did indeed say how she owed it all to her deputy manager, the incomparable Chels. Perhaps that was all she really wanted to say.

"It's nice of her to say that. I would never let her down." She checked the car park, which was still deserted. "But the truth is that I'd be nothing without her."

"I don't understand. You're so . . . confident. I mean, anyone can see that you've done remarkable things in the past, whatever they are. How could you be nothing without Sylv? I don't believe you."

She looked at him, wanting to say something. The face she had first thought pinched and vulpine now seemed open and trustworthy. He had shown with Councillor Phil that he was something more than a moody boy. She still did not know what to make of him, conscious as she was that she was starting to see him with different eyes. Oh Mia, she thought, you're lonely yourself. You should tell him something, anything. You should trust him a little. He's earned that much. But even as she opened her mouth, she knew she wasn't ready. He would have to wait, if he really wanted to know.

"I just think I would."

He retreated, aware that he had failed in his bid to win her confidence. He looked down at the thermos. "Well, she's a great woman. She's been kind to me, too." Mia gripped the steering wheel in frustration. She felt cold; she felt old. Would it always be like this? "But you're staying? I mean, you sounded at the start—you know, when you first came to see us—as if you might move on quite quickly." Did it sound as if she cared? And would it matter if it did?

He ran his hand through his hair again and smiled. "No, I'm not going anywhere. Not yet. Do you think I'd leave the two of you to Councillor Phil's tender mercies?"

"Good." Christ, she meant it. How strange was that? "How about some tea, then?"

The hours passed. There was no sign of life in the car park, not even the glow of a desk light from the offices behind. After a while, an athletic-looking young man, his vagrancy betrayed only by his clothes, leapt over the wall and ran off with the trolley, as if the Trolley Police were only seconds behind him, sirens wailing, lights flashing. His T-shirt was soaked from the damp air and the sweat of the runner. Of course, she thought: He'll go to the supermarket and collect the pound-coin deposit, if there is one. And then he'll continue his mad circuit of the neighbourhood, his pursuit of small change, and his furious flight of the soul from the station of the beggar, frozen by fate to the pavement.

She and Rob talked about the centre, about Councillor Phil, about what might happen next. He made her laugh with a surprisingly good impersonation of the councillor's reaction to his outburst: She had assumed that Rob had been much too preoccupied by his own rhetoric to notice the effect he was having. She asked him if his big mouth had ever got him into a fight, and he had stayed silent just long enough to make her burst out laughing again.

They played the game of choices: Sylvia Plath or Ted Hughes; linguini or gnocchi; Germany or France; *Star Wars* or *Star Trek;* the Sex Pistols or the Clash; Sean Connery or Roger Moore; Jerry Springer or Lucian Carver; Matisse or Picasso; J.Lo or Britney; Bach or Mozart. They disagreed on almost everything. He talked about living with his mum and how they drove each other mad, loved each other. He told her about his band and how terrible it still was. She asked whether she could come and see them sometime. He blushed, paused, and agreed reluctantly to let her know the next time Thieves in the Night had a gig. He warned her not to hold her breath, and, taking a big bite from her bacon sandwich, she said she wouldn't.

"Mind you," he said, "it might be all I've got if Councillor Phil gets his way. I mean, the horrible truth is that we could all be looking—"

"Shut up, Rob."

He put his sandwich down in its tin foil. "What? I was only—"

"Look. Look. Look at the car park."

It was hard to see much clearly in the gloom of the late afternoon. But the streetlamps were already flush with their first glow, and light from the adjoining shops leaked onto the tarmac of the car park. So it was just possible to make out the shape emerging from the door that Mia had correctly identified as the entrance to Councillor Phil's office. In silhouette, the shape looked at first like a centaur, one form composed of a tall half and a shorter rear. In the light, however, the form broke into two: a squat little man, his arms grabbing and groping, and a much taller woman, squirming and giggling as he did so. Rob and Mia watched in stunned silence as Councillor Phil reached up to kiss Eileen with the desperate enthusiasm of an ageing satyr who had just been told by the woodland deity that, sadly, this would be his last outing and to make the most of it. The man who had seemed so sedentary in their meeting was now frenzied with activity, his hands unsure whether to scale Eileen's impressive chest like a mountaineer or to concentrate on squeezing her bottom, which was wrapped in a skirt of even greater brevity than Mia remembered. His passion was vile to behold, although astonishing in its ferocity. In his office, she had thought that Councillor Roberts didn't really care about anything. Wrong: He cared about *this*.

And then she remembered the plan. The plan! Where was the camera? At Rob's feet. She scrambled over him and grabbed it, her hands shaking. It had been years since she had used it, and she had not checked that it worked. A thousand pounds' worth of gear, bought for her by Ben for Christmas, now at last put to good use. Or so she hoped as she looked through the viewfinder, rammed Rob's head against the headrest to get him out of the way, and brought Councillor Phil and the lovely Eileen into focus. Oh yes, she thought as their blurred features hardened into clear lines. Oh yes. Beautiful. There it is: a dirty little councillor, self-proclaimed family man, fresh from a frantic rutting session with a junior member of the council staff. In full fleshy Technicolor—and this she had remembered to check—on film sensitive enough for the poor light. *Click. Click. Click.* Who's stuffed now?

With one last grope, Councillor Phil sent Eileen packing into the night and went back into his office. She stumbled a little as she walked across the car park, tottering in her heels. But she was smiling. She was smiling. Mia thought, not because she could possibly have enjoyed what had just happened, but because she enjoyed the feeling it left her with. She could sit opposite Maureen Stove and sense the eyes of fifty men in the open-plan office undress her every day as she walked back and forth with trays of coffee, and she could think to herself, I am protected, as you are not. Whatever you think of me, I have the upper hand. And she could see Councillor Phil in the paper and think of the havoc she could wreak in his life, too. That was why she smiled.

"Fuck," said Rob. "She's heading over here. She'll see us."

"No, she won't," said Mia. But she was not so sure. Eileen was bearing down on them, dodging cars, which tooted appreciatively, to get to the other side of the road. She did up the zip on her leather jacket and pulled out a cigarette. She was standing directly in front of the Transit. The tip of the cigarette glowed as she inhaled deeply. She looked each way. Mia and Rob sat, immobilised, daring not to breathe or blink. If she sees me, I'll drive off, thought Mia. No, no: If she sees me, we're dead anyway. The plan won't work. The plan will be dead. We'll all be dead. *Don't look into the van.*

Eileen looked but didn't see. She dithered interminably by the bumper of the Transit, only a few feet from Mia, who was still holding the camera in trembling hands. She looked at her nails and then picked her nose for a few seconds. Her mouth opened as if she was going to say something to herself. She rummaged in her bag, found what she was looking for, and then looked at her watch. Some inner process of cogitation had not yet run its course; that much was clear. The brain of Eileen, however small it might be, was running a programme of some kind. And then, suddenly, it was over and she was gone, heading off to the main road and the cluster of bus stops.

"Oh Christ," said Rob. "Oh, Jesus Christ. That was close."

Mia was slumped on her seat, breathing heavily. "Too close. Too bloody close. Oh God, that was too much."

Rob flung himself round to face her. "Did you get them?"

She handed him the camera and put the key in the ignition. The engine spluttered into life and she checked her mirrors. It was time to go home.

"Well? Mia?" They were near to the lights now. She changed lanes to avoid a bus. "Did you? Did you get them?"

Putting on the hand brake as they waited for the lights to change, she turned to him. "Oh yes. I got them all right."

AND SO IT WAS that a week later Sylvia received a letter of epic politeness from Maureen Stove, written, it was clear, with the greatest reluctance by a woman, it was also clear, who had been warned that she would be out of a job if she did not do exactly as she was told. Mrs. Stove said first how much she had enjoyed meeting Sylvia and her colleague Miss Taylor. She was also grateful to Miss Taylor and her colleague Mr. Eastwood for taking the time out of their busy schedules to explain the background to Councillor Roberts. She was pleased to say that Councillor Roberts was very impressed by the case they had made and had asked her to pass on his gratitude for all that the centre was obviously doing for the community. The planning subcommittee had met on the following Monday, Mrs. Stove continued, and had resolved, in light of Councillor Roberts's strong recommendation, to close the enquiry into the Echinacea, all outstanding matters having now been resolved, as required "under the terms of the legislation." However, she was pleased to advise Sylvia that the subcommittee had also decided, in light of the structural defects which were identified a decade ago but ignored due to an unfortunate bureaucratic error at the town hall, to recommend a reasonable grant be made to the centre to assist with any work that might have to be undertaken as a result of this earlier oversight. Mrs. Stove looked forward to receiving builders' estimates from Sylvia so that she could process these with her colleagues in the Finance Division. In the meantime, she hoped that Sylvia would not hesitate to contact her—or her new assistant, Michele—should there be any way in which they could be of further assistance. "Yours faithfully," etc.

That was all it took, thought Mia as she poured champagne into Sylvia's glass that evening. One picture. One picture slipped in a brown envelope under the back door of Councillor Phil's office. Mind you, it was a good picture, by any standards. A bit grainy—she was cross with herself for that—but clear enough to see who was groping whom. Hands everywhere, if you looked. A funny little man all over a much younger, taller woman. It made you laugh, when you thought about it. Just one picture, with the rather cryptic words "Our foundations are fine, Councillor. How about yours?" written in black marker pen across its glossy surface.

Chapter NINE

THE TOPIARIES ON either side of the walkway were clipped in the shape of peacocks braced for flight. Silhouetted in the flames of the blazing torches, they looked like strange beasts of the night, guarding the marquee and its secrets. Only the flashes from the press cameras behind the red rope, blasting light into the enclosure, revealed the birds for what they really were: nothing more than a meticulously crafted artifice, the first joke of the feast.

The shoes were giving Mia more trouble than anything. After three hours in Bond Street, she had settled on the simple backless, bias-cut Versace dress, which shimmered when struck by light. With the help of a Japanese man in a tight black T-shirt, she had found a miniature Gucci bag that went perfectly with the dress, and, at Fenwick's, tiny diamond studs well within her budget. But the new black satin Jimmy Choos were killing her. It was years since she had worn heels, and Claude was making no concessions to her, in spite of her mumbled complaints. Too late, she remembered what he was like on a night like this. He could not wait to get into the fray, to see who was there, to drink whatever was go-

ing and schmooze with whomever he considered worthy of his attention. He was in his element, overexcited and impatient, already irritated,
she could see, at her nerves and the drag she might become as the
evening developed.

"Claude," she whispered as they walked along the red carpet.
"Claude. Slow down. My feet are giving me hell."

"What?" he asked, speeding up as he spoke. "What's the matter?
We're nearly inside. Oh, look, there's Hermy."

"Hermione Lane?"

"Who else? God, you have been on another planet, haven't you?
She's got her own shop in Notting Hill now. Very fashionable."

"She was just somebody's girlfriend when I last saw her. What was
the name of that rich Italian?"

"Bruno Da Ponte. Long gone. She dumped him when she got backing for the shop. She's being chased by some pop singer now, according
to Harry. The game is to guess which of them has pumped more Botox
into their face."

They were greeted at the entrance by a woman in a long black skirt
and starched blouse. She wore the Bracknell insignia on a brooch and
an identification card round her neck: Security was tighter than usual
this year, as the committee had bagged not only the normal quota of
aristocrats, film stars, Cabinet ministers, and Arab princelings but two
younger members of the royal family. Mia had already noticed a number of men whispering into their lapels and trying to fade into the background. They looked ridiculous. But this was part of the Bracknell's
pantomime of self-importance. She remembered it all now. She remembered how bitter she had been the year she was invited to be a member
of the committee but had been seconded at the last minute to
Washington for six months, thus denied the power to treat all her enemies—and friends—like shit for most of the autumn.

"Ah, Mr. Silberman," said the greeter. "Welcome to you. How many
is this?"

"My twelfth," Claude replied. "They get better every year. Is that Mick Jagger over there?"

The greeter smiled. "We never reveal the names of our guests. Even to other guests. Table twelve. Enjoy your evening, sir."

Claude grinned gleefully. "Of course, of course."

The interior of the marquee was a scene of breathtaking opulence and imagination. Vast drapes of Ottoman design hung from its ceiling, their brocade matching the tapestry which ran seamlessly for hundreds of yards round the inside of the tent. The tables were built into its land-scape of fountains, vegetation, and bridges. Some were on a higher level, set in four little pagodas. There was a stage and a dance floor, and, at the centre of the marquee, a lush garden in which real peacocks strutted moodily, guarded by two keepers in Bracknell polo shirts. By the en-trance, where she and Claude took their first glasses of champagne, was a large meeting area and a bar. There, she saw one of the royal party flashing his famous smile at an Oscar-winning actress, who had already moved on to the Stoli. The barman laughed to himself at this sight, a picture for which the tabloids would have paid a very large amount. The actress was whispering into the young man's ear and then smiled, re-vealing teeth of supernatural perfection; he blushed and gulped down his champagne. Gyrating lights overhead re-created the whirl of a disco. But in the corner, a string quartet played Vivaldi, a pocket of stern con-centration as the bacchanal warmed up around them. The musicians' backdrop was the massive video screen of the chill-out room behind, still deserted at this early stage of the evening, but lined with the leather couches on which exhausted guests would snooze and embrace many, many hours later.

"Isn't this heaven?" said Claude. He was right, at least in his own terms. Mia looked at him in his velvet jacket, new dress shirt from Turnbull & Asser, and patent-leather shoes and realised that this was in-deed what Claude meant by the word "heaven." Outside, the chill of winter expressed perfectly the chill of those excluded from this great event. And to be excluded was unthinkable to Claude. This year, his friends from the Pisces Club—the Oxford dining society where he had first made his mark as a coming man—had organised a table. One of their number, Harry Startt, was a member of the committee and had fixed it. This was, of course, quite impossible. Everybody knew that the Bracknell was arranged by double tickets only, absolutely no tables, absolutely no groups, absolutely no exceptions. That was the whole point of this most decorous and democratic event: that an eighteen-year-old just down from public school might find himself next to Gwyneth Paltrow or a Saxon princess or a First Lord of the Admiralty. You took pot luck. But Harry had fixed it for the boys. A whole table, on one of the pagodas, near the stage. What a fucking star. "There's Natasha," said Claude, grabbing two more flutes. "Let's go and see her."

Natasha Chapman. Tash Chapman. Good old Tash. How long had it been since Mia had seen her? Long enough. They had been inseparable at Oxford, swimming hand in hand on a sea of white wine and Pimm's through affairs, essay crises, and parties. So many parties. Afterwards, they had seen each other at least once a week for years, their meetings diminishing in frequency only when Mia's career began to command most of her time. But Tash had always been part of the scene: Tash, with her incorrigibly long brown hair, the little mews house in Kensington her father had bought her, and the pretensions to be a playwright. What did she do all day? It had never seemed to matter. Mia had loved her once. And then, when darkness fell, she had thought of other things and forgotten people such as Tash. That their lives had carried on since she left them behind was strange indeed. If she imagined them at all, she imagined them as she had last seen them before the night of the picnic: innocent, brash, irrelevant.

"Darling," said Claude. "You look ravishing. But you know that." Natasha was wearing a white silk dress, black scarf, and black evening gloves. She was more slender than Mia remembered her. Her features were a little drawn, gaunt even. But her smile was unchanged. She kissed

Claude on the cheek, and smiled again with the lack of commitment which fills in the gap before an introduction is made.

My God, thought Mia, she doesn't recognise me. She thinks I am just Claude's latest bit of stuff, passing through their world, somebody to tolerate before the next one comes along. If he says my name is Francesca and I live in Monaco, she'll look at me with vacant eyes and tell me some dreary story about how much she loves Monaco, then forget about me forever. What does she see? Mia wondered. She sees a small, vaguely familiar woman on the arm of a man who has remained her friend, who has not left the group behind, or gone into exile, or forced them all to confront the embarrassment of tragedy. Not like me, the friend who vanished. Yes, looking at the woman on Claude's arm, she sees his date—no more, no less.

"Well, Tash," said Claude. "Aren't you going to say hello?"

Natasha looked again; this time, something in her synapses clicked. Could Mia detect a draining of colour behind the rouge, a sudden wish for flight? What does the pride of lions do when the sickly creature returns to the veldt? What feral twitches, the remnants of instincts long suppressed, enable humans to signal to one another: Not Welcome? Perhaps it was her imagination. Natasha collected herself. She screamed with delight and jumped up and down before flinging her arms around Mia.

"Oh my God!" She looked her old friend up and down. "It is you. It *is*. I don't believe it. It's been *so* long, darling. How long? Four years, five? Wait till I tell David and Mands. Oh—you know they've got a little boy?"

"Yes, I do," said Mia. "Claude told me. It's good to see you, Tash. You look fabulous."

"Told you I'd find her, didn't I?" said Claude. "I had to go to bloody Holland, but I found her."

"Holland?" asked Natasha. "I thought you said she was somewhere in the middle of nowhere. In the East End or something?"

So that was it: cover blown entirely. Oh, well. "I think Claude was trying to be funny about how far east he had to go to find me. Weren't you?" She turned to him. "Darling?"

"Of course, of course." He drew on his cigarette and smiled. The manipulations and tricks of the evening were already pleasing him enormously. He knew well enough that Natasha was squirming with horror, and that Mia had little to say to her old friend, either. There would be plenty more where that came from, too. Mia could see the relish in his eyes, and she felt a spasm of hatred. But no: She had known what to expect. That was the point of the evening for Claude. The petty power games and the opportunities to cause discomfort were its true glamour. That was why he loved the Bracknell. And that, if she was honest, was probably why he had invited her. To watch her take the bait and then see her facing people who now treated her as a long-forgotten missing person, a woman whose skeleton would be found under a patio many years hence and who would be remembered briefly as a good sort.

"Come on, you two," he said. "Let's see if we can find Lord Harry." Natasha linked her arm with Mia's and the three wove their way through the gathering crowd, heading towards another part of the marquee, where a muscular fire-eater with a mouthful of glass was being more or less ignored. She recognised many faces and said hello to one or two people without feeling or meaning. None of them, she realised, had yet gone through the image processing which had made Natasha turn pale. They were simply observing the rituals of their class, the careful acknowledgement of a dimly recognised face. She might have been a ghost, for all they cared, these men in tailored tuxedos and Nehru jackets, and women in gowns of awesome beauty and expense. It was not so much that she had come back. Most of them, in truth, had never really noticed she had left. Ten years before, ten years after, their behaviour would have been exactly the same. Time meant nothing as this dance of empty etiquette was performed beneath the twinkling of a disco ball.

"Who's your date, Tash?" Mia asked as brightly as she could.

"Date?" She laughed. "Oh, Mia. My darling. This is what happens when you disappear on us. I'm married now. Didn't Claude tell you?"

"No. No, he didn't." Another flute arrived and was taken gratefully.

"I've been married—oh, six months now. And you'll never guess who to."

"Amaze me."

"No, you have to guess."

"Oh, all right. Tom?"

"Tom!" she screeched, spluttering champagne into her hand. "Tom! I'd never have married him. He was desperate to, mind you. House in the country, kids, Labrador. Had it all worked out. A flat for him during the week. Near here, actually. A place for him to have his affairs while I got on with breeding. But—darling—" She yawned theatrically. "In bed, he was a whole lot of nothing. My feet were asleep."

"I see. I never had Tom down as one of those. But there you go."

"Guess again."

This was irritating. She would give it one more go. "Oh, I don't know. Stephen Dee?"

"Warmer. He proposed, too. I thought about it, but then I found him shagging my sister at a ball. Not good."

"No, not good." This was an easy point to concede. "Tell me, then. Who's the blushing groom?"

"Lucian Carver."

Mia's father had once told her that the true mark of a lady—or a gentleman—was the ability to absorb a piece of truly disgusting news just after one has taken a mouthful of fine wine. This was precisely the position in which she now found herself. Lucian Carver? Natasha might as well have said that she had recently wed Jack the Ripper or Pol Pot. It was hard to see how any woman in command of her faculties could willingly engage in conversation with Lucian Carver, let alone promise to spend the rest of her life with him. Natasha had always been eccentric. But this lifted her into the category of the criminally insane. She had evidently lost her mind at some stage over the last four years. But Mia was determined to pass her father's test. She swallowed the champagne and considered her response.

"Lucian? Wow. That's . . . that's fantastic, Tash. How long were you seeing each other?"

"Do you know, that's the amazing thing. We were in Hampshire at a house party one weekend and just hit it off. Lucian took me off one afternoon for a spin in his Porsche and we sat on a hill and just talked and talked. And I fell head over heels for him. He was—is—the sweetest man, you know. I know what people say about him. But, believe me, I didn't walk down that aisle for nothing. Oh, look, here he is. Darling!"

Through the throng came the dyspeptic form of Lucian Carver, lumbering and barging his way towards them. In spite of Natasha's claim to the contrary, he looked exactly as he had always done: furious, rude, outraged at the world's shortcomings, liable to punch somebody at any moment. It was this persona that had made him a considerable success on his notorious television chat show, *The Carve-Up,* a weekly outpouring of political bile, on which he subjected *bien pensant* guests to the most ferocious humiliation. His reactionary views were well known, and no more remarkable than what a taxi driver might say in a traffic jam. But it was Lucian's willingness to see his opinions through to their logical conclusion, and often far beyond, that had made the show a hit. Its ratings had soared after he had reduced one female governor of the BBC to tears live on air, claiming she was a "pointless pudding of a woman, whose only two purposes in life were to remind people why Britain lost its empire and to encourage celibacy in the male population." He had accused a highly respected bishop of representing an institution "committed only to atheism, pederasty, and the surrender of national sovereignty." Invariably dressed in a pinstriped suit and florid tie, he often called for the return of hanging and flogging on air, demands which were always backed up by interactive polls of his viewers. His most recent stunt, which Mia had heard about but not seen, had been to make a live telephone call on his show to a homosexual novelist who had written a furious essay in *The Independent* attacking *The Carve-Up.* Lucian had asked the novelist a series of superficially innocent, but obviously well-informed questions about the school he had attended and a particular choirmaster, recently deceased. The novelist had been stunned into silence as 5 million viewers watched the host's lascivious grin. The next morning, the novelist's body was found by his maid, hanging from a beam in his kitchen. An angry debate had ensued in the press about the propriety of such television shows, and whether or not they were rotting the moral fabric of the nation. Lucian did not care: The following week, his ratings were up by half a million.

"Silberman!" Claude turned round to find Lucian Carver jabbing a finger into his chest. "Silberman! This is your fucking fault! I want a scotch, and all I can get are these girls' drinks." He pointed in disgust at a tray of vintage Krug and sea breezes passing them by.

"Lucian," said Claude, shaking his old roommate's hand. "Lucian, your wish is my command."

"Don't be so Jewish," Lucian continued. "So bloody craven. You were always like that. Even at Oxford. Bowing and scraping before the goy. Like some horrible little Fagin."

"Now, darling," Natasha said, taking his hand, and running her fingers through his thinning black hair. "Remember what we agreed? No anti-Semitism. It's not nice."

"I'm not being anti-Semitic. Some of my best friends—in fact, as you can see, my best bloody friend is Jewish. I'm just giving Claude some advice. He shouldn't be so bloody servile."

"Okay, then," said Mia. "Get your own bloody scotch, you stupid bigot."

The group fell silent. Lucian peered down at her. Natasha's eyes rolled in horror. Claude gazed ahead with the look of a man who wished he could make himself invisible at will. This is Lucian Carver, Mia thought. He could easily hit me. He's mad enough. I remember him from before he got famous, drunk and slapping women about. She wondered if there was anything sharp in her handbag which she could drive into the fat man's groin if things got nasty.

Suddenly, Lucian burst into peals of delighted laughter. In seconds, they had all joined in, even Claude, relieved that what had looked like a disaster had become an unexpected moment of triumph. It was very, very rare that Lucian laughed at anyone, apart from himself. He removed his glasses and whipped a large spotted handkerchief from his pocket to wipe his eyes. "Priceless," he said. "Priceless. Genius. She should be on the show, don't you think?" He put his glasses back on. "Now, madam, may I ask—if that's okay, and you won't get too upset— who the fuck you are?"

"Don't you remember me, Lucian?"

"No. Why should I?"

"It's Mia. Mia Taylor."

Lucian stared at her again through his thick glasses. "Little Mia. Well, well. I thought you were dead. Caught in a conflagration, or whatever it was." His lip curled.

"Still alive, Lucian. Sorry to disappoint you. But, anyway, congratulations on your wedding. I'm sorry I wasn't around at the time."

"Thanks. And don't worry. We wouldn't have invited you anyway!" He burst into fits of laughter again, breaking off to abuse a waiter and saying that if he didn't bring him a large scotch immediately, he, Lucian Carver, would send a television crew round to the home of the waiter's mother and broadcast images of her in her dressing gown, putting out the rubbish, to the entire nation. The waiter replied that his mother had been dead for some years but that he enjoyed the show and would be honoured to get Mr. Carver his drink.

"Bloody hell, Taylor," said Claude. "That was a close one. You haven't lost your taste for diplomacy, I see."

"Jesus," she said, turning her back on the Carvers. "How did that happen? Tash Chapman marrying that monstrosity? I remember him at your parties, singing SS drinking songs."

"Oh, just high spirits, I'm sure. And anyway, that's not the point."

"Well, what *is* the point?"

"The point, my dear, is that Lucian has got his own production company now. What nobody knows, apart from him and me—and I told Tash when I was drunk—is that he's going to sell it later this year. He's already on a huge salary. But when he sells up, he'll be a *seriously* wealthy man. I mean, miles more than the pretty boy bankers she used to run with."

"And that's it?"

"And he's a star. Don't forget what Tash is like. He goes to all the best parties, everywhere. You saw how that waiter acted. Lucian calls people idiots and they ask for his autograph. That's his gift. You know, they had dinner at Number Ten last week? He gave the prime minister a piece of his mind, said the Cabinet was full of gays or something, and the PM just laughed. It was in all the diaries. Get real, Mia. It's exactly what she wanted."

They started to move towards their table. The lead singer of a group which had had a string of hits in the eighties was singing Chet Baker songs by a piano, his floppy hair still falling over his eyes as it had a generation before. On the other side, applauding between numbers, was a boy she had once gone on a date with. Richard? No, Roland. That was it. Son of an actor, struggling to make his name in the computer business all those years ago. He did not notice her, which suited her fine. The crowd clapped as the pianist struck up "The Thrill Is Gone." She looked up and noticed for the first time a cage of parrots and other tropical birds, jumping from perch to perch, squawking miserably in competition with the vapid chatter that rose from below.

Up on the pagoda, Harry Startt was waiting for them with his girlfriend. He gave Claude a fierce bear hug and they exchanged some strange Latin greeting, which she guessed was a small remembered ritual of the Pisces. Claude, Lucian, and Harry had all been members together, eschewing the more obvious clubs for this more secretive and violently drunken masonry. The Pisces had existed only since the thirties, founded by the sons of three earls, but its hold on its alumni was considerable. Years before, she had been baffled by Claude's selection of a particularly dud trainee at Robinson as an associate on one of his more prestigious accounts. When she asked him about it, he had mumbled platitudes. But she had pressed Claude into revealing that the boy had been a member of the Pisces and that he was more or less honour-bound to look after him, idiot though he undoubtedly was. She had threatened to take the matter to Kingsley. Claude had smiled and told her that she was welcome to do so but would be wasting her time: Kingsley was a Piscean, too.

Harry Startt had not done as well as Claude or Lucian, but he had done all right. His father, the seventh Viscount Lilling, had despaired of his eldest son ever taking an interest in the family estates and so had set him up instead with the capital for a small publishing venture. Harry printed specialist magazines and technical manuals: His company rarely turned a profit, but it stayed afloat. His private wealth was such that it did not matter very much: The flat in Bayswater and *gite* in Provence were never under threat. But it mattered to Harry, who managed simultaneously to be podgy and insubstantial, and was conscious of this embarrassing paradox. He wanted to have something to show for his years since Oxford. He spoke often of wanting to be "his own man," as do those who never will be.

Mia stood awkwardly at the table, looking at the placement, hoping that she would not be next to Lucian. Peering at the ornate calligraphy on the embossed Bracknell cards, she saw with relief that she was between Harry himself and Anthony Wentworth-Crawford, an inoffensive lawyer with an offensive wife; although not a Piscean, Anthony had attached himself to Claude somewhere along the way. The Wentworth-

Crawfords were a uniquely dull couple, whose occasional presence in Claude's entourage tended to ensure the early dispersal of the party (or, on one memorable night, a brilliantly coordinated pretence on the part of all the other members that they were going home, only to regroup in an hour, sans Wentworth-Crawfords, at a downstairs dive in Mayfair). Anthony had found out about the ruse, but did not mind, knowing that he was essentially an impostor and regarding such indignities as a small price to pay. He understood that he was only included in Claude's nocturnal adventures on sufferance, rather than as of right, and that his inclusion could be terminated completely if he made a fuss. But he had not told his wife, Melanie, about the trick that their friends had played on them. Furious, desperate Melanie, with her two children and her endless talk of schools, holidays, and houses: She would have been quite incapable of dealing with the knowledge that she and her half-successful husband had been the victims of such a plot. Lively in her youth, Melanie had, in Claude's unforgiving phrase, "headed south" since leaving Oxford. Her face was a pale, caked mask of disappointment. Her shrill voice—"For Christ's sake, darling, just sort it out!"—could be heard above the hum of many a party. Her husband was a bore, broken by a decade of such treatment. But at least he was not Lucian.

Harry had indeed done well by his friends. From the vantage point of the pagoda, Mia could see the whole of the party, now in full swing. Each table was individually lit by candles and by strategically placed spotlights. Lanterns twinkled on the garlanded pillars which held up the marquee, their light reflected by the glitter scattered on the wooden floor. Behind the garden, she could see for the first time, was a spectacular fountain, a kitsch tribute to Versailles or perhaps the Piazza di Trevi, its painted papier-mâché trunk swathed in blinking fairy lights. Through the trellis of the pagoda, she could see Lucian, talking this time to a pretty young waitress, blond and vivacious. She evidently knew who he was and was laughing loudly at his patter, holding a tray of drinks aloft with one hand as he performed. He was asking her something.

With her free hand, the waitress smoothed the front of her waistcoat, visibly nervous at the presence of this dangerous and famous man. She smiled as he spoke and nodded uncertainly. At the next table to their own was another group of friends, evidently fixed up by someone on the committee in the same way as Harry had the Pisceans: A supermodel ran her index finger absentmindedly around her gums while talking to a young peer whose sister had been in Mia's dorm at prep school. The tousle-haired singer of a band five years past their sell-by date, but still welcomed in London society for their extraordinary commitment to hedonism, pressed his fingers to his temples and screwed his eyes shut. He reached desperately for a napkin folded in the shape of a bird and was quietly sick into it. Mia noticed that none of his party saw this. Or if they had, they chose to ignore it. It was early yet.

"Mia, my dear." Harry walked across and reached down to kiss her hand. "We are replenished. We are complete. Claude has brought you back to us."

She kissed his cheek. "Hello, Harry. It's good to see you. How have you been?"

"Desolate, my dear. Desolate. Wondering when you were going to turn up on my doorstep and agree to marry me." His chubby features creased into a grin of sad generosity, the face of a cherubic Falstaff. "Gave up, I suppose. Had to make do with Lucy here." The diaphanous blonde at his side extended a limp hand, which Mia took as one might the hand of an invalid. Her sheath dress did little to conceal her painful thinness. No dairy, no wheat, Mia thought. Probably no anything. Toothpaste in the handbag and therapy at a hundred quid an hour. Not much has changed since I went away.

They sat down. Serving staff swarmed around them with fresh glasses of champagne—this time of a more fabulous vintage, sponsored, their menus revealed, by a particularly enterprising bank. Worth every penny, too. She sipped and remembered the two horse pills she had dropped as she got ready at her flat, full of nerves she could not banish by breathing exercises or rational deliberation. A bad idea, probably. Two of those would have a moody elephant snuggling up to its keeper. And already she had added a bottle or so of champagne to the tranquillising cocktail within. No wonder she was starting to feel woozy, her head spinning like the disco lights in the bar. Lucian Carver's face was a ruddy blur on the other side of the table. He was whispering something into his wife's ear. Natasha looked at him, apparently aghast, and then remembered herself, smiling. He raised his eyebrows with grotesque suggestiveness. Some transaction had been made, some dark deal in the basement of the soul. Mia could only guess at its horrors.

"So, then," Anthony Wentworth-Crawford said. "Long time no see."

The day before, when she had confessed to Ringo about her crazy excursion, he had bet her a curry in Brick Lane that, first, somebody at the ball would say "Long time no see" before ten o'clock, and, second, that she would find this infuriating beyond belief. She surreptitiously checked her watch and saw that it was 9:45. Yes, she owed Ringo that curry.

"Anthony," she said, allowing him to kiss her. "It has been a long time, hasn't it?"

"Years and years." He blinked behind his glasses. She noticed that his shave was comically imperfect on the left-hand side; beads of sweat clustered on the Velcro patchwork of his sideburn. "Melanie and I were talking about you only the other day. Jessica has started school already, would you believe?"

"Really?" This, she realised, was what had changed in the past four years. When she had left these people, they had been completing the rituals of courtship, settling on husbands and wives, or rejecting them, choosing partnership or declining it, confusing the ticking of the biological clock with love, signing deeds, buying houses. Now they were producing children. And that was what they wanted to talk about, exactly as they had talked about money and cars and drink and sex a decade ago. Reproduction and its long aftermath was their chosen theme, their common denominator. She had no idea what to say to Anthony Wentworth-Crawford about Jessica's progress to school. Was it unbelievable, or extraordinary, or odd in any way?

"So what have you been up to, Mia?" he asked, digging into the extravagant pyramid of lobster, avocado, and caviar on a bed of ice which had just been placed before him. She noticed that he wrinkled his nose like a rabbit as he prepared to eat. A few of its capillaries were broken. "Claude says you've gone east."

"Yes. I suppose that's right." What else had Claude told them over cocktails in St. James's? That the old girl had gone mad? That he had tracked her down in some sort of terrible commune hundreds of miles from anywhere? That she dressed like a student now and drank cider? That grief had disfigured her, ruined her, changed her beyond recognition? Was that what Claude had said as the others shook their heads and said nothing, agreeing silently to be tolerant, unembarrassed, civil to their fallen friend when they met her at the Bracknell?

"Pay well, does it? This job?"

"Well, not as well as Robinson did. It's . . . it's a bit different. I'm managing something. A small business. Nothing fancy."

"Right, right." Poor Anthony: He was not up to this task. He was not up to much, if the truth were known. Hosing down Melanie took up most of what little energy he had left after the punishing hours he turned in at his law firm, chasing the partnership that would bring the rewards that might shut her up for at least part of the time. He was not equipped to deal with the return of Mia, Claude's psychological parlour game for the evening. "But you enjoy it?"

"Yes. Very much."

"That's the main thing. Can't say I really enjoy my work. But it pays the bills. And boy, do we have some bills in our house."

She laughed politely. She had known Melanie before Anthony, when she had been going out with one of the stars of her generation, who had since gone on to become a promising Tory MP. Now you saw his face on the television almost as often as Miles's. Melanie had loved him deeply, a love that even she sometimes mistook for mere ambition but which was something much more simple. The sadness of her life was that she had known from the start, as they ran through cloisters together and lay in punts with their friends, that she would not end up with him. That she would have to settle for Anthony or his equivalent. Her tastes were too expensive, her needs nonnegotiable; she needed a workhorse who could be relied upon for forty years or more. She would have to settle for something less than love, something other than excitement. Melanie was captive to her own refusal to compromise. It had made her amusing at first, then boring, and finally insufferable. Mia did not want to talk to her, or to have to explain herself. She tried the first wine—a crisp white Burgundy—instead.

The horse pills were doing their work. Time became elastic. There were agonising longueurs at the table, followed by hours which seemed like minutes. As course followed course, wine followed wine, she divided her attentions between Harry's tales of frustrated business acumen and, latterly, loveless relations and Anthony's audit of his children's schooling and wife's new car. Neither conversation remotely interested her. Better, though, than the interrogation she had feared. Their fascination with her was little more than antiquarian. She was an exhibit from a past life, located and dusted down by Claude as part of the evening's diversions. They were more interested in whether the Hollywood actress had sneaked off to one of the Bracknell's notorious "changing rooms"—the well-appointed little cubicles by the cloakroom, supposedly for guests to change from one outfit into another, but invariably used for earthier purposes. They were more interested in how much each wine would cost in a restaurant (Claude had calculated that they had, thus far, got through two grand's worth of booze a head). They were more interested in themselves. They sang songs to which only the men knew the words.

After the fifth round of brandy—she had reverted to champagne, as had Natasha—the music began and they left their seats to mingle. It was already two o'clock. Claude took her by the hand and led her through the crowd to talk to a client he had spotted across the room. It was darker now. The clusters of people were more fluid, the faces less fixed suddenly, colliding, merging. She felt she was at a masque, a masque held in a mausoleum. All honesty gone, all truth disguised. Complicity and bad feeling at every turn. Her drunkenness made her see things differently now. And as she lost interest in Claude's vacuous business chatter, she turned and watched the dancing, the gargoyles in black tie, the human features which melted in the flashing light and became the faces of birds, pecking greedily. Arms in tailored black or long gloves were wings, wings beating with sudden brutality. The colours of the dance bled into the darkness hanging in the air. She was not safe. This was not a safe place.

She turned back and Claude was gone. How long had she been watching the cavalcade? She was alone on the dance floor now, nobody she recognised close at hand. A young man with lipstick on his cheek, his tie already undone, grabbed her arm and tried to dance with her. She pulled away, heading for the table. She thought she heard someone call her name, but she did not turn round. She wanted only to make it back to the pagoda, to find Claude, or Natasha, or even Anthony, somebody to anchor her in conversation, however disjointed or dull. Like a swimmer caught in a riptide, she struggled against the flow of guests edging noisily towards the fountain and the dance floor. They were as one: a human river of pleasure-seekers heading out to sea.

The table was deserted. She fumbled in her bag for her mobile phone and, without thinking, rang Rob's number. Christ, what was she doing? It was so late. It rang and rang, and then, to her relief and panic, clicked on to Rob's message service. She wanted to say something, but she didn't. She would sound mad. She didn't want him to hear her like this, to guess at her weakness. So why had she called him?

"Mia, my dear." An arm wrapped round her waist and a hand patted the small of her back. It was a few inches away from indecency. Harry Startt was drunk as the lord he would eventually become and had evidently lost Lucy, or been ditched himself in the throng. His lechery was halfhearted. He slumped a little. "On your own? Me, too." She disentangled herself from him. He sat down and poured himself a glass. "Me, too. She's gone off. God knows where. I dread to think. Probably in one of those bloody changing rooms now. Saw her ex. That photographer, Mike, still keeps her up to her eyes in coke. Well, she says it keeps her appetite under control. What appetite? She doesn't eat. She looks like a fucking tuberculosis case." He relit his cigar.

She felt sorry for him. He was not boorish with drink, as she imagined the others were by now. Harry, poor Harry: He cut a sad figure, left behind by his cokehead girlfriend, who was doubtless pleasuring her ex in one of the changing rooms. Even Anthony Wentworth-Crawford did not have to deal with this particular indignity. No, he would be groaning under the full weight of his wife's fury at the moment, as Melanie insisted on leaving and fussed about their transport home. Mia remembered dimly that getting back from the Bracknell was always a nightmare. Once, she had walked. On other occasions, she and her friends had hired a driver for the night. But one thing was for sure: Whatever arrangements Anthony had made, Melanie would find them wanting.

Mia could see that Harry, his polka-dot bow tie stained with red wine, was desperate for her company. He did not want to make a fool of himself on the dance floor, or look for friends elsewhere. He had reached the stage of the night—the morning, actually—when he craved only a shoulder to drink on. Harry would happily down a bottle or two more and rant at her about the injustice of his situation before passing out on the table in an hour or so. She heard him mutter something to himself about "being a fucking committee member" and "what's the point?" and realised that she did not want to hear another word of it. She dared not sit down, for fear that she would not be allowed to stand up again. "Harry," she said, puncturing his reverie. "Harry, have you seen Claude?"

He looked up at her, billowing cigar smoke as he did. "Claude? That—well, no, I won't say it. Claude. I haven't seen him for a while. Snaking around and schmoozing as usual, I bet. I think he went to the changing rooms, too. Fucker. I wouldn't be surprised. Sit down. Mia. Tell me what you've been up to."

"No. I mean, thanks. But I really want to find Claude. I think it's time for me to get going, actually. I'm out of practice."

Harry turned to her with an expression of sudden seriousness. He paused. "Tell me something."

"Sure."

"Is it better where you are?"

"What do you mean?"

He scratched the pale skin of his cheek nervously. "I mean, everyone knows why you left." He waved his hand in a gesture of solidarity and understanding. "Sorry for mentioning it. Terrible, awful thing. Awful. I understand. I'd go and hide in Siberia, if it was me. You know. The same thing. But what I want to know . . . is why you stayed away. Is it because we're so terrible? Or did you find something better? That's what I want to know. Why did you stay wherever you went?"

What could she tell him, this shambles of a man, with his stained tie and his cheating girlfriend? There was nothing to say. Not to someone like Harry. There were things someone like Harry could not know, should not know. Was not entitled to know. She mustered another smile.

"I'm doing all right, Harry. Things are okay for me."

He fidgeted with a cigar cutter. "So are you coming back?" A couple, laughing hysterically, stumbled towards their table, realised their mistake, and retreated. "It seems like everyone is leaving."

"Harry." She put a hand on his shoulder. "I really do need to find Claude. Do you know where he is?"

He patted her hand but did not look up. "I'd try the changing rooms. That's where Lucian went."

At the edge of the dance floor, a space had opened up and a small troupe of Chinese acrobats was spinning in the air, their golden costumes luminous and ornate. Three men with flushed faces had shed their jackets and were trying to mimic the gymnasts' dazzling manoeuvres: One lay on the ground already, stunned and breathing heavily, having landed on his head while performing a blubbery cartwheel. His girlfriend, swathed in electric blue silk, was calling for an ambulance. Mia turned towards the bar and the chill-out room, which was now packed with exhausted guests. As she approached, she could see what looked like a long, loose formation of amber stars in the depths of the room. Some of them floated from side to side, as if part of a fluid constellation. Some went out, only to flare into life again. They were, she realised as she got closer, the glowing tips of joints being passed around the sofas. Stuffed, drunk, and exhausted by the dance, the guests were skinning up as the strains of Moby wafted through their cavernous retreat. They would wait for a second wind and then resume business, some of them dancing till six or seven.

The changing rooms were to one side of this sedated chamber. They lay behind a thick black velvet curtain, guarded by a tall, immaculately dressed doorkeeper. The man did not have the bearing of a bouncer. His white tie was unruffled by the many hours he must have worked already, and his hair, slicked back and dark, was at one with his smooth features and public school cheekbones. Yet he exuded danger. The changing rooms, especially at this late stage of the night, were the Bracknell's sanctum sanctorum. To gain access was difficult—and expensive—enough. Once in, guests expected not to be disturbed. This man's task was to ensure that no such interference occurred. In his eyes was the manic glint of Cerberus.

"Excuse me." Mia had never been into the changing rooms before, but she knew full well how difficult this would be.

"Madam. May I direct you to wherever you are heading?"

"I wondered if you could let me in. I need to speak to someone."

"I am afraid all of the rooms are in use at present. Guests are using them for changing purposes. I am so sorry, madam."

Mia felt herself stagger a little. Horse pills, drink, heels. Damn. "I believe my host is using—he told me he would be in there. Why don't you ask him?"

"Madam, I assure you I have no instructions from any of the guests. Now, perhaps I can arrange to get you a drink from the bar. Or are you in need of transportation home? Our concierge is over there. . . ."

She reached over and put the notes discreetly in his hand, four red bits of paper, which might not be enough but which would certainly secure his attention. "It's Lucian. Dear Lucian. He said I should join them and . . . well, I got lost." She smiled coquettishly. "I must be a little drunk. Silly me. He'll be *so* disappointed. Poor, sweet Lucian. I don't know what I'll tell him. He was very specific. *Very* specific, if you know what I mean."

The white-tied Cerberus looked at her and weighed up his options, as well as the cash in his clenched fist. "Well, madam, I . . . You could try cubicle four." With the flourish of a vaudeville conjuror, he swept the black curtain aside and let her in.

It was bigger inside than she had expected. There were six cubicles in all, three on either side, walled off from one another. At least one was not in use, and she could see from its open door that the partitions were thick, perhaps even soundproofed. In the gloom, there was what looked like a console table with a large vase full of lilies. A low-wattage lamp lit the atrium just enough for her to pick out where she was going. On the first door on her right was a gold numeral. Cubicle four. You could try cubicle four. She turned the handle and walked in.

Her eyes had not yet adjusted properly and the light within the cubicle was even dimmer. But it did not take long for her to establish the main points of the tableau before her. The facing wall of the room was not a wall at all, but a mirror, lined by a velvet banquette. To the side, there was a smaller stool with the same style of upholstery. She could just make out that resting on it was a mahogany tray, on which there were at least three thick lines of white powder and a platinum credit card. There was a large sum of cash, too. On the couch, Tash, oblivious of Mia's arrival, slumped against the mirror, her eyes flickering as if she were barely conscious. The blond waitress Mia had seen Lucian talking to earlier was sitting beside her and kissing her cheek; her hand caressed Tash's face and stroked her long hair. Tash's mouth opened and closed, as if she was murmuring something, words of distress or lustful encouragement. With her other hand, the waitress was unbuttoning her own blouse, her waistcoat already discarded on the floor.

Lucian Carver surveyed all this with approval. He was in profile to Mia, but she could see enough of his face to tell that he was happy with the show so far. He stood with his arms akimbo, his jacket thrust aside to make him look like some overfed lord of the manor inspecting his lands from the crest of a hill. His trousers formed a preposterous little pile around his feet, revealing old-fashioned garters and tartan socks. The position of Lucian's hands also cleared the way for the waiter—the man he had so brutally threatened only a few hours before—whose right arm was now curled around Lucian's torso. The waiter was the only one of the party to have seen Mia's entry, and he stopped whatever it was he was doing to look at her. His expression was blank. She saw something which looked like a leather paddle fall at his feet. But she could not be sure. Lucian turned round sharply and screwed up his eyes to see who had dared to interrupt proceedings. He achieved a state of incandescent fury with the speed of a sports car hitting sixty.

"You! What the fuck are you doing here?"

Not for the first time that evening, Mia had no answer.

"Christ, the impertinence. You shouldn't be here at all," Lucian spat.

"Spoiling our night out. *Our* night. Fucking impostor." He delved deeper, his arousal merging with his rage. "Should have burnt with the rest of your family."

Still she said nothing. The waiter continued to stare, his arm now locked around his patron's shoulder. Tash and the waitress held hands and nuzzled, a wall of drugs insulating them from the intrusion and eruption.

Lucian Carver, trouserless, his capacious buttocks, she could now see, still smarting from the last blow of the paddle, completed his thought. "Typical Irish. They can't even bomb a place properly. Bloody micks. Left one standing, didn't they? Didn't they? Look at you. Pathetic. Now fuck off back wherever you came from."

She turned around and closed the door behind her. Lucian's rant continued as she crept away, the words "bloody Claude" were just audible and then, more quietly, "Yes, dear boy, please do." After the cubicle, the light in the atrium seemed bright again. She walked out briskly, brushing past the gatekeeper, who seemed about to ask her something but then thought better of it. She went to the ladies' and was sick in the sink.

Shall I cry? she asked herself. Shall I slump to the floor here in the loo, at four in the morning, at a ball I should never have come to? No. Not because I'm brave, but because I might never get back up. If I crumple now, who will lift me, cradle me, and take me home? They think this is my home. It isn't. It isn't. I am far from home now.

She turned on the tap and, trying not to gag, cleaned up the sink. Then she splashed water on her face for five full minutes, feeling its gorgeous sting, the shock of cleanliness it brought to her skin and the accumulated toxins of the evening. She dried off and applied the barest amount of makeup so she looked presentable. Five deep breaths and she checked herself in the mirror. Well, not bad. Under the circumstances, not bad at all, actually.

Mia marched out of the ladies' and ran straight into Claude. His face was full of the anxiety which only severe public embarrassment, or its prospect, could prompt in him.

"There you are," he said. "Thank Christ. What have you been doing?"

"Looking for you. You weren't where I looked, though."

"William just told me. The doorman. He told me you'd interrupted Lucian. You bloody fool, Mia. Why did you do that?"

"I was looking for you. Harry thought you might be with Lucian. You weren't, I'm glad to say." She rounded on him. "But perhaps you wish you had been?"

"Now look—"

"No, Claude. You look. That monster you call your friend just subjected me to the nastiest, most vicious attack I have ever experienced in my whole life. And he had the temerity to do so halfway through getting spanked by a waiter. Oh, and by the way, part of the deal seems to be that his wife gets it on with a waitress at the same time. Just thought you should know. Now, if you don't mind, I would like to leave this hellhole and get back to the real world. Thank you for a lovely evening." She headed off towards the cloakroom, foraging in her handbag for her ticket as she did so.

Claude gave chase, catching her up at the counter and, to her surprise, presenting his own ticket. "Mia," he said. "Don't."

She turned to him. She wanted the night to be over, to go home and sleep for a day. She wanted to wake in the early evening, have a long bath, and then go and see—whom? Ringo? Rob? Yes, Rob. He would make her laugh as she told him of the horrors she had been through. At least he would make her laugh.

"Don't what, Claude?"

"I—I'm sorry about Lucian. He's appalling. Listen, let's go now. Come back to my flat. It's only five minutes in a cab. We can have a drink, unwind." She looked at him sceptically. "I—I really want you to. Mia, please."

Could he actually be expecting her to sleep with him? Could he be that crass, or that deluded? No, that was not it. His eyes spoke of a deeper longing. He wanted something; that was clear enough. For him to speak to her like this, to leave the Bracknell so early: Claude needed her in some way she had not guessed. The night was not over for him. And as much as she was filled with contempt for him, and rage at what he had put her through, his behaviour triggered her curiosity. She wanted to know what lay behind all this.

"All right, Claude. All right. I'll come back for one drink. And then I am on my way. Okay?"

He looked at her with relief. He was more drunk than he was letting on, his bloodshot eyes betraying his true state. "Okay, Mia. Thank you."

Outside, the frost had fallen. Once they were clear of the marquee, the walkway, and the car park, the grass crunched underfoot and the wind pricked at their faces. The effect was cleansing, the air of the London night snapping them back from the strange place they had been. Mia and Claude walked in silence to the road, their teeth chattering. They passed parked limousines, Bentleys, and booked taxis, the drivers sleeping at the wheel as they waited for the ball to spew forth its human wreckage in a couple of hours. At the roundabout, they stood for a few minutes and then hailed a cab. Its light was not on, but Claude saw that it was empty. The driver was on his way home, but he happily accepted a twenty-pound tip up front to take them across the river to Claude's flat in Pimlico.

A quarter of an hour later, she was slumped on the long white sofa that dominated his drawing room. The flat was larger than she remembered. She remarked upon this as he opened a bottle of malt and poured two hefty drinks. No, he murmured. He had bought the next-door flat two years ago and knocked the wall down. There was more room for his books, his gym equipment, his computer stuff, his plasma screen, his toys. He had wall space for the art in which he had invested. The kitchen was new. Space and light everywhere. That was the idea. No frills, no fussiness. Anything not to be cramped. Claude fell into the armchair opposite her. He reached over the glass table in front of him and grabbed a remote control on a stack of books about chic hotels and modern-art museums: the second act of *Don Giovanni* filled the room. He turned the volume down a little and emptied his glass. At the end of such a night, Claude ought to have been exuberant, tiggerish. But she had never seen him so subdued.

"You hated it, didn't you?"

"What, the Bracknell? I knew what to expect."

"You haven't answered my question. I'm sorry it was so awful for you."

"Claude . . . I—I wish I could say that it was easy for me. Leave aside the revolting Lucian for a moment. I haven't seen these people for years. I used to see them all the time. They don't know what to make of me. I think some of them think I'm mad. The others think I'm cured and I'm coming back. Or don't care either way. It's very hard to explain to them what's happened to me. I'm not sure I can really explain it myself."

"Don't worry about Lucian." Claude rubbed his eyes. "He's out of control. I should have warned you about his . . . tastes. I honestly didn't think he'd be damn fool enough to get up to any funny business tonight. The fact is, it's all going to catch up with him pretty soon. One of the papers has a reporter on him full-time, looking to catch him out. Can you imagine if you'd had a camera in there? He'd be finished."

The face of Councillor Phil Roberts flashed into Mia's mind. She smirked involuntarily. Yes, Lucian would certainly have been finished. She was good at that sort of thing.

"Anyway, I'm sorry he was beastly to you."

"Forget about it. I'm cheered up by what you say. I look forward to reading about his downfall."

Claude filled their glasses. "Don't worry, you will. They'll destroy him: 'The Carver Carved,' it'll say. I just hope it's after he sells the company, so Tash gets a reasonable bit of cash when it all goes pear-shaped."

"She was out of it. Poor Tash."

"Yeah. Poor Tash."

They sat in silence for a while. He was deep in thought, she could tell, his physical exhaustion vying with the need to speak. He rested his chin in his cupped hand and looked out of the bay window at the darkness.

"Come on, Claude. What is it?"

"What do you mean?"

"Look, it's gone five. I said I'd come back. I can see you've got something on your mind. I'm actually quite relieved, to be honest. Because if you have, it means that I wasn't just your party turn for the night. Maybe you dragged me all this way to say something important to me. I hope so."

"God, is that what you thought? That I'd dragged you back after all this time just for a laugh?" He shook his head. "Were we really so shallow when you used to hang out with us?"

She laughed. "Harry asked me the same thing. I couldn't really answer him. Don't forget, I was part of it once: the Bracknell, Tash, you, even Lucian. It was my life for years. I have no right to judge anybody. I'm just not part of it anymore."

"I know. Of course you aren't. But you must believe me when I say that this was not a joke or a setup. I . . . . What I mean to say is that I've been thinking about this for a very long time, and now you're here, and it's late and I'm drunk. I don't really know what to say or even if I should say it at all."

"Try me. Just try me, Claude. You've got me this far, after all. You found me. You got me into a designer dress for the first time in years. You got me to see Lucian Carver engaged in sexual congress. So what harm could it do to tell me what this is all about?" She finished her drink, the angry whisky too much for her taste but still welcome in her belly as it spread its relaxing warmth.

Claude put his hand to his forehead as if he had just thought of something. She realised that he was frightened. He looked over her head at the abstract painting, a riot of pastel cubes, hanging on the wall behind her.

"I wish it was easy. I've wanted to talk to you for years, really. Well, since it happened. But I didn't. And the anniversary . . . well, each year it got harder not to say something. And so I decided that this time I would find you, would talk to you. And so I did."

"What anniversary?"

"The fire. The bomb." She saw his eyes were full of sudden tears. "The end of everything."

"What do you mean, 'the end of everything'?"

Moving now with the solemnity of a ghost, Claude stood up and went down the corridor. He was gone for longer than made sense, and she wondered if he had passed out on his bed. When he came back, he was clasping a silver frame to his chest, shuffling towards her. He gave it to her and fell into his seat again, shattered by the effort of what he had just done.

The picture in the frame was a black-and-white photograph. It showed Claude and her brother on holiday—in Italy, she thought. Yes, she remembered them going. Six, seven years ago, maybe more. A villa party. They were laughing. Ben, tanned and handsome, was wearing a linen shirt and jeans, Claude a T-shirt and chinos. Behind them was a landscape of heartbreaking beauty: the rise and fall of hills, spotted with olive trees and distant vines. The shadows of midafternoon fell on the scene like a gentle blanket. She could almost smell the perfumes of the season, the fruits and flora, and sense the light-headedness of the heat. The picture spoke of uncomplicated happiness: a long lunch, lying by the pool, glasses of ripe local wine, slow evenings in a piazza. It reminded her of all that was good about Ben, a memory which confronted her with a moment of abject misery. She fought it off and looked at Claude. And then she realised from his face and the devastation etched into it what she should have guessed years before: something so obvious, so close at hand, she had never thought of it. Something that had never crossed her mind in a thousand phone calls with her brother, in all those careless conversations with Claude, in a million dreams of the world she had lost.

"Claude. Claude. I'm so sorry. I had no idea."

"It's not what you think. It wasn't like that. Nothing . . . Nothing ever . . . I just miss him. Each day. I miss him."

She reached out and took his hand. "I know. So do I. So do I."

He wrenched his hand away and stood up. Before she guessed what he might do, he had grabbed the picture and, with a low animal howl of despair, hurled it across the room, where it hit the marble surface of a side table, shattering in a spray of fragments. There it was: on the floor of his flat, years of pent-up fury and guilt. Claude's porcelain heart broken into a hundred pieces, the mask of nonchalance fallen forever.

She ran over to him and clutched his wrists, fearing he would lose control completely. "Claude. Claude. For fuck's sake. Now look at me, Claude. It's late. It's late. And you are drunk. Come on now. Sit down with me. We'll talk about it."

He was trembling as he joined her on the sofa. She had never seen Claude in such a state; indeed, the personality she had known so well was founded on a determination never to be so reduced. The fact that he was capable of such a lapse was more shocking than the outburst itself. In her arms, he seemed smaller than she could ever remember, his collar drenched in sweat, his hands clammy and limp.

"I'm sorry," he said after a while. She poured him another large whisky, which he drank in one go.

"That's all right. Are you feeling better? I mean, do you want to talk?" She looked at him, this time with hard eyes. "I think you do. I think it's time." He gathered himself with an effort that he could not conceal. All this, she could now see, had been dragged from the deepest recesses of his heart: the visits to the Boltons, to Henty, to Mile End, and now the Bracknell. All had been agonising preparation for this private moment, alone with Mia, in his flat, in the dead of night. He had been steeling himself for this for years. She could see that even now he was not sure if he was ready.

When he spoke, it was with a distant voice. "The thing is . . . The thing is . . . I think it was all my fault. All my fault. I knew from the moment I heard. I should never have introduced him to those people."

He was rambling now. Dangerously so. She did not like the terrain towards which he was dragging his damaged soul. "Don't be absurd, Claude. What are you talking about? You lost a friend; I lost a brother. I lost a lot more than a brother. You know what happened. It happened, and there's nothing either of us can do about it. Don't insult my family's memory by indulging yourself. Don't you dare, Claude."

He stood up again, then went and sat down opposite her. "What happened. Ah, yes. Listen to me, Mia. Or rather—no, let me ask you a question, and I want you to answer honestly. Do you really believe that crap about Ronny Campbell and Ulster and the breakaway Provos? I mean, come on. Do you really believe that *for a single second*?"

"Of course I do."

"Do you? I don't. Not for a minute. A bomb goes off, kills five people. Nobody knows why. It's inexplicable. Then the press find out that the next-door neighbour is political. He's got a history. He's a big Loyalist, lots of enemies on the Republican side. So the reporters start making enquiries in Northern Ireland. And—guess what?—one of the splinter groups jumps up and says, 'It was us!' And everyone heaves a sigh of relief. Case closed."

"Well, what's so mad about that?"

"I don't buy it. Never did. Come on, think as you used to do, not as you do now. Those Mickey Mouse splinter groups don't do stuff like that—mainland stuff. I don't believe it. Of course, they claimed responsibility for it, given the chance. Got them a few days' headlines for free, didn't it? But it was all too neat, all too quick. Can't you see?"

"I don't see why. Don't get confused, Claude. None of us could bear the fact that it was all a big fuckup. All for nothing. That was the worst. This is my family, remember. They all died for *nothing*. They all died because of that scumbag Campbell and his loud mouth." She looked away, desperate not to cry hot tears of rage. "It was just a fucking *mistake.*"

"Was it? I wish. Why are you so sure that nobody wanted to kill someone in your family? I mean, why are you so sure that it wasn't meant to be an attack on Ben's house after all?"

She stood up. "I'm leaving."

"Sit down." The tone of command had returned to his voice. Embarked on his perilous course, he had recovered his poise. To her surprise, her reflex was to obey.

"What are you talking about?"

"The worst thing in the world is what I'm talking about."

"Talk sense, Claude. I won't let you jerk off over this. No riddles."

"Listen, Mia. This is hard stuff for you to hear. But listen anyway. Did you ever ask Ben what he did?"

She shifted in her seat. "Yes. Well, I mean, I asked him in general terms."

"And what did he say?"

"Well, you know what he was like."

"I do. I did. That's why I'm asking you."

"He always said he was doing financial services. That he had learned a lot in the City but that he wanted to get away from Dad's shadow. He wanted to branch out, and the firm let him do that. It made sense at the time."

"Yes. But what did the firm do? What do you think it did?"

She let her hands fall to her lap. "I don't know."

"That's what I thought. Well, I know. I know, because Ben used to tell me what he was up to. You see, your brother was smart, smarter maybe than you ever realised. I think your dad knew how clever Ben was and I think it frightened him a little. I think Jeremy knew that Ben was reckless. Which he certainly was."

Bad things, Beatrice. She remembered her father's warning to his mistress, relayed to her years afterwards, when both he and his son were dead. Bad things.

"You see, Ben did plenty of legit work. Of course he did. But he had also spotted something. Which is that what rich people want is security. Poor people think they do, but rich people really want it. They want to be safe. They understand that being rich changes everything. That you can't go back. That it's better to die than go back. And the trouble is that more rich people than you can possibly imagine have got rich doing things they'd rather not talk about."

"So what?"

"So that's where Ben came in. Oh, he did lots of normal stuff, too. But his real talent was cleaning people's money for them. Making things tidy."

"What? Money laundering? You're joking."

"No, it was more sophisticated than that, really. *Laundering* doesn't do justice to it. I mean, he was brilliant. He moved money around the world, from account to account, from country to country. He was dazzling. I guess he'd have been found out in the end, but it was amazing while it lasted. I don't even pretend to understand how he was doing it, not the technicalities anyway. And none of his clients did, either. They were just happy with the results. So happy that they paid his chunky commissions with a smile."

" 'Chunky commissions'? He wasn't that rich, was he?"

"The truth is, even I don't know. Much, much richer than you think, that's for sure. I know most of it was hidden away in his electronic maze. He wanted to get out in a few years, retire completely." Claude's face fell. "That was the plan anyway. A place in London. A place in Italy."

"You sound like you knew a lot about it."

"I did." His voice was level now, the voice of the dead. "And I introduced him to a lot of his clients. Lots of them. You think you were the first to go east? I was there years ago, Mia. I used to take Ben to all my haunts late at night. Bow, Stepney, even Leytonstone sometimes. There were people there with lots of money. Lots and lots of money. They'd cleaned up over the years in the rackets, extortion, drugs, robbery, the lot. Big firms with more money than they knew what to do with. And they wanted the cash cleaned. You see, things were changing. They wanted out. They didn't want to go to Spain anymore. They just wanted peace and quiet. So they needed Ben. And, of course, once they met him, they liked him."

"You must be mad. Ben doing dirty work for East End villains?"

"Oh, not exclusively. He dealt with everyone. Arabs, Russians, all sorts of people. He was flying to Germany, Spain, everywhere. That was why he did so well. And, naturally, he didn't deal with many people directly. There was always a middleman."

" 'A middleman'?"

"Someone to do the deal. A buffer. I doubt Ben knew who half of his real clients were round there. But it didn't matter. He was making it big, fast."

"So what? Even if all of this is true, so what?"

Claude leant over. He shook his head. "Like I said, your brother was reckless. He was greedy. The one thing I do know—the thing that keeps me awake at night and makes me drink too much the rest of the time— is that he had started skimming off the top."

The silence between them was deep and nasty. " 'Skimming off the top'? What, taking more than his percentage?"

"Yes. Exactly that. He thought the hard boys up east were just thugs. The work was so complicated that he thought they wouldn't spot it. I didn't realise what he was up to till it was too late. The truth is, I didn't know how much business he was doing with these people. One minute, we were drinking afters in these back-room places in Dalston, Hackney, wherever, and the next, Ben was up to his eyes in it. But he underestimated them, how clever they were, and how vicious they could be. I mean, these guys may wear camel hair coats. But they're no fools. I warned him so often not to be stupid. I said there were no second chances in that world, only punishments. And he always said he would take care. But I knew he was lying. He loved secrets, did Ben. In that respect, he wasn't like you at all. He couldn't keep himself out of trouble. And you know what? It finally caught him up with him that night. I think it killed him, and your family." He caught her eye: There, it was said. At last, at last. The poison extruded.

Mia stood up, walked over to Claude, and slapped him hard in the face. He looked up at her and flinched, too late, as she slapped him again, harder. She was white with anger, ready to hit him again, this time with the first weapon that came to hand. She was ready to kill him.

"Tell me." She said no more. He blinked, unsure how to answer her. "Tell me."

"What?" She raised her hand again. "Stop it!"

"Tell me."

"You don't want to know."

"Tell me." She picked up a corkscrew from the table and held it before his right eye. She was no match for him physically, a foot shorter, at least five stone lighter. Yet he was not sure that he would win if he took her on. The spike of the corkscrew hovered before his face, her knuckles a motley red and white as they tightened around it. Her will was stronger than his.

"All right. All right." He pushed her away. "Fucking madwoman."

She stepped away from him, waiting. The corkscrew was still in her hands. In any other circumstances, it would have looked ridiculous, a kitchen tool clutched to a black evening gown. But in Mia's hands, he realised, it was no such thing. He had brought her to the edge. She would not be denied.

Claude let out a long sigh of surrender. Years of indecision, guilt, and self-hatred were crammed into a single second. He peered up at her. "All I know is what I blame myself for. The name of the middleman was Micky Hazel. At least that was the name of the guy I introduced Ben to.

He ran a car showroom in Stratford. But that was just a front. He dealt with everyone. He was the man. Everyone knew that. That's all I know." He let his head rest on a cushion. The music, unnoticed by either of them for so long, was swelling to a conclusion as the statue called out to Don Giovanni, summoning him to hell. Calling the dissolute to account. *"Pentiti, scellerato!"*: "Repent, you scoundrel!"

"That's all I know. And believe me, it's enough." Claude closed his eyes. Sleep was creeping through his limbs at last, claiming him, demanding an end to his long resistance. His voice fell to a whisper. "You don't know what you're getting yourself into. Don't go near these people, Mia. Don't go near. I'm telling you. All you need to know is what I've told you. You know the truth now. Maybe I should have told you years ago. Maybe not. But now you know. Why it happened, and why we're both so fucked up. And whatever you do now, you can't punish anyone more than I've punished myself. You can't. It's my fault. Isn't that enough?" His voice trailed off. "Oh Christ. Ben."

As Claude spoke to himself, Mia collected her belongings. She would not say good-bye. Not now. Would she ever see Claude again? Probably not. But she felt no need to say anything at all to him. All those years, knowing that about her brother. In this room, he had squirrelled away this dirty secret, allowing her to believe a convenient lie which had suited everybody, a fiction to smooth out the ragged edges of tragedy. Here in the expensive playroom he pretended was a home, Claude had wondered what to do with the knowledge that he had introduced Ben to smiling killers, hard men who had waded waist-deep through blood and shit to make their money, and would, of course, slaughter anyone who tried to take it away from them—without thought, without compunction. They would punish a stupid young man full of greed with a ball of fire that would rip him from history. It would be as though he had never existed. And all this Claude had known, sitting on his chair, rocking in the night, mourning the friend he had loved and to whose door he had ushered death. He deserved the pain he felt.

Outside in the street, she waited five minutes—or was it longer?—before a cab glided towards her. This time, the driver was pleased with the fare. He was on his way back to his home in the Isle of Dogs, and Brick Lane was more or less on his way. He tried to engage her in banter about a football match, then a soap opera, and then the unplanned pregnancy of a female film star, news which was, apparently, all over the morning papers. She did not say a word, and wished she had the energy to tell him to shut up. Instead, she stared out of the window as the car sped past Tate Britain, into Parliament Square, up the Embankment. The river, shimmering with the lights of the bridges and the penthouses, with the flickering memories of the centuries, drew her home. Trees, stone, water merged into one: The elements of ancient times rose up again, mingled, and dragged her with them. The water took her all the way to Tower Bridge, where the cab turned left, snaking through Brick Lane to drop her at her doorstep. She paid the driver and gave him a five-pound tip.

It was not yet light and the streetlamps on her road were still at full strength. She could see her breath billowing in the air. It was as cold as she had feared, pitilessly so. She needed to get inside, drink tea, calm herself for the long sleep she required before she could begin to think about what to do with the burden Claude had passed on to her. Yes, she needed sleep.

As she started to walk down the stairs to her flat, she saw something piled at the bottom of the flight by the door. A funny little mound of rags, plastic bags, and what looked like an old boot. It was only on the bottom step that she realised it was the frozen, lifeless body of Tommy Bonkers.

Chapter TEN

IT TOOK HER SEVERAL minutes to drag the body into her flat. Curled and rigid, Tommy was peculiarly difficult to manoeuvre over the doorstep and then through the little hallway in which her coats and bags hung. He's light even for a small man, she thought as she strained to edge his slight frame across the fur of the doormat: seven stone, seven and a half at most. Through the soaked cloth of his jacket, she could feel only his shirt and bone. And yet the fetal position into which his body had wound itself—grimly comic in its unyielding form—made an obstacle course of the few feet which separated her porch from the carpet of her sitting room. By the time she had dropped the cadaver to the floor, she was sweating and exhausted.

Mia turned on the light and looked up at the clock on the fireplace. It was 6:30. Was it really only twelve hours since she had met Claude at the Ritz for a drink to warm them up for the ball? In the intervening time, she had stumbled upon an orgy involving a television celebrity. She had discovered that her dead brother had been a high-tech money launderer, and that his greed had killed him and the rest of her family.

And now she had the corpse of a lunatic vagrant in her living room. There were better ways of spending a night.

Now she would have to call the police and spend the morning explaining how the mortal remains of Tommy Bonkers—No, Officer, I don't know his real name—had ended up outside her door. Hardly suspicious circumstances, of course. But that wouldn't matter. It would take hours, as the ambulance was called, and the body covered, and the formalities concluded. For the second time in her life, she would make tea for policemen and talk about death. Yes, Miss, these things happen. We find it quite often. These kind of drifters, it's very sad—they attach themselves in their minds to someone, possibly someone who's never met them, and when the moment comes, they try to find that person. Very distressing for you, Miss, I'm sure. Thanks, Miss, three sugars. That's what they would say. Did she feel sorry for poor departed Tommy? No. She didn't have any space left in her heart for that. Tommy had chosen the wrong night to die on her. Sorry, Tommy.

Suddenly, a long susurration filled the room. It was like the call of a tiny bird, a shrill rattle, piercing and plaintive. Then it stopped. She gasped. The silence that had enveloped her since the taxi dropped her off was deep, alien to London even at this time of morning. It was as if a part of the city had died, too. Now a noise from the netherworld had interrupted that silence, filling her with dread and confusion. But no, she quickly realised, that was wrong: There was no need for dread. No need at all. The noise was coming from Tommy's lips, quivering into half-life as the battered tramp dithered in the no-man's-land which lay before the valley of death. The tip of his tongue, blue and repulsive, issued from his mouth. He was still, by some quirk of fortune, alive.

He coughed, billowing foul air into the room. She wanted to retch, but she knew that she must act fast. The easiest thing to do would be to call an ambulance. Within minutes, sirens would wail outside her door, and calm men in green jumpsuits would perform the art of resuscitation and remove this moribund scarecrow from her home. It could all be over in half an hour. She would be in bed by 7:30. Thank you, Tommy. If you'd died, that would have been the whole morning gone. This was just a minor inconvenience by comparison.

She reached for the phone; then something within her, something instinctive and dutiful, counselled caution. She looked at Tommy, a bag of bones in a dead man's suit, wheezing at the margins of life, still unconscious, and likely to hallucinate from drink or its withdrawal if he did indeed regain consciousness. She had seen this man, mute and maddened, most days of her life for the past three years. He had smiled at her, signalled to her, clanked past her with his bags of bottles on the slow bridleway to death. Had he reached his terminus? Maybe. One thing was sure: If she sent him to hospital now, he would be dead in days. There was no way that Tommy Bonkers would submit to the care of an institution, however benign; no way he could, really. She did not know him, but she knew enough of him to guess that what made him carry on breathing each day was the knowledge that he was not imprisoned, that he could walk from green to green, from corner shop to corner shop, from hovel to hovel, a trail of bottles in his wake, and nobody would try to stop him. If they put Tommy in hospital, his last act would be to escape. They would find him in the morning, as she had, outside the driveway, stiff and smiling. This time, death would not be cheated.

On the sideboard was a Spanish fruit bowl which Henty had given her after the nanny's first holiday abroad—a trip suggested and paid for by Jeremy when he discovered that she had never been farther south than Plymouth. In the bowl, Mia kept a strange mix of junk and essential items. There were old pens, keys that would never turn a lock again, a tube of glue, a roll of undeveloped film, and some antiseptic cream. There was also a card with a name and number on it: Dr. Robert Armitage. Uncle Gus had given her this when she had moved into the flat. Robert Armitage, he explained, was a first-rate doctor, as well as an old friend of his, who happened to have a private practise in the area.

Most of his calls were made during the day, his patients overwhelmingly middle-aged men of the City with heart conditions, slipped disks, and prostate trouble. But he would see Mia anytime, day or night. Gus had fixed that. The bill would go straight to the trust, without details of the treatment. Gus guessed she would want to find a local doctor, and that was fine. But if she needed something a bit more urgent, then Robert Armitage was her man.

Mia had taken this to mean that Robert Armitage was a high-class quack, who could sort out any little needs she might have, quickly and discreetly. She had never liked Gus much and liked him still less after the episode with Beatrice, when he had put his misplaced devotion to his dead brother before his responsibility to his living niece. He had, to Mia's disgust, connived in Beatrice's manic surveillance out of some ridiculous sense of fraternal duty: as if what Jeremy had wanted was for his bereaved daughter to suffer even more distress. Still, she had kept the card. And now she found herself dialling the handwritten number on the back, to wake Robert Armitage at home and summon him to a part of the East End which she doubted he visited very often. He answered the phone with a speed peculiar to his profession. Befuddled with sleep, he asked her first what time it was. She told him, and announced herself as Gus Taylor's niece. She heard the rattle of spectacles being put on, and the stirring of Mrs. Armitage beside him. Ah yes, he remembered. Miranda, was it? No, Mia, of course. Was she in need of treatment? Where was she? She explained that she was fine but that . . . a friend, yes, a friend of hers had fallen sick and needed urgent help. Could he come? He said he would be there in an hour, if it could wait that long.

She sat down and realised that she was still wearing the Jimmy Choos. This made her laugh as she slumped back. She was beyond exhaustion, probably on the verge of hysteria. But if she stopped now, she would find it hard to start again. The cushions of the sofa welcomed her, soothed her body, told her to lift her tired legs up and sleep awhile. She closed her eyes and felt fatigue crash down upon her. She would sleep,

sleep for an hour. But as her senses begged one by one to be excused from active duty—sight, touch, hearing, taste—she found herself overpowered by a smell. A smell of criminal degradation, utter horror. It was the first time she had noticed it, and it was enough to snap her back from limbo into a state of blinking anxiety. She looked down at Tommy and realised that, dead or alive, he stank more than she had believed it was possible for an object of any kind to stink. As she focussed on it, she retched again. This would not be easy.

What day of the week was it? Saturday. Yes, Saturday. The day between death and resurrection. Well, Tommy smelt of death. His chest moved gently up and down and his mouth still trembled. But his body reeked of decomposing flesh, as if its organs and juices did not believe that reprieve had been granted, as if its very fibre was preparing to melt wetly into the ground, to follow the last instruction—the self-destruct programme—imprinted in its genes. Tommy's body would have to be persuaded of its error, scrubbed and scrubbed until the ghastly odour was at bay. This was a chore she could have done without at the best of times. But she had no choice.

She went into the kitchen and fetched two black bin liners, half a dozen J Cloths, and a big sponge. Then she dug out from her wardrobe the largest T-shirt and sweatpants she could find. She took these into the bathroom and turned on the taps. Steam rose from the bath as piping hot water filled the tub. She squeezed in half a bottle of bath gel, until, after a few minutes, a mountain of bubbles rose up beside her, a sight of comforting domesticity after a night of unhinged drama. She tested it with her hand, wished she could climb in it herself, and went back to get Tommy.

His body was no longer frozen and, with great effort, she was able to lift him up, holding him to her breast. His limbs hung from her arms; his face showed no reaction. She felt herself grimacing even as she breathed carefully through her mouth, desperate to avoid vomiting for the second time in twelve hours. What little hair Tommy had hung lank from his forehead; his skin was scorched, as if sunburn and frostbite had colluded to do their worst. They turned the corner into the bathroom, Mia trying hard not to hit his head against the door frame. His boots dragged against the ground as she struggled not to collapse.

She caught sight of herself in the mirror. There she was: odd little Mia, cradling a half-dead tramp. What was she doing? Whatever next? She wore a thousand-pound evening gown, smeared already with Tommy's dirt. Her expensive haircut was a distant memory. In her arms, a dying man, a vagrant who could not speak and was known only by his nickname, a man upon whose unmarked grave no tears and much rain would soon fall. In the nimbus of steam which encircled the room, with Tommy in her arms, she looked like a grotesque pietà, her face twisted not by grief, but something closer to earth. Oh God, Tommy, she thought. Don't shamble into my crowded life. Please: Let it not be for my sins that you suffer.

At last, she dropped to her knees and dumped him on the bathroom floor. She slumped, so tired that she longed to weep, but she knew she could not. She started, instead, to undress the foul creature who lay before her. Each item of clothing seemed more soaked than the next. A brown suit jacket peeled off his back and ripped as she pulled it from his elbows; the lining had long gone. There were a couple of leaves inside one of the pockets. His shirt and vest were wet with sweat. Next, she pulled off his boots, remembering still to breathe through her mouth, doing so rhythmically to a count, so that no air could, accidentally and fatally, invade her nostrils. As she worked, she put the clothes into the bin liners, persuading herself that an orderly approach would mitigate the disgust which still overwhelmed her. Finally, she pulled off Tommy's trousers and pants, which were full of shit. Jesus Christ. No wonder he stinks. She put her hand to her mouth and closed her eyes. No turning back now. All or nothing. She jammed the last clothes into the bag and cleaned up the worst of his mess with one of the J Cloths, then another, then another. Then, as she had planned, she tied the drawstrings of the bags tight and ran—faster than she would have thought herself capable—barefoot and without her coat out onto the street, heaving them in the dumpster. She could not bear to see the bags a second longer, let alone have them in the same room. That much she insisted upon.

Back in the bathroom, the emaciated body of Tommy Bonkers lay naked on the floor. His breathing was now deep, and the rasping from his chest more even. But he seemed no closer to consciousness. She hauled him up once more and edged him into the bath. The sudden shock of the hot water caused him to exhale soundlessly and his skin to flush. She took the sponge and began to wash him. Within seconds, she could see caked filth rising to the surface of the water, which had already turned a shade of grey, Tommy's years of grime overwhelming the innocent white of the bubbles. She continued to sluice water over him as his body adjusted to an experience long forgotten and crusted dirt was shed like a skin, the geological layers of Tommy's life on the road dissolved by a few suds. She kept the water hot. After half an hour, her work was complete, or as complete as it needed to be. She pulled him out, his skin soft and pink. She had put an old man into the bath. Now she took out an infant with a straggly beard. She laid him on a towel and patted him dry with another. Then, at last, she sat behind him and, leaning him forward, pulled the T-shirt over his head. It was, she noticed for the first time, a souvenir from her trip to New York, and she had never worn it. The questing arm of the Statue of Liberty looked ridiculous on Tommy. This kept her going as she yanked the sweatpants onto him and then dragged him by the armpits back into the living room and onto the sofa. She threw a blanket over him and then collapsed on her armchair.

Mia fell into a deep sleep for what could only have been a few minutes. As a blazing bird circled over her head, its eyes amber points in the night, its talons poised for the kill, as a troupe of acrobats danced in attendance to her death and a thousand dangerous smiles glinted in the night, there was a knock at the door. She leapt up and opened it. There in his heavy herringbone coat and trilby, carrying a large leather bag, was

Dr. Robert Armitage. He was a more impressive figure than she had expected: tall, overweight but carrying it well, a dark moustache and glasses adding to the impression of professional calm. Less than an hour ago, Dr. Armitage had been snoring beside Mrs. Armitage in his house—in Islington, he revealed—dreaming, no doubt, of their next trip to Saint Lucia or the Napa Valley or Bayreuth (Dr. Armitage looked like a man who could tell you a thing or two about wine, or opera, or both). He smiled, shook her hand, and asked if he might come in.

She mustered what politeness she could. "Thank you for making a call at this unearthly hour, Doctor. I'm extremely sorry."

"Not at all. Not at all. Your uncle told me that you were moving into the area and that you might call me in an emergency. That was a few years back, mind you. Happy to help out. How the devil is old Gus?"

Old Gus. Oh God. If there was a Pisces Club at the hospital where they had trained together, her uncle and Armitage had definitely been members of it. "Uncle Gus? Oh, fine. You know, we don't see each other very often. I don't get out as much as I used to."

Dr. Armitage looked at her gown and laughed as he took off his coat. "Well, you look like you got out last night. Dare I ask if you were at the Bracknell?"

"I was. Yes."

"Well, good for you. I haven't been to a Bracknell for—oh, thirty years. My daughter went last year, though. She adored it, of course."

"Of course."

"So. What seems to be the trouble?"

Tommy, she noticed, was now barely visible beneath the blanket she had flung over him. Only a wisp of hair, newly washed and sprouting proudly from his head, gave away his presence. Dr. Armitage was surprised to discover that there was, indeed, a third human being in the room. He pulled aside the blanket and sighed, shaking his head. He put a hand on Tommy's forehead and then leant over to hear his breathing. He returned with a stethoscope and a thermometer, taking his new patient's pulse, examining his chest, and listening, listening, listening. Mia could tell that he did not like what he could hear.

As much as she wanted to dislike Dr. Armitage, she found the examination captivating to watch. Seconds after paying homage to "old Gus" and the marvels of the Bracknell, he was enacting the rituals of his profession, its tiny miracles and silent practices. As he tried to understand what was wrong with Tommy, his personality subsided and his mind became a vessel only for his skills. His brow furrowed with thought. Hands, eyes, ears, instruments—all were deployed to discover what had driven this drunken scrap of a man to the point of death. Reactions were tested, glands examined. His eyes narrowed and, aiming a penlight at Tommy's face, he lifted the tramp's eyelids and looked deeply within. Then he stood up again, his investigations at an end. He clasped his hands together.

"Miss Taylor."

"Mia. Would you like some tea, Doctor?"

"Mia. Yes, thank you. Darjeeling, if you have it. White, no sugar. Mia, I'm afraid that this man is in a terrible state. He has bronchial pneumonia, for starters. There is evidence of jaundice. I dread to think what condition his liver and kidneys are in. He is very ill. You say you found him outside?"

She nodded.

"My guess is that if you had gone away for the weekend, he would have been dead by this evening, assuming nobody had found him. That's just a guess. But in this weather, a man in his state, pouring booze into his system and maybe other things, too, with no proper diet to speak of . . . Really, it's a miracle that . . ."

"Tommy."

"That Tommy is alive at all. He must be moved to hospital without delay."

Mia made Dr. Armitage his tea. She sat down and explained her dilemma. The man was mute, possibly deranged. If he was moved to a hospital, he would run away and would probably not last the night. The doctor sipped his tea and frowned. She explained why she had called him. She was frank. This impressed Dr. Armitage, who was evidently used to frank men in vast offices speaking frankly to him. She had a need, though not the kind Uncle Gus would have predicted. The question was whether the doctor could help her. She would take responsibility for Tommy for the next few days. She would make sure he ate and slept and took whatever medication Dr. Armitage prescribed. She would prevent him from drinking, or at least she would try. Then, she proposed, Dr. Armitage should return—say on Wednesday?—and they would review the situation. In the meantime, she would keep him posted on the telephone. If Tommy's temperature did not drop, or the infection did not start to clear up, she would of course alert him immediately.

"You're taking a risk, you know? And so am I."

"I am aware of that, Doctor. But I know what I'm talking about with this fellow. Believe me, it's the only way."

"Well, I can't say I'm a hundred percent happy. This man needs a hospital and then, I imagine, a proper programme of institutional care. But I hear what you say. So I'm prepared to give things a try, with all those provisos."

She thanked him, but he brushed aside her gratitude, as if to say that such petty deals were what made him the kind of doctor he was, and were the reason that Uncle Gus had given her his card in the first place. He gave Tommy two injections, without telling her what they were. He wrote out four prescriptions and left detailed instructions on how to administer them. He also scribbled some basic advice about Tommy's diet and liquid intake over the next few days. Then he shook her hand and left. As she watched him scaling the steps to the pavement, she wondered how much Dr. Armitage would sting the trust to cover this little excursion. Doubtless he would tell Mrs. Armitage exactly how much as he sat down to a cooked breakfast in his well-appointed Islington kitchen and reminded his irritated wife that, for all their inconvenience, such calls were what filled the cellar and enabled the two of them to fly business class.

Mia read the instructions and forced some water between Tommy's parched lips. The prescriptions would have to wait till the afternoon. She walked into her bedroom and fell onto the bed, asleep before her head hit the duvet. The bird was back above her, although she knew she was lying facedown. Had the world turned on its axis to confront her? The eyes and the beak were not far away now, swooping from constellation to constellation in readiness for attack. She was the bird's prey, staked out in the desert, helpless against its screaming dive. Claude and Ben walked over to where she lay. "Oh, Mi," said her brother. "I'm sorry. I made a mess, didn't I? Claude thinks it was his fault, really. What do you think? You should never have left the picnic. Then we could have talked about it." Claude whispered into his ear and shook his head. They vanished. Lucian Carver drove up in a secondhand car and asked her directions to Micky Hazel's showroom. There was somebody in the passenger seat she thought she recognised, somebody with something important to tell her. But she could not hear. Lucian could hear, and he drove away immediately, trailing dust and a line of white powder behind him. There was definitely somebody else in the car, some secret she was not yet permitted to hear. The bird, its eyes the colour of hate, hovered and prepared for its final swoop.

It was five o'clock in the afternoon before she stirred. Her hangover was prodigious and inclined her to think that she had imagined the entire night. She took off the ball gown at last and wrapped herself in a towel. There was half a bottle of tepid Evian by her bed, and she drank it in one go. Aspirin? Where were the fucking aspirin? She shuffled into the sitting room on her way to the bathroom and saw that Tommy Bonkers was still lying comatose on her sofa. So that much, at least, had not been a dream. Which probably meant the rest had been real, too. She went into the bathroom, locked the door, and lay in the bath for an hour. Her phone rang a couple of times while she was lying in the tub, but it did not occur to her to get out. She needed to clamber back to the world at her own pace, blinking and nursing her headache. She had run out of fucking aspirin.

The man at Banerjee Late Night Chemist's was alarmed by the scale of her purchase. "Bloody hell. All this for you?" He held up the prescriptions like a hand of cards.

She could not face a conversation. "No. Only the aspirin." Please give me aspirin. No, make it the strongest aspirin in the world.

"Well, make sure it is only the aspirin. Some of these fuckers wouldn't mix at all well with painkillers. No." The pharmacist shook his head vigorously, as if his shop were the daily venue of premature deaths, as customers recklessly took painkillers together with—well, with one or another of these fuckers. She nodded feebly to let him know she had got the message.

On the street, it was already as dark as it had been when she had found Tommy. She pulled her fleece tightly around her, glad of the jumper she was wearing underneath, the thick combats, and the beloved trainers. She was returning to a cocoon of unexpected duty, unsure how long she would be confined in it with the convalescing Tommy. The hectic flow of Brick Lane—the clubbers and kids and waiters—cheered her up. In spite of the cold, a lone DJ had set up his equipment in the courtyard of a bar and, encased in a puffer jacket, was playing loud jungle music to a group of teenagers dancing in their winter clothes. She had been wrong to think that something in the city had died. Even as she walked down the steps to her burrow, it was roaring into life above her, defying the frost, its hot, dirty blood coursing through the veins of its young.

After she had forced the pills down Tommy—his swallowing reflex just enough to do the job—she listened to her answering machine. The messages were from Rob, asking her whether she wanted to go for a coffee or a drink over the weekend. He said he had a date for his next gig, but he still wasn't sure whether to tell her or not. Then he had rung off. She sat down opposite Tommy. She wanted to call Rob but felt too wretched. There was too much to say, and she was far from ready to say even half of it. Instead, she pulled out one of her most trusted mega-death videos—whose main scene of action was a twenty-fourth-century starship invaded by murderous clones—and watched the first hour blankly, soothed by the ferocious exchange of laser fire and the destruction of a small planet by nuclear explosion. Tommy slept throughout this intergalactic carnage. Halfway through, she pressed the pause button and made herself an omelette, which she consumed without enthusiasm. She started to watch the film again but had lost interest. It was barely eight o'clock, but she knew that the day had nothing left to offer her. Only sleep could repair her battered cells and mend her damaged compass. Where next? Not a clue. Not yet.

This time, her sleep was dreamless. She set her alarm for eight o'clock but awoke before then, her headache receding and her limbs beginning to feel less tarnished. She lay awhile, and drank more water. Then she dressed in her room and went out to the sitting room to see how Tommy was. To her horror, he was awake and sitting bolt upright, an alien being in his T-shirt and sweatpants. His eyes darted nervously from side to side and he chewed compulsively at his lips. She had not given thought to what she would do when he became conscious, and now it had happened, she was scared. She had no reason to think that Tommy would do her harm, but she had no way of knowing that he would not. Even Sylvia had urged her staff to take care with the desperate cases they often dealt with. Not all had started as victims, she said. Plenty were wife-beaters and thieves who had ended up on the street. It was important, Sylvia said, not to get sentimental. Now Mia wondered whether she herself had got sentimental, and would pay a heavy price for it. Tommy's feral features gave nothing away. She tried to work out whether she would make it to the door if she decided to flee. Even in his weakened state, might he intercept her before she could escape?

Armitage was not coming till Wednesday. It was only Sunday morning. Armitage had offered to come on Sunday morning. Stupid girl. She should have said yes.

Then she noticed the bottle of cherry brandy on the table and the flecks of vomit on Tommy's New York logo. It was a bottle Ringo had won at a residents' association event and given to her as a joke. She had hidden it at the back of a cupboard, unable to throw it away, but sure she would never drink it. It was the only hard stuff she kept in the flat. Tommy—emaciated, mad, mute Tommy, rattling with pills and stricken with pneumonia—had searched her flat while she slept, looking for what he needed. He had found it, drunk it all, and, to judge from his clothes, thrown up a good proportion of it. She realised that his expression was one of panic rather than murderous intent. And, with that in mind, she also realised that she had finally had enough.

She stormed over to where he sat and swiped the bottle to the ground. "Tommy! You stupid bastard. Do you know how stupid you are? You nearly *died* yesterday, for God's sake. Did you know that? Can you remember that? Is any of this getting through to your stupid boozy brain? Do you know that I spent a fucking fortune getting a private doctor out so that you wouldn't have to go to hospital? And I'll tell you something else. If you'd had the kind of night I had on Friday, you would know that it's me you should be feeling sorry for, not the other way round. And this is the way you pay me back? Getting wasted in my sitting room. Throwing up. Disgusting. Tommy! Are you listening to me?"

His eyes rolled heavenwards, as if there was nothing that could be done when people lost their temper. This only compounded her fury. She turned around, rubbing her fist against her brow in frustration. "What am I doing? I mean, what a waste of time. Of my life. Tommy! Do you understand a single word I've said to you?"

"It's Thomas, actually."

The words, once said, could not be unsaid. They changed everything, and made no possible sense. The voice that had uttered them was a steady baritone—that of a middle-aged, middle-class man trying to bring order to things. Was there an edge of patrician impatience there, too? She could not be sure. But her judgement, she knew, could not be trusted on this. She was still absorbing the fact that the words had been spoken at all. So her response, when it came after many seconds, took what eventually became a conversation no further at all.

"What?"

He coughed into one hand and put the other to his chest. "Excuse me. I simply said that my name is Thomas. That's what I prefer anyway."

Mia sat down opposite the tramp. "You can talk."

"Very observant," he said, laughing. "Why on earth shouldn't I be able to talk?"

"Well, the fact that you're a mute might have something to do with it."

"I'm not a mute. I just don't talk to people. There is a difference."

The disparity between Tommy's appearance and his voice made her head throb. It was as though the scrawny body of this wizened little tramp had been possessed by the spirit of a man twice his size: a man of poise and confidence. Not, perhaps, the match of her father, but certainly someone who, by the sound of his voice, could see off Dr. Armitage on the golf course. She had heard only a few sentences, but the timbre of Tommy's words reminded her of the men who had come to the Boltons for dinner and parties when she was a girl. Men in suits, or perfect sports jackets, comfortable in their skins and with the trajectory of their lives. Men who knew they were not Jeremy's equal but who enjoyed the warm glow of his orbit.

"I see." She paused, thinking. "Did you take your medicine?"

"Yes, thank you. I followed the instructions on the bottles. And I had my liquids and managed to keep half a banana down, as per the piece of paper headed 'Daily Diet.' "

"But you didn't manage to keep the cherry brandy down?"

"That was less successful, I will admit. But, as you can see, the victim of my failure was me, rather than your sofa. I will, of course, wash your clothes for you, if you would be kind enough to let me borrow a change while I'm doing so. As for the brandy—forgive me, but I suspected that you were unlikely ever to drink it."

"That's not the point."

"No, but perhaps it should be. You know well enough that a bottle of brandy is quite something for a man like me. And you obviously didn't want it. So why not let me have it?"

"You should have asked."

"You were sleeping. And my needs were . . . well, pressing."

"You shouldn't be drinking. I promised Dr. Armitage I would stop you drinking while you get better."

"I don't want to get better if I can't drink. Dr. Armitage knows that. And so do you."

"You are an ungrateful sod. Did you know that?"

Tommy laughed again. The tendons in his neck looked as if they might snap from this exertion, and he started to cough violently. She went into the kitchen and fetched him a glass of water, which he drank, clutched between shaking hands. He closed his eyes and breathed deeply, his chest rattling. She remembered how very ill he was. The voice had chosen a feeble frame to inhabit, in this unearthly act of ventriloquism.

"You're quite right. I owe you an apology for my rudeness. And a debt of gratitude for looking after me. Thank you."

She did not acknowledge this, anxious that he might sink back into silence before he had answered her questions. "Why don't you talk to people?"

He began to rub his hands on his knees. At first, she thought he was embarrassed. Then she understood that he regarded the question as important and was struggling for a precise answer which would do it justice. "I suppose because it wastes time. I talk to the trees, to the roads, to myself. But not when people are looking. It's not that I have anything against them. I would say, as someone who's conducted a pretty extensive experiment in what it's like to be vulnerable, that people are better and kinder than they're generally given credit for. The trouble is that they only want to talk about me, tell me what to do and how to improve myself. And there's not much to say. So when I came here, I decided I wouldn't talk to anyone. And it worked. They leave me alone in the hostels, around where you work, and in the shops. Oh, I get things thrown at me, and the occasional kicking. But nobody expects anything of me. Nobody tries to save me from myself."

"Why did you come to my flat?"

He sucked on his gums. She realised that many, if not most, of his teeth were missing. "Oh, I don't know. I was in the area. Something old-fashioned like trust, I suppose. I thought you were somebody who could be trusted. Isn't that how you see yourself, Chels? Everybody else seems to."

I trust nobody, least of all myself, she thought. I have been sundered from trust. I am on the precipice now, looking down into a dark, unknowable time. "You can call me Mia, if you like. Chels is what Sylvia calls me. It's just a nickname."

"Like Tommy Bonkers."

"Yes, like Tommy Bonkers. How did you pick that up?"

"Oh, the kids round here asked me my name a few years back and I wrote down 'Thomas.' And—well, you can imagine the rest."

They sat in awkward silence. It was disconcerting to find that the man she had assumed was a pickled vegetable was, in fact, a highly articulate gentleman. How resilient the rituals of the middle class are, she thought. Years on the road, awash with drink, have ruined his body. But he has not forgotten how to speak, how to conduct a conversation, the little courtesies. Those habits have not been shaken from him by the pulverising forces of his life. They will be with him until the light is finally extinguished. I am looking at the man as he is now, but I am speaking with the man as he was a long time ago.

"You should wash. I'll get you some clean clothes. And you should sleep. You're very ill, you know."

"Yes, I do know. I think I will sleep."

She got up and caught his eye. "Listen, Thomas. I know you'll want more drink. And you're right: There's nothing Armitage and I can do about it. But you shouldn't go outside. It's freezing. I'll get you some—probably not as much as you want, but some. And you must promise to stay inside for a few days. Deal?" He considered her offer, but not for long, and nodded.

When he awoke late in the afternoon, she was sitting with him, reading. A bottle of Famous Grouse stood on the table, alongside the bottles of pills, the water, and the fruit. He smiled and stretched. "Goodness. Do you have a glass? It's not often I get the chance to use one, you see. A plastic cup occasionally." She looked for a whisky tumbler but could not find one. He would have to make do with a wineglass. She handed it to him and helped him count out his pills, which she insisted he take with water rather than, as he proposed, a large scotch. He could wait thirty seconds for that, she said.

She made herself tea and allowed him to drink some of the whisky alone. The gasps and gagging she heard filled her with a sense of futility. The medication in his body would be fighting not only the infection but the booze. She did not want to watch the battle, or at least its first and most bloody phase. After a while, the noises subsided. She went back into the sitting room and sat down again.

"That's better," he said.

"I doubt that very much. But you've heard it all before."

"How funny. Sheila used to say that."

"What?"

"Towards the end, in the months before I left home. 'You've heard it all before.' That's what she would say. As if she knew that there was no point. Of course, she was quite right."

"Who's Sheila?"

"Oh, my wife. Well, ex-wife. This is eight, nine years ago I'm talking about. A long time. A long time."

Almost by accident, Tommy found himself telling his story to Mia. It took several hours, and, as the time passed and he drank, she wondered why he was bothering. Perhaps, she thought, he feels it is all he has to offer as recompense for my nursing services. He is settling his bill by baring his soul, the only goods he has to barter. Perhaps he wants to tell someone what really happened before he dies, and I administer the last rites. Am I his confessor? Is that what I have become? For Beatrice, Claude, and Tommy? The shadowy figure on the other side of the grille, nodding and muttering an ancient prayer, dispensing absolution before it is too late. Are these the last days?

Tommy—Thomas Williams, Esq., MA Cantab, BCL—had been a successful lawyer, with a large house in Enfield, a wife, and two children. He read a lot, a habit of his youth. He took his family on outings. They could afford two holidays a year, one abroad and one in the West Country. There were two cars parked in the drive, which he walked past on his way to catch the Tube into work very early each morning. He was secure in every way. The future looked bright. But he had known for years that he was heading for the exit. He had known with an absolute, deadening certainty. It was a corrosion within him, scraping out his insides. Mia asked him how he could know such a thing. It was patently ridiculous. Sadness swept across his face like rain.

"Loneliness. I knew the loneliness would catch up with me. I knew it would drive me away. I would have to leave it all."

"That doesn't make sense. You had a family. You had a life."

"Yes, but that's not what I mean. I was so lonely in that life, you see.

I was surrounded by people at work, at home, demands, plans. There was no time for anything. I . . . You can't imagine the loneliness."

"Don't be so sure."

"Yes, well, perhaps you can. Most people can't. They think people end up like me because of great catastrophes. But it isn't always so, not at all. The strange thing was that the drink was never the point. It was only a means to an end, a way of being alone, and not lonely. It was the way I broke free, the only way I could, really. I had to contrive a way to be unbearable to live with. I had to find a way of breaking free."

"I still don't understand."

"I don't expect anyone to. That's why I don't talk to people." He half filled his glass and drank it all, his body reacting less violently this time to the assault of the whisky. "It's all about what you hope for, and what you get, and the difference between the two. That's the gap I tumbled into. You see, the truth is that I loved my wife. More than anything. More than life itself. And I had only wanted to be with her. Nothing more. And somehow, after I don't know how many years, I found my-self in a world where that wasn't the point at all. Our home was like a small business. Everything had to be planned, regimented. Oh, there was plenty of love in the conventional sense. We all loved one another. But there was no real love. Not what I had wanted, anyway."

"So it was all about Sheila?"

"Yes."

"And did you tell her?"

"Yes."

"And?"

He smiled his old man's smile. "And here I am."

Mia tried to imagine Sheila, still a student at Cambridge, meeting Tommy—or Thomas, as he then was—and seeing comfort and affec-tion written into his face. Not feeling the intoxicating passion which had consumed her husband-to-be for the first time, mistaking his ardour for her own, more prosaic enthusiasm. He, deluded that his soul's needs had been answered; she, convinced that all would be well. The years passing, roots being planted, children being born. Tommy's despair hatching within him, growing as his life became officially perfect, a life which separated him from the only thing he had ever truly wanted. Sheila's failure to understand, her impatience. And then, finally, drinking. First, more than he should in the evenings. Then at lunch with colleagues. Then at lunch without them. Then all the time. Rows, confusion, perhaps even violence. Sheila Williams, furious and frightened, mystified by the chaos which had engulfed her life, doing her best to help her husband, realising that she could not, and then, at last, her instinct for self-preservation kicking in, rejecting him utterly. Middle age heralded by decline and disaster. Had he left once, or several times? As he walked down the first of many streets, had he looked back to see the faces of his children pressed against the glass? Or only forward, to a thousand bottles and a life of needless squalor?

Tommy continued: "I simply knew one day that I couldn't be with them anymore, didn't want to. That's the terrible thing. People think that it's something you can't control, what I do, how people like me live. Well, I made my choice. I know it must be hard for you to believe, but this was my decision. This is the life I choose to lead. It really is."

"Don't you ever think of going back? I mean, aren't you curious?"

"I was. I was. Even after the divorce. I wondered about Sheila and the kids and whether I would ever see them again. And then I did, three or four years ago. Or at least I saw Sheila. She was in Columbia Road, at the flower market, with her new man—I couldn't tell whether they were married, but I assumed so. She had had her hair done differently—you know, shorter, new colouring. More glamorous, I suppose. But it was definitely her."

Tommy scratched his beard. "I was outside the shop, drinking with a few of the others. Just a six-pack, if memory serves. Just a Sunday-morning pick-me-up, you know? I was about to nod off, actually. Then I saw her. And him." His expression faltered with the burden of memory. She could see him trying to fight it off, and failing. "She looked . . . I don't know. So different. Happy, I suppose. Not like when we were together, and I would arrive home from work late, and she would be waiting in the sitting room, pretending not to be waiting. Or when I would try to explain how I felt to her, and she would smile, and I would know she hadn't understood a word. Not like that. I remember they were wearing matching coats and each carrying a big bag of plants. I realised that I must be nothing to her now. I mean, it's common sense that I should be. But it was only then that I knew for sure, myself."

"Did she see you?"

"Oh yes. She saw me. But she had no idea who I was. You know, I used to have a short back and sides and wear a suit."

"You still wear a suit."

Tommy laughed. "Yes. But these days, it's from a charity shop. I was just a bearded old alky, sitting on a wall, probably begging, certainly not violent. Just part of the scenery, albeit rather an unsightly part. That was the weird thing. Seeing her again was such . . . such an important moment in my little story, you know. Monumental. The end of the story, I suppose. And it was nothing to her. Absolutely nothing. She carried off her plants, and her man opened the door to their car, which was parked opposite. And they smiled and drove off, and I never saw her again."

Neither of them said anything for a while. She felt too weary to soothe him. On the other hand, she was also too weary to tolerate the silence. "Did you feel regret?"

"You bet I did. I regretted only buying a six-pack. I dug out my reserve ten-pound note, bought a bottle of bloody rough cooking brandy, and was out cold for twelve hours."

"And now? Don't you get lonely now?"

"Being solitary isn't the same as being lonely. I know what you must think when you see me shambling past your shop with a bag full of drink. Or when you find me outside your house. But I never feel lonely."

"Why not?"

"I'm not sure. Partly because I know it'll all be over soon enough. Loneliness is a form of vertigo, I think. You look up and around, and you see no limits, no end to anything, to all the demands. You get dizzy. That's what I used to feel. But now I know the end will come. I'll just pass out and won't wake up. So simple. I half wondered whether this was it, actually."

"Thanks for choosing my porch as a morgue."

"I apologise for that. Let's just say it seemed a good idea at the time."

H E S L E P T for most of the day. She called Rob and told him about Tommy. He said he would tell Sylvia and that they would not expect her at the centre before Wednesday. She told him that was fine. Then she asked him about the gig and whether she would finally get the chance to see Thieves in the Night. He was bashful and said he would think about it. She suggested to Rob that he think about it over a drink. He arranged to meet her in Brick Lane on Tuesday.

The soft growl of Tommy's breathing grew louder as the hours passed. He was taking his pills and drinking, she imagined, about a quarter of his normal intake. She made him soup, which he managed to keep down, and a baked potato, which was less successful. He asked her to read to him from a newspaper—his eyesight was going fast, he said—and she was struck by how absolute was his disconnection from events outside his own mobile bubble of booze. Current affairs had ended about seven years ago for Tommy. He was genuinely amazed when she told him the identity of the prime minister—"You're joking? *Him?*"—but was amused to hear that the leader of the opposition was exactly whom he had expected it to be. She told him about football teams, the state of the economy, soap opera developments, a fresh impasse in the Middle East, trouble in the subcontinent, the strength of the euro, the number-one record, a new movie. She offered him a précis of key events he had missed in the world of politics, military conflict, culture. Just as his body was healing and recovering its taste for food, so he remembered how he had once known all these things. He was enthralled by the crash course, patchy as it was in places. He asked her about writers he had read before he left home, and directors whose films he had seen. What she did not know, she made up, or bluffed her way through. It was important not to falter. If she was to be his guide—Virgil to his Dante—she could not slip and lose her own footing.

On Monday, he asked her about herself. He could tell she had not grown up in the area. It was obvious that she was overqualified for her job, however much she loved it and was loved by the people there. He did not want to pry, he said. But he wondered what it was that had made her so unhappy. He trusted her because of her unhappiness. But he was sorry that so kind a person should be captive to such misery. She wondered how much to tell him, and arrived at a half-truth. It was the best she could do.

"You know, there isn't much to say. I think some of the people round Nantes Street know bits of it, and I don't really talk about it much. To be honest, I came here so I wouldn't have to talk about it. A bit like you, really."

He closed his eyes. "Mourning is a terrible thing. I can see that."

Had he overheard conversations, or was he guessing? It didn't matter. "Yes, it is. It really is. The thing is, my family died a few years ago in . . . in a terrible accident." She thought of Claude, and Ben, and the vengeance of the cheated men. "It was just one of those things that happen, but you never think they'll happen to you."

"Yes, yes." He reflected a little longer. "Did you ever read D. H. Lawrence? My mother used to read me Lawrence when I was twelve, perhaps a little older. The poems, mostly. I used to love it. What I loved was that she loved the poetry so much. I didn't understand it all. Couldn't, really. But it was the first time I saw my mother as a woman, not just as a mother. We lived in a house in Ealing. I remember her face as she read to me, and a big bay window behind. There was a great oak in the garden, and in the summer, the light played through its branches onto her face in the evening. I can see it now."

"What did she read to you?"

His own face was alive now. His learning, suppressed and stultified, was rising again to seep through the pores. "About the gentians. 'Bavarian Gentians.' Do you know the poem?" He began to recite it: " 'Not every man has gentians in his house in soft September, at slow, Sad Michaelmas.' " He continued from memory for several lines.

"What does it mean?"

"Dis. Persephone. The old legends. People can get stuck in darkness. That's what happens. They fill their houses with gentians, dark flowers, and they never escape. That's what Lawrence meant."

"How can you be sure?"

"I'm not. I'm not sure. It means what you want it to mean, doesn't it?"

"No. No, I think things mean what they mean."

He fixed her with a look that was suddenly powerful, freighted with bitterness and experience and warning. "I think you live in a gentian house, Mia. I do. I think you are stuck in darkness. I know I am. Stuck somewhere I chose to go. But the difference is that you can get out." He lay back, surprised by a wave of exhaustion. "When I see you every day, you stand out a mile."

"Oh God. And there's me, thinking I blend in. Incognito."

"No, I don't mean it like that. I mean that you look . . . You are full of fury, if only you knew it. You have a task. There is something you want to do. You think you came here to escape, but that's only partly true. You came here to make yourself ready for something. I can't be sure what it is. But I think you know. And I think you should do it, what-ever it is. I can't. It's too late for me. I chose this; you didn't choose. But you can choose to free yourself."

"Maybe I don't want to be free."

"Oh, but you do. You do. Your story has barely begun." He trembled as he spoke. "Can I have the rest of that brandy now, please?"

For supper, she cooked him a chicken breast, which she served with some plain potatoes. His appetite was improving, and his temperature was almost normal. She phoned Armitage and left a message saying all was well and that they were looking forward to seeing him on Wed-nesday. She watched a little television with Tommy, but she switched it off when Miles came on the screen, holding forth outside the House of Commons about the other party and its stupidity. She headed for bed, leaving Tommy snoring contentedly. She turned back and felt his brow. The raging heat had gone. Was he well? Of course not. But she had made him better.

In the morning, she awoke early, put on a T-shirt, and went to take a shower. Even as she walked into the sitting room, she knew that he would be gone. The pile of bedding, neatly folded on the floor beside the sofa, told its own story. Had he taken the hundred pounds in cash on the mantelpiece? No, only two bottles of whisky and one of decent German wine, which she had hoped to drink with her supper. Besides the bottles of pills—the course of medication incomplete, the fool—there was a note, written in an old-fashioned looping italic. Only the oc-casional slips betrayed the shaking hand which had written it:

> Dear Mia,
>
> Thank you for looking after me. I feel much replenished after my stay with you. I cannot begin to thank you for your hospitality and for the kindness you have shown me. You are a truly good person, and I believe I am not exaggerating if I say that I owe my life to you.

I think, however, that it is time for me to move on. I do not know how long is left to me—a little longer than I thought, at any rate, thanks to your care. So I feel bound to go somewhere else for a while and see what that has to offer. Five years is a long time to spend anywhere. Who knows where I may end up?

Remember what I said to you. You must move on, too. The moment is not far away. Do not be afraid. You will be equal to it.

Yours faithfully,
Thomas

P.S. I have stolen your trainers. Sorry.

Bastard. Bastard, bastard. She could not believe that the drunken bastard had taken her trainers. She would have preferred him to take the cash. Now she would have to make another trip to Aldgate. She would have to explain to Armitage that his patient had flown. He would suck breath through his teeth to imply that his indulgence had been rewarded with failure. She would be made to feel that Tommy's abscondment and imminent death were a direct consequence of her misjudgement. Sylvia was right: Don't get sentimental. Bastard.

That night, she met Rob at a bar on Brick Lane. He was waiting for her, reading a discarded newspaper. In his leather jacket and baseball boots, with his mussed hair and hopeful eyes, he reminded her at once that not everything was the way it had been over the past five days. She leant over and kissed him on the cheek.

"Christ," he said, folding his paper. "What was that for?"

"Nothing. It's good to see you."

"And you. Well, you look like you've got a story up your sleeve. Hang on; I'll get the drinks in. And when I get back, you can tell me all about it."

So she did. She told him everything.

→ Part THREE

THE END OF THE RIVER

Chapter ELEVEN

THE FORECOURT to the showroom was a carnival of bargains. Translucent strips of blue plastic stretched across the windscreens of the cars; on each of them, long strands of white lettering explained why this was the only vehicle you could possibly want. A black Mercedes was going for the "unbelievable" price of £11,500; the mileage was "low, low, low!" An older station wagon, with 170,000 miles on the clock, was on sale for the "once-in-a-lifetime bargain price" of £7,500. Next to it was a beautiful amber red Merc convertible—the sort of car Ben had driven towards the end of his life—yours "for a song" at £30,000. The winter sun flashed off the polished surfaces of the cars' bodywork, promising speed, power, and value for money. The forecourt was a triumph in doublethink: Each car advertised itself as the only car worth having. By implication, all the other cars in the world were useless, a con, trash cans that would fall apart a mile down the road, if you were fool enough to buy them. And yet the twenty vehicles on display managed somehow to coexist. Their free-market exuberance was such that, defying the laws of logic, if not the laws of economics, they did not quarrel with one another.

For all the gravity of her mission, the whole concept of Michael Aitch Motors amused Mia. She liked the fact that Micky Hazel, thinking of what to call his enterprise, had chosen the formal version of his Christian name—which, she imagined, nobody used—and then, in a cheeky flourish, had tacked on the phonetic spelling of the first letter of his surname. This said: I am a man who abides by the rules, a serious man, not a shyster. But—and this was where the Aitch came in—I like a giggle, too. I'm a geezer, me. I like a laugh. You've got to laugh, haven't you? As she wandered around the cobbled patio, pretending to inspect the cars, she formed a picture of Micky: mid-fifties, a long fawn coat, new driving gloves (a present from his daughter), silk paisley scarf, and a white-collared shirt. A hint of the seventies there, maybe, but certainly nothing garish. Micky would drink pints with the lads but stiff G&Ts with his wife when he got home. Capped teeth and bouffant hair. He would have a West Ham sticker on his car, but a small one. Yes: a geezer you could trust. A connected man.

A woman in blouse and skirt came over and shook her hand. "Miss Taylor? Good morning. I'm Janine, Mr. Hazel's PA. I think we spoke on the phone. If you'd like to follow me, I'll show you to the office. He's just on a call to one of our suppliers. It's been an unbelievable morning. We're shifting cars quicker than we can replace them. Mr. Hazel's worried we'll have run out of motors by the weekend. I said he can give us all the day off if we do!"

Mia smiled and followed Janine across the grey plastic floor tiles and past the electric fountain at the centre of the showroom. She counted four salesmen. None of them seemed especially preoccupied, which was hard to tally with Janine's claim of record demand and frenzied selling. But there was doubtless an answer to that, too. It was probably possible to have your best morning ever, without, technically, having your best morning ever. Micky Hazel would see to that: The rules of philosophy would bend to his will.

Janine left her in a little waiting area outside her boss's office and offered her coffee, which Mia declined. She was nervous, light-headed. It was hard to square the bullshit factory that was Michael Aitch Motors with the syndicate of death described by Claude in his ravings. The idea that Janine might be one rung down from the man who was one rung down from the men who had killed her family was laughable. She wished she could walk away now. Rob, of course, had tried to stop her from coming at all. In the bar, after listening with great care and patience to her story, he told her that Claude had obviously gone mad and that four years of silent grieving for Ben had evidently made him believe a paranoid conspiracy theory of his own devising. For some obscure reason, Claude blamed himself for the tragedy and, his talent as a fantasist finally pushing him over the edge, had constructed a version of the truth to correspond to his self-loathing. Rob could well believe that Claude had introduced Ben to some dodgy customers on his nights out. But did she seriously think that her brother, with all his acumen and talents, would have got in so deep with these people that they had killed him and the rest of her family? With a calm wisdom that surprised Mia, Rob urged her not to go to see Micky Hazel. What good could possibly come of it? Did she really think it was a smart idea to march up to an East End car dealer and ask him if he had been involved in a conspiracy to murder five people? A crime for which a notorious terrorist group—if he remembered the reports correctly—had already claimed responsibility? When he put it like that, she had felt foolish and sent him to the bar for more drinks.

And yet she could not forget the fear in Claude's face. Perhaps this was nothing more than insane grief mutating into psychotic dread. Perhaps not. She had never seen Claude properly scared before. He had spent years waiting to tell her what he had told her that night. He had gone to elaborate lengths to find her, and then to pass on this horrific knowledge. Could it all be nothing more than a delusion, the most complex, the most destructive of Claude's many games? Unfortunately, there was only one way to find out.

"Miss Taylor? I'm Micky Hazel." She turned with a start, to see an outstretched hand, manicured but free of jewellery. "I'm sorry to have kept you waiting. As I'm sure Janine told you, it's been a busy morning. I hope you haven't been here too long. Have you been offered coffee? . . . Good, good. Come on in."

The man welcoming her into his office was definitely more Michael than Aitch. Much more. He was younger than she had expected, no more than forty, and his suit was less flash than she would have predicted. He was tall and slim—a regular at the gym, she guessed—and his hair was parted. He wore reading glasses and brogues. And his voice—his voice!—was like something from her school days. Not a hint of geezer, not a whisper of West Ham car stickers about it. Micky Hazel sounded like a history teacher at a minor prep school, or a BBC newscaster. She felt humiliated already. What would this busy, respectable man, running his successful firm, think of this funny little woman with her mad questions? He would humour her, of course, and then, if he had any sense, call the police to make sure they weren't looking for anybody on the run from a mental institution. She had no idea what to say.

"It's good of you to come in. See anything you like?"

"Oh, I'm not really looking. Not at the moment anyway."

Micky Hazel grinned. No capped teeth. "Don't worry, I'm not going to give you a sales pitch. The customers are fed up with the rubbish we used to talk in our trade. The East End has changed so much, too. The kind of people who walk into this forecourt these days are as likely to work in the City or a publishing firm as they are to be local boys who are flush with a bit of cash. Ten years ago, the guys who bought Mercs and Beemers round here were making a statement. It was the biggest purchase they would ever make; it showed they were players, hard boys to be reckoned with. Now most of my customers are just middle-class people buying prestige cars to get to work. Rich is driving out poor. This city is always hungry, Miss Taylor. It sucks in money like a monster, and spits out poverty if it can. We go with the flow at this firm."

"I can see all that. Well, I live off Brick Lane. It's changed even since I've been there. I bumped into one of my favourite novelists the other day."

"There you are. So that's what my boys have to face up to. Can they sell a car to a novelist? That's it exactly." He shifted on his black leather swivel chair. Behind his head were a series of plaques, trade awards celebrating his achievements, and a framed photograph showing the opening of a new branch somewhere—Leytonstone, she thought. "Now, how can I help you? Janine says it was a personal matter about a member of your family. Is that right?"

He was looking her square in the eye. Does he know who I am? Or is this going to sound as mad as I think it will? "Mr. Hazel. First of all, thank you for seeing me. I know how much you have to do today, so I'll try to be brief. Second, I hope you won't take what I'm going to say personally. I'm trying to find out something—I'm not sure what exactly—and I'm afraid I'm having to follow all the leads I can. I'm talking to lots of people, and I'm embarrassed to say that I'm wasting a lot of people's time in the process. But I have to do it." Her lie sounded unconvincing. Hazel would know from her nervousness that he was the first person she had seen. If he was as smart as he looked, that is.

"I'm intrigued. Call me Micky, by the way."

"Mr. Hazel—Micky, I mean. I think you knew my brother, Benjamin. Ben Taylor."

She had taken the plunge. His face betrayed no reaction whatsoever. He tapped a Mont Blanc pen against his lip. He continued to scrutinise her. "Ben died four years ago in a fire. You may remember it. The police—"

"My God, Ben! Are you Ben's sister?" Micky Hazel reached across the table and took her hand. "I am so, so sorry. Forgive my stupidity. I could not believe it when I read about it in the paper. I remember wondering whether there was going to be a funeral, and then it said that the service was private. So . . . But how terrible. My heart goes out to you. To lose your whole family." He shook his head as if he had just heard the news. "I am so pleased to meet you. But I am so sorry it is this that has brought you to me."

"So you did know my brother?"

"Oh, yes. Of course. I mean, not that well. We used to end up at a few of the same clubs. Mostly in the area. We had lunch once or twice, too. He was excellent company. Very able."

"And you knew Claude?"

"Of course. You couldn't have one without the other. But you knew that. Do you mind if I smoke?" She shook her head, and he lit a Marlboro Light, then inhaled deeply. Was he nervous? "I think it was Claude who introduced me to Ben, actually. Late one night in a place I go to occasionally in Stepney. I'm afraid we were both pretty drunk. We had some good times, played cards, that kind of thing. I always enjoyed bumping into them." He looked straight at her. "So how is Claude?"

No, Mr. Hazel, I'm not playing your game. You'll have to earn information like that. "Oh, Claude? He's well, I think. I don't really see that much of my old friends, you see. When it all happened—well, I rather needed to break off from my old life, as you can imagine."

"Well, I can only guess how hard it must have been for you." He had not taken his eyes off her. It seemed, indeed, that he had not blinked. His skin, she noticed, was pale and cruel.

"Yes, it has been hard. The thing is, Micky, I am trying to sort out some unfinished business my brother left behind. The fact is that I didn't really know what he . . . did, not exactly. Until quite recently, that is. And there are one or two things I need to find out, for personal reasons. For my peace of mind. I am sure you'll understand that it matters to me to know as much as I can about what my brother was doing before he died."

Micky stubbed out his cigarette and lit another. He buzzed Janine for an espresso. He was edgy. Was he anxious, or merely bored? "I see. Well, how can I help?"

"What do you know about my brother's work?"

"Not much. He didn't really talk about it. Claude was always—if you don't mind me saying so—the show-off. Always bragging about big-shot clients and fuck-off accounts. Frankly, it could get quite boring. But Ben didn't say that much about what he did for a living. Financial services of some kind, wasn't it? He always talked about cars and wine and sport with me. Stuff like that. Not much shop."

"Yes. It was financial services. I knew that. What I didn't know un-til quite recently is the nature of those services. I think some of the fi-nancial products Ben offered were not exactly the sort of thing you get at your bank on the High Street."

His eyes were now thin with suspicion. Was it her imagination, or had a touch of local accent crept into his voice, too, a whisper of Aitch fighting to climb out of Michael?

"I don't follow you."

"You see, I have been told that some of the people Ben met round here—you know, at the clubs you went to—used him to sort out their money for them. Clean it up a little. I'm told Ben was rather good at that. Handy with computers, if you catch my drift." She could hear the quiver in her words; he must be able to tell how frightened she was. "That's what I've been told. I just wondered if you could help me. If you might know something, or someone I could talk to."

Micky Hazel stood up. She wondered if this was the prelude to an angry dismissal. It was conceivable that he would have taken offence at her insinuation. Who was she, after all, to ask an honest businessman such a question? Did it do her brother's memory any honour to indulge such fantasies? But no. He walked to the window, looked through the slats of the blind, and surveyed his little kingdom. His expression was not one of fury, but of deep thought. He was dwelling upon what, exactly, to say to her, choosing his words with care. He turned round to face her.

"Miss Taylor. Mia—if I may? Let me ask you a question. How long have you lived here? I mean round here, as you put it."

"Not long. Three years."

"Exactly. Not long." He walked towards her, his expression blank once more. "You like the area. You may well love it, quite possibly. People do, if you believe the property prices. But you don't *know* it."

"I suppose not."

"Well, I do. I really do. I've lived here all my life. I grew up in Stepney. My whole family, all the men, worked on the docks, one or two as printers, a couple of taxi drivers. My dad busted a gut his whole life. Dropped dead of a heart attack when he was fifty-six. I was lucky. I got a scholarship to the Hewlett School when I was seven, and picked up qualifications like confetti. First in my family to do so. God, my old man was proud. That's why I talk the way I do—they more or less beat the accent out of you at places like that, or they did in those days. Oh, I'll bet you were wondering about that, the way I speak. Well, that's fair enough. People do. The point is, appearances can be deceptive. I may talk a bit like your brother and Claude did, but I belong round here. I could have gone to university—I had the grades. But I wanted my own business. I cleared a hundred and fifty thousand pounds last year, basic. I'll clear more this year. I'm a winner. And part of the reason I'm a winner is that I go with the flow. I take my cue from the city. I don't question it."

Back off, little girl, he was saying. Back off now. Your questions are not welcome. We won't answer them. We don't answer questions like that. And we'll get seriously pissed off if you keep asking them.

"I'm sure you're right. I just wonder if you can help me. That's all."

Micky had returned to his seat and was lighting up once more. He buzzed Janine again, annoyed that his coffee had not arrived. "I can help you, and I will. The fact is, I have no idea what your brother was up to. He always seemed a very straightforward guy to me. But, I admit, you never can tell. It's possible that he was up to a bit of this and that. Unlikely, but possible. The question is, What do you gain by going out and asking about his business? Let's say—just for the sake of argument, you understand—that he had been up to no good. And let's say—"

"For the sake of argument." She returned his cool stare.

"Yes. Yes. For the sake of argument. Let's say that he ended up in some sort of trouble as a consequence. He's been dead four years. I'm sorry to put it like this, and I hope you won't take offence, but do you think anyone gives a fuck anymore? Do you think people will tell you what you want to know, even if it is true? Let me tell you something, and I want you to understand exactly what I mean. I want you to listen, harder than you listened to whoever has been whispering in your ear already: *Even if it isn't true, people won't tell you that, either.* You are wasting your time. And, at the end of the day, whichever way you look at it, you are wasting mine, too." This, then, was the dismissal she had been waiting for. "Does that help?"

She stood up. "Yes. Yes, that is helpful. Thank you for being so candid, Micky. I think you may have saved me a wild-goose chase. It's difficult for me. But you have—you've put things in perspective." Bullshit, she thought. He won't buy that for a second. I wish I could find out the name of the person he's going to call the moment I leave his office. That would tell me all I need to know.

"Good. Sorry to be blunt. But I think I owed it to you. It was nice meeting you." He offered his hand. She noticed it was a little clammy—just a little. "Really. I liked your brother a lot. I hope you'll come back and see us sometime. And buy a car—maybe we will persuade you next time."

"Who knows? Thank you for your time, Micky." She smiled. "I'll let myself out." As she left, she nearly knocked over Janine, who was bringing in the espresso at last.

It took her more than an hour to get home by bus, and for half of that she was caught in traffic caused by a diversion at Old Street. There was a message blinking on her answering machine. It was Claude. He sounded distraught, begging her to call him the minute she got in. Christ, had Micky Hazel got to him already? Put the frighteners on him? She imagined Claude, probably not himself the last few days, sitting subdued in a meeting at Robinson, hauled out to take an urgent telephone call that the secretary had been told simply could not wait. His face, already ashen, draining of all colour as he listened to the whispered words at the other end of the line. No, that was too fanciful. There was no way that could have happened in the time it had taken her to get from Stratford shopping centre to Brick Lane. Was there? To find out, she would have to call Claude. And that she would not do.

IN THE MORNING, she walked into work and told Rob what had happened. It had been her day off, and he had guessed what she would do. She had expected him to chastise her, say that she was playing with fire, but instead, he asked her what she was going to do now. She had been preparing her defence, her justification of what she had put herself through, and what she might have started. But she had no answer to his question. What should she do now? Micky Hazel had given her nothing. He had told her nothing, other than to warn her that her very enquiries were dangerous, irrespective of the truth about Ben. She was asking things that should not be asked, ever. She was parading the ignorance of the outsider, transgressing the rules of the tribe without even knowing it. She remembered what Claude had said: There were no second chances in that world, only punishments. Perhaps Micky Hazel really had been trying to help her. She had escaped death once, by a whisper. Why march towards it a second time?

Rob had other things on his mind, too. That night, his group were due to play at a pub on London Fields called the Four Bells. It was a shithole, with a rough crowd, and no stage. But it was a gig. He had invited Mia, with some misgivings, and Ringo, with even more. He did not want to make a fool of himself in front of her, and having now met Ringo a couple of times, Rob knew that he was an expert. She wanted to talk to him about the chance that she might get gunned down by East End villains, or find a horse's head at the end of her bed. He tried to concentrate, but she could tell that he was more worried about his amp, which was playing up. How strange men are, she thought. He is more concerned that he might not impress me than he is that I might be the victim of a gangland shoot-out. You couldn't chat up a girl when she was full of bullets. She thought of pointing this out to him, then decided to go over to Ringo's instead and tell him where to meet her that evening.

Ringo was moving a pile of twelve-inch records, mostly imports, from one side of the shop to the other. He looked up at her as she walked in and, to her surprise, smiled only weakly. Had Aasim been back?

"Hello, you," she said. "How's the master of the steel wheels?"

"I'm okay," he said, pulling out a stock sheet and writing on it with a blue ballpoint.

"Only okay?" This was unusual. "Christ, you're going to be a barrel of laughs tonight. Poor Rob's antsy enough as it is. He keeps muttering about his amp. And he's scared stiff because he knows you know what you're talking about. Personally—"

"Chels." He put a box down on the counter. "Chels, man. What are you doing?"

His tone was serious, more so than she could ever remember. "What do you mean?"

"I mean exactly what I said: What are you doing?"

"I'm not doing anything. What are you on about?"

"My cousin called me from Brick Lane earlier today. He keeps his ear to the ground. Talks to lots of characters. He heard you charged in to see Micky Hazel yesterday."

Shit. This was not good. She could feel her knees buckle. "I didn't *charge in* to see anybody. For your information, Micky Hazel did some work with my brother years ago that I want to know about. He said he didn't know anything. That's it. End of story."

"No. Wrong, Chels. Beginning of story. Whatever you said to the man, the word is out. There're people asking questions about you, the shop, everything. Even Aasim and his crew had heard about it, you know? What did you say to this guy?"

She leant against one of the record racks, a bin marked EARLY TECHNO. She felt faint with fear and leaden with embarrassment. "I didn't say much. Honest. I—somebody told me that Ben—my brother—was in too deep with some guys Micky Hazel knew. I think he might have been in some trouble. That's all. I had to see Hazel. I had to ask him."

"So you just went in there and asked him, right?"

"Yeah, I did. And the truth is, he sent me away with a flea in my ear. Didn't take kindly to my questions. Told me I was a fool to be asking them."

Ringo grabbed her arms. "He's right. Stop messing about, Chels. I tell you, these boys don't muck about. They don't like some chick with a posh voice asking all sorts. If you were a bloke, you'd probably be in the emergency room by now, with teeth in a basket, maybe worse. Whatever it is you're trying to do, drop it. Drop it, Chels."

She broke free. There were tears in her eyes. "How can I? He's dead. Don't you understand? My brother. Ben. They're all dead. My family. All I have left is the chance of finding out who did it. That's all I have. How would you feel? What would you do?"

He relented a little. "I know, man, I know. I've always known how hard it is for you. Not the details. But you know, it's obvious. All of us who love you round here know that. Sylvia—God, she cries when she talks about it. But listen to me. You have to listen, Chels. This is not a game. This is not cheeky Cockney chaps, man. This is hard bastards who don't give a fuck. And they're sniffing around. They're making enquiries. Just let it go, Chels. Let it go. If you leave it now, they will, too. That's the way it works."

She wiped her nose. He was right, of course. She had been foolish, courting trouble for herself, and possibly for others she cared about. If she kept her head down, she might just get away with it. That was the best she could hope for. "Okay, Ringo. Okay, I'll drop it. Thanks for tipping me off."

He smiled broadly, his anxiety thawing, and embraced her. "That's my job. Your eyes and ears, right?"

She smiled back. "Right. You certainly know your way round, that's for sure. Why can't we get a couple of these characters on Aasim? That would wipe the grin off his face."

"Yeah, for sure."

"Listen, I just came over to say that the gig starts at eight. I'll see you there. All right?" He nodded, smiled again, and she left.

THE FOUR BELLS was a dive without even a large-screen television to boost its modest clientele. The landlord, Dave, was an Elvis fan who loved rock'n'roll. He also enjoyed violence, as long as he was not personally involved and his property did not get damaged. He paid peanuts to give local bands the chance to play, and gave his punters complete freedom to humiliate the acts if they were as bad as they usually were. Mia had been to a gig there only once before, by mistake, where she had seen a bluegrass band called Phil's Billys last five minutes before they were pelted off. Ringo had told her that the gigs had a reputation for trouble, which was why people went along. There would be

no record company executive at the bar, weaving his way to the front of
the crowd after the final encore to offer Thieves in the Night a three-
album contract. There would be a bunch of tough nuts full of lager,
looking for a fight. The only bright lights Rob could expect were the
ones on police cars.

When she arrived, Ringo was waiting for her at a table, a pint of
cider already set up. He was eating a packet of nachos and talking into
his phone. He waved her over, but first she went up to see Rob, who was
fiddling with his guitar by the pinball machine.

"Hello," she said. "So this is your band?"

He was bent over the troublesome amp, and looked up, flushed and
anxious. "Oh, hi. I'm glad you came. Yeah, this is the band. That's Steve,
the drummer. Heavy, our keyboard player. And Malc on bass."

"And Rob on vocals and guitar. Right?"

"Yeah. I guess." He bent over again. "If I can get this fucking amp
to work, that is." He plucked a string on his guitar. An unholy hissing
rose from the speaker. This was not, she guessed, what he had hoped for.

The band members had grunted to her as he introduced them. They
were trying hard to look cool and unflustered, but it was clear that this
was very far from the case. Grey-haired Steve, the oldest by several years,
she guessed, was sweating heavily in his denim shirt, trying to fix the
leads into his electric-drum kit. Heavy, who was tiny and quite bald,
lurked in his LONDON CALLING T-shirt behind a terrace of keyboards,
which she imagined would kill him if they tumbled over. Malc, the bass
player, looked the part more than his fellow band members: He wore a
loose black T-shirt and tight grey jeans, his skin tanned and his hair
spiked. In all honesty, he was the only one of them who vaguely resem-
bled a rock'n'roll musician, rather than a nervous mature student. The
image of Christians and lions flashed through her mind. There was
much fidgeting and short-tempered muttering. She could hear the word
fuck being repeated in different accents and with different rhythms; the
effect was that of a profane Morse code. It was not obvious that any of

them, including Rob, claimed leadership of the group, or deserved it. They did not seem ready to breathe fire. Poor Rob. She did not want to embarrass him.

She went and sat with Ringo, who had finished his call. To his amusement, she drank the cider down in one swig. "Well, I needed that. And I need another. Same again?"

"I'm all right. Let me get it." He returned quickly with her second pint.

"He's really worried." She pointed at Rob, who was now squatting before his squawking, malfunctioning amp. "Do you think he'll be all right?"

"Dunno," said Ringo, trying to conceal his giggles. "I don't know much about this guitar pub rock stuff. I'm a DJ, man."

"Oh, fuck off. Listen to you, Fat Boy Slim. Give him a chance."

"I am giving him a chance. I'm here, aren't I?"

"Yeah. I'm not sure we're helping much, though." She told Ringo the story of Rob's mum coming to rescue him from the dangerous gig, which only added to Ringo's mirth. He slapped the table in delight. They sat and drank while Rob, Heavy, and the others continued their preparations like dead men walking.

The pub was filling up now. There was a crowd of twenty or so obvious regulars, all male, several in football shirts beneath their thick winter jackets. They stood at the bar and cackled at the band's self-conscious sound check. But there were also thirty or forty other punters, who were less easy to categorise: teenaged couples, a group of black kids, some girls with piercings drinking Bacardi breezers, and a few older customers who, Mia prayed, might just be interested in the music rather than in looking for a fight. One of the regulars, a fat bloke wearing dark sunglasses and a gaudy gold earring, was holding court. She heard him say, "Like she was dead or something!" which was enough to make his little entourage explode into laughter. The black kids were playing the pinball machine, which was bleeping and playing jingles noisily. They did not even acknowledge the band, which had just finished setting up a few feet away from them. It was 8:30.

Rob slung his guitar over his shoulder and stepped up to the microphone. He looked good in a plain white shirt, jeans, and boots, though she could tell he was giddy with nerves. "Good evening," he said with more diffidence than was strictly proper in a rock singer. "We are Thieves in the Night, and this is 'Candid.' " They started with one of their own numbers, which Ringo said was a gamble. If the crowd didn't know the song, they could lose interest immediately. This was ominously borne out by the response, or lack of it. The music was fast and angry, and the band tried hard, in spite of their useless sound system. Rob strummed his three chords and sang the words he had written himself, his eyes closed. Heavy's little fingers moved with surprising dexterity across the keyboards as he stared ahead with a pleasingly manic intensity. They were not completely useless, thank God. But the drinkers in the Four Bells were indifferent. One or two who were engrossed in conversation turned round and glared at the noise, which had interrupted them. A few left immediately, not even deigning to scorn the nonevent in their midst.

The number ended without applause, and Thieves in the Night played another of their songs, and then another. Still, the crowd acted as if Rob and his group were not there. Beads of sweat rolled down his forehead. Mia winced at the rhymes of a song called "Learn Nothing," apparently a critique of the educational system, in which "the man in the coat" was pilloried for forcing people "to learn by rote" and then, if her hearing didn't deceive her, ended up "in a moat." Or was that "gloat"? She wasn't sure if she wished she could hear better, or not at all. Rob would certainly ask her later on what she thought, and would force her to be honest. That was what worried her.

She finished her third pint and turned to Ringo. To her surprise, he was concentrating hard, his chin cupped in his hand, his foot tapping, his expression focused. "Be honest," she said. "How bad is it?"

"They're too loose," he said. "They haven't rehearsed enough. But there's something there. Rob's all right, and the keyboard player is really good. They don't believe it yet, though. I tell you, man, they need to connect with the audience, do a cover version of something the crowd know. They'll die if they don't get a reaction soon." He pointed at the dwindling audience, some of whom were starting to sing their own football anthems.

As if reading his mind, Rob stepped up to the mike and said: "You might remember this one." Someone in the melee called out, "You're fucking useless, mate." Rob peered over the heads and said, "Oh, hello, Mum. I thought I saw you." A ripple of surprised applause coursed through the little mob. Then Heavy attacked his keyboards with the unmistakable first chords of "Oliver's Army."

Rob was no Elvis Costello, and Thieves in the Night were not the Attractions. But he knew the words, and they knew the tune. "Don't start me talking," he sang with a nicely nasal drawl. "I could talk all night, my mind goes sleepwalking, while I'm putting the world to right." The girls drinking Bacardi breezers screamed in recognition, as if the useless band had been replaced by a golden oldie karaoke machine. They rushed to the front and began to dance frantically, bopping and bouncing up and down. They were making fun of the group, squealing with laughter, but it didn't matter. The black kids liked what they saw and joined in. So did some of the teenagers. "If you're out of luck or out of work," sang Rob, "we could send you to Johannesburg."

At the end of the song, the crowd clapped and the girls demanded more. Rob had got the message. He turned and said something to the band, who broke immediately into "Gene Genie." The pulsating stomp of the opening bars, instantly familiar even to those who did not know the name of the song and had probably never heard of Bowie, drew more people to the dance floor, including some of the hard cases from the bar. Mia could see Dave pulling pints in a stained polo shirt one size too small. He looked impressed. The boys and girls were jumping up and down and buying big rounds to keep them going. Dave liked to watch a good fight, but he liked this even more.

Rob was on a roll now. He shouted at Steve, the drummer, to keep playing at the end of the song, and she realised that they were storming straight into "Lust for Life." Clever boy, she thought. This lot don't know who Iggy Pop is, and don't give a damn, but they sure know this song. By the time Rob was singing "Well, I'm just a modern guy," there were at least forty people, mostly kids, roaring along with the words and pogoing on one another's shoulders. She finished her pint, then took Ringo's arm and dragged him onto the dance floor.

Thieves in the Night had taken the temperature, sussed the crowd, and come up with the right answer. They followed with "The Passenger"—Iggy again—and then "Should I Stay or Should I Go?" and then "No More Heroes" and then "Town Called Malice" and then "She Sells Sanctuary." If they could not play their own music, they would play the music that had inspired their own. And in the new world of back-to-back retro nights, of TV adverts, of movie themes played again and again in malls, the crowd found that they knew these songs, too, for quite different reasons. Mia was soon swaying with them, shaking her head, enjoying the cider, the freedom, and the chance to forget about Claude and Micky Hazel and all that stuff. It was hot as hell on the floor, and she threw her jacket onto her stool and shook her whole body, with Ringo at her side. She was not a great dancer, never had been, but she was dancing.

Then the band stopped. Rob turned to Steve, said something, and he and Heavy nodded. Rob stepped up to the mike and said, "Thanks. This one's for a friend of mine called Mia." She recognised his choice instantly: It was "She's Lost Control," an old song by Joy Division, a band he knew she loved. This time, the rhythm was different, more menacing, Spartan. The electric guitar ripped over a primitive beat and dark bass line. Had they tried this earlier, the band would have been heckled off the stage. But the crowd were in their hands now, desperate for music and instantly moving to the angry electro filling the pub. "And she gave away the secrets of her past," sang Rob, "and said I've lost control again." Yes, this was her song all right. It was not a ballad. It was something much more intense than that, a cry from him to her, as if to say that he understood, that he knew her better than she had guessed and better than he had yet dared to tell her. She lost herself in the forbidding sound, dancing to the front of the crowd, gyrating only yards away from him, glad of the drink she had drunk, the sweat on her brow, the chance he was giving her. She did not want to catch his eye, but she wanted him to know. She would dance as long as he played.

The song ended. The crowd applauded wildly and Thieves in the Night put down their instruments and walked off, as if the whistling and clapping and shouting were happening somewhere else. Instinct was biting. They had commanded the stage, and now was the time to go, to leave the audience desperate for more, to raise the prospect of another night and another dance. She could see how hard Rob was trying not to show his relief, how badly he wanted to leave and be somewhere else. She grabbed his sleeve and said, "Come back to mine. We can have a drink there. To celebrate. In an hour?" He smiled at her, nodded, and left as Steve and Malc went back to pack up the kit.

The crowd subsided, unimpressed by the music Dave put on over the sound system in an effort to keep them dancing. Ringo bought another round and agreed with her that it had been a great evening. She nodded as he made observations about the band and their style, how good they could be, how much work they had left to do, but she could not concentrate. She wanted to leave and go back to her flat. She let Ringo talk and finished her drink as quickly as she could. Then she said she was tired, kissed him on the cheek, and walked out into the cold night.

She looked at her watch and realised she would have to get a taxi. As she reached the end of the park, by the children's playground, a black cab sailed past and she screamed for it to stop. The driver, just hearing the tail end of her shriek, pulled over as if in an emergency. He laughed when he saw how distraught she looked. "What, you in labour, love? Climb in." He drove off, turned into Hackney Road, and had her home in less than ten minutes.

She turned the lights on, ignored the letters on the doormat, and went straight to the fridge, where a good bottle of white wine was waiting. She poured two glasses and found herself checking her appearance in the mirror, playing with her hair, smoothing her T-shirt. The answering machine was blinking—Claude again? Something worse?—but she had no intention of listening to it. Not now, not tonight. Her expectations were not high. But, for the first time in a long while, she did not feel trapped. She put on a Groove Armada CD and sat down, trying to unwind. She lost track of time and could not tell how long it was before she heard feet coming down the stairs from the pavement.

She went to the door and opened it before he could ring the bell. Rob looked at her with great seriousness, as if he had grave news. He said nothing as he walked in, and neither did she. He saw the wine and heard the music, then turned to her. She returned his gaze, waiting. He moved towards her, a barely perceptible shift, but enough to tell her all she needed to know. And then he was kissing her, hard and with desperation, as if she would flee his arms once he let her go, as if he would never see her again. She felt him pressing against her, and, even as she returned his kiss and reached out to caress his face, she pushed him away a little. She did not want him to panic, or squander everything for nothing. His fervour was too much.

"Not in here," she whispered. She took him by the hand and led him into her bedroom, turning the light on as she did. He was breathless and confused, overwhelmed by emotion and desire. After the turmoil of the past fortnight, she felt only release, too exhausted to feel anything else. More than she had ever suspected—although, in the midst of everything else, she had suspected it—she wanted this.

He lunged towards her again, and she could see the gleaming tears of youthful lust in his eyes. Again, she put her hand softly on his chest and looked into his eyes. "No, don't," she said. "Let me." She took off her T-shirt and unhooked her bra, letting it fall at her feet. Then she took him in her arms and held him for a while. She could feel his hardness pressed against her belly, and the racing of his bursting heart. How long was it since she had touched a man? Almost four years: not since New York. Not since a squalid little episode involving a fabulously handsome magazine writer in a restaurant rest room. Not like this.

Now, Rob was submitting to her. She made space between them and moved his hands up to her breasts, guiding him at first, until he understood what she liked and what she did not. She undid his jeans and watched them drop in a comic heap at his feet. They laughed, as if to confide in each other how nervous they were. She looked at him again. "I do want this," she said. "I do. I want you."

They tumbled onto the bed, and he became more urgent, pulling at her slacks, pushing her knickers down, and kissing her more vigorously now. She responded and gasped, astonished as the ferocious impulses of sex returned to a body that had almost forgotten them. And then he was inside her, and it was too soon, but it was too late to tell him that, and she tried to slow him down, to give her time to relax, and her lip curled in discomfort, but he did not notice, for by now he was whispering the inconsequential mantras of absolute need into her ear, holding on to her with a strength that was both gentle and uncompromising, rising above her, his body taut, finishing as he called out her name, then letting his head rest on her shoulder, shedding tears at last onto her pillow.

The room was cooler than she had thought, and looking through the window of her bedroom, she could see a clean blue half-moon perched above a chimney stack. Somewhere, a cat bayed, low and demonic. She stroked Rob's head as he breathed long and slow, letting him cleave to her body, wanting him not to fear what they had done. She did not want to think about it, or talk about it. After what seemed like hours but was probably only minutes, he looked up, disconsolate, expecting her to be embarrassed or disgusted. He started to speak. "Hush," she said. "Let's go to sleep now." She helped him take off the rest of his clothes and then she eased him back into her bed. She went into the bathroom and brought them both a glass of water. Then she turned out the light.

She drifted into sleep in his arms. The nightmares began almost immediately, and they were ferocious. This time, there was no narrative: only a bombardment of horror, without form or sequence, a timeless vista of fire and faces and heat. Her whole body was invaded by the sensations of loss, of fear, of being an impostor. Was that Lucian's face in the eye of the storm? Or the sad smile of Tommy Bonkers? No, somebody else, somebody carrying with him an infinite hoard of pain and unresolved anguish. Ice and fire merged into one, icicles aflame and driving straight into the lacerated core of her heart. These were the bad times. *Bad things, Beatrice.*

She awoke and fled to the sitting room. The sick creature needed solitude before it could grant release to its suffering. In the safety of the sofa's corner, she broke into sobs of pure affliction. Her body shuddered with a misery she had not felt for years. This must stop. There must be an end to this. Even as she wept, she realised that this was the problem. Into the white noise of her unhappiness had crept a new voice: the stammering voice of hope, introducing itself, wondering if she would recognise it. That was what was so intolerable. The sudden recollection that her abject condition was, of course, an outrage, and must be escaped.

"Christ, are you all right?" He was standing at her side, vaguely ridiculous in an old terry-cloth robe that was too short for him and barely stretched to his knees. He reached out, and she flinched.

When he spoke, it was with the low voice of a long-felt dread which has just been justified. "I'm sorry. I'm sorry. I've gone and made things worse for you, haven't I?"

"Rob—"

"No, it's okay. I must be mad, stampeding into your life like that." He looked at her and smiled with pitiful sadness. His hair still had the asymmetry of recent sleep. "I'm sorry. You'll have to—I just got carried away. I'll go now." He picked up his bag and went back into the bedroom.

She stayed still, and did not speak when he returned fully clothed. He said good-bye but did not try to touch her this time. As she listened to his footsteps, heavy on the steps and then disappearing into the night, she wanted to tell him that he was wrong. That what he'd said was the opposite of the truth and that her pain was the pain of long-felt despair wrestling now with something new and worth cherishing. It was easy to expect nothing. Harder when hope seeped into your marrow once again.

She sat until it was light, her sadness turning to anger and then resolve. It was time. Time to call in a favour.

Chapter TWELVE

HE LOOKED rubicund now, not rosy-cheeked as she remembered. He was fleshier, too, as if the intervening years had been filled with too many dinners, too many constituency functions, too few afternoons in the gym. A stone, maybe a stone and a half heavier? He had lost some of the sheen she had spent hundreds of hours giving to him. She suspected—no more than a suspicion—that his socks might be threadbare, his belt a little frayed. The kind of thing true ambition could not afford. But his smile was the same: as winning as it was impenetrable.

As she so often had, she met Miles in Central Lobby at the House, just by the statue of Sir Stafford Northcote. It had been a long time since she had leant on the plinth and examined the stern folds of Sir Stafford's Victorian attire, his imperious brow, and his features, which pledged stern reform to the MPs, peers, and visitors who scurried past him. Just above, a smaller effigy of Henrietta Maria looked down from a century even more distant. Mia craned her neck to see the mural of Saint David over the archway, then up to the ornate ceiling with its inscriptions and adornments. The great atrium was a museum into which a nation's history had been crammed, as if there were nowhere else for it to go, an old curiosity shop of collective memory. The present tenants of Parliament—the frantic leaseholders of its power—swarmed through the lobby, indifferent to the faces, sculpted and painted, and the wisdom they sought to impart. Two screens, one red, one green, flashed with the business of the Upper and Lower Houses.

"Mia," he said. "It's wonderful to see you. You look quite beautiful." Miles leant over to kiss her. His breath, she noticed, was minty and fresh. Good to see he still remembered some of the discipline she had forced upon him. She was uncomfortable to the point of panic as she stood in their old corner, by the desks covered with blotting paper, where MPs stood and wrote notes with pens on chains. This was the marketplace where, in a former life, she had prospered most: a cross-roads between the two Houses, through which the traffic of the polity passed, back and forth, all day. Once, the smell of this ancient space had been enough to fire her with adrenaline and—sometimes—with venom. Now, she felt nothing but a sense of her own irrelevance. She wore the only business suit she had kept from her Islington wardrobe, a grey pin-stripe which was a little too large for her now, and doubtless out of fashion, along with a pair of shoes that, she knew, were not quite right. She did not look the part any longer. She had raided the dressing-up box and come as an unconvincing version of herself five years ago.

"I'm sorry I'm late," he said. "My train from Birmingham was delayed and then I had a meeting here with the poverty task force that I couldn't cancel. I'm sorry. You would have organised my day a lot better, I can tell you."

She smiled. "No, it was nice to have a look around. I haven't been here in so long. Of course, I don't have a pass anymore, so the policeman had to stop me at St. Stephen's and remind me to go through the metal detector. That was odd. I think the last time I did that was the first time I came to see you here."

"Probably was. I'm sorry about the hassle. Maybe we should have met at a restaurant, but I thought you might like to see the old place again. Better than the Home Office anyway."

"Definitely better than the Home Office." She tried hard to be bright and assertive, and to match his memory of her. Miles was not a man of imagination. He would not understand any of what had happened to her. She would have to do all the work.

"Are you hungry? I booked a table at the Churchill. If that's okay. I thought that might be nice."

"Yes, I'd like that."

He led her through the warren of lobbies and corridors, past men in frock coats, policemen, women in pantsuits on the telephone, numbered lockers, shelves of books, tearooms, ancient peers, fresh-faced MPs, postmen, journalists, waiters, frowning lobbyists. It was as she remembered it, a strange collision of industry and indolence. Everything was serious; everything was an in-joke. It was hard to disentangle the air of high sincerity from the looks of smirking fraudulence. There was no design to the place, none whatsoever: It was an assembly of chaos, a labyrinth leading nowhere and everywhere. Miles led with confidence, nodding and smiling as he went. Yes, she thought, his journey has continued since we parted company. He is a made man now, and his colleagues acknowledge that. They say that this place doesn't matter anymore, that power is made and broken in the television studios across the road. But this is still the clubhouse. This is where the boys make their deals and the girls try to join in. I was once part of this gang.

They sat down in the restaurant and Miles ordered a bottle of champagne. "Yes, that Veuve, George. Is it properly cold? Great, thanks."

"What are we celebrating?"

He clapped his hands and then held them together as if in prayer. "Reunions. The team reunited. I was worried I'd never sit at a table in this place with you again. It's been much, much too long." There was an awkward pause. "I was so surprised—I mean pleasantly surprised—to get your letter."

She had written to Miles a few hours after Rob had left. Still in her bathrobe, she had dug out some decent stationery from the bottom of a drawer and composed a letter which gave away none of her purpose but conveyed the urgency of her request in language which she knew he would remember. Lovers part, but the codes they use survive like Rosetta fragments, to be unearthed in later times. Miles would have known from her brief but cordial greeting that her need was great. His private office had called her mobile two days later and said that the minister suggested a dinner at the House the next Thursday, if that was convenient. The minister. Milesy the minister. Who would have thought it?

She had thought it, of course. She had invented the idea. She had groomed him, prepared him, chosen his clothes, and slept with him. At one time, she thought she loved him. And now she sat opposite her creation, the minister, and wondered what to say next. The waiter poured the champagne for Miles to taste and then made his way round the table to fill her glass. She wondered if he would propose a toast, which had always been one of his more irritating—and, she thought, gauche—habits. But he drank pensively. He was no less nervous than she.

"So, Miles. You have done well. I'm proud of you. Really."

He looked across the table. Was there a pearl of mournfulness in his expression? He was so hard to read, always had been. He swept his hair, still thick and dark brown, off his brow. She remembered the little mole just below his right ear.

"Thank you. Well, I need hardly say that I wouldn't have a red box and a driver today if I hadn't had you around at the beginning. I mean, I really do owe you an enormous debt. It's amazing how often, even now . . . You know, things happen and I remember what you said, and how right you were."

"Jesus." She could not help basking in the flattery. "Like what?"

"You remember you told me not to trust Luke? You remember that night at Christopher's, when you got upset with me? I remember it in detail, actually. Toe-curling detail. What a prat I was, not listening to you." Luke Robbins had been the other shooting star of Miles's generation, a favourite of the prime minister and the press, and a close friend of Miles. Years before, one of the hacks had told Mia very late one night in the bar what Luke really thought of Miles, and, more alarmingly, his strategy to ensure Miles's removal as a future rival. The reporter had then tried to put his hand up her skirt, which had brought the meeting to a swift conclusion. She had passed the intelligence on to Miles, who had shrugged and said that you could never trust the reporter in question, except when it came to putting his hand up women's skirts.

"Yes, I do. That's going back a bit. What's Luke doing now? I don't keep up as I should."

"Nothing, if I can help it. Still in a junior job at Environment, and his boss'll get the chop next time. Turns out the little bastard was putting it about that I was okay as a campaigner but that I couldn't run a fish and chip shop. Plus, he made up all sorts of stuff about a deal between the two of us—you know, a nonaggression pact. The point being that Luke would be the beneficiary of this. You know, suspiciously similar paragraphs in feature articles which linked us as allies but always made it look as if he was the senior partner."

"Of course."

"Well, perhaps not. What Luke doesn't know, you see, is that the party supremos now have chapter and verse on his little escapade with the police on Hampstead Heath after Oxford. Every last cough and spit, if you'll forgive the image." His face darkened. He looked older. "*Terrible* how they get to hear these things. Not even the tabloids know about that, and how his father had to pick him up at the station. Although, come to think of it, perhaps it's time they did. All in the interests of transparency and public accountability, you understand."

Careful, she thought. Don't get bitter, Miles; it clouds your judgement. If you have a single round in your revolver aimed at Luke, wait till you really need to fire it. And that day will come. Late one night, years from now, when the prize is near and the last few obstacles must be removed. When your blood is thin and you are all alone. Then you will need your darkest weapons, your secret arsenal. That will be the moment. But I will not be there to share it with you.

"Shall we order?" she said. Miles chose celery soup and steak, while she asked for arugula salad and sole. The champagne was poured again. She felt herself relax a little. From their window table, she could see across the terrace to the lights of the barges and pleasure boats, and across to County Hall, where a laser display announced an arts festival about to open in the capital.

"My God, Mia Taylor?" She looked up and saw a face she knew she should recognise instantly but, to her horror, did not. "The last time I saw you was in a Blackpool hotel room, and you were on your knees, mending a gadget I had foolhardily dropped. A very pleasant sight it was, too. An angel of mercy come to save me."

Thank God: Recollection of that unforgettable moment triggered every other memory she needed in order to get through the encounter with the tall grey-haired old man before her.

"Hello, Eddy." She shook his hand. Edward Brownlow: "the least impressive home secretary of the past thirty years," as *The Times* had described him, somewhat generously. Who was this home secretary thirty years before, who had been worse? Eddy had failed on every conceivable score, except as the delight of newspaper cartoonists, and survived in the Cabinet in the newly created post of minister for European development only because his departure would have given the prime minister's enemies in the party so much pleasure.

He grinned haplessly. She had forgotten all about him, and how epically useless he was. That year in Blackpool, after a summer of prison riots, controversy over asylum policy, and a botched bill on ID cards, Eddy had needed to make the speech of his life to the party's annual conference. He had called in Miles to help, and, at 2:00 A.M., the night before Eddy's big moment, Miles had paged Mia, who was in a bar on the other side of town but had battled her way through a seafront gale and tight security to get to Eddy's room in the official conference hotel. The home secretary had been conspicuously drunk and roundly abusive when she arrived. His researcher and suspected mistress of the time was crying in the corner. Miles was on the floor, trying to mend the computer which Eddy had hurled across the room. Mia took over and managed to get the Compaq to work in about half an hour. Her efforts, it turned out, were wasted: The text, as it stood, was useless, the worst-written suicide note in history, as she later described it to Miles. She had been hoping to spend the night with Miles, but she soon realised that the needs of her lover were now rather different from those he had alluded to in an earlier text message. She had asked for a glass of wine, sat Eddy down, and told him to explain what two points—two, and no more—he really wanted to make. They were both predictably dull. But she was able to distil from his rambling—mostly a hugely personal attack on the chancellor—what he wanted to say. At 3:30, she sent Miles and the researcher away, and Eddy to bed, then started to write. By the time the home secretary awoke with a ferocious hangover at 8:30, stumbling from his bedroom, demanding a Bloody Mary, she had written a half-decent speech, with three passable sound bites, all of which were running on the news by six o'clock that evening. ("A nation of conviction, not a nation of convicts" was meaningless, but it had got Eddy out of a hole on prisons.) How typical that all the ungrateful bastard could bear to remember was the fact that she had repaired the laptop.

Eddy looked at Miles and then back at her. "Glad to see you're back keeping this one in line again. He's missed you. Mind you, he'll be in the Cabinet before you can say 'knife,' so I should watch what I say. Isn't that right, Miles?"

"Well, you were a good teacher, Eddy. Let's see if Number Ten agrees."

She wanted him to leave them alone. "Actually, this is just a social call. I'm a civilian these days, Eddy. Just another voter. So you really have to be nice to me now."

He bowed and kissed her hand. "My dear. No excuse is necessary." Miles shifted with irritation in his seat. "And now I shall bid you both a good evening and return to the exciting company of my Belgian opposite number. A most entertaining man." He shuffled off, deluding himself, no doubt, that he had left with a flourish.

"Christ," said Miles. "The sooner he goes, the better."

"And the sooner he goes, the sooner another chair becomes vacant in the Cabinet. Right?"

"Right. But he won't go. The PM has made a thing of it. Not giving in to the press and all that."

"Not giving in to the chancellor, you mean."

"Just so. So I think we could have Eddy for the duration."

Their first course arrived, and they talked affably of nothing much. Miles had honed the politician's talent for small talk, offering her morsels of gossip but expecting nothing in return. He asked her a couple of times if she found her work interesting, without asking her what her work actually was. She asked about his department, and he amused her with his portraits of his colleagues. Two of the junior ministers refused to be in the same room together, which meant that officials had to dart between their respective offices in "proximity talks" modelled on the Middle East peace process. The other minister of state, technically Miles's rival for preferment, spent most of the day logged on to a Web site dedicated to Afghan hounds, which he bred at the weekends. Miles's boss, Eddy's successor, was reaching the end of the road. He was not in line for the job. But if there was a new home secretary next year, then there would be more changes in the Cabinet. It was possible, just possible, that Miles might get the call, if only to run a small department. He would be thirty-eight in May. He was not too young. She looked at him and thought back to the schemes they had hatched in bed for hours and hours: the plan, the plan. He had not strayed from the plan, not yet. He was still on course.

They drank a good Pouilly Fumé over the main course. He had chosen steak and would, she knew, have preferred a robust claret. But he deferred to her choice from the menu and joined her in a few glasses of white. The wine was well chosen, crisp and fruity. Another thing she had taught him. The falcon and the falconer. Now she needed the falcon's help.

"Miles, I came here for a reason."

He wiped his mouth and put his napkin on the table. "I imagined you missed the pleasure of my company."

"Miles, I'm serious. I need a favour. I wouldn't ask if it wasn't a last resort. No, I don't mean that the way it sounded. I mean that I wouldn't bother you unless I had nowhere else to turn."

He considered this. She knew what he would be thinking: He would not want to get involved in anything tiresome, time-consuming, or in any way risky. He had closed her file long ago, and would not want to reopen it unnecessarily. On the other hand, his politician's antennae would be alive to the prospect that he might be able to grant her a favour easily and that she would then be in his debt. That was what politicians did. He would be curious as well as cautious.

"You know what?" he said, signalling to the waiter for the bill. "I fancy a nightcap. It's hard to talk here—properly, I mean. Eddy Brownlow and his friends stalk every corridor. And you obviously don't want any disturbances—which there will undoubtedly be if we stay here. Let's go back to Selbourne Terrace."

"My God, you kept that place? I assumed you'd be somewhere else by now."

"I am, officially at least. A flat on Albert Embankment. All very nice, I suppose. Spent most of my inheritance on it. It's near here, of course, and it's been done up properly by—what shall I call them?—the friends, who have got it into their heads that I'm a security risk just because I've been on telly a couple of times with the mullahs. Well, you remember. All those shouting matches with Saffi and Aziz. So they spent six weeks doing the flat up. Entry phones, panic buttons, the works. Very impressive, the friends are. They asked me if I had a cat. Apparently, they do special security cat flaps these days."

"So why did you keep Selbourne Terrace?"

"Oh, I don't know. The trouble with the new place is that I don't really feel at home. It's a bit soulless. Very functional. I like my old flat. I can relax there. I know where everything is."

You lying bastard, Mia thought. You kept Selbourne Terrace so that you can take your girls back there, away from the private office, away from the reporters, away from the twitchy "friends." You still need a love shack, after all these years, you stupid boy. She imagined Miles emerging at lunchtime from the Home Office in Queen Anne's Gate, slipping into his car, his driver shaking his head and smiling as they raced off to the little flat in Butler's Wharf, just in time for Miles to open the door to some party official, or secretary, or junior civil servant, his latest conquest in a long line. She imagined the wine in the fridge, the hurried sex, the lack of tenderness, Miles showering, the return to the office. She imagined his smugness at his first afternoon meeting, his superior manner with the permanent secretary as he enjoyed the feel of a fresh shirt. She imagined it all. She remembered it.

"How does that sound?" Miles smiled at her. There was a lubricity to his expression, the merest hint of presumption on his damp upper lip. Even as he had gone to seed over the past three years, Miles had retained his priapic edge. His urges had evidently not declined with his sinews. The effect was not pleasant. She was watching the dawn of middle-aged lechery.

She had fallen for him more or less instantly when Kingsley had introduced the two of them at Robinson's annual summer reception. She remembered admiring his confidence and his cheek and his slim frame. He had shown her his new cuff links, which were a gift from the Japanese ambassador. He made jokes at his own expense. She had wanted to go to bed with him that night, and had done so only a week later, after their first professional meeting. The sex was vigorous, exciting. Pushing her over the sofa in his flat and calling out her name, he made her feel from the start that he could not bear to be apart from her. There was an urgency to his need which would have seemed pathetic in another man but was captivating in Miles. She had taken Tash Chapman out for dinner a few days later and confided in her old friend about her new lover, the two women giggling noisily at her usual table at Le Caprice. She told Tash drunkenly that she could imagine marrying Miles. Their lovemaking, she believed, was unimprovable, exactly what sex should be. Only at a distance could she see that it was nothing more than the continuation of politics by other means. Their ferocious attraction to each other was the attraction of like to like, the love ambition has for itself.

Now she was in his ministerial car, driving past the policemen at the entrance to the Commons and turning off Parliament Square onto the bridge. At this time of night, it would take no more than ten minutes to get to Selbourne Terrace. Miles engaged in badinage with his driver, Sam, who acknowledged her presence with a polite insouciance, which she found eloquent. Twice, she caught him looking at her in his rearview mirror, doubtless comparing her with Miles's recent trophies. He would discuss her with the other drivers the next morning as they laughed over the antics of their respective ministerial cargoes. Whatever it was, the drivers always knew first. That much she remembered. She wondered how big Sam's last Christmas bonus had been, and how much bigger the next one would have to be.

Miles looked at his card of appointments for the next day and noted with pleasure that he was not expected at the Home Office until eleven.

"You know what, Sam?" he said. "Why don't you take the morning off and go shopping with Mary? You know how much she wants to go and get that kitchen sorted."

"Oh no, sir, I couldn't do that."

"Seriously. I can make my own way in. Believe me, it'll be good for your marriage."

"That's very kind of you, sir."

"No problem. Pick me up at the office at two. I've got to meet some cops in Southwark."

They were driving round the maze of Butler's Wharf now, through the little lanes of stacked loft conversions and chic restaurants. After he came down from Cambridge, Miles had bought his two-bedroom flat in Selbourne Terrace for what seemed like a lot of money. His father helped him out, having promised to subsidise Miles's political ambitions for five years. They had agreed that if he had not been selected for a decent parliamentary constituency by the time he was twenty-seven, he would think again and find another career. But the Andertons, father and son, had not had to wait that long. Three days short of his twenty-sixth birthday, Miles had been selected for a constituency with a majority of ten thousand, thanks almost entirely to the pressure brought to bear by the party machine. His father had agreed to pay the mortgage for five more years. He was dead now, and he had left everything to his only child. Mia doubted Miles had a mortgage any longer.

The ground-floor flat was set in the back of a building but had a small front garden, which was much better tended than she remembered. She watched Sam turning in the road as Miles got out his keys.

"Do you let him take time off like that often?" she asked.

Miles tried not to smile. "Oh, not that often. He's a great guy. I've been really lucky with him. He makes me laugh. Always knows what's going on. Told me the best story ever about Trish Hughes the other day."

"Where is she now?"

"Minister of state at Health. Definitely being groomed for the Cabinet. Apparently, she's having it away with her fitness instructor. She and her driver go and meet this guy at his studio, which he closes for her. Which is just as well, because apparently Trish has been getting very busy on the pec deck, if you know what I mean. Sam thinks her husband doesn't know."

"How can Sam tell?"

"Sam knows everything. Here, look at this."

Mia saw that the front door lock had been rebuilt. There was now a large black box with a keypad beside it. He entered a six-digit number and the bolt was released with an electronic bleep.

"The friends found out I was still using this place and practically had a nervous breakdown. I was given a kicking by the permanent secretary. Big row, all this stuff about taxpayers' money being spent on the Albert Embankment flat, asking me what was the point. Well, you can imagine. Anyway, I had to meet them halfway, and they installed this stupid lock. It helps that I'm the only one in the block who uses this particular entrance. So I'm the only one who knows the number." He pushed the door open for her. "I was told it couldn't be anything related to me personally, so I chose your birthday. How's that?"

They made their way down the corridor. "Well, Miles. I don't know what to say. I should be grateful, I suppose. Immortalised as a PIN number."

Miles turned on the lights and shut the door behind them. The flat had been redecorated, but the furniture was as she remembered: the belongings of an unreconstructed bachelor. The walls were lined with books, newspaper cartoons, and photographs. She was reminded of Councillor Phil's collection of memorabilia, a low-rent version of Miles's tribute to himself. In pride of place was a picture of the president of the United States shaking Miles's hand at a private function in London and smiling as if Miles had just informed him that a constitutional amendment had been passed which would enable him to stand for a third term in office. There was a more artistic black-and-white shot of Miles speaking at a conference, jabbing his finger into the air. There was a picture of him running the London Marathon for his favourite child-poverty charity. And there was a picture of Jean.

How long was it since Mia had thought of Jean? There had been a time when she and Miles's Commons secretary had spoken ten or more times a day, steering him in the right direction, tracking him down, exchanging women's confidences. She was in her late fifties then and wore the cardigans of an older woman. She loved Miles, though she would never tell him so, and he loved her in return. He revelled in her mild reproaches and her anxiety on his behalf. She took care of him, as Mia had realised from the start. She worried about him as a mother would, and filled the void in his life left by his parents. Mia remembered sitting on the edge of her desk in the Commons, talking about the future of this brash young man as if it were the most important thing in the world. "He needs to be taken in hand, that boy," Jean would say, looking up archly at Mia, as if it were obvious what she meant. It was obvious what she meant. Mia always wondered what Miles had done to deserve this pillar of loyalty, decked in pearls, resplendent even in her ugly clothes.

"Jean," she said, almost to herself. "How is Jean?"

Miles handed her a glass of wine. "Jean? Oh God. I should have told you earlier."

"What?" She followed him and sat down. "What, Miles?"

"It's bloody awful, I'm afraid. She's got cancer, has for two years now. They've done all they can, but she's decided not to have any more treatment. It was tearing her to pieces. She lost her hair and—" He put his hand to his head and closed his eyes, wincing at the very words he was uttering, the pain they stirred. "Nothing left to do, really. She's a day patient in a hospice down in Bellingham, not far from her house. I've been once or twice to see her. Not often enough."

"Christ, Miles, I'm sorry. I know how much she means to you."

"Yeah," he said. She remembered the tone of bitterness in his voice, always there when he had talked of his mother's death. His father calling him at school to tell him. He shrugged, as if there was nothing that could be done about the return of the fates to conspire against him. "There's not much to say about it, really."

So it is that I come to sit opposite you once again, Mia thought. When we were lovers, death was only a memory: the bad dream of a mother leaving a young boy alone with his father, and the pain hammered on the forge into the iron of ambition. That was you, Miles. And me, too. Immortal in our own eyes, in our bed. We would go forth and conquer, lay claim to all that we wished and discard the rest. We were golden, untouchable. Now I am here with you, a small woman, still in the weeds of the bereaved. And you are angry again, angry this time at Jean for leaving you. We all leave each other, sooner or later.

"I saw you on television the other day," she said. "You were on the green outside the Commons. Very angry about something."

He laughed into his drink. "What was I on about?"

"Not sure. Your opposite number was being 'crass and ridiculous,' I think."

"Small Dave? Oh, that must have been about the militants' bill. Dave thinks I'm cracking down too hard on the mullahs. Civil liberties stuff."

"You've kept going with it? I wasn't sure you would."

He frowned. "Why ever not? It's even bigger than it was when you were with me. Islam, the fundies, and all that. Dr. Muhammad and his friends." He took his jacket off and threw it over the back of his chair. "It's terrific box office. The focus groups love it. You know, standing firm, cracking down on terror, not being pushed around by towelheads. The PM says he'll back me all the way."

"What about the home secretary?"

Miles snorted with derision. "He's too frightened even to talk about it. Said he doesn't want to get involved. Muslims in his constituency, all the usual. Which suits me. He's left me an open goal. And if I put the ball in the back of the net, I'll be in the Cabinet this time next year. Simple as that."

She accepted more wine. She had run out of things to say to him and knew that she must broach the subject before he lost patience. "Miles, I need a favour. That's why I contacted you. I really wouldn't have bothered you otherwise. But you are the only person who can help now."

She had his attention. He blinked as he did when he was concentrating. "I guessed it was important. After all this time. Your letter . . .

well, let's say it was more interesting for what it didn't say than for what it did."

"I knew you'd understand. I remembered how sharp you are. It helped when I was writing it." She sipped the Sancerre. "And I didn't want to put anything in writing that would embarrass you. It was marked 'Strictly Confidential,' but I knew it would get opened. I don't know your code mark—you know, so the officials know to leave it alone."

"I can give you that. But anyway. What's up that you have to call a minister?"

She told him about Ben and Claude and Micky Hazel and her visit to Michael Aitch Motors. His eyes widened as he listened. She continued, explaining her fears, how Micky Hazel had reacted, her need for information. She imagined that this was precisely what he had not wanted to hear from her. A case long closed, pointlessly reopened by prying, meddlesome Mia. Too much emotion invested. Too much danger. No rewards in prospect, either. No benefit to anyone. What was to be gained? Every line in his face asked that question as she concluded her story. She could see what he thought: that the sharp wits he remembered in her—which he had, perhaps, loved—had decayed into a tedious, reckless paranoia.

He went to the fridge and opened another bottle. "God, you have been a busy bee, haven't you?"

"Can you understand why I wrote to you? I need your help."

Miles, still in the kitchen, turned to her sharply. "How can I possibly help?"

She looked into her lap. "I'm not really sure."

He poured the wine, put the bottle on the table, and sat down. His mood had changed. "Listen, Mia. You went through hell. And you lost everything. Absolutely everything. And I lost you as a result. Don't you know what that was like? You meant the world to me. I hated you leaving like that, just disappearing. But I half guessed you would, and I had to accept it. It was bloody hard. I often think about what might have happened. Who knows? I'll tell you this: You are the only person I have ever thought of proposing to. I came close even when we were together. That night in Vienna? Yes, you remember. If you hadn't been so tired, I would have asked. And then it was over. I had to accept it."

She looked into his eyes to see if he was lying. They were opaque, unyielding. "I had to get away," she mumbled, the words dead even as she spoke them.

"I know. The point is that you can't do what you're doing. You just can't. Your family's case was closed more than three years ago. If you stomp around town accusing people of doing it, you could land in all sorts of trouble. And that's only the legal position, which is, frankly, the least of your worries. Listen, what your friends are saying is right. If Ben was up to no good—let's just say—you've no business looking into it now."

"I don't believe the case is closed. Do you believe it is? Do you, Miles?"

"Do I believe that your family was the victim of a ghastly blunder? Yes. Yes, I do." He paused and leant forward. "I wasn't sure what to think about it all to start with. But you know the funny thing with this job is that you realise how useless the human race is. I mean, you imagine it's all run by conspiracy, and that the things that go wrong go wrong because of cunning. But it's not true. Day after day, I have to wade through files about suffering and crime and killing, and most of it's just a load of nonsense. It's bullshit. Mistakes, arbitrary attacks, anger spilling over. Nonsense. I remember thinking that when I heard about what had happened to your family. It was just nonsense. Pointless. That's how things happen. I wish it weren't so."

No, she thought, you're glad it is so. You're very glad. It makes your job easier, to be able to sit there smugly and say that such things happen. To tell me to calm down, when all I want is the truth, or something close to it. "Do you know what, Miles? It took me more than three years to come to terms with that 'nonsense,' as you call it. And now I have to face the fact that it was something else entirely that killed my whole family. Everything I was told, all the rubbish that was in the papers, was a lie. That is more than a minor detail to me, I assure you. I'm not trying to be awkward. I'm not trying to rock any boats. I'm just"—she could hear her voice rising, and tried to control her fury—"I'm trying to find out what really happened. That's all. Is that so bad?"

"Of course it isn't. Of course not." He put his feet up on the table. "I'm just not convinced that you're right. I don't believe that's why your family died. I'm sorry, but I don't."

Last chance. Last chance to force his hand. She breathed deeply, closed her eyes, then opened them again. "I'll ask only once. And then I won't bother you again. Look: Micky Hazel is obviously more than a car salesman. Perhaps you'll allow me that. And what I need to know—all I need to know—is whom he represents. His boss. His real boss. Who was he warning me off? I need a name. That's it. It's the sort of thing you can find out with one phone call. A minute of your time. I know that, and so do you. And here's the thing, Miles. Here's the thing." She caught his eye. "You fucking owe me, Miles. You really fucking do."

He owed her more than the favour she was asking; that was for sure. When he had been moonlighting for Eddy Brownlow, she had been astonished by what senior ministers saw, and how easy it was for them to gain access to information. She and Miles had spent a gleefully macabre night drinking champagne and reading out the gruesome details of one of the twentieth century's most notorious murder cases from a brown Whitehall folder. She remembered Miles, naked, with a flute in one hand and the file in the other, standing on the bed and describing the incision of a Stanley knife, as recorded in a coroner's report. It made her feel sick to think of it. That was how easy it would be for Miles to find out who exactly Micky Hazel's boss was, and whom Ben had crossed when he got greedy. Less time than it took the minister to order up a copy of a parliamentary report from the library, or to complain about the filling in his sandwich.

"I do owe you, Mia. I do indeed. But I won't break the law. I won't help you with some vigilante escapade. Think back. What would the Mia of four years ago have told me to do?" His hands clasped the arms of his chair. "What would she have said?"

She stood up and put her bag over her shoulder. "I don't know. Something insufferably knowing, I expect. Just the sort of thing you wanted to hear, I imagine."

"Where are you going?" Now he was on his feet, too.

"Where do you think? I came to see if you would help me. And you've made it very clear that you won't. So I'll be on my way."

He stood in her path as she headed for the door. His shirt was hanging out now and two of the buttons had come undone, revealing more flesh than she remembered. His features were saturnine and heavy. "Don't be ridiculous." He smiled. "Come on, Mia. We'll talk about it. It's early yet. Have another drink."

"I've had enough to drink, thanks. And so have you, by the looks of things. Now, if you don't mind."

She tried again to get past him. To her amazement, he grabbed her. She struggled, thinking he was acting from reflex, then realised that he knew exactly what he was doing. "Come on," he said, his grip tightening on her arm. "I've missed you. Don't leave just yet. You look so good. Let's go next door. For old times' sake. Come on. Don't tell me it hasn't crossed your mind."

Then she was trembling, but not from fear. Laughter took hold of her body like an alien force and sent it into spasms which shook her free from his grasp. She could not help herself, though she knew that he would take it badly and that things might become ugly. He was pathetic, so pathetic. As vulnerable as she had felt at the start of the evening, she now wondered why she had ever imagined such a ridiculous man could ever help her with her task. Lunging at her like a silly, spoilt schoolboy. Not safe in taxis. Not safe in the Cabinet, either: That would be his punishment. So greedy, so cunning, but foolish in ways that his elders would have noted. The rulers of the party would with-hold the prize from him.

He called after her as she marched down the corridor and out of the front door. She was glad that he did not chase her out into the night, that she was spared a second tussle with the shambling minister of the Crown. She welcomed the air and the walk over the cobbles towards Tower Bridge. Maybe she would walk all the way home. Yes, that was what she would do.

She made her way down the terrace towards Bell Street. She thought she saw fleeting movement in the shadows opposite Miles's building. No more than the hint of another presence, something or someone scrutin-ising her as she fled. Was there a figure, wraithlike, lurking in the black-ness? Was that the flash of a ring or a mirror, or nothing at all? She stopped for a second and looked again. A cat ran across the cobbles. The wheels of a car screeched somewhere. She resumed her escape, faster this time.

It was not as late as she had imagined, and couples were still emerg-ing from the restaurants, full of wine and unguarded intimacy. Glancing through the windows, she could see the waiters closing up, the barman pouring a drink for a blond coat-check girl of astonishing beauty. It was a generous measure. Four floors above, a man was braving the chill and leaning out of his apartment window, smoking a cigar and surveying the river. A tug rumbled past her, its lights rotating and sending beams cut-ting sharply across the new and old stone of the riverbank. Seeing a mound of human debris huddled in a sleeping bag by one of the little walls, she wondered where Tommy Bonkers was and whether he was still alive. She could still hear the long, disapproving silence down the line as she had told Dr. Armitage of her failure and confessed that his patient had escaped her custody.

She walked up the stairs to the bridge and made her way across. It was a walk she had always loved, especially when there were few people in the way, only the insect drone of passing cars to disturb her thoughts.

She looked down the river, towards the distant winking tower of Canary Wharf. I am at home at last, she thought. This is my home now. Not the neighbourhoods with their high walls and gossip and tribal codes, but the whole city through which I walk at night, which claimed me long ago as its own. I am safe in its darkness, the long streets, upon which only slivers of light fall until dawn comes.

As she walked, she reached into her bag and got out her mobile. She dialled the number and called. He was not asleep.

"Hi," she said. "It's me."

He was silent for only a moment. "Where are you? You sound miles away."

She enjoyed the inadvertent pun. "I'm on Tower Bridge, walking home from dinner. It's such an incredible night. I was thinking about you."

"Really?"

"Really. Look, do you want to get together? I'm not sleepy."

"I can't believe you still want to see me. I thought I'd blown it."

"Oh, shut up, Rob. Just meet me. Okay?"

"Okay. Where?"

She liked the sound of his voice, its familiarity. "At that bar on Brick Lane. It'll be open. I'll be there in about half an hour." She clicked her phone shut.

In the morning, she woke in his arms. She looked at the clock, saw it was ten, and realised that they had slept through the alarm. Somebody was ringing the front doorbell with mounting irritation. She reached under the bedclothes, grabbed him to wake him and to remind herself what he felt like. She kissed him on the mouth and realised that she had not taken off her makeup. He blinked awake and she pounced on him, straddling his naked body.

"Bloody hell. What's that racket?"

She rolled off and put on her bathrobe. "I don't know. Somebody wants me."

"I want you," he said, trying to grab her.

"Even more than you do, child," she said, and ran to the door.

Standing in the portico was a forlorn motorcycle courier carrying a clipboard, desperate to give up but receiving stern instructions from his radio not to do so. She could hear the voice of his controller crackling out of the ether: "Two-one, try again. Keep trying. This is a code blue. Repeat, code blue."

The courier spoke into his mike. "Two-one here. Er, success at last, I think, Steve. Wait five and will confirm. Over and out for now." He inspected Mia, with her crazy hair and bathrobe. "Are you Miss Mia Taylor?"

"Yes."

"Package. Please sign." He handed her the clipboard, indicating two boxes. "Print name and sign here."

She scribbled in both boxes and took the big brown envelope, which was stamped ADDRESSEE ONLY. She shut the door and went into the kitchen to put the kettle on. As it boiled, she ripped open the envelope, and took out a grainy photocopied form, a black-and-white photograph, and—separately—three more pages of typed A4, on which was stapled a piece of unheaded notepaper. It was not signed, but she recognised the handwriting. It said, "There's no such thing as a free lunge. You win."

The form was almost completely illegible; the original had been folded over, so that most of it was obscured. All but two of the boxes had been whitened out. In the first was her brother's name: Benjamin Simon Taylor. In the second, marked "Suspected Activities," was scrawled "Evidence of computer fraud, illicit cash transfers. See par 2(d) below. Recommend referral."

The photo, obviously shot with a telephoto lens, showed a man in his sixties, or perhaps older, getting out of a dark car. He was wearing a black coat, a white shirt, and a tie, on which a pin could just be made out. He was gaunt and looked tired. But his face bore the mark of an iron will: The lips curled down in displeasure and a sharp, battered nose stood at the centre of craggy, imperial features. He had a full head of hair, white with a little grey, cut above ears that had been mauled in the boxing ring and probably elsewhere. His eyes were blank, the eyes of a kestrel.

The attached enclosure was a samizdat file of some sort, a hastily made photocopy, third generation at least. It was addressed to somebody whose name had been deleted with whitener. The reference number had also been erased, as had another code at the top of each page. There was no departmental letterhead. But as she read on, she guessed that this was a confidential memorandum by a political adviser to a minister. It was impossible to tell when it had been written, or precisely why. But it told her all she needed to know.

ALFRED (aka "freddy") ELLIS

You asked me to provide you with some basic information on Ellis before your meeting today. You have seen the police file and will know that he has two convictions, one for armed robbery, and the second for grievous bodily harm, and has served a total of six years in prison in two stretches. He also breached a probation order in 1976.

This is only the tip of the iceberg, as you predicted at the 9:00 A.M. last week. It is no secret that Ellis, who is believed to be 68 (69?), has, at various times, controlled much of the criminal activity in the East End and in some other parts of the country, too. He is understood to have extensive interests in narcotics, prostitution, and extortion, although I am told that we have "not come close" to prosecution in any of these areas.

The memo described an awesome network of criminality, developed, it seemed, with near impunity, over three decades. She remembered mentioning Ellis when Ringo was ranting that he would get protection from Dove's crew. Some protection. This was a man of terrifying power, whose savagery was matched only by his elusiveness. Everybody knew what Ellis was up to, but nobody was able to prove it. And here, the anonymous author wrote, lay political danger. The risk of total failure.

> It is generally believed that Ellis is now a very wealthy man. However, IC4 have been unable to find evidence of this in his domestic accounts. Information on offshore accounts is also limited. We must assume that Ellis has taken steps to insulate himself from systematic enquiry on this front.

The memo hinted darkly at payoffs to the police, mysterious interventions on Ellis's behalf, and a chase that was unlikely to be worth the bother.

> Having spoken to all relevant divisions, I am convinced that Ellis is a bad target for the crackdown you propose. The politics of success are obvious: big scalp, press coverage, etc. But failure carries significant risks. Ellis is a folkloric figure in his neighbourhood, although it is many years since he lived there (he is thought to divide his time between Chelmsford and his villa in Spain). I would strongly advise against action of the sort SH suggested, although it may be politic to go through the motions at your meeting, given the sensitivities involved, which we discussed last week. I have spoken to P.W., by the way, who agrees with the above analysis.

The sensitivities involved. She wondered when this shabby exercise in political evasion had been written, to whom it was addressed, and where it had been filed. No matter: As she'd thought, it had taken Miles only a matter of minutes to come up with the answer she had sought.

Probably no more than a muttered aside to the person he trusted most in his private office. Now, she need never speak to him again. He had provided her with what she was after. She felt the loneliness of knowledge, the final barriers to action swept away at last. She tore the document in half and put it in the bin.

Rob walked in and took her in his arms, stroking her face. "Who was that?"

"Oh, just recorded delivery," she said, stirring at his touch, allowing him to move his hands inside her robe.

"Did he bring anything interesting?"

She looked up at him. "Oh, nothing much. A repayment on one of my accounts."

Chapter THIRTEEN

THE GREY frost crunched under her feet as she left the emergency room and walked down the ramp, through the pool of bright light, and out onto the street. What time was it? She wasn't wearing her watch, and she didn't want to ask the bouncer standing at the door of the Mexican pub. The woman at the desk had offered to book her a cab, but she decided to walk home in spite of the bitter cold. She wanted to clear her head and try to understand what had happened. She needed time to think about it all, to think about nothing. She noticed for the first time that her own hands were still caked with blood from the fall. Where she had hit the curb, perhaps. That was probably it.

She walked down Whitechapel, passing the curry houses and the pubs. On the wide pavement, groups of drunken men staggered their way towards the Tube station, shouting abuse at one another. She kept her head down, startled occasionally by the rumble of a bus passing by, its light flashing through the leaves of the trees. Outside a fried-chicken joint, a woman in a shiny tracksuit was vomiting. Her boyfriend, who wore a football shirt under his leather jacket, was berating her furiously between swigs from a bottle. An old Muslim man in a thick body warmer, his beard full and grey, looked on in rapt horror at this vignette of brutal hedonism. A police van approached and the girl straightened up and pulled herself together. Mia felt a twinge in her right ankle. She was in more pain than she had expected, or admitted.

It was only two days since she had found Irene—the lonely widow who had been a regular at the Echinacea Centre—and bought her a cup of coffee. Irene had wanted ordinary instant coffee, of course, and told Mia that she "could not be doing" with all the fancy lattes and mochas and skinny this and organic that on offer these days in the café. She said that there was no need for all that fuss, that it held people up in the line because they did not know the answer to all the questions they suddenly had to answer about perfectly obvious things. Why did there have to be so much choice? She didn't understand. Irene smiled as she held forth. Mia wondered how long it was since she had been bought a cup of coffee. Her complaint had the garrulousness of the lonely.

She had found Irene in the community centre off Mare Street, which was a favourite of pensioners on her estate. It had started serving Costa coffee to attract business from young professionals. Still, most of the people sitting at the new pine tables in its café were Irene's age or older, some wearing suits, most of them silent. A couple in the corner played Scrabble. A black man in a trilby ate his egg and cress sandwich with infinite care, as if his method was being appraised by a panel of experts. Irene was on her own, sitting with her knitting and a magazine. She looked up when Mia walked in but did not recognise her. She returned to her magazine, flicking the pages without reading. So this was how Irene spent the long watches of the afternoon, when the shopping was done, after a little lunch at home, before an evening with her cat in front of the telly and bed by ten. An outing to the pop-in centre, and the meagre comfort of being with other people counting the hours in the same way, her brothers and sisters in solitude. Mia remembered Irene telling her once with great pride that she had laid flowers at Reg's grave every week for five years without missing a visit. These were the rituals of the widow, the observances that formed the contours of her life.

It was important that Irene not know that Mia was looking for her, that this was, in fact, the third place she had looked in. To get the moment of pretence over with, she walked directly to her table. "Well, hello, Irene," she said. "Is this one of your haunts, then?" The older woman peered at her through her thick glasses, her features screwed up with the effort of identification. She revealed a plate of ill-fitting dentures as she smiled broadly in recognition.

"Well, Chels, dear. This is a lovely surprise. You on your way somewhere?"

"I am actually. I'm looking at some computer things for Sylvia, but I'm gasping for a coffee. I didn't know they'd done this place up. It's nice to see you. Is this near where you live?"

"Just a few minutes' walk, love." Irene motioned for her to sit down. "I like coming in here in the afternoon. Nice and cosy."

"It's very nice. I've never been in here before." She took off her gloves and muffler. "Fancy seeing you here. You haven't been by the centre for a while. We've missed you."

"Oh, well. You know how it is, Chels. My foot's been playing up again, and if it's not one thing, it's another. Busy, busy. I've been meaning to come down. I do enjoy those classes." The Scrabble-playing couple had finished their game and were putting the pieces back in the box. They were talking about sausages and supper.

Mia went to get the coffees and returned, to find Irene staring out of the window at some kids in school uniform who were milling around at a bus stop, comparing the enormous quantities of sweets and crisps they had just bought. A redheaded girl with the skin and eyebrows of an albino was twisting the arm of a smaller boy to make him release a big pack of crisps. The boy cried out in pain, swore viciously at his tormentor, and gave her the bag. He then walked over to another boy, who was reading a comic book, and kicked him in the shins. The second boy began to cry at once—the kick must have broken skin—but did not retaliate, or complain at the brute injustice of what had happened to him. His tears provided the group with a fresh focus. They turned from their junk food to his misery, pointing at him and mocking him.

Irene shook her head. "These kids, Chels. I don't know. Oh, thank you, dear." She took the mug. "I mean, we were always naughty when we were little. I used to pull my sisters' hair all the time. Running around the house. Drove my old dad mad, we did. Said girls were worse, why couldn't he have a son to keep him company? Well, he ended up with three girls, didn't he? It's potluck, isn't it?"

"I suppose it is."

"Well, that's what my mum used to say to him anyway. We were a handful, I'm sure. But we weren't so . . ." She searched for a word, scrolling through years of experience to express the difference between then and now. She looked as if the task had defeated her. "Well, I don't think we were so cruel as these youngsters are now. That's all."

Mia sipped her decaffeinated cappuccino. She had postponed her little visit for a few days, mostly because she knew that Rob's suspicions had been aroused by the courier, but also because she did not know what exactly she was looking for. She could not speak to Rob, Ringo, or Sylvia about what she had discovered. She could not possibly tell them that a government minister had passed to her some deadly information, and that the way in which she used that information was intimately linked with her prospects for survival. The trail was no longer cold. It led now to a door of unknown horrors.

Freddy Ellis. Probably well into his seventies now. A legend, as the unknown memo writer had reminded his boss. Perhaps even more powerful than Jack Dove, and certainly more dangerous. No longer photographed as he once was, arriving at exclusive West End discos or opening a new boys' club. A recluse these days. But still, she now knew, a man whose lieutenants protected his interests and policed what remained of his empire. How many Micky Hazels did Ellis have at his command, even now? More, probably, than the politicians and detectives who had given up hunting him could possibly guess. Wherever he was, Ellis had outwitted the custodians of law and order, made them look like fools for so long that their political masters had instructed them to give up. Between him and the rest of the world stood men like Micky, smiling, cleaning up, making sure that nobody—nobody, nobody—got within a mile of the man who had run it all, the man who made things possible. It was the voice of Ellis she had heard creep into Micky's accent when he warned her off that day in Stratford. It was the voice of quiet, murderous confidence. Ellis had won, and he wanted to make sure it stayed that way. Poor Ben. Poor clever Ben, with his flashing screens and his schemes and his juvenile greed. He never stood a chance against these veterans of avarice and bloodshed.

But Mia needed to find this man. She needed to ask him, even if she signed her own death warrant in doing so. Ellis would understand why she had to ask, why this was a matter of self-respect rather than vengeance. More than Micky, he would admire her for trying at all, for chasing him to find out why, and how, he had punished her brother and killed her family. He would nod and speak softly of the terrible things of this world, with his dead eyes and manicure. And then, she imagined, he would have her followed—perhaps not that day, but another day, soon. And she would be hit by a car, or feel the cold steel in her belly, or perhaps even the barrel of a gun. The end, when it came, would be swift. But first she had to find him.

And in her frustration, sitting sleepless on her sofa, it had come to her: Irene would know. Not where Ellis was, of course. But she would know where to start, the places where the man used to be seen when she was a younger woman and his dominion in the East End was public and flamboyant. She would not know much, but enough. She would tell Mia what she knew, without asking too many questions or probing too deeply. And she, unlike Ellis, would not be hard to find.

They talked for a while about the centre and its troubles, about Rob and how he was settling in. Mia blushed when Irene said that what Mia needed was a nice young man to treat her right. Irene asked her whether she would stay in the area, and Mia said that she did not know. She took advantage of the question to ask how the neighbourhood had changed over the years. Irene warmed to the theme.

"Changed? If only you knew, love. It's like a whole new kind of people—like a—what's the word?—*species,* that's it—came out of nowhere and landed on top of us. Bang on top. Nobody can afford to live here anymore." She shook her head and nibbled her biscuit. "It's for people like you now, Chels. Not for people like me. It's just the way things are, I suppose."

Mia did not meet her eye, but she tried to make her question sound lighthearted. "What about all the legends? You know, the shooting in the Blind Beggar? Jack Dove and Freddy Ellis? Is it all rubbish?"

"Jack Dove! Would you believe that he asked me to dance once? More than thirty years ago, we're talking about now. At a club in South Woodford, it was. Reg used to go there, and he took me along one night when they had a band. Well, guess who was there? Only Dove and his cronies. All wearing beautiful suits, polished shoes. Brylcreemed hair, of course. Men were smart in those days. But I was terrified. I mean, I didn't want to be in the same place as a chap like that." Irene looked around conspiratorially, as if somebody might be spying on them. "I asked to leave, but Reg said, 'Don't be silly. They own the place. Where's the harm?' "

"What did you do?"

"I had a stiff gin for starters, dear. And then probably another. I don't recall. Then Reg and I danced a bit. And then we sat down for a breather, you know. And suddenly I look up and it's only Jack Dove himself, isn't it? I mean, poor Reg. I think he was having to pay a bit of protection every week on the dry-cleaning business to one of Dove's men. Thank goodness he was prompt with the payments. But actually to have to speak to the man himself! Well, it was Reg who was spooked now, not me. I got a good look at him and he wasn't half handsome, Chels." She laughed, and Mia joined in. "A real heartthrob, he was. Tall and dark. Like Cary Grant or something. And he said good evening to both of us and asked if we were having a good time, and could he get us a drink. And then he says that he couldn't help noticing what good dancers we were, and how he wasn't half as good as Reg, but would Reg mind if he took a turn with his good lady wife. And Reg—well, he was flabbergasted. But he just shook his head, and I looked at him and thought, Well, you can't say no. I mean, can you? So I stood up, terrified, of course. And we were just about to go on the dance floor, when one of Jack's men comes up and whispers something in his ear. All urgent like, pointing outside. And he says he's terribly sorry but something's come up, business, and he's got to go, and would I forgive him. And he shook my hand and Reg's, and then he was off."

"Did you ever see him again?"

"Oh, no. Didn't expect to, either. And then, of course, things got harder for people like him, all the publicity, and you didn't see them around these parts anymore. But I dined out on that for years, I can tell you."

"What about Freddy Ellis? Did he ever ask you to dance?"

Irene scrutinised her. Her expression was less carefree now. "Oh, dear me, no, love. Not Freddy Ellis. You didn't dance with Freddy Ellis. You stayed out of his way. He was a vicious piece of work. No gentleman at all. He hurt a lot of people didn't deserve it."

Mia tried to conceal her interest. "How do you mean?"

Irene frowned, as if the question were vaguely indecent. "Oh, you don't want to know, Chels. Really. Thank goodness them days are over, is all I can say. Good riddance. We're all better off."

"Why?" Mia's laugh sounded forced even to her own ears. "Was it that bad?"

"It was worse." She fell silent, as if debating whether to unburden herself of some hideous knowledge. She seemed to take a deep breath, and set her knitting aside. "My Reg had a friend called Johnny Prentice, you see. He was an odd-job man round the estates and he kept things spick-and-span. Drank most of his wages away, mind, and the rest of it went on the horses. But harmless, you know? Reg and I used to buy him a fish supper when he was short, which was most of the time. Sweetest fella you could hope to meet, and he and Reg had known each other since the army. They were quite tight, in their own way. In the way that blokes are."

"I see. So what happened?"

"Freddy Ellis and his firm used to spend most lunchtimes in a big pub up in Dalston called the Jake. It was Freddy's favourite place in the day, you know? When he wasn't in swanky places up west in the evenings, he was in the Jake. It was sort of their headquarters. They used the back office and had a bunch of tables reserved for them and their friends. It was no place for a lady, I must say. I only went in there once or twice, and it was awful. But Johnny liked it because it was near a place where he used to get a bit of work. Plus, there was a bookie's next door." Irene rolled her eyes. "Anyway, Johnny was there one lunchtime on his own, having a pint, minding his own business. And Ellis and his lot come in as usual and, of course, nobody takes any notice; everyone gets on with it."

"When was this?"

"Oh, ages ago, love. Late 1960s, I suppose. Not much later. Anyway, Johnny's attending to his pint. And then there's a big row at Ellis's table. And his boys have drunk a lot, and one of them is having a set-to with the other. The bloke's name was Tony Snell, and he was Ellis's hardest man. Vicious. Broke more fingers than you've had hot dinners. A lot worse, too. And he was having a row with the other bloke—I don't know what his name was—about a darts match. You know, who was the best player. Nothing much. But it turns ugly. Tony Snell started to pound the other bloke like there's no tomorrow, and the whole pub falls silent except for Johnny, who's laughing at something the barman said to him and hasn't really taken in what's going on. So there's these two blokes being pulled apart to stop them kicking lumps out of each other, and Johnny's laughing."

"That can't have looked good."

Irene nodded sadly. "No. You're not wrong, Chels. It didn't look good at all. Not at all. And what happens is this: Ellis whispers something into the ear of one his gorillas, and they go and grab Johnny and bring him over. And Ellis says that he can't see why Johnny finds fighting funny. Doesn't he know that fighting's bad? Doesn't he have kids and want to set an example? And Johnny doesn't know what to say. I mean, he's scared out of his wits. Never the sharpest knife on the block at the best of times, so he's just stunned into silence. Gawping like a goldfish. And this makes Ellis even angrier. He thinks it's dumb insolence. So he asks Johnny to help him sort out their little problem."

"What problem?"

"About the darts."

"How could he sort that out?"

Irene looked at her. This time, her voice was firm and clear. "Two of Freddy's men held Johnny against the dartboard, with his face over the bull's-eye, and Tony Snell and the other bloke had a game, didn't they? A game of darts. They were at it for about half an hour, or that's what I heard afterwards. Johnny passed out quite quickly, of course, but they kept going. He lost an eye and needed a hundred stitches." She finished her coffee. "He died about ten years ago, I think. Poor sod."

Mia stared at the pine table. She remembered the photograph of the old man with the blank eyes. She expected to feel fear, but she felt something closer to sadness. "Didn't somebody do something?"

"Oh no, dear. You didn't interfere. Reg told me—he knew the barman at the Jake, you see—Reg told me that Johnny screamed for a full ten minutes and nobody did a thing. Either ordered more drinks or made themselves scarce."

"How terrible."

"Funny. It all happened a very long time ago. Seems like yesterday, though. You'll find that when you're my age, Chels. It doesn't make much difference whether something happened yesterday or thirty years ago. You remember it in the same way."

Mia nodded. She didn't want Irene to start rambling. "So do Ellis's men still hang around this pub? The Jake."

Irene regarded her with eyes that were suddenly knowing. "Oh, I doubt it, dear. I doubt it very much. It hasn't been called that for years. Changed its name a long time ago, I think. Goodness knows what it's called these days. Something silly, I'll bet."

"Probably. You're probably right. More coffee, Irene?"

"No thanks, love. No, I'd better be off now. Time's getting on, you know. Got to feed the cat and do a bit of housework. You know, keep the place shipshape. And you've got your errand."

"Errand? Oh, yes, of course. Yes. The computer."

"That's right, dear. Don't want to make Sylvia cross now, do we?"

"No, you're quite right. I'd better get on myself."

Irene gathered up her knitting and her bag and put on her woolly hat and mittens. She seemed small again, smaller than the stories she had told. Mia wanted to say something to her, but she found herself struggling for the right words. Irene patted her arm and said good-bye. She got to the door and then turned round. "You're a lovely girl, Chels. Lovely. Bright as a button, too. Don't do anything silly, will you?" She smiled again and left the café before Mia could reply.

IRENE WAS RIGHT about the Jake. It was no longer the Jake, and had not been for fifteen years. But the betting shop was still next door, and that gave away its location. According to the man in the hardware store a couple of streets down, it had changed its name to the Apple and Pear, and then became something else entirely a few years back. When she pressed him, the storekeeper, who was sweating heavily in his overalls, told her that the place was now—if she didn't mind him saying so—a tableside dancing club. No place for a lady, he said. No place at all.

From the outside, Spangles club for gentlemen looked ridiculous, rather than dangerous. A neon light in the shape of a champagne bottle hung unlit above the doorway. The windows had been blacked out and a number of plastic notices screwed to the wall advertised the special licence awarded to the premises by the local authorities, as well as the strict age and dress code imposed by the management. A tubby man in a brown coat and heavy shoes went into the club furtively as she waited to cross the road. It was only noon. You had to be pretty keen on tableside dancing to want to experience its pleasures so early in the day.

She walked across, dodging a cyclist who had been hiding behind a bus and then swerved into her path. As she reached the entrance, she realised how out of place she must look in her old suede jacket, combats, and bright white trainers. She was almost certainly breaking the Spangles dress code, quite apart from the fact that, as a young woman, she was unlikely to blend in with the crowd—such as it was on a dreary winter Tuesday. She was glad that Rob had taken the afternoon off to go with his mother to a medical appointment. She would not have to explain what she was doing, or apologise for her persistence. She did not need Rob to tell her that her behaviour was, at best, eccentric, and, at worst, certifiably paranoid.

Inside, it took a while for her eyes to adjust to the light. Spangles, even at this time of day, was frozen in the twilight appropriate to its purpose. The cavernous pub of Irene's description had gone: no sawdust now, no stained tables, no dartboard. The club was dominated by its chrome bar, along which twinkled tiny lights built into the metal. The row of optics was impressive—mostly, she could see, clear spirits and the other ingredients of toxically powerful cocktails. At one end of the bar, a man with a goatee polished champagne glasses and put them beside a stack of ice buckets. What was the markup on a bottle of house bubbly, she wondered. Ten quid? Twenty? Depended on who was sitting on your lap at the time, she imagined, and what stage of the proceedings had been reached.

The big barn which had once been the playground of Freddy Ellis's men was now dotted with small round tables, their marbled surfaces matching the black of the seats. The floor itself was a latticework of translucent tiles, underlit and flashing halfheartedly in time with the music which was pumped from overhead speakers. It was music for women to dance to, a beat to arouse men's desire and make them part with their money. There were partitioned areas, too, which offered greater privacy, and what looked like a video jukebox in the corner, surrounded by a small dance floor. Beside it, a bouncer, vast and muscular, sat in a dark suit, sipping a Diet Coke and reading the *Sun*. There was nothing to occupy him in the club, no hint of trouble or brewing danger. No doubt his big hands were kept busy on Friday nights, when the room would be full of drunken men groping and leering, their eyes narrow with lust as they watched the women perform.

Mia thought she could count three customers, although the design of the club and the gloom made it hard to be sure. One of them was the man in the brown coat, who, she now saw, was wearing a matching brown suit beneath. He sat at a table, stiff-backed and miserable, drinking a glass of champagne. On the chair next to him was a blonde, who was barely bothering to conceal her boredom. Her own glass sat untouched on the table. She was skinny rather than svelte, and her poor complexion was partially hidden by heavy makeup. She wore what looked like a negligee over a glittering bikini, with stockings and high heels completing the outfit. She had an arm round the man's shoulders and was asking him perfunctory questions, which he was answering with sad little grunts. There was no way this girl could give him what he needed, whatever it was.

Mia walked across to the barman with the goatee. He did not see her, or pretended not to, busy instead with his polishing.

"Excuse me," she said. He spun round, as if astonished that somebody should be at the bar at all.

"Yes, darling. Are you looking for directions?"

"Directions?"

"Well, I assume you're not here as a customer. This is a gentlemen's club, you know."

"Yes, I know."

"So how can I help you?"

"I'm looking for the manager."

"Derek? I'm not sure he's in yet."

She looked round the club. The blonde was dancing for the man in the brown suit now. She gyrated without conviction or rhythm, straddling him briefly in a way which obviously gave him no pleasure whatsoever. She was chewing gum and looked over his shoulder at a screen above the barman's head; the set was tuned soundlessly into an Australian soap.

"I see," Mia said. "Do you know when he will be in?"

"Not really. Derek keeps his own hours. Doesn't usually leave here till threeish. So we sometimes don't see him till late in the afternoon. Especially early in the week, you know, when things are slow. Can I get you a drink?"

"No thanks. Is there somebody else I can speak to? It's a business matter."

"If it's business, Derek's your man. Your best bet is to call and make an appointment. He's out and about a lot of the time. You won't always catch him on spec."

"I'm looking for somebody who used to come here quite a lot."

The barman grimaced, affronted that she would expect discretion to

be breached so readily. "I wouldn't know about that. We see a lot of people in here. It's a popular place. On a Friday night, you'd have a job getting to the bar at all."

"I'll bet. Listen, I just need to talk to someone very quickly. Then I'll
be on my way."

He stopped polishing. "You're the law, aren't you? I thought there
was something funny about you. Look—"

Mia flushed. "Of course I'm not. Look, I work locally and I'm looking for someone who used this place a lot before it was . . . well, whatever it is now. I just need to speak to somebody who might be able to
help."

The barman relented a little. "Well, I don't know. You could try Ray,
the floor manager. He looks after the shop front of house. He might be
able to help you. I'll see if I can find him. Why don't you sit down
Miss—"

"It's Miss Taylor. Thanks, I will."

The barman went over to the phone on the wall and dialled a number. She could see him shrugging and gesticulating. Ray, you could be
sure, didn't want to be bothered by some blonde sort asking questions.
He was savaging the barman over the phone line. She sat at a table not
far from the bar and waited. In a cubicle opposite, three girls in variations of the uniform worn by the first blonde were chattering over cups
of tea. One of them was laughing hysterically at a story told by her stat-
uesque black friend, whose tresses shimmered in the half-light. The
third girl was trying not to smirk as she applied her lipstick. They did
not notice the small woman in trainers watching them from across the
floor. They wouldn't have cared if they had.

A door by the bar opened and a flustered man emerged, looking
angrily around the room. The barman pointed at Mia and the man
adjusted the jacket of his single-breasted suit, which was too tight, and
ran his fingers nervously through his hair. He made an effort to look
friendly and marched over to her, his shoulders rolling over a corpulent

frame. He was wearing pointed black shoes and tartan socks. His tie was a garish colour—purple, she thought. There was a clownish quality to him. But his hands, she could see as he approached, were hands that clenched easily, that were happy as fists. The bouncer put down his newspaper as Ray entered the room.

"Hello, Miss. I'm Ray. I gather you were after Derek. Can I help you at all?"

"Yes, hello. I'm sorry to bother you."

"Mind if I join you?" She shook her head, and he squatted on a chair beside her. He turned round to the barman. "Barry, usual for me. Drink?"

"No thanks."

"Please yourself. Now, what can I do for you?"

"Well, I'm not sure if you can do anything. It's—it may not be something you can help with, really. It's unusual."

"Unusual?"

"Yes."

Confusion swept across Ray's face. He ran the back of his hand over his brow. He was not sure he understood her. "Miss, you do know what sort of club this is, don't you? I mean, it's for gents only. That's it. No offence, but we don't do . . . *specials* here. You know, no odd stuff. Just girls with men, no combos. Good clean fun. I'm not quite sure what you're after, but—"

Christ. Did they really think she was looking for company? "No, that's not what I'm here for. Not at all. I'm trying to get in contact with somebody. Somebody I gather used to be in here quite a lot."

Ray relaxed visibly. He was not being ask to fix up any specials. He was not expected to arrange a combo. What horrors, she wondered, must come his way as friends of the management, or people who said they were, demanded favours late at night, took a fancy to one of the girls, or more than one of the girls. His job must be one of endless fine judgements. Whom to offend, whom not to. Which requests to grant, when to throw a customer out, when to say yes, when to tell a girl to get on with it, or lose her job. No wonder Ray looked pulled apart by stress, ruined by booze and fast food. Barry arrived with his drink, which was an elaborate cocktail in a tall frosted glass. Ray drank half of it in one go and then returned his attention to her.

"Lovely. So who are you trying to contact, Miss? We get a lot of people through here. I'm sure Barry told you."

"Yes. He did. But I'm not looking for a customer. The man I'm looking for is Freddy Ellis."

Ray was about to take another sip of his cocktail as she uttered the words. They triggered an instant reflex within him, one which made his features twitch. But she could not tell what his reaction would be. He stared at her with eyes full of contempt or outrage, or something worse. The air between them was suddenly thick with words about to be said, words she could only guess at. She felt nauseous. The lights on the bar flashed more brightly, as if marking the rhythm of approaching punishment.

Ray's shoulders began to move and his face curdled strangely. His hands were on his knees and his eyes were shut now. He looked as though he was in terrible pain. Except, she realised, he was not in pain at all. He was laughing, laughing so much that he was making no noise. She saw the tears begin to run down his cheeks, the tip of his nose redden. His ears seemed to have changed colour, too. He looked like a crazy gargoyle perched on a big bovine body. Then, at last, he roared out loud. He could not help himself, and gestured to her as if to say so. His laughter came from some deep space within; it was quite beyond his control. She sat in silence, waiting for something to happen. After a while, he was able to speak. But it was not to her that he spoke. "Barry! Barry! Come over here, mate. Sorry, love, but he's got to hear this."

The barman bustled over to see what all the fuss was about. His face suggested he was still expecting trouble. Even the girls, she saw, had been diverted from their gossip by the floor manager's seizure. The bouncer looked on with interest, sipping his Diet Coke.

"What's up?" asked Barry.

"Tell him who you're looking for, love. Go on, tell him."

Mia looked at Barry, who was smiling, too, now in anticipation of some unexpected fun. She did not want to speak. She did not want to compound her humiliation.

"Who are you looking for, then?" said the barman. She looked at Ray, furious and frightened. He raised his eyebrows, prompting her to perform again.

"Oh, go on. You can tell Barry. Really."

The standoff continued. She looked at the door and wondered how many steps, how many seconds, it would take to get out of the place.

"Oh, you're no fun. I'll have to tell you, Baz." Ray beckoned to the barman to come closer so he could whisper into his ear. When he did, Barry's face crumpled quickly into laughter, too. This got Ray going again. The two men shuddered with mirth at her question, at her stupidity, at the very fact of her presence in such a place.

"Oh, you're fucking joking aren't you? You are?" said Barry. Ray shook his head in delight. "You asked that? Really?" Still she said nothing. The barman was thrilled. "Are you on a gangland walking tour or something? Got lost, did you, love? No, I'm sure we can find him for you. Easy. I tell you what. If you hold on, I'll just go and get Jack the Ripper, too. He's having a drink with Reggie Kray out the back."

This set Ray off yet again. His laughter was so all-consuming, so compelling, the mere sight of it was enough to make the girls join in. All three of them were now giggling at the floor manager's performance. The bouncer was smiling. The man in the brown suit had halted the blonde's dance and was staring at Mia with contempt. Barry sniggered and patted Ray archly on the back, as if the exertion might cause him serious harm if he did not calm down soon. He laughed, on and on, the sound stabbing through to the core of her throbbing brain. Nothing could retrieve him from his dangerous ecstasy.

And now, as she sensed herself surrounded, as the all-too-familiar stench of danger became overpowering, her body took over. Fear flooded into her bones, supplanting frustration. She was in the house of the mad, the wicked, the lawless. It was intolerable to stay there a moment longer. She bolted, knocking the table and spilling what remained of Ray's drink as she did so. She ran to the door and pushed at it. It seemed to be locked. Flustered, she grabbed the handle and shook it desperately. The bolt must be on. No, no, that could not be so. She could not be confined with these people, not for another second. She yanked at it with all her strength and the catch gave way, releasing her into a sudden blast of cold light.

It was freezing outside, but she did not stop running to do up her jacket until the pain in her chest was so bad that she knew she would be sick if she ran any farther. Leaning against the wall of the post office, she breathed desperately through her tears. Colours and shapes swam through her vision. Her hands shook. Her T-shirt was drenched in sweat. As the worst of the panic attack subsided, she realised what a pathetic, comic figure she must be: a little woman in the street who had lost control.

This was the end of the line, then. Not a confrontation with Ellis, or even someone like Micky Hazel. Not even that. Just a fat pimp and a barman screeching with laughter at—at what? Her audacity? Her paranoia? Or something else? Would they even now be whispering to each other in disgust, or would Ray be phoning the same people Micky Hazel had talked to after her visit to Michael Aitch Motors?

Mia went into a café across the road and ordered a cup of tea. Her hands were still shaking as she lifted the cup to her dry lips, and she could see from his expression that the man who brought it to her table thought she must be on something. Probably some clubber up to her eyes in speed, or coming down from a trip. He turned away and walked back to the counter, but she saw him shaking his head. It was half an hour before she felt able to stand again. Her breathing was still irregular when she did. The prodigious asthma of panic had not released her yet.

She took a black cab back home and phoned in sick. Sylvia asked if she wanted her to come round with some soup later on, but Mia said she would be fine. She called Rob and, with much effort, asked how his mother was. She did not want to speak to him at all, but she did not want his suspicions to be aroused, either. She said that she wasn't feeling great and would see him at the centre. She drank some mineral water from the fridge, took three pills, and went to bed. She slept fitfully for fourteen hours and then, able to sleep no more, lay on her sofa, watching television until it was light. Some fat people had been sent to a boot camp to lose weight and were being shouted at by a sergeant from the Parachute Regiment. They bounced up and down gelatinously, only to be screamed at again when they stood on the scales and were told that they had lost not a single ounce. A woman called Rita told the interviewer that she had decided to commit suicide if she did not lose five stone by March. The camera cut to the interviewer nodding sadly, as if Rita's ultimatum to herself was unfortunate but entirely appropriate. This televised torture absorbed Mia until dawn, when she took a long bath, full of some expensive salts she had saved at the back of the cupboard for just such an occasion.

The steam rose from the surface of the water, blue with the herbal infusion from the granules. She stretched her leg up and noticed that she needed to shave. Not now, though. She closed her eyes and touched herself absentmindedly. She thought of Rob. Little by little, her body was thawing, returning from its long hibernation. She enjoyed being in bed with him more than she could possibly have imagined a few months ago. Lying in his arms, her head on his heaving chest after their lovemaking. Drifting in and out of sleep. His hand between her legs, probing gently. The abrasion of his stubble on her neck as he lay on her back. These were new and wondrous things. They were not to be squandered for nothing, for madness. She drenched the sponge and laid it on her face.

"Let it go": That was what Jenny used to say to her. She remembered her mother in the kitchen when she was small—five, six?—saying these words to her. Mia would present her with a problem, something intractable, unconscionable. She would explain that a friend was no longer a friend, that Ben was being bad to her, that she could not find the door to her dollhouse. Jenny would sit her on her knee and stroke her head and listen to the injustices of a child's life, the petty afflictions of the nursery and the playground. Mia would demand revenge, or judgement, or recompense. And sometimes, Jenny would deliver these things, taking her daughter by the hand and leading her to the place where there was a solution. But not always. There were times when Jenny kissed Mia and told her not to fret, to forget her worries. There was no answer. The kind, wise face looking down at her. "Let it go, darling. Let it go."

The word would be out again about her. That much seemed likely. Ringo might get to hear of it and chastise her, more fiercely this time. But she could tell him, truthfully at last, that it was over for her. In the dark recesses of Spangles, she had been given her answer, which was no answer. In that lustful little asylum, the world had spun and spun around her, until she realised that it was not going to stop for her benefit. There was not going to be a moment of deliverance. This time, when she knocked at the door, she had been greeted only with brutal laughter. Micky Hazel had told her, and it was true: Whatever she asked, however she phrased the question, wherever she went, they weren't going to tell her. They weren't going to tell her anything. Ray's laughter was the sound of their scorn, their outraged amusement that she should presume to ask them these things. Like her brother: She just didn't know her place. But that was all over now.

She got dressed, had a glass of apple juice, and walked to work. The three book boxes that raised the centre a bit of cash were already out in the porchway and Sylvia was distributing some dog-eared novels among them.

"Hello, my love," she said. "You feeling better?"

"Yes, thanks. What's that? Joanna Trollope? No, put it in the one-pound box. Remember the system."

"Here, you do it. I don't want to trample on your territory. Anyway, I've got to talk to the new Pilates teacher. She's upstairs—Elly. She's ever so nice."

"That's good. The class is filling up nicely. Almost full. Have you seen Rob?"

"No. He doesn't work Wednesdays, remember?"

"Christ, yes. My brain is going."

"Bit distracted are we, Chels?" said Sylvia, wiping her hands on her smock. "Well, well. Anyone would think you were in love or some-thing." She smiled to herself and went inside.

Mia spent the morning doing the books, updating the computer, and showing Elly where everything was. The new instructor was a tall brunette from the south, who said earnestly that Pilates had "changed her life—no, really!" Mia did not quibble with her, but she sat her down in the back room to fill in some employment forms.

She phoned Rob, who had gone to inspect a new rehearsal room for the band, and arranged to meet him for lunch at Prospero's. They sat side by side on a bench in the pub, sharing a sandwich. She held his hand occasionally, and laughed as he told her about a drunken bust-up between Steve and Heavy over the merits of Neil Young, which had ended with Steve dangling Heavy out of a window until he conceded that *Harvest* was a great album. This was the first proper row to beset Thieves in the Night, and it worried Rob, who had managed to get them a bigger gig in Islington after somebody at the venue had heard about their triumph at the Four Bells. She did not tell him about Freddy Ellis, Spangles, Ray, or Barry. She smiled at his stories and agreed to go with him to Brighton, where his brother ran a bookshop. They would wait until it was at least sunny, and then play hooky for the day. Mia liked Brighton, but she hadn't been there for fifteen years.

They lingered well into the afternoon, sipping pints of lager. When he had gone, she returned to the shop and got on with her paperwork. She still needed to submit three sets of builders' estimates for the cost of the work on the foundations of 12 Nantes Street, which, thanks to the roving eye of Councillor Phil Roberts, was to be subsidised by the town hall. After two hours of this—and frequent interruptions by Sylvia and Elly—she grew bored and went and stood on the porch. There were no evening classes, so the two other women left for the night. Erica had gone home at lunchtime, after the only yoga session of the day. Mia finally had the Echinacea to herself. It was already dark outside and her breath made bursts of mist in the air. A dog—a terrier of some kind— was dashing between the parked cars, full of schemes and panting joyfully.

At first, she did not realise that the noise she heard was coming from Ringo's shop across the road. But when she looked over and saw Aasim's scooter parked outside, she grasped immediately what was happening. She could see Aasim, his sharp, sinuous figure silhouetted against the light from Monsoon's, beholding some sort of drama within. She stepped into the street, leaving the door open behind her and clutching at herself for warmth as she crossed to the other side. She could hear the sound of a man cursing loudly. It was Ringo. She quickened her pace.

Aasim was standing by the curb, one hand on his scooter's handle-bar. He was wearing a thick Nike top, its hood down, and a jogger's hat, which concealed some, though not all, of his earrings. He was laughing quietly to himself, his fine features a vision of satisfaction. She wondered how long he had been standing there. The noise of something being smashed came from within. She heard Ringo cry out in rage again.

"What's going on?" she said. "What's all this racket, for God's sake? Aasim?"

He looked at her but said nothing, taking a swig from a can. He turned back to whatever was going on inside the record shop. She stormed past him and pushed open the door to Monsoon's.

By the counter, Aasim's brother, Ali, was grabbing a pile of records. Ringo was just behind him, but Ali was too fast. Even in his heavy leather jacket and gold chains, the boy was fleet of foot, dodging Ringo and running round the record stands, successfully avoiding capture. He laughed as he did so, pulling the disks from their covers and breaking them as he ran. The floor, she now saw, was a shiny sea of black fragments where Ali had tossed the smashed records. He had pushed over a tower of cassettes, too, and trampled on them, so that one corner of the shop was now paved with the crazy brown spaghetti of old tape ripped from broken cartridges. The window of the door leading to the back office had been smashed. Yes, the boys had done a real job on Ringo this time.

She looked over to her friend and saw now why Aasim was smiling as he was. Ringo's face was streaked with tears. There was rage in his features, and panic as well, but the contortions she could see were mostly a sign of pain. All around him, thousands of hours' worth of loving selection, collection, and preservation was lying on the ground. Much of his stock, she knew, was all but irreplaceable. It was the only asset he had, and now it was in sudden ruins at his feet. Ali may as well have ripped out his heart and danced on it before his eyes.

"Stop it!" she cried. "That's enough, Ali! You've made your point. Just go!"

Ali, dancing from one aisle to another, turned around and sneered when he saw who it was. "You? Mad bitch. Fuck you."

Ringo stopped pursuing Ali and faced her, breathing heavily. He pointed at her. "Chels, stay out, man. I'm going to kill him. I'm going to catch him and tear his fucking head off. I swear."

Ali hopped onto the counter. "Are you? Come on, then? Come and rip my fucking head off, then. I'm shitting myself." More plastic was broken. More shards fell to the floor.

She was inside the shop now, only a few feet from the counter upon which Ali was cavorting in his tight pants and white socks. "Ringo! For Christ's sake, he's fucking out of control. Leave it. I'll call the police."

"Don't you dare," snarled her friend. "Don't, Chels. I'm going to settle this now. I'm going to make him—"

Before he could finish, Ali jumped down from the counter, whooping as he made a dash for the door. She tried to grab him, but Aasim's brother was too nimble and too determined for her to stand a chance. Ringo lumbered behind him, shouting obscenities out into the dark. She followed them, and saw that Ali had run across the road, gone straight into the Echinacea Centre, and slammed the door. Clever boy. That would keep Ringo at bay and Ali would escape out the back. She could see the boy celebrating in the front room, shouting gleefully through the window at his victim. She got her keys out, readying herself for a second confrontation with Ali.

Then she felt herself falling and realised that Aasim had tripped her as she ran. She hit the ground hard, her hands breaking her awkward fall against the curb. She could smell the grime and industrial disinfectant of the drain in the gutter before she knew what had really happened to her. She was stunned by the impact, suddenly listless and soaked with fatigue. Aasim walked past her and spat on the ground. "Fucking mad," he said, and went over the road so he could see properly what was going on in the centre. His business in Ringo's record shop was done.

She was not yet able to get to her feet, so she did not see the car until it was at close range. It was a black Mercedes with darkened windows, and it had careered into Nantes Street at high speed. Now she heard the brakes screech as it slowed down to a crawl outside the Echinacea. She thought, too, she could hear the buzz of an electric window and then the smash of a window, as if something had been flung from the car towards the centre. The Mercedes screamed instantly into reverse, and as she squinted to watch it speed backwards, she caught a glimpse of something in her peripheral vision. A sudden flame lit up the innards of the Echinacea like a spiteful flare. A second passed, hovered in the air as time decided whether or not to stop, whether to wait awhile, or to carry her forward on its tide. Then, Mia was deaf, deaf from a noise out of the bowels of the earth, both deep and sharp, the noise of a scream, of fury and death. She thought she could see a fireball, a sudden inferno where there had been darkness, and the flames from a hundred nightmares made real at last: not memory, it turned out, but prophecy. The nagging intuition of a horror to come. The whole street was caught in the light, seared by its heat and soldered fast. She could feel the blaze from across the road scorching her cheek and the palms of her hands, the fingers of the fire reaching out to the pavement where she lay. Its rage lasted longer than she thought possible. Then there was rain of ash and glass and droplets of flame falling from the sky, dappling the road in a thousand places. She lifted her head again and thought, as she drifted in and out of consciousness, that Aasim had probably saved her life.

Aasim. His was the first voice she heard, and his the first figure she saw as her vision returned. He was screaming, no longer with scorn, but with the terror of a child. He was calling out his brother's name, but no sound came in return, apart from the noise of glowing timbers falling into the charred remains of the centre's ground floor. Aasim was running into the burnt-out husk of the Echinacea, through the door which had blasted open, howling for a mercy he already knew would not be his.

She struggled to her feet and felt again a blast of hot air as another wooden rib of the building crashed to the pavement. Ringo was on his knees in front of the centre, dazed and in shock, lucky to be alive, let alone conscious. He blinked as she staggered past him, holding up his hands, which were bleeding as if from stigmata. He had a wound on his forehead and his face was black with dust. But he seemed to have escaped the main force of the blast. His mouth opened and closed, and then he slumped on his side again. He was not ready for the hellish vision of her blasted workplace, or the body which Aasim was already cradling, his howls silent now as he gathered the charred remains of his brother to his breast and wept.

Mia stood by the porch. She wondered how Aasim could stand the temperature within. What remained of the Echinacea Centre looked as if it might collapse at any moment. She could see melted paint, the desk torn in two by the explosion, and a small crater where there had been a display cabinet. The back office had survived, but most of the store and the first flight of stairs had been destroyed. Little pools of fire still burned on the floor. She looked up and saw that the blast had taken out much of the ceiling and that most of the joists above were now gone or had been exposed. The fragile skeleton of the building was laid bare and, she thought, must soon give way.

She called Aasim's name, then again, much more loudly this time. She could see that he had heard but had chosen to ignore her. He rocked back and forth with his brother in his arms, resisting her intrusion into his grief. She put her jacket over her head and ran into the room, coughing as smoke billowed from the dying fires. When she grabbed his shoulder and shook it, she expected him to stiffen and snarl. But his body was yielding and limp, craving help at last. She realised as she saw the devastation of Ali's face and flesh that Aasim could never let his brother be seen this way. She grabbed his wrist and told him what they had to do. He looked at her and blinked agreement. Then she rushed into the back room, snatched the throw from the sofa, and returned to the store. This old bit of paisley linen would be Ali's shroud. She handed it to Aasim and he laid it on the ground. She breathed through her mouth, fearful of what she might smell if she did not. Then together they rolled Ali onto the throw and closed it. She gestured to Aasim and they carried him out of the door and into the street. As they shuffled out onto the pavement, another payload of plaster crashed into the room. The whole building was on the brink of collapse.

Outside, there was now a group of people, one or two barking into their phones. An elderly woman from one of the houses on the next street was tending to Ringo. A man in jeans and an England football shirt was shouting into his phone, telling someone to "get a fucking move on." She and Aasim bore their burden to the other side of the street and laid it to rest on the pavement outside Ringo's store, near where she had fallen. They sat on the curb, their makeshift catafalque, one on either side. Neither of them said anything or caught the other's eye. They kept a strange vigil as the street filled with people and light.

It was many hours before she was able to speak to Aasim. She had put her gloves back on in the ambulance, and nobody had noticed the minor wounds on her hands. Her face was dirty from the explosion, but after a brief checkup to see that she did not have concussion and was not in shock, she had been left to her own devices in the A&E reception area. She sat and watched the waiting room fill up with frightened old people, tramps, children with minor injuries, drunks, a girl who needed her stomach pumped. A little boy with an eye patch and a bandaged arm came up and said his name was David. She looked up and smiled. He offered her a mint and she shook her head. He ran back to his father, a fat skinhead in a denim jacket, who stood up every fifteen minutes and berated the first nurse he could find. The white walls of the room closed in on its desperate occupants, who were hunched on yellow plastic chairs.

It was almost eleven before Aasim emerged from the corridor and spoke briefly to the receptionist. Mia moved to stand up, but he walked straight over to her and sat down, staring in front of him. She looked at him. A single tear ran down his cheek. His was no longer the face of a scowling street fighter, but of a teenager for whom childhood was a recent memory. He clasped his hands before him and rocked a little. When he finally spoke, it was in a whisper.

"He's gone, man," he said. "Gone."

"I know. I'm so sorry." She did not know what to say. She did not know where to start, how to tell him the terrible truth. She feared that when she did tell him, he would try to kill her. She would not blame him. But she had to tell him.

He turned to her in a moment of pathetic pride. "You know something? You'll never guess. He was *alive,* man. When we got here. Can you fucking believe it? Still alive. He was always the toughest, Ali. He was a tough mother. He only died about an hour ago and—" His voice cracked.

"Aasim, I— Do you want me to call your parents?"

He looked at her, genuinely shocked. "Of course not. I have to tell them. Who else is going to tell them?" He shook his head, as though, even in this darkest hour, she could not quite bring herself to behave properly, with decorum.

She waited awhile. He seemed in no hurry to leave. She guessed that he knew that they had business to do first. But she did not know where to start. She asked him if he wanted a cup of tea and he said he didn't. She put her head in her hands.

"Aasim . . . I can't say anything that'll help. But I need to say something before you go. I don't really know what happened tonight, any more than you do. But I know it had something to do with me. What happened tonight was meant to get me, not your brother. Whoever was in that car was after me."

"Yeah."

"What makes you think I'm right?"

"You're trouble, man. Everybody knows that. You're always digging your nose in. People ask questions about you. You know, 'Who's this nosy bitch?' Stuff like that." He shrugged.

"Who asks questions?"

"How the fuck should I know? You're the one with the problem. All I know is that they *asked.* I hear things. It's my business. But that's it. The details, that's your problem, man."

"I know. I know. I'll tell you what I know. I lost—something terrible happened to my family a few years back, and I thought I knew why it happened, and then, not long ago, somebody told me that I was wrong all along. There was a whole other reason for what had happened. And you're right: I asked too many questions. And I think"—she felt the quaver in her voice, a sudden surge of guilt tearing through her guts— "I think that what happened tonight was my fault. You must hate me. I would hate *you*. But I owe it to you to say what happened."

He was regarding her coldly now. He adjusted his hood and smoothed his jeans. "So. Nosy bitch. Who were you asking? Who were you looking for that caused all this mischief?"

"I was looking for Freddy Ellis. That's who. I know he had my family killed. Don't ask me how, but I know it was him. Believe me, if you knew how I found out, you wouldn't doubt me. It was Ellis who had my brother and my family killed four years ago. And it was Ellis who sent his people to get me tonight. It was Ellis all along."

Aasim took some gum out of his pocket, unwrapped a stick, and began to chew. He didn't offer any to Mia. Why should he? He was listening hard. She took a deep breath. "I went to see the person who got my brother mixed up with Ellis in the first place. In Stratford. He warned me off. I should have listened. Instead, yesterday, I went to a club he used to hang out at. I daresay he still owns it. It doesn't matter. It was a mistake to go there, a big one. I was going to drop the whole thing. But it was too late. You're right: I'm a nosy bitch. Tonight was Freddy's payback for me being a nosy bitch. He tried to finish me off. And I expect he'll try again."

Aasim spat out the gum and looked at her. There was cruelty in his eyes but also something approaching condescension. "You're joking, right? I mean, you're taking the piss?" He spat again. "Fuck. You *are* crazy."

"What do you mean?"

"Ranting on about Freddy Ellis. Freddy Ellis? For fuck's sake, girl. Freddy Ellis has been dead for, like, seven years, eight. At least. I mean, don't ask me where he's *buried*. But he's dead. Everyone knows that. Even the fucking cops know that. They never got him. Lived like a cripple in Spain for years before he popped."

"A cripple?"

"Yeah. He was in bed for the last five years. Or that's what I heard. Never knew the geezer. He was the fucking *past,* man. He was, like, long-ago history. I mean, his crew still had a few things, snooker clubs and that, but nobody gave them respect. Do you think I could run like I do if somebody like him was still around? Do you think I could take money and cars and shit if a geezer like that was still in the chair? That's the *whole fucking point.* They're gone, which leaves space for me, OGs like me. It really is true, man. You *are* fucking crazy. Freddy Ellis!" He shook his head again at how preposterous she was. He could not get over it: She really believed that a man who had done his last real work—what, ten, fifteen years ago?—had returned from the grave only hours before to rain fire on them. She felt her head spinning.

"But maybe . . . maybe somebody close to him did it? I know it had something to do with him and his firm, even if he is dead. Otherwise—"

"No." Aasim shook his head with absolute certainty. He turned to her. "Listen. It wasn't fucking Ellis. It wasn't fucking Ellis's firm. It had nothing to do with Ellis. Get it straight. I know it wasn't any of that."

"How? How do you know?"

He looked away in cold fury. "Because I saw them, bitch. I fucking *saw* them."

"You saw the people in the car?"

"Only for a second."

"Did you recognise them?"

"Course I fucking didn't. Do you think I'd be still sitting here if I did?"

"So what are you telling me?"

"What I'm telling you is that I saw faces. They were Asian."

Asian. How could the men in the car, who had come to punish her for going to Spangles, for bothering Micky Hazel, for Ben's greed—how could these men possibly be *Asian*? There was no sense in it, no order. There was nothing comprehensible in any of it. Maybe Miles was right. It was all nonsense. It resisted the constraints of rationality. That was why she was sitting in an emergency room with the hardest teenager in the neighbourhood, whose brother had just been burned to death. Asian.

Aasim got up to go. He turned to face her. "I could cut you and string you up to bleed. You fucking deserve it. But I think I need you. I think the only way is through you, man. Yeah. The only way. I don't know what you did to piss these people off, but they're *angry* with you, girl. I never seen them before, never seen that car, either. But I'll tell you one thing: They weren't no amateurs. And when they realise that they messed up, they'll come again. Or you'll find them. You're mad enough. And when you do"—his voice was low now—"when you do, I fucking want to be there. Hear me?"

She nodded. He reached into his back pocket and pulled out a card. It was one of the calling cards that you get out of a slot machine, a sad little symbol of how he saw himself, his posturing. It said "Aasim" and then, in larger letters, "NUFFINK." His mobile number was below.

"Be speaking to you," he said. Then he turned and left.

Half an hour had passed since he'd walked off into the night, but it seemed much longer. The pain in Mia's ankle returned as she walked down Whitechapel towards Brick Lane. The police van which had slowed to investigate the argument between the drunken girl and her boyfriend purred past her, the officer inside surveying the human wreckage on the street. She tried not to catch his eye.

Chapter FOURTEEN

THE FAMILY plot was almost derelict. She had instructed
Gus to set aside a sum every year to ensure its upkeep, knowing that she
would not go herself. But the money had not stretched very far. The
headstones themselves were in reasonable order and clear of dirt and
cobwebs. Someone, it seemed, ran a cloth over the engraved letters once
in a while. But there were no flowers, and the turf was overgrown with
weeds. She wondered if anyone had been to the plot in the past four
years, or if she was the first. The birdsong in the graveyard was sensuous
and calming—at odds with the nervous desolation of her family's resting place.

There were four stones, the one for Jeremy and Jenny a little larger
than the others. The epitaphs were simple, which she liked: "Beloved
Husband of," "Only Son of," "Youngest Daughter of," rather than the
more florid language she noticed on some of the edifices with their
trumpeting angels and mourning Madonnas. She was not sure about
the stone itself, which was a brownish marble. She could not remember selecting the colour and guessed that this task, like so many, had
been left to Gus. She imagined him ticking the first box he got to in

the options offered by the funeral directors. A tasteful marble? Yes, that would do.

The graves were in the shadow of a great oak, in one of the cemetery's more exclusive corners. Jeremy and his family were surrounded by the better class of lawyer, generals, and a handful of junior aristocrats, one of whom, a twenty-five-year-old heroin addict, had been buried less than a year ago. The lawn on most of these plots was immaculate and a few bore fresh flowers. She knelt on the grass in front of the graves and laid a rose on each, two beneath her parents' stone. She had expected to be burdened by a sense of ceremony, but she felt only crushing self-consciousness. The plastic wrapping in which she had carried the roses was taken from her hands by the wind and flapped like a translucent bird up and away, until it snagged in the branches. Looking through the black railings, she could see kids riding on their bikes, performing wheelies and screaming profanities at one another. On the other side of the oak, an old man in a suit and blue coat sat on a bench, lost in deep thought. He twisted and turned a yellow handkerchief in his fingers, and his feet moved, the motion barely perceptible. When he had finished with the handkerchief, he started to drum his fingers on the bronze plaque at his side, as if awaiting a delayed rendezvous. She wondered whose death the plaque on the bench commemorated, and whether it had anything to do with him.

She heard voices behind her and watched a couple walk by, the man in his forties, the woman a little younger. The man was strikingly good-looking, the woman less so. She linked her arm with his and tried to comfort him. "Honestly, Mike, you can't do more than you already do," she said. He looked down at the gravel on the path and shook his head. The woman tried again. "If Lydia won't come and do her bit, that's her business. She was always a bit funny about your mum. You've got the studio to worry about, and the kids. I think coming once a month is plenty. You should stop eating yourself up with guilt, you know." They walked out of earshot.

ONE MORNING in Camden, about a month after she moved, Mia had decided to come to the cemetery. The new flat was too small to spend her days in, and so she had found a series of places where she could while away the hours, reading, watching the passersby, drinking tea. Her favourite was Bert's, a café where you could buy a mug of tea at nine in the morning, and Bert, a stocky man in his fifties, with his sleeves rolled up, would bring you refills until it was past noon. At least he brought refills for her. She liked him and his mild flirtations. He said that if she spent any more time in the café, people would talk, and Mrs. Bert would give him hell. She said she was sorry that he was already married, and that she would stay a bit longer, if that was all right with him. He said that she looked like she needed feeding, and that he would have a word with her boyfriend, if he ever turned up. She smiled at him. He left her alone. Why couldn't they all leave her alone?

The police had been the easiest to shake off. She remembered how to deal with them, how to nod and agree and listen. They knew how her family had died, or at least they quickly found out, and this made them circumspect with her, as if she was owed respect as a veteran of suffering. Aasim told them nothing, except that he had seen a car and then an explosion. He did not mention that he had seen faces, and that those faces were Asian. He, too, knew how to deal with the police. Ringo could not even remember the blast, and he had only the dimmest recollection of his fight with Ali and their twilight chase. After the fire, he shut up the shop "until further notice" and went to stay with his mother to recover. Mia wondered whether he would ever return to Nantes Street. They'd had one awkward meeting three days after the attack, when he was still on crutches. He had smiled at her and made jokes, as if nothing had happened, as if they were meeting in Prospero's for a pint after work. She'd asked to try his crutches and each mocked the performance of the other. But his eyes were glazed: The flames of the explosion still gleamed in them. She could see that, without knowing how, with more fear than confidence, he, too, believed that she had brought this devastation upon them, that she carried a curse with her. When he embraced her, she could feel the recoil in his lean body. She could feel an end to it all pulsing through his sinews.

But Ringo had nothing to tell the police. They did not even ask him about her, why she was called Chels, anything. And when it was her turn, she realised quickly that they did not grasp that the bad magic was hers, that she had brought darkness upon this place. Their line of questioning made her think that they had missed the point completely, and the scale of the horror they were dealing with. They saw a dead Asian boy, the brother of a local troublemaker with pretensions to be a gangster, killed in a horrible accident, which they considered to be the unfortunate by-product of petty feuding in the area, rather than something much more sinister. Whoever had tried to kill her had a long and terrible reach: That much was clear to her now. But the police did not understand that at all.

They believed the fire to be related, somehow, to Aasim's vendetta against Ringo—or Mr. Patel, as they properly referred to him. Was she aware that the lad and Mr. Patel had had many disagreements in the past? Yes, she was. Did she know that Aasim was trying to drive him out of his shop? Yes, she did know that. Had their confrontations been violent before? Not as far as she knew. Was Aasim's gang capable of such an act? She doubted it. Did Mr. Patel have any underworld connections or criminal contacts that might be involved? The idea was risible, she told them. She could see that they did not know where to start, and that they hated the case. But they were not really interested in her. They interviewed her three times after the night of the blast, but they asked her few questions about her past, except to say that they knew how difficult it must be for her to go through another episode of this sort. They told her to contact them if she heard anything—anything at all—which might help them with their enquiries. The chief investigating officer left a number and said she could call him day or night.

Sylvia was sedated when Mia went to see her. She lay dozing on her sofa, with Ravi curled up on her chest. Her flat was a mess, and Mia did the washing up and some cleaning before sitting down to talk to her friend. Sylvia had not yet been to see the wrecked building; she had been told by her doctor to stay at home for a few days and to take it easy. There would be plenty of time to deal with the insurance company, the adjusters, and the town hall. First, she needed to recover from the shock of hearing that her life's work had been destroyed in one pitiless moment.

The cat purred as Mia sat down on the chair beside the sofa. She reached out and stroked its long fur, tickled its chin. It stood up to walk over to Mia, waking up Sylvia. Her eyes were red and sunken. She recognised Mia and started to get up, tears welling as she did so.

"Chels, darling, I—"

"Don't," Mia whispered. "Don't. Lie still. I didn't mean to wake you. Mike from next door let me in."

"I was so worried about you. I was so worried that they had taken you away from me."

No, thought Mia. I have taken everything from you. You have protected me and loved me, and this is your reward. I have brought death into your midst. I have destroyed, just as you have created.

"I'm fine. I only got a few cuts and bruises where Aasim tripped me. Just needed some TCP." She laughed, trying to hold back her tears. She took Sylvia's hand. "I'm very lucky."

"No," Sylvia said, reaching out to touch her face lightly. "I'm lucky. I've still got you."

Mia turned away. Ravi nuzzled against her face. "I don't know what to say to you, Sylv, I really don't. It's impossible to explain all this. It's madness. It's my fault."

"Don't be silly. That's rubbish. How could it be your fault? Nobody knows what happened yet. It's a mystery. Everyone keeps saying that it's the gangs—Aasim's lot and all the fighting with Ringo. You know, they're saying that we were just caught in the cross fire or something." She sniffed. "I don't know. Ringo wouldn't hurt a fly, and Aasim—well, he's just an annoying little kid, isn't he? Poor bastard. To lose his brother like that. I don't understand why all this happened, Chels, and neither do you. But there'll be an explanation. This isn't the first time somebody's burnt out a place in this part of the world. I just got on the wrong side of someone, I guess. Didn't pay up for some yoga mats or something."

Mia looked down at the wreckage of her friend's face and marvelled at her strength. All that Sylvia had lost was as nothing compared with what she thought she still had. She would not let her friend Chels believe that she was to blame, even though some sense of the truth must surely be dawning on her. She would expend what little energy she had left making sure of that.

"It's funny, isn't it?" Sylvia said.

"What?"

"The way things happen. I mean, the way you and I met each other. And then Vic left. And then along came Rob. And now this. I used to believe that you had to fight for disorder, that everything was conspiring to keep us in line. I fought against those forces; I really did. And now I wonder if they're really there at all. It seems—well, it all seems a bit more random than I thought. Some of it is so good. I thank whatever brought you to me. And the rest of it?" She waved her hand. "Well, God knows. How does something like this happen? It makes me laugh. When I think about the town hall trying to close us, and everything you did to stop that. You're so fucking clever, Chels. You really are. Maybe it gets you in trouble sometimes. But I don't mind. I think you came out of the sky to help us all. To help me."

"Well, the computer's safe. I checked that. That's one thing you won't need to buy."

"Oh, great. Got a computer, need a new building." They laughed, and then a small embarrassed silence fell between them.

"Listen. I came to say that I'm going to go away for a while, okay? I just need to get away."

She could see from Sylvia's expression that she knew what her friend was saying. "But you'll be back. Won't you?"

Mia blew her nose and tried, wretchedly, to feign insouciance. "Oh, sure. Of course. All that paperwork—I wouldn't miss it."

Sylvia sat up. Ravi jumped back onto her, his tail up. "Where will you go?"

"I'm not sure yet. Just somewhere so I can sort myself out a bit. I just need to be by myself."

"You're not as good as being on your own as you think. You really aren't. You do know that, don't you?"

"I do. This— I am not running away from people. It just isn't right for me to stay."

"We need you more than ever."

"Try to understand."

Sylvia looked at her and smiled. "I do, Chels. I do understand."

There was nothing more to say. She could not explain her act of desertion to Sylvia without having a conversation she was desperate to avoid. She was not even sure what she would say if pressed to make sense of her behaviour. But her first instinct was to get away from those she loved, to save them from the danger that clung to her like the shroud she had wrapped around Ali. These were not things she wished to talk about with Sylvia. She leant over and kissed her, said good-bye. Sylvia nodded through closed eyes, and kept them closed until Mia had gone.

She went to her flat to pack. There were two old holdalls in her wardrobe, and she filled them with whatever she could lay her hands on: clothes, toiletries, a couple of books. She needed enough to live, and nothing more. She went back and forth between her bedroom and sitting room, dividing what she owned into categories of necessity, filling black garbage bags with things she would never need again. Henty's bowl would have to stay. Yes, that and dozens of other keepsakes. But a few things were too precious to leave. She took from her bedside table a framed picture of her mother, a loose photograph of the whole family when she was twelve, and a letter from her father. She took it out and read it again:

> Darling Mi,
>
> I just spoke to Benjamin, who says you are off to India a week earlier than we thought. Will you be missing the last week of term, or am I doing my sums wrong? Your grandfather always took the last week off on principle because he said that the undergrads were so drunk that there was no point in teaching them. But that's another story. . . .
>
> I thought of leaving a phone message, but knowing how these things get lost I decided that I would drop you a line before you go. Of course, Mummy and I hope you will have a wonderful time and—boring Dad bit—that you will be careful and sensible when you are travelling.
>
> Remember to take your emergency credit card. The fact that Ben always forgets his is neither here nor there! He is the sort of chap who thinks sleeping at Third World bus stations when you have run out of cash is fun or in some sense an "authentic" part of travel. You, I think, do not share this delusion.
>
> Anyway, all the above is a paternal excuse to get to the main bit, which is to say how very, very proud I am of you and all you have achieved. I know you and the others think Mummy and I are having you on when we say that you are the best things in our lives. But it really is true. You are doing amazing things already, and I watch your progress, bursting with pride.

You are all that any father could possibly hope for in a daughter, and much more. So there!

Have fun, and call us when you land.

All the love in the world,

Daddy

What had prompted Jeremy to write such effusive words? Had he returned flushed with guilt from an afternoon with Beatrice? No, these were not the phrases of guilt. She imagined him, more than a decade ago, sitting at his desk, fidgeting with his fountain pen, and suddenly missing his daughter. Lost in the room, lost in himself. Perhaps feeling the first intimations of old age creep into his joints, wanting to reach out to his adored child, the child he loved most, to seek comfort even as he offered it. That was the truth of it. Jeremy had been a lonely man.

There was a pile of bills and leaflets on her doormat; well, the pile was going to get bigger. She wondered how long it would be before she was visited by debt collectors, having failed to turn up at the county court. Would they break in? Would it be legal if they did? And what would they say when they found the furry sandwich in the fridge, a riot of mould, and the bestial stink of the months-old milk? The envelopes addressed to her were the moorings which linked her to normal life, the ties of money and status that identified her as a person, located her in the scheme of things. It was these ties that she must now lose. She would leave behind another life, this time for something less comfortable, less cushioned with unexpected love. On the move again, in flight from God knows what.

"Why didn't you call me?" Rob stood at the door, which she had left off the latch as she took out the garbage bags.

"I'm sorry." She stood up as he closed the door behind him.

"I don't understand. I don't know why you couldn't have called to say you were all right. You could at least have done that."

"I know. I'm sorry."

"Do you know how I heard? I heard on the fucking news. That's how. And I've been looking for you ever since. Couldn't find Ringo. Had to call Sylvia at home to check you weren't hurt. No answer here. No answer on the phone. I didn't know what to think. And then I went to see, where the street's cordoned off. . . . Christ, Mia."

She walked over to him and laid her head on his chest. He was still cold, the metal of his jacket buttons chilly against her cheek. He put his arms around her, gripping her tightly. She tried to return his embrace but found she lacked the strength to do more than pat her hands on his back. She had made him suffer, for nothing. But what was she to do? How was she to make it all right? She took him by the hand and led him to the kitchen, where she made tea for them both. They stood in silence for a while. They were beginning, she noticed, to acquire the habits of a couple, no longer needing the constant reassurance of conversation, the arousal of verbal jousting. The contest was over now. Two selves were beginning to lock into each other. Their quietness was affable, free of resentment. Some of his tension drained away as she stroked his arm. They fitted well. But it was too late.

"Are you leaving?" He met her eye.

"Yes."

"Why?"

"It's too dangerous to stay."

"Did you go looking again?" Now she avoided his eye. "Tell me. I just want to know."

"No— Yes, I did, but I didn't find anything. It's not what you think. It's not what I thought. I was wrong about Ben, I think. Or at least I was looking in the wrong place. But somebody doesn't like the fact that I'm looking at all, that's for sure. Whoever did this knew that I'd been asking around, and they didn't appreciate it. And they'll come back. I know it."

"You can't run, Mia."

"Can't I? I've been running for four years. I don't see why I should stop now."

"You can't just leave."

"How can I stay? Oh, Rob. My darling. Look what they're capable of. That was just a car pulling up in the road, and a firebomb hurled out of the window. It was *nothing*. Nothing, just a warning shot. And now somebody's dead. Just a kid. If I stay, they'll kill more people. They'll kill you, Sylvia, God knows who."

"Who's 'they'? Come on, Mia. You've got to explain."

She contemplated telling him what Aasim had told her about the faces in the car, and thought better of it. But she did not lie to him. "I don't know. I really don't know."

He would not let go. "Look. You've got to go to the police, tell them everything. This has got out of hand. Let me help you, anything. You can't do this alone."

She went back into the sitting room and flopped down on the sofa. She saw the feet of children running past on the pavement and then a woman with a pram. "The only way I can possibly do it is alone. I can't look after myself and have to worry at the same time about what might happen to other people. It's too much." She put her head in her hands. "Too much."

He sat beside her and took her hand. "You can't push people away like that. It's not just your choice. Don't you see? You can't walk away from this."

"Yes, I can. That's all I can do now."

"Would it make any difference if I said that I loved you?"

Now he had said it, the only words she had hoped he would not say, and there was nothing to be done. She could cope with rage, irrationality, or self-pity. But she had no answer to this. Nothing to add to what he had said, or to offer in return. She had hurt him already, and now she must hurt him again. She waited, to be sure that she was right. Then she shook her head slowly, but long enough for him to see what she was doing. She looked into his eyes, as the seconds passed, and watched the nakedness of what he had just told her mutate into shock and then anger and then something closer to despair. She saw what it had cost him to say it, and that he would not have said it if he had known she would respond as she had. She remembered how he had left the flat the first night that they spent together, the confusion in his face. But this was different. His expression spoke, finally, of exhaustion. He had offered her everything and it was not enough. He was not what she wanted, or needed. He had nothing left to give her.

She watched as he stood up and picked up his blue satchel. He moved with great care, deliberately, as if he might fall. He was oblivious now of her scrutiny and concentrated only on the business of leaving. He put on his jacket and walked over to where she still sat. He put his hand on her head and she felt his fingers begin to stroke her hair and then, when he thought better of it, withdraw. "Take care of yourself, Mia," he said. Then he was gone. She curled up on the sofa and dug her fingernails into the back of her hand until she drew blood.

THE NEXT day, she found an accommodation advertised in the classified columns: a single room with bathroom and kitchenette in Camden, for a modest rent, including utilities. She went to meet the landlord, Mr. Hilly, in the afternoon. The house was a six-bedroom Georgian structure in poor repair. The paint was flaking off the front door and alarming odours rose from the basement, where, Mr. Hilly explained, he had lived since his wife died six years ago. His clothes reminded her of Ted's: the unidentifiable monochrome of the single man in late middle age, the same plastic shoes and forlorn trousers. Gales of halitosis emanated from Mr. Hilly, but so did much goodwill. He asked her if she needed any help moving, as his son was around for the day and had a van. She thanked him and said she would be fine. She asked if he would be happy to be paid weekly in cash, and he said, "That'll do nicely," as if it were the funniest line in the world, and one which he had personally minted for her amusement.

The room itself was at least clean, and larger than she had expected. The pink floral pattern of the curtains matched the three-piece suite and the lamp shades. There was a small bookcase against one wall and a mantelpiece with a gas fire on the other. The bed was in the corner, a few cushions thrown over it in a halfhearted effort to make it look like a second sofa during the day. As she looked around, she said that she had some academic work to do, rather urgently, and that she hoped the house was quiet and that not much would be expected of her. Mr. Hilly said that everybody kept to themselves, and he put his finger to his lips rather too melodramatically. There were, he said, three other lodgers at the moment: Kay, who said she was a singer; Leonard, a student from Ghana, who liked the house to be quiet, too; and the mysterious Mrs. Arbuthnot, who had lived in her room for five years, paid her rent with immaculate regularity, and had managed only three abrupt conversations with her landlord in all that time, two related to faulty plumbing during a cold snap. Three new people, she thought: each new name bringing a new history and a new world with them. Except this time, I shall not know any of them. I shall hide myself from their worlds and save them from the contagion I bring in my wake. I shall never know if Kay is really a singer. Mrs. Arbuthnot will have to remain mysterious.

She paid him a month's rent on the spot, which made him even more cheerful. He said he was looking forward to having her as a tenant. Then she went to get the Tube back to Aldgate so she could collect her bags and lock up the flat. She wrote to Gus, to whom she had spoken briefly in the small hours after the fire. She told him she was going away for a while, asked him to deposit ten thousand pounds in her account immediately, and prevailed upon him not to bother her. She walked out to the street and posted the letter. Then she went back to the flat and checked each room to see that she had not left anything essential behind. She took a cab to Camden and was in bed by midnight.

It did not take Mia long to settle into her new routine. She would sleep till nine, wash, and then go to Bert's or the juice bar on the other side of the road. Nobody knew her name, because nobody asked. She had feared that she might be bored, without company and occupation. But she found that the time passed more quickly than she would ever have expected. She walked for hours at a time, up to Highgate village and back. She listened to the radio and rediscovered the intimacy of hearing the same presenter for three uninterrupted hours, rather than for a few snatched minutes in the morning. She read with a voracity she had not known since she was a teenager, when she would lie on her bed in the Boltons, during the school holidays, and read a book a day, ploughing her way through junk and classics alike. It was at Oxford that she had lost the reading habit, limiting herself to the bare minimum of what she needed to read to get the degree she wanted. In her first month in Camden, she read more than fifteen novels, starting with *Anna Karenina,* one of the many classics she had never got round to, and then been forced to pretend she had read. She finished it in two days, dividing the book into fifty-page sections, going for a walk after each section to stretch her legs and absorb the prose, until the screaming of Tolstoy's train ended the story. This was the strange paradox of reading, she thought: that only when she had disconnected herself from the world to which these books gave meaning did she finally have time to read them properly.

She became a familiar face at the library and at Pencil's bookstore on the High Street. People treated her a little differently than they had in the past, with delicacy and understanding, as if she might shatter in their hands. She realised that she had begun to exude strangeness, that her wanderings in a small area were conspicuous to those who lived and worked there. They must have wondered who this curious little blond woman was, with her unwashed hair and her book bag. At first, she could not guess why they smiled so inanely at her when she took out a book, or when she bought one, or when she paid for her groceries, until she realised that they were mirroring her own detached expression. Every neighbourhood needs its prophet of the last days, and I am theirs, she thought. I am the woman who is reading every book that was ever written before the last night falls and all words are hidden forever in the darkness.

It was not enough, though. As mired as she was in her belief that some sort of end was near, that she would not have to wait for long, there were still things she had to do, unfinished business to which she could not attend when she was living in Brick Lane. One morning in Bert's, she pushed aside her paperback and realised that her drifting could not last forever. She remembered the colour of the fireball, and Aasim's screaming, and all it implied. There was a reckoning ahead, and there should be tidiness. That much she could demand of her fate. She decided that she must do two things. She must visit the grave, and she must go and see Jean.

THE TRAIN to Bellingham was slow because of engine trouble. It took her more than an hour from Blackfriars, three times as long as it was meant to. But the hospice—St. Francis's—was only ten minutes' walk from the station, through the maze of council estates and across a green with a playground and abandoned tennis court. She had called in advance to check that Mrs. Jean Moss was indeed a day patient. The nurse was reluctant to give out such details, but when Mia said that she was an old friend and wanted to surprise her, the nurse said Mia wouldn't be disappointed if she came on most weekday afternoons between one and five. She could take her chances if she wanted.

The hospice was hidden behind a tall brick wall and surrounded by a modest garden area and forecourt, in which its ambulances and vans were parked. The building looked more like a university science block or a municipal office than a consecrated place where people came to make their peace with God. Mia found the reception desk, which was deserted. Above it hung a luminous tapestry with a picture of Saint Francis surrounded by animals and a psalm verse in clumsily stitched Gothic script: "Lord, Thou hast been our dwelling place in all generations." With the prayers on the walls, candles, and religious statues, the effect was that of a sad little grotto. A vase of lilies stood alongside three phones and a reading light on the table. The receptionist had used fridge magnets to stick postcards to the side of her filing cabinet—from the Holy Sepulchre and Lourdes, as well as Tenerife and Orlando. There was also, incongruously, a picture of Brad Pitt, dapper in suit and wide-collared white shirt.

The receptionist returned. A small red-haired woman, she was wearing a nurse's uniform underneath a blue cardigan. She spoke in an Irish accent, with the undertow of a lifetime in south London.

"Oh, I am so sorry to leave you in the lurch," she said. "Dear me—we're short-staffed today, what with all the flu, so I've been helping sister with a birthday party and dashing back and forth from the desk. Not ideal, but there it is. How can I help you?"

"I am a friend of Mrs. Moss. Jean Moss. I understand she's a day patient here. She's not expecting me. I was hoping that she might be here so I could surprise her."

"Well, you're in luck. She didn't make it in yesterday. Feeling a bit poorly, I think. But she's in today. I just saw her in the dayroom. I'll show you where to find her."

The receptionist—or was she a nurse who had to be a receptionist, too?—led her through swing doors and into a dark corridor. "It's the large room at the end. Nice view of the gardens." Mia thanked her and walked towards the door the receptionist had pointed at. The smell of medical hygiene was overwhelming; it gave the place a giddying bleakness, reinforced by the religious icons on the walls and the drooping plants. There were two wards on either side of the corridor and a small television room. An old woman in a dressing gown and nightdress stood with her walker, shuffling her fluffy pink slippers without moving forward or back. Mia thought she could hear someone saying "I'm scared" again and again within one of the sepulchral wards. A man in the television room was calling for a biscuit.

The dayroom was less gloomy: Its linoleum was of a brighter colour and there was ventilation of some kind. One of its walls was glass from ceiling to floor, allowing the patients to sit and look out at the lawn and trees. Two children, a boy and a girl, were playing with a ball on the grass and waving to an elderly woman in a head scarf slumped in an armchair. Mia could see her hand moving a little in response to their gesticulations. There was a table covered with board games and a chess set, a small group working on tapestries with a teacher, and a cart of books parked in the corner. Next to it was a hissing tea urn on a table, with a jug of milk and a bowl of sugar, which had been spilt all over the tray.

There were a dozen or so people in the room, including the staff and visitors. The deep-cushioned armchairs had been arranged in little groups, and a few were set off on their own for patients who wished for some privacy. A long, sagging sofa in ancient oatmeal dominated the right-hand wall and was strewn with old newspapers and magazines. A man in pyjamas was making an effort to tidy them up with his walking stick. Pages fell from his feeble grasp and landed on the floor.

"What do you want?" The woman standing in front of her must have been eighty, and she wore a housecoat and flat shoes. Her face, wrinkled and unapologetic, flashed with anger. She wore earrings and there was a smear of lipstick at the corner of her mouth.

"I'm sorry," said Mia. "I'm looking for Mrs. Moss. Is she here?"

"What do you want?"

"Yes, I'm looking for Mrs. Moss. I can't see her anywhere, I'm afraid."

"What do you want?"

"Oh dear. Listen, is there someone—"

"What do you want?"

A woman Mia assumed was the head nurse bustled over. She spoke with the same lilt as the receptionist but was a good twenty years older. She took the woman by the hand and spoke to her kindly. "Now, Barbara, what are you up to, for heaven's sake? Bothering the nice young lady with your nonsense. Look, she's a lovely thing, and here you are, showing her no sort of welcome."

"What do you want?" offered Barbara, this time with a measure of regret.

"I'm sure she knows perfectly well what she wants, Barbara. But why on earth should she tell some funny old lady who jumps on her the first moment she walks in the room? Now why should she tell you?"

"What do you want?" her patient grunted.

"I'm sorry," said Mia. "I don't mean to be any trouble."

"Oh, it's no trouble," said the nurse. "Barbara's always doing this to visitors. Aren't you, darling?"

"What do you want?" Barbara nodded in concession as she repeated her incantation.

"Her friend Ernie counts them, you know. On a good day, he reckons she'll say it five or six hundred times. That's just the ones he can count. And she'd say it more if she didn't sleep so much. You know, the medication knocks her out, poor soul. Now, how can I help you, dear?"

Mia looked around the room again. "Well, I'm looking for Mrs. Moss. Jean Moss. But I can't see her. Maybe I should come back another time."

"Oh, Jean. She's over there. She was playing gin rummy a little earlier, but I think she's having a nap now. Careful you don't give her a shock when you wake her up. Her nerves aren't all they were."

Mia thanked the nurse and walked over to the corner she had pointed to. There were two women sleeping in their chairs, neither of them Jean. Mia wondered where she had gone, and hoped she had not missed her. The hospice would certainly not give out her home address. The women might know when she had left—if they had still been awake. Mia saw that one of them was stirring, a tiny thing lost in the battered cushions of the armchair and her blanket, which was marked as property of the hospice. She wore a yellow cardigan and a string of pearls. Her hair was a strange ruby colour, the curls impossibly neat and tight: a wig. Mia saw the woman's feet twitch as she emerged from her slumber. Her face bore the crow's-feet of pain endured, and her skin looked a little jaundiced, but there was a puckishness to her features, too, a resilient liveliness. This was a woman, Mia thought, who would laugh at her own slow, public erosion. Whom, years ago, she had heard laugh at many lesser evils. She was barely recognisable now. But it was definitely Jean.

She pulled up a stool and sat at her side as she awoke. Her eyes blinked open, but Mia could see that she was not yet fully conscious. The old rhythms of sleep and wakefulness were confusing when you were being tossed around by the tides of disease. Mia smiled but did not speak until the woman's eyes began to blink with anxiety.

"Hello, Jean," she whispered. "It's Mia Taylor. Miles's friend. I've come to see you. Do you remember me? We haven't seen each other for a while."

Jean's confusion did not subside. Her mouth opened and she tried to speak. Mia could not hear her, so she leant over. She thought Jean was saying "Drink." There was a bottle of mineral water and a tumbler on the table, and Mia poured her a glass. Jean's hands fumbled for the glass, so Mia guided it to her dry lips and watched as she drank, most of the water spilling down her front.

It revived her. She smiled at Mia and peered at her watch. "Thank you, dear. Have you come to take me home? It's early yet."

"No, Jean. I haven't come to take you home. It's Mia. Do you remember I used to work with Miles? Mr. Anderton?"

The woman looked scandalised, as if too great a demand was being made of her. She considered this deeply, first as an affront, looking at Mia out of the corner of her eye, and then, on reflection, as something less insulting. She looked again.

"Mia? Is it really you?"

Mia smiled and took her hand. "Yes. I came to see you. As a surprise. Miles told me where to find you." This was almost true: He had told her she was in a hospice in Bellingham, which was remarkably precise for Miles.

Jean's grin was broad and knowing. She rolled her eyes. "That boy. If he knows where to find me, why doesn't he bloody well find me occasionally?" They laughed, instantly retrieving the intimacy that had been based on their conspiracy against Miles, their plot to keep him in line. "Do you know, I still remember his birthday? Send him a card and a present. And he still forgets mine, and then a fortnight later realises he's forgotten and sends a hundred pounds' worth of flowers. What a waste of money. I said to the nurse, 'Why doesn't the silly boy buy a calendar?'"

For a while, Mia attended to Jean's needs. She had medication to take and then wanted to go to the loo. All this took time. Then she asked for a cup of tea, strong, with milk and two sugars. Mia set the cup down in front of her and went to get one for herself.

"How do you like it in here? The staff seem very friendly."

"Oh, it's all right, dear," Jean said. "It gives me something to do. Only so long I can bear being cooped up at home, especially as I can't really do my garden anymore. There's a nice man who looks after it for me once in a while. He stays for a cup of coffee sometimes, to pass the time of day. But it's not the same."

"How are the other patients?"

Jean snorted. "They're a bunch of idiots, most of them. Half have just been dumped here by relatives who couldn't take any more, you know? It's sad. But there are one or two I like. Pearl, here"—she pointed at the still-sleeping woman opposite—"is lovely and has a gorgeous grandson who comes in to see her, and he brings me things, too. And I play gin with a few of the chaps. It makes the afternoons go by. And I can sleep here without worrying. They look after you if you have an . . . well, an episode."

"I'm glad you like it. Are your family making a fuss of you?"

"Well, I've been a widow for seven years now, would you believe, so there's only my son, Ian, these days. I suppose he does his best. But he's living in Ashford now, and Suzi—that's Ian's wife, you know—doesn't like making the journey too often. Truth be known, they're longing for me to fall off the perch so they can cash in the house. Oh, don't look so shocked. You remember me telling you about him. Do you know, the other day he was telling me about some tax dodge or other so they don't have to pay full death duties. I mean, can you imagine? Here's me, trying to plan a dignified exit. And there's my own son with an accountancy textbook, telling me how to get the best deal when I do."

Mia laughed again. She remembered conversations like this on the phone or at the Commons, every day at one time. Jean, at her best, was magnificent, a legend on her corridor and beyond. Miles was considered lucky beyond all measure to have secured her services, although he rarely acknowledged his good fortune properly. She had played as great a part as Mia in grooming him, acting as his gatekeeper, lying to the press and to party officials about his whereabouts, spotting infelicities in his speeches as she typed them up for release.

"You look thinner," Jean said.

"So do you." She said it without thinking and was appalled at herself, until she saw Jean giggling at her tastelessness. She blushed.

"So, dear. Tell me how you found me."

"Oh, I ran into Miles and we had dinner together. He's doing so well. It was really good to see him. And he told me you had been in the wars. So I thought I would come and see you."

"How nice. How long has it been? I suppose five years."

"About four, I think."

"Have you found a job yet?"

"Oh, Jean, stop teasing. Of course I've found a job. I'm not a complete fool, you know." Yes, she thought. I used to work in a health centre, but after that was destroyed by a firebomb, I decided to wander around Camden, reading the classics and talking to myself.

"But you're keeping all right?"

"Oh, you know. Ups and downs, even now. I'm doing okay."

"Anyone special?"

Yes. Yes, there is. But I drove him away, told him to get out of my life with a single gesture. "Not really," she said. "I go on the occasional date."

Jean shook her head. This did not please her, not at all. She bridled like a fishwife. "I'm still cross with Miles, you know."

"Why?"

"Well, really. He's a spoilt child. He should have married you when he had the chance. You were the best thing that had ever happened to him; that was plain as a pikestaff. Best thing that was going to happen to him, too. I told him as much. He'd stopped chasing after girls and found one who could make him happy. Who had his measure, more to the point. And he let you go, Mia. He should have run after you when you moved away. But . . . you know what he's like. The truth is, dear, he couldn't cope."

"It was my fault, too, I guess. I mean, I shut him out."

"I daresay you did. So what, I say. He should have kept trying."

"No, I was so bloody angry, Jean. I didn't want to know. I couldn't believe what he'd done. It seemed so crass, given the circumstances."

Jean squinted with confusion again. "Why were you angry, dear? What did he do?"

"Well, you know. He should never have left me standing at the airport like that. I mean, imagine how I felt. I suppose it was bad luck on his part. But it was the wrong night to be selfish."

"Selfish? That's a little harsh, dear. I mean, I know he wanted to wait for you that night. He told me as much, how badly he felt. But, really, he didn't have any option."

"I don't see why. He could have just hung around a bit longer."

"Oh, no. The policeman was very insistent. He told Miles to come with him immediately when he met him at the gate. Well, they were so jumpy, of course. About the diary. You know how these things are."

"What do you mean, Jean? What diary?"

"You remember the break-in? Honestly, what a fuss about nothing. The silliest fuss. But I suppose they were only doing their job."

"I don't have the slightest idea what you're talking about, Jean."

She looked at Mia and raised an eyebrow. "Surely Miles told you about it? Oh, you remember. He was in a proper state about it, I can tell you."

"Why was he in a state?"

"Because it had lots of private stuff in it. You know, ministers' private numbers, and personal details. All scribbled, of course, but just about legible."

"What did?"

"Miles's diary, dear. The one he kept himself. Almost a notebook. Well, it was locked in my desk and when the break-in happened, it was the only sensitive thing which had disappeared. Some petty cash and a camera. But the diary was the thing that got the police going, naturally."

"Why?"

"Well, Miles was getting threats all the time. Mostly just weirdos and hoaxers, of course, but some they were starting to take seriously. I mean, he was so outspoken. Too outspoken, if you ask me. He went looking for trouble with those Muslim groups, and they didn't disappoint him. It was a bit of a game for him, I think, the tussle with the Islamics. But then they heard that Saffi's lot—not the official organisation, but the people he represents—were really after him. They were raising the stakes, looking to make an example of someone prominent. Or so the police had been told."

"Saffi Muhammad?"

"Yes. You remember him, don't you, dear?"

She did. She did remember Saffi. She had written briefings on Saffi for Miles, along with all the other fundamentalist leaders he was taking on. There were plenty of them, ranging from hoodlums with a taste for fiery rhetoric to misunderstood holy men. But Saffi was different from the others, much smoother, better connected, certainly better funded. He had never been prosecuted, never even held on remand. He spoke well, better than Miles, and was his most compelling adversary on television. His links with extremist groups at home and abroad were well known, which was why Miles went after him. But in public, Saffi never missed a beat, denouncing "the violence of American imperialism" and the complicity of "the poodle prime minister," although remaining carefully vague about what form of retaliation his own allies were entitled to take. He would not condemn acts of terror, but he would not applaud them, either. He spoke of "the forces persecuting global Islam," but he never called for "holy war." He hated America, but he had studied for his doctorate there. He drove himself around London without a bodyguard. He seemed untouchable. She remembered standing in the wings of a BBC studio, watching Miles debate some civil liberties point with Saffi, who was soft-spoken and perfectly groomed. He had bested Miles with ease, although she had lied to her lover about that afterwards. She had thought then that Saffi Muhammad was formidable.

"Yes. Yes, I do remember him. What does he have to do with this?"

Jean sat up. "Well, they got some low-grade intelligence from some sort of informant that Saffi, or his people, I suppose, were planning something nasty. And that got Miles's attention for a while, I can tell you. It happened that week, I think, the break-in, but it was only while he was in Frankfurt that I noticed that things were missing. I was in the office, picking something up, and I realised what had happened. God knows when they'd been in, and I must say they weren't very exciting burglars. Anyway, I was straight on the phone to him, and to security.

The policeman who met him at Arrivals was very strict. I know the plan was for you and Miles to go to Selbourne Terrace to work that night, but the policeman said he had to come straightaway."

But that wasn't the plan. That wasn't the plan at all. Mia interrupted her: "Didn't he tell the policeman that he was waiting for me?"

"Certainly not. He didn't want to drag you into it all. As it turns out, you had plenty on your mind anyway."

"So Miles told you he was expecting to take me back to Selbourne Terrace?"

"Yes, that's right. And the policeman said they were taking him straight home, where they could keep a guard on him, apparently. Just a precaution while they worked out what had happened. He had someone with him for a week or so, one of their tough guys. And then the whole thing fizzled out. I thought it was a bit of a storm in a teacup, to be honest. I mean, it was just some petty thieving. There were loads of confidential letters and documents which they left. It wasn't the worst theft I saw in all my years at the House, not by a long chalk. With all those people wandering about, doors open, late nights, things go missing all the time. But I suppose the police had to go through the motions. Miles made them a bit nervous with all his speeches."

Mia tried to absorb what she had been told, but she found herself reeling. "And did the diary turn up?"

"Oh, goodness, no, dear. No more than the fifty quid or the camera. We weren't going to see any of that again. And then it all got forgotten pretty fast. The police got over their little panic. And everything moved on. I mean, Miles was subdued for quite a while after you disappeared. He went off the radar a bit himself, to be honest. And I didn't give it much thought after that. I was too busy trying to cheer him up, fixing things for him to take his mind off you. I'm surprised you've forgotten all this, dear. Mind you, I suppose you had other things on your mind."

"I never knew any of it. It's all completely new to me."

"Really? That's strange, isn't it?" Jean licked her lips. "Could you be sweet and get me another cup of tea? That's so kind."

Mia lingered at the urn, trying to keep her focus, to contain the nausea that rose within her. There it was, at last. Had it been there all along, and had she resisted it? Was there any sense to the little quest that Claude had sent her on, or was the final indignity that she should discover this by accident, after she had stopped looking? All along, she had known that somebody was keeping the truth from her. There had always been the stench of lies coming from somewhere. But she had been looking for treachery in the wrong place. Treachery had held her hand, soothed her, told her fresh lies to avoid detection. She cast her mind back to the documents Miles had sent her. Yes, Jeremy had been right to worry about Ben. Claude had been right about the laundering. Miles had found out that her brother was under investigation, that the authorities were closing in on him; perhaps Miles had known it all along. But Freddy Ellis? The dates on the memo had been deleted: It was years out of date. And Miles knew she had no way of knowing that. She had taught him too well. He had become too good at concealing the truth, creating falsehoods, forcing those who got close off the scent. He had fooled them all. He had even lied to Jean about where he was meant to be going that night. Liar, liar.

She put Jean's tea down for her and listened to her talk as she took sips from the mug. The nurses, she said, didn't take her as seriously as she would like. They nodded when she talked about the politicians she had worked for, and she knew that they weren't listening or didn't believe her. Still, it broke up her days, and she would keep coming in until the day came when they finally moved her to one of the wards as an inpatient, when she could no longer be left alone at home. She did not know when that would be. She was having one of her good days, but the day before had been murder. There was a fete at the hospice the following week: Would Mia come along with her? She wasn't sure that Ian would be able to. She wanted to enjoy it with somebody. Mia said she was sorry but that she couldn't. Jean did not look surprised. Another time, she said. Yes, said Mia. She would come and see her again. When she could.

After a while, the nurse came over to check that her patient had taken her medication.

"So, Jean. Nice to have a visitor. And such a lovely one, too."

"Oh, it's wonderful. Wonderful. Do you know, I haven't seen Mia for four years? And here she is. Such a treat for me."

"I'm sure it is. You must come again and keep Mrs. Moss entertained, Mia. When you've had the kind of life she has, there's not much we can say to impress her. She's a clever old soul. Knows lots of people on the telly. Don't you, Jean?"

Jean's face darkened. Mia could see that she felt patronised and helpless.

"Oh yes, I'm sure I'll be back soon. Thanks for helping me out earlier."

"My pleasure, dear. Come back anytime."

The nurse left them. Mia leant over and kissed Jean on the forehead. She said she would return soon, but when Jean asked for her telephone number and Mia said she had just moved, she could see that Jean knew she was lying. She squeezed Jean's hand and set off.

Miles. Miles, his traitor's mask torn off at last. His obscene sin laid bare after all these years. But no, that was not the whole of it. That was not even the most important part. For it was she, not Miles, who had led death to her family's door, who had ushered horror to where they were waiting. It was she who had decided their fate. It was she who had forced Miles to put Ben's address and the details of the birthday party into his diary, insisting through her giggles that he write it out in full so that he would not forget. All there, in the diary that had gone missing, and then been forgotten.

Barbara was waiting for her by the door. "What do you want?" she said. But Mia did not even have time to smile.

Chapter FIFTEEN

THE DUST on Holloway Road rose like a dirty nimbus and scattered over the pavement. Trucks and buses thundered past her as she walked by the old furniture shops and the resale stores. Though it had been raining, nobody had bothered to move the desks and filing cabinets inside, or to cover them. The chipboard tables, warped already, gleamed with water, a vision of futility. These were shops that sold nothing, that nobody visited. Only a few paces separated the bookstores and restaurants of Islington from the grey hopelessness of Holloway. The road stretched like a dead artery to Archway. This was where the gallows used to be, she remembered: where the thieves and the murderers drank ale handed to them by the mob before swinging to their cheers from Albion's fatal tree.

She knew this walk well now, from the Tube station by Highbury Fields up to Seven Sisters. It had been been a long haul, the work of three weeks. Up and down, back and forth, every detail considered and settled. Now it was done and there was nothing left to prepare. Tommy had been right. There was, indeed, something for her to do, a task for which she had been readying herself all this time without even knowing it. She was primed for it now, purified by the fire and unburdened of all other concerns. She had turned her back on Sylvia and Rob. She had left a place where she was loved, and the name they had given her there. All these things were in her past. And at the hospice, she had found out what the task was.

There were ten pubs on the walk, and, as was her habit, she divided them into three categories. There were those, like the Devonshire Arms, that nobody sane would dream of entering: silent, failing joints in which the hard men from Finsbury Park drank to get drunk while their bull-dogs slept at their feet. There were the merely dangerous establishments, like the Overspill, in which young men with Arsenal shirts played the quiz machine and punched one another occasionally. And then there were the rest, grimy north London pubs which were trying to attract the curious customers from Upper Street, the blackboards outside offering cheap spritzers and, with unseasonal genius, "bargain-price Pimm's." She was never bored as she walked.

It took her twenty minutes to get to the turning which led to Monk Street. She had been here so often that she wondered whether the locals were beginning to recognise her. Probably not: She always came after dark and did her best not to be noticed. She stood at the bus stop or in the café, kept on her hooded top or her jogger's hat, avoided eye contact at all costs. There was a newsagent's, a Laundromat, and a long-closed pub, its windows boarded up and covered with flyers. At the end of the street was the chicken wire of a school and its playground. The gates were always bolted by the time Mia arrived. There were few passersby in Monk Street.

The Islamic Community Centre was a tall brick building not far down from the café and the pay phone. It lay snugly between the old pub and a Quaker meeting house, and might have been mistaken for a run-down family home if not for a small plastic sign at the gate in four languages. Down the left side of the building was a parking space for two cars, safe behind a high grilled gate with a double padlock. The centre was the nearest thing Dr. Saffi Muhammad had to a public office and it was here, Mia had discovered, that he spent the end of each weekday. He drove his BMW into the alley at about four, locked the gate behind him, and entered the house by a side door. His study was on the first floor at the front. This she had worked out by watching the timer light in the stairwell go on and off as he went in. He would spend three hours—sometimes more, sometimes less—in this room. Then the lights would go off and he would emerge, put his briefcase on the backseat, straighten his tie, open the gates, and back out. The centre, according to its leaflets, offered daily consultations from 4:30 to 5:30 with Dr. Muhammad—"business trips overseas allowing"—and there was no shortage of plaintiffs seeking help and judgement from this man. She watched each day at six as the disappointed families who had not been able to see him left the building tutting and shaking their heads in dismay. She would later see some of them at the bus stops, heading to east London or farther north. People travelled miles to see Dr. Muhammad. They expected him to give them deliverance.

He was not as tall as she remembered. But that was the confusion of stature and height in her mind's eye. There was a slowness to Saffi's movements which she had not spotted in the studio: an aristocratic refusal to rush, and perhaps a caution born of long intimacy with danger. Yet there was no hint of wariness or anxiety about him. He strode from house to car with the aura of invincibility she recalled. He did not seem to have changed much in five years, his hair still jet black and swept back, his complexion smooth, and his features refined. When he talked to visitors outside the building, she could see that they deferred to him instinctively, their body language signalling complete recognition of his authority. He smiled and spoke softly to them. There would be justice: if not now, then soon. That much he could promise.

She had stalked Saffi for weeks and she was beginning to know what he would do before he did it. She knew that he always wore a dark grey suit. She knew that he rubbed his finger up and down his nose when he was distracted. She knew that he sometimes sat alone in his car for ten minutes after work, as if absorbing the lessons of the day or dozing or praying. She knew that at 5:30 a member of his staff—there were never more than three—brought him tea and what looked like pastries from a bakery round the corner. And she knew that at 6:10 every night he sent whoever was left in the building home. He almost always had half an hour of work to conduct on his own. That was his way.

She hid in the dark and saw all these things, noted them, processed the information she needed. She did so with a singleness of purpose that she would never have thought possible. Her parents had given her a love of order and method, and she was quick to acquire skills and impose sense upon the tasks she undertook. But Jeremy and Jenny had not taught her to be a fanatic: That, she had taught herself, in four years of exile and a few months of madness. She was free now of inhibition and had lost her distaste for irrationality. She had discovered these reserves of strength within herself without looking for them. They had been found for her, forced upon her. Between Camden and Holloway, day after day, she honed her intentions, considered her actions, burnished her resolve. There were no distractions now.

She looked up to the first floor and checked her watch. It was 6:10: The light was on and the car was parked in the alley. She crossed the road and walked quickly into the Quaker meeting house. It was warm inside and the benches in the main room looked inviting. It would be pleasant to sit down for a few minutes. But that would be to disrupt her plan.

"I'm shutting up in five minutes. Sorry, love." The caretaker, whose nightly ritual she had watched many times, was locking the door of the bookstore inside. He would attend to the back room next, she knew, then turn out the lights, then make a deeply irreligious call to his girlfriend on the office phone, and then let himself out. He was in late middle age and had the quiff of an elderly teddy boy, with crepe shoes to match. A badge on his tank top said RIP THE KING—Elvis, she assumed, rather than Jesus. He smiled apologetically.

"That's okay." She took a deep breath. "I tell you what. I'll be out in a sec. I just want to take a quick look."

"Well, I'm not sure."

"Don't worry. Look, you get on. I'll close the door behind me. You'll hear it slam."

"All right. But I mean it about five minutes."

"Thanks." She asked the next question with all the nonchalance she could muster. "By the way, do you have a loo I could use?"

"Oh, sure. The ladies' is over at the side, just there."

She thanked him and walked over to the room she had inspected on four previous occasions. She closed the door behind her and counted to twenty. Then she ran back into the main hall, took hold of the front door handle, and slammed the door as loudly as she could. She returned quickly to the loo and closed her eyes, praying that the caretaker would have no business to check in there. She heard him walk in from the back room, his keys jangling. "Jesus fucking Christ," he said. "No need to make such a racket. I'm not fucking deaf. Stupid fucking cow."

A few minutes passed. The hall was plunged into darkness. She could hear whispering, the sound of the man speaking to his girl. The words did not carry into the little room, but she could guess the gist of what he was suggesting from his tone and priapic cadences. The call did not take long. The front door closed, and she was left alone in the building. A Quaker tomb in which all was silent, no further clues offered. No place to spend the night.

Blinking as she adjusted to the dark, she put the toilet seat down and stepped onto it. For the first time that day, she noticed that her heart was pounding, her hands shaking. Dizziness descended upon her. No, not again; not now. She could not yield now. She took three long breaths, in through her nose and out of her mouth, closed her eyes, and tried to keep at bay all rational thought about what she was doing. There was the window to worry about first of all. She unscrewed the lock and hoped it would push open. It was jammed. Quickly, she thought, I must act quickly. If it was painted shut, she would have to use her penknife to open it up, chiselling away at the edges to prise the window from the frame, a procedure which might take a long time. But she could not believe that the window was never opened. The room was not stuffy or rank, and there was no other ventilation. She tried once more, her face screwed up with the effort. Nothing. She leant against the tiled wall, recovering her breath, sweating freely. Last chance. She pulled at the window with all her might. It sprung open, letting in floods of icy air. She pushed it up and, hopping from the seat, clambered up and through.

The alleyway was empty apart from the car. She looked out of the gate and saw that there was nobody about, not even at the pay phone. She reached up and used her fingers to ease the window shut behind her. This time, it slid easily, the sash no longer snarled up. She looked above the side door to the centre and saw through the little window that the stairwell was dark. There was no sign of life on the upper floors. It was 6:25. He would be alone now.

The front of the car gave her cover to crawl over to the other side of the alley to the side door. Again, she checked out of the gate. What if there was a motion sensor which turned on an outside light? No, she would remember if there was such a thing. At least, she thought she would. She leant against the car: Its bodywork was freezing and made her start. She must move fast. She could not afford to linger where anyone passing could see her reckless intrusion, the absurd sight of a young woman hiding behind a BMW parked outside a community centre.

She crawled over from the car to the door and stood up. Now or never. If it was locked, she would have to run, climb over the gate—was she agile enough?—and hope that nobody spotted her as she sprinted down the street. There was no letterbox, so there was no chance that she could reach in to turn a handle within, or pull up a latchkey. But Saffi always had to lock the door behind him. A single lock. That much she was clear about. That much she remembered. But what if she was wrong? No, that was impossible. She gripped the handle and turned it as slowly as she could. The door opened.

There was no light inside the porchway after she closed the door behind her. She could see nothing, hear nothing. There was the smell of shoes and, distantly, of spices. But she could not see the stairwell window, through which at least some of the light from the street ought to be leaking. She realised that there must be another door on her left. Fumbling, her hand found the fabric of a gabardine coat hanging, its pungent odour evidence of a recent walk in the rain. She moved her hand to the side of the coat and felt the smoothness of paint on a door. Down a little, she found another doorknob, which she turned gently. The door stayed shut. There must be a key. Yes . . . yes, there was. Just below. She took another breath and turned it, fearful that the sound of the lock giving way would carry up the stairs. It opened, and light fell into the porchway from the landing window.

The stairs were wooden and carpeted except at the edges. The question was how to make the least noise as she went up. Logic suggested that she should walk on the carpet. But she remembered from her childhood that stairs creak less at the side, where they have borne fewer footfalls. She shuffled over to the wall and with great care put her left foot on the edge of the first stair. It made almost no sound as she shifted the sole of her trainer from side to side, experimenting. Then, with her back to the banister, she put her full weight onto the wood. The first step, then the second. Each time she moved, the wood groaned a little. But not much. No, not much. Not enough to disturb anyone, unless they were expecting the noise. Unless they were waiting in silence on the floor above, waiting for her arrival.

There were eighteen stairs, divided by the landing. She treated each

354

of them as a project, a discrete task to be completed efficiently. She kept her face to the wallpaper and moved up, one foot onto the step, then the next. She would count to ten, listen for movement upstairs, then continue her progress. Her pulse was hectic, but she kept her breathing low and under control.

The main landing was carpeted in the same way as the stairs, and at the end of the corridor, a faulty night-light flickered on the wall. She could see his office from where she stood. There were three doors, but only one had the illuminated border. She thought she could hear a calm baritone from within. The final telephone calls of the evening. Or was it the rumble of the distant traffic? The house, which thronged with activity during the day, was still. Some buildings speak to you, Jenny used to tell her; they whisper their secrets to you. But not this one. This one kept its secrets close to its heart. It did not welcome strangers with confidences.

And now she must act. She was in. His door was—what?—six paces away, seven at most. And now she must go in and confront him. There was no way back, no escape from this moment. A debilitating wave of fear coursed through her bones and her guts, but she fought it off. This was what she wanted, and what she had planned for. There were no more choices to be made. What would Ben have said? This was the end of the river all right.

"Don't move." She felt something cold against her neck. "Don't move at all."

"I won't," she said, unable to think of anything better. She gasped as a hand frisked down her front and into her trouser pockets with practised speed. The cold metal did not move. A finger probed the inside of her trainers, looking for a concealed blade or anything else.

"Walk to that door," the voice said. "Don't look around." She walked towards his office. "No, not that one. The one before."

They walked together, joined by the muzzle of the gun, through which flowed his power over her. He reached out with his free hand, opened the door, and flicked on the light. The room was bare, white-walled, with a single lightbulb hanging from the ceiling. The only furniture was a battered desk and a chair on either side. In the corner was what looked like a tool bag, spattered with paint. There was nothing else.

"Sit down." The voice was gentle, as if the possibility of resistance did not even have to be addressed. It was the voice of natural, uncontested command. "Don't say anything, please."

He moved into view for the first time, still keeping the gun aimed at her. He looked older at close quarters, the bags under his eyes deeper than she remembered, the skin more pitted than it had seemed at a distance. His eyes were soft and brown, but still freighted with menace. He did not blink as he considered her; did not blink at all. There was no flash of recognition or interest. In spite of the gun, he communicated irritation rather than alarm. The irritation of a respected community leader who has apprehended a female intruder, doubtless psychotic and looking for drug money.

"Give me one good reason why I should not call the police straight-away."

She sat in silence.

"You can speak now if you wish. One good reason."

"Do you remember me, Dr. Muhammad?"

"Of course not. Why should I?"

"We met a few years ago. At the BBC."

"I am involved in hundreds of broadcasts every year. I can scarcely remember everybody I meet."

"I'm sure that's right. But you remember your broadcasts with Mr. Anderton. Don't you?"

He sat down. She could see him ruminating. She knew he would remember that encounter. And there were other reasons why he should recognise her. Why continue the pretence? He breathed sharply through his nostrils and scratched his chin. "What are you doing here, Miss Taylor?"

"You should know."

"I can hardly guess what you mean. But I am sure we can both agree that your presence here—your breaking and entering, I should say—is a foolish step. I would have thought that you, of all people, would be aware of the risks. Shall we agree on that?"

"You haven't heard me out yet."

The gun was still ranged on her. Under the naked lightbulb, she recognised it: a British army–issue revolver, similar to a model her father had had in his collection. "What makes you think I am remotely interested in what you have to say?"

"I am not here to make any accusations."

"That's good. I wouldn't advise you to try."

"I am here to make a trade, Dr. Muhammad."

"A trade? You are joking, I assume."

"Not at all. You have something I want. And I have something I think you might want. I want to trade."

He could not contain his sneer. "What could you possibly have that is of interest to me?"

"Forgive me for coming without an invitation. Let's just say I wanted your complete attention. I don't think you'll find I'm wasting your time. In my breast pocket, there's something for you. I would take it out myself, but I know you don't want me to move."

For the first time, his features twitched. His disgust gave way to calculation. "If this is a trick, I warn you that you will be very sorry."

"No tricks."

The gun was in her face, inches from her eye, as he leant over her and searched in the pocket of her jacket. Scent wafted from him. What was it? Sandalwood? He pulled out the piece of paper and withdrew behind the desk again, never once letting her out of his sight. He sat down and unfolded the single sheet, then looked at what was written on it. No reaction, nothing. He folded it up again and put it in his suit pocket.

"Yes," he said. "Yes, you are right. That is something valuable. I will admit that, Miss Taylor. Now, what are you asking in return?"

"I want you to tell me what really happened—to my family. I'm not interested in anything but the truth. I am not going to the police. They closed this case years ago. And as you can see, I am unarmed. You could kill me now, and dispose of my body without difficulty, I imagine."

He shook his head. "You think too much of me, Miss Taylor. And too little. Do you really imagine I enjoy having to aim a gun at you? Indeed, do I look like a man who enjoys using weapons? Hardly. You know my academic pedigree. I keep this weapon out of bitter necessity. For occasions such as this, which, I am pleased to say, are few and far between. Don't forget, you broke in."

"But you have to admit—"

"I have to admit nothing. There is no 'have to' about my position. In contrast to yours."

She remained silent for a while. "Yes. I accept that. But we wouldn't still be speaking if you were unwilling to say anything at all to me. I don't think you will take what I have given you without some sort of payment."

"You seem very confident of that."

"Let's just say that I suspect you have a sense of honour, Dr. Muhammad. So let me put it to you in a way that you might not find offensive: Is there anything you can tell me?"

He put the gun down on the desk and sighed. Suddenly, he had the bearing of a man who bore a heavy burden and had to deal constantly with people to whom that burden was impossible to explain. "I wonder when you ask me that question how you think I operate. How we operate. I have many friends engaged in many forms of activity. Some of them are teachers, youth leaders, people involved with charitable work. Religious men. I speak to people all over the country. And I speak to people elsewhere, too. My brothers, for whom daily life is somewhat different. All of us are engaged in different struggles, but we have learned over the years, in many nations, that the only friends we have are one another. There is no compromise to be had anymore. The other side is not interested in negotiation or coexistence. That is the basis of all our struggles. Against ill health, against poverty, against ignorance, against oppression, against imperialism. We do not answer questions of the sort you ask, because there is no point in doing so. That is what you cannot, will not, understand. There is simply no point."

"I see. Well, let me put the question differently: Why do you think your brothers tried to kill Miles Anderton that night?"

He allowed himself to laugh, a terse grunt. "If I knew the answer to that question—a question of empathy, I suppose—why should I tell you?"

"Because, Dr. Muhammad, as I think you acknowledge, you are in my debt. Whether you choose to repay that debt is, you are right, entirely up to you. It's entirely a matter of honour."

He grunted again and smoothed his tie. "How can I put this to you? Let me tell you how I would see Mr. Anderton if I were engaged in the struggle which afflicts my brothers every day. Remember, I speak hypothetically. I see Muslim children all over the world suffering because they are denied pharmaceuticals. I see Muslims all over the world being driven from their homes, with the complicity of the West, sometimes more than complicity. I see fire raining from the sky on these homes, on schools, on hospitals, on mosques. And then, here, in your comfortable, decadent country, I see a young loudmouth, lionised by your media, spreading poison, locking up the innocent, changing the law to do it. No ordinary enemy. A man who has chosen my people as his target, not even as the expendable casualties of some defensible purpose, but quite maliciously, as the people he will single out to hurt. To advance his political career. Well now, Miss Taylor, you are, if I recall correctly, a clever woman: Imagine how you would respond to that."

She fixed him with her eyes. "And if an innocent family dies? People who had nothing to do with any of that? People who just happened to be in the house where Miles was going to go but never did? What do your brothers have to say about that?"

He slammed his hand on the desk, and she could feel herself flinching. "Innocent? What makes you think you are *innocent*? Let me tell you about innocence and guilt. Let me. I watch television every day, and I see the bodies of innocent Muslim children being pulled from the ruins: in Lebanon, Sudan, Gaza, Sarajevo, Kandahar, everywhere the same. And this is 'collateral damage.' I am told this by your smiling politicians. I hear generals use this term. Always. Collateral damage. The acceptable price of conflict. You see, Miss Taylor, we live in a new age. There are no innocents now. There will never again be innocents."

Her heart was still beating furiously. She collected her thoughts. "Even so, you missed him, didn't you? He got away. What use was it to kill five other people? You didn't even claim responsibility. You let some tin-pot little Irish outfit say it was them."

He waved his finger at her. "A gauche attempt to trick me into admitting involvement. And that I will not do. But I will say this. There are operations which succeed and operations which fail. That is the way of things. Do you think my brothers falter *for a second*? Do you imagine they lose faith, or that their will deserts them? The opposite is the case, Miss Taylor. The opposite. It only bolsters their strength. They become only more determined."

Feeling a cramp curling into the core of her leg, she shifted gently in her seat. "And then I suppose they get angry? When somebody starts asking questions? Like me, I mean."

"I have no idea. That is a question only they could answer. But again, I appeal to your common sense, such as it is. Even I heard about your clumsy investigations, the people you pestered. It is the sort of thing I hear about. You are not a subtle woman, Miss Taylor, not subtle at all. You raked up the past, which is never wise, in my experience.

Digging around, flailing about. I assume you angered people along the way. I assume that they believed you had foolishly renewed your association with Mr. Anderton, and that they were aggrieved by that. I assume some people felt you were becoming a liability. That would seem a very safe assumption to me."

"Very safe, yes. But . . . these people, they missed again, didn't they? A young Muslim boy got killed this time. Burned to death before his brother's eyes. I was there."

"Yes, that was not expected. By any of us. My heart was full of sorrow. But that is the way of the world in which we have been forced to live. That is the way of things."

"Is it? I'm not sure I think it is the way of things, Dr. Muhammad. It is your way."

He pushed the gun across the desk. "I want to show you something. I want to show you what I am talking about. An experiment, if you like. To focus your muddled mind for a moment. Now, listen to me very carefully. Take the gun. . . . Yes, that's right. Take it—exactly so—and shoot me."

She raised the gun to the height of his face and looked down the sights. Her hand was shaking, but the range was so short that she could not miss. One shot to the forehead, a single round, a final report in the little room: an end to the blood feud. That was what he was inviting her to do. A mess of bone and blood against the wall to settle accounts once and for all: That was his offer. She thought of Ben, Ben with Claude, her father, Beatrice, her mother carrying the twins, the impact of loneliness, the sudden absence of love. The golden thread, burned through, reduced to dust. She looked down and let her arm fall. No, she would not do it. She toyed with the gun in her hands below the level of the desk. She wondered what he would do next.

He brought his hand down on the desk again, this time in triumph. "That's it. That's it *exactly*. Do you see? You thought about it, of course.

But not for long. You had decided not to finish the job even before you had taken aim. And I knew that. It's the truth of it. You are full of rage, of course, but you are weak. You had the wit to get here, but not the strength to complete the task. Always the same. You have the might to humiliate my people. But you always withdraw in the end, drifting away on a tide of doubt. That is the lesson of history. That is why we will win. It is why I persist. Oh, I know full well what will happen. One day, men will come here and kill me, or take me away and put me in a cell to rot and go blind. That is precisely what Mr. Anderton intends. And it will happen. I have no doubt of that. How could it not? But when it does, another will fill my place. And then another. And then another. Until the battle is won."

She put the gun back on the desk. He stood up. "You cannot possibly imagine what you have stumbled into. It is not your fault. You are the victim of your culture, your upbringing. You have been seduced by comfort, by the illusion of being guiltless. It is imprinted on you from birth. That, and the belief that victory is yours by right. But you are wrong. The accidents of life have given you a glimpse of what living is like for most of the world's population, Miss Taylor. How precarious it is, and how painful. But only a glimpse. You haven't seen how resolute people become when this is all they know. This is what you have yet to grasp, any of you. That we will prevail in the end, because we have right on our side. We have God on our side. Your friend Mr. Anderton plays with fire. He takes us on to impress the public, as part of some little political battle he is fighting. Pitiful. For us, there is no other battle. There is only the fight for survival."

No, she thought. It is you who are wrong. There is more to it than you say. There is the battered love that has tumbled down the mountain and still stands up. There is my anger with my father and my adoration for him. There is my memory of my mother, Ben, the twins. There is Rob. These things I have are modest before the flaming wall of your certainty. But you cannot wish them away because you feel wronged, because a billion voices rise in fury within you. Voices rise within me, too.

"And now," he said, "I suggest you leave before I lose my temper. I suggest you leave the way you came in. And I suggest you leave quickly."

She stood up and turned for the door. The gun was still on the desk in front of him, within his grasp. Was he deciding whether or not to shoot her in the back?

"Miss Taylor," he said. She looked round. "This will be the last time we meet. I am sure of that."

She left the room and took the stairs two at a time. Through one door, then the next. In the alleyway, she felt her gorge rise, and she coughed bile into her hand. She wiped her glove against her sweatshirt and breathed deeply. She wanted to cry. Soon, she would fall to pieces as the last surge of adrenaline ended and her body took revenge for the suppression of its reflexes. But first she must decide how to get out. There was the gate, but she would have to climb over it, which would be noisy and difficult. No, Saffi was right. She should retrace her steps. The window of the Quaker hall was still unlocked. Pressing her fingers against the glass, she was able to edge it open and then push it up so she could climb back in. The street was still deserted. She was fortunate.

Clambering through, she perched on the toilet seat again and locked the window behind her. Then she jumped down and went into the hall. As she edged open the front door, she saw that there was a man outside, talking into his phone. She looked through the crack and could see only his back: short black hair and a denim jacket. His conversation—in Italian—was sharp and furious. She longed for it to end, but the man seemed rooted to the spot. A minute passed, then another. At last, he clicked the phone shut, swore vigorously to himself, spat on the ground, and was on his way. She waited until he was out of sight and then slipped out.

Her call on the pay phone took less than a minute. Then she walked into the café and up to the counter. The man was fiddling with the coffee machine, from which steam was pouring unhealthily.

"Hello," she said. He turned round, hot and exasperated. "Could I have a cup of tea, please? And do you have the time?"

The man broke off and wiped his hands on a cloth. "There's a clock there, love. Help yourself." He pointed to the wall.

"Oh, seven o'clock. I thought it was later." She took off her hooded top and smiled at him so that he might notice her face. With luck, Saffi Muhammad would still be on the telephone, calls which would be logged and timed. This was her alibi, or as near as she could get to one.

"Well, yeah," said the man, wiping the counter and looking at her as if she were mad. "It's usually later than you think. Did you say tea?"

She looked at him again, trying to make him feel uncomfortable, so that he might just remember her. "Yes, please, tea. If that's all right. Tea."

He scrutinised her, clearly convinced she was a madwoman, then threw the cloth over his shoulder. "Coming up. Take a seat."

The bar by the window was a good vantage point. She could see the centre, which was about fifty yards down to the right. His office light was still on. The car was still parked in the alleyway. By now, Dr. Muhammad would normally be straightening his tie, or sitting in the driver's seat, lost in contemplation, or unlocking the padlocks. But tonight, she had given him some extra work to do. He would be late. But he would not be that late. She hoped that she had been quick enough, that she had left enough time.

It was twenty minutes before she saw the scooter pull up. He parked it at the end of the street, a long way from the centre. She watched him walk, his stealthy lope, how he became part of his surroundings. He had made a ghost of himself, a being who could not be seen. His dark clothing—head to toe, apart from the white of his trainers—was part of his camouflage. But there was something more to it than that. He merged with the concrete, with the pavement, with the boards of the derelict buildings. He was a child of the city, rising from its subterranean heart, mastering its terrain. She watched as he climbed over the gate, feline in his agility, and went in through the side door, as she had told him to. Then she did not see him again for ten minutes. When he came out, he thrust his hands straight back into his pockets. Back over the gate and onto the street. Did he stagger a little? No, that was her imagination. He did not miss a beat. Another thirty seconds and he was gone, the tires of his scooter screeching against the tarmac and off into the night.

It had been her task to find Dr. Saffi Muhammad, and Aasim's task to do whatever he had just done. She could have finished him off herself. He had given her the chance. But he had done so knowing that she would not take it; could not. Had he been directly involved in her family's death? She could not be sure. Not sure enough to pull the trigger. But he had admitted responsibility for Ali. That he had done. And that had meant it was time to call the number on Aasim's card and to tell him what he needed to know. Aasim had been right the night he spoke to her at the hospital: "The only way is through you, man. . . . And when they realize that they messed up, they'll come again. Or you'll find them." She had found them first. And she had kept her promise to him.

Of course, she had done more than that. She had made sure that Aasim had an advantage as he scaled the steps to the little room. She tried to imagine Saffi's face as he realised what she had done. No, she could not envisage fear on his stony features. She took the bullets out of her pocket and counted them. They were all there. All six. Oh, Daddy, she thought. The absurdity of it. Of all the lessons you taught me in your study—that this should be the one. It was just a game then, a secret from Mummy. But not now. It was so easy, easier than I'd thought. Even with trembling hands, I remembered how to do it. Even while he mocked my weakness, I took out the rounds under the desk. One, two, three, four . . . He didn't pick the gun up again, Daddy. He didn't know what I had done. The trap I was setting.

She looked into her tea and watched the little vortex of froth as she stirred it again. Yes, she had left Saffi enough time before Aasim's visit. He would have worked fast; she knew he would. He would have called straightaway with the news of the evening's unexpected gift, to give instructions or to take them. Her visit was irksome, no doubt. It raised the stakes. What if she had told someone where she was? It meant that he could not kill her there and then, but that he would certainly have to kill her soon. He would have to find her, track her down, erase her from history before she did more damage. Another errand to run in the name of the great struggle. But her visit had not been a waste of his time. Far from it. This is what he would have whispered into the phone. He knew at once what she had given him on the piece of paper, and the need to act swiftly. It was something he had been looking for, a prize that had eluded him for a long time. Oh, there was no doubt about that. Six digits. Not much, really, but enough. Six numbers, written in black ballpoint. That was all. The six numbers that opened the security lock to Miles Anderton's flat. The date of her birth transformed into a numerical code. She remembered the movement in the shadows in Selbourne Terrace, the glint of metal, the sound of a car leaving. Yes, what she had given Saffi would be put to good use. It was a generous gift by any standards.

Now she was weary. She felt nothing but the clasp of fatigue creeping through her limbs to the centre of her being. She needed to sleep. The nausea had gone; the panic which she expected had yet to invade her bones. Time now to leave, to leave the whole thing, and to sleep. She wished that she could sleep where she was. Just for a few minutes. To let her head fall, to close her eyes, and to surrender to the void. Not for long. Only awhile. Was that asking so much?

"More tea, love?" The man was at her side. He looked solicitous, and she wondered what she must look like. A funny little urchin. No makeup, lank hair. On her own in a Holloway café. Going nowhere, really.

"No thanks. How much is that?" She paid him and slid off her seat.

He pointed at the clock. "Look, it's later now. You were right. Sort of anyway."

She smiled. He would remember her. "Thanks. See you again."

Then she was back on Monk Street, walking fast, wrapping her jacket around herself. It had become even colder while she was in the café. The air tasted of ice and petrol fumes. She looked down, tried to avoid stepping on the cracks in the pavement. From time to time, she would close her eyes, to see fire, flames lapping up, the faces of the lost, the forest burnt to the ground and silent. She kept moving, turning corners, left, right, left, no longer on her normal route, but darting across roads, turning back on herself, huddled and afraid. She could hear footsteps behind her. Yes, there they were again. Sharp, inevitable, only a few seconds away, just round the corner.

And now the chase was on, as it was always going to be. You knew this would happen, she said to herself. All the premonitions, the dangers sensed, the phantoms in the shadows. You always knew this moment would come. That it would be the last moment. She quickened her pace and looked back. Nothing. Not yet. Ahead, a fog was forming. Thick and sudden, it enveloped the street, made the lights look like eyes. She could no longer see the cracks in the pavement, could not see where her feet fell as she moved on at a half run. She was breathing heavily now, exhausted and unequal to this last challenge. Her chest began to burn, her legs to buckle. This time, she would fall.

She turned again and saw the figure. Slender as a knife, moving more slowly than she was, but still gaining ground. Dark as the nightmares she had had, this was the person whose face she had never quite seen, the last face in the world. Yes, this was the one. She knew him at once for what he was. She recognised the rendezvous they had planned together for so long. She turned and began to run. The fog rose and embraced her. Now she could see nothing, and everything. Nothing that was present. All that she saw, swirling before her, was the past. Claude, weeping and broken. Lucian Carver, gleeful that her punishment was upon her. Sylvia at the desk, working in the burnt-out ruins. Ray and Barry, still laughing. Her mother, smiling, wishing peace upon her. Her faithless father. Ben, saying good-bye. Saying good-bye. No time for good-byes. No time to tell them that it was all her fault. Time for nothing. A few more paces, into the light. The figure running now, too. Faster than she. The footsteps getting louder, nearer. Seconds away. And now she was falling. At last, she was falling. The ground reached up and swallowed her whole, and then all was quiet.

She floated in the nothingness. There was no feeling where she was, no sense of time or place. It was calm, a great pool of silence. She lay back and watched the stars fade one by one. Then she sensed something on her vein, the pressure of a finger and thumb. The surface of the pool was being punctured. Sounds forced their way in under the door of the chamber. The stars blazed above her. The hand stayed on her wrist for a while. As she rose up from oblivion, slowly, blinking, she realised that somebody was taking her pulse. Cool fingers busied themselves as he counted. She felt the hand on her forehead now, checking her for fever. Her head was in his lap. They had not moved. She could see the fog, the tires on the parked cars, the tufts of grass by the tree. She was inches away from a puddle reflecting the light from the streetlamp overhead.

"It's okay," he said. "Just take it easy. You just took a fall. You ran too fast and tripped."

She recognised the voice. But she could not explain it. This was not how it was meant to be. This was not what she had been made ready for. The face in the dream was someone else's. Wasn't it?

The words began to order themselves into sentences. "You really took a tumble," he said. "I'm not surprised you feel a bit groggy. That's it. Just lean against me for a moment."

She tried to speak but could not. She coughed to clear her throat. Her mouth was dry. "What are you doing here?"

Rob laughed. "Couldn't keep away, could I? I knew you'd be needing me."

She coughed again, bringing up more bile. She gasped for breath. "Shit. I feel rough. Why did you run after me, you bloody idiot?"

"Well, why were you dashing around like somebody was after you? I thought somebody must be following. And then you hit the deck."

"Thanks a lot. Next time, stay at home."

He helped her up. She had grazed herself and was shaken, but she could walk. Rob told her that his car was parked a few streets away, and, too tired to argue, she took his lead, occasionally leaning against him and the shoulder of his leather jacket.

After a while, she turned to him. "How did you find me?"

"Wasn't hard. I came to see you the night you moved out, and you were just getting into the minicab. So I drove behind, all the way to Camden. Nice place, by the way. Looks like a squatter's house."

"Thanks. But how did you know I'd be here?"

"I didn't. After the first night, I guessed that you wanted to be left alone. I mean, that you meant it."

"But?"

"But—well, I missed you. And I knew you'd be up to no good. I was going to confront you one evening, tell you to stop being so bloody foolish, and then you left the house and I followed you up here. I couldn't work out what you were doing in Holloway, and I still can't. Anyway, I plucked up the courage to try again today. I went to the house and you weren't there. So I guessed you'd be here. And you were."

"So you've been following me, basically?"

"Not very well. Only a couple of times. You should be flattered."

"Oh, very flattering. What a creep. It's against the law, you know."

"Is that right? Well, you'd know all about that, I'd guess."

He opened the door of the car for her. She got in and waited for him to walk round the side. He turned the key and switched on the heating. They sat in silence for a while. She recovered her breath. He blew on his fingers.

"Did you really miss me?" she asked.

"Of course I did. What do you think?"

"I don't know. I've been out of it for a while."

"Oh, you don't say?"

She wondered how angry he really was. She waited. "Listen, Rob—"

"Not tonight. You need some rest first. You can tell me tomorrow."

"No, some of it you need to hear now."

She told him the bare bones of the story. He listened, nodded, let her finish. If he was shocked, he did not show it. When she was finished, he said he had to think. He rested his head on the wheel and tried to decide what to do.

He reached behind him and grabbed his satchel. He told her to put the bullets in it, and anything else she needed to get rid of—Aasim's card, the leaflet about the centre. All of it. They would go to Brighton, he said, as they had planned. They would go and see his brother in the morning, and he would let them stay at his place for a few days. It was better that way. It wasn't a good idea for her to be in London anymore. She needed to get away for a while. They both needed it. She took his hand and started to speak. But he put his finger to his lips. They had done enough talking for now. It was time to drive.

She wanted to think it through, but she realised that all her energies were spent now. She tried to get comfortable as he turned the engine on, put the car in gear, and edged away from the curb. It would be hard to settle, to persuade her body that its task was over, to force the furies from her tendons. Yes, it would be hard.

After a while, before they had even reached the end of the Holloway Road and the top of Upper Street, she fell into a deep sleep. He looked over at her. She was beautiful, he thought, even with those perfectly oval, luminous eyes closed, even with her features crushed against the headrest. Her face would tell anyone who cared to look the story of her life, or some of it. There was love there, the imprint of love. The nagging scratches of hope. Something darker, too. It was as though death and life crisscrossed within her. As though there were forces surging inside her, riptides she couldn't control: memory, and other things. Rob hoped at first, for her sake, that hers was a face at peace, and then he changed his mind. Perhaps, after all, it was a face of penitence. Yes, that was it.

Upper Street, he noticed, was clear for the time of night. He saw the road sign and headed east.

ACKNOWLEDGEMENTS

The idea for this novel arose on long winter walks around the East End with Zac d'Ancona. His newborn brother, Teddy, brought the breeze of summer to the completion of the U.S. edition. I send them both my love. In London, my editor at Hodder, Sue Fletcher, was magnificent in her support and guidance, as were Karen Geary and Swati Gamble. In New York, Nan Talese offered me faith, wisdom, and patience, which is all that a writer can ask. Lorna Owen was inspiring and meticulous. I owe them both a great debt of gratitude. Lois Wallace, my U.S. agent, provided flawless advice, and made me look forward to checking my e-mails.

The inspiration of Giles Gordon, my UK agent and trusted mentor, made this book possible. My deep sadness at his death is matched only by my sense of gratitude for all that he taught me. *Ave atque vale.*

My family, as ever, supported me wholeheartedly at every stage. There are no words to express the debt that I owe my wife, Sarah: so this book, which is for her, will have to do.

A NOTE ABOUT THE AUTHOR

MATTHEW D'ANCONA was born in London in 1968.
He is the deputy editor and political columnist of the
Sunday Telegraph. He lives in East London with his wife,
Sarah, and their sons, Zac and Teddy.

A NOTE ABOUT THE TYPE

This book is set in Adobe Garamond. Designed by Robert Slimbach
in 1989, this contemporary digital font is drawn from two
sixteenth-century sources: the roman typefaces of Claude Garamond
and the italic types of Robert Granjon.